THE
SORROWS

BOOKS BY RANDY LEE EICKHOFF

The Fourth Horseman*
Bowie (with Leonard C. Lewis)*
A Hand to Execute
The Gombeen Man
Fallon's Wake*

THE ULSTER CYCLE
The Raid *
The Feast*
The Sorrows*

NONFICTION
Exiled

*denotes a Forge Book

THE
SORROWS

Randy Lee
Eickhoff

A TOM DOHERTY ASSOCIATES BOOK
NEW YORK

THE SORROWS

Copyright © 2000 by Randy Lee Eickhoff

This book is printed on acid-free paper.

A Forge Book
Published by Tom Doherty Associates, LLC
175 Fifth Avenue
New York, NY 10010

www.tor.com

Forge® is a registered trademark of Tom Doherty Associates, LLC.

ISBN 0-312-87028-0

First Edition: March 2000

Printed in the United States of America

0 9 8 7 6 5 4 3 2 1

For Mícheál O'Ciardha

. . . an lëigheand labhraid cléirigh
's ar n–ealadha Fhirchëilligh,
cë a–dera siad ind d'obadh . . .

Acknowledgments

I wish to thank my daughter, Leone Eickhoff, for the lovely illustrations that accompany this work.

A large debt of gratitude is owed to Michael Carey; Jacques de Spoelberch, my agent; Robert Gleason, my editor; and Tom Doherty, whose vision made this possible.

A very special thanks to my wife, Dianne, for her patience and for being the first reader.

Contents

INTRODUCTION

FIRST MUSICIAN. I have a story right, my wanderers,
That has so mixed with fable in our songs
That all seemed fabulous. . . .
—William Butler Yeats, *Deirdre*

Ancient Irish tales generally appear in medieval manuscripts, where they are usually divided into four categories:

1. The Mythological Cycle
2. The Ulster Cycle (sometimes referred to as
   The Red Branch Cycle)
3. The Fenian Cycle
4. The Historical Cycle

On the surface, such a division would seem to form didactic categories, yet the tales and sagas do not follow rigid lines that preclude them from association with tales in other categories. These categories are loosely arranged to establish a time line, but not all of the tales follow a time line. The poets in Ancient Ireland did not memorize the required poems according to cycles to fulfill the demands of their school. Rather, they memorized poems according to categories:

Of the qualifications of a Poet in Stories and in Deeds, here follows, to be related to kings and chiefs, viz: Seven times Fifty Stories, i.e. Five times Fifty Prime Stories,

and Twice Fifty Secondary Stories; and these Secondary
Stories are not permitted [assigned] but to four grades
only, viz., an *Ollamb*, an *Anrath*, a *Cli*, and a *Cano*. And
these are the Prime Stories: Destructions, and Cattle-
raids, and Courtships, and Battles, and Caves, and Voy-
ages, and Violent Deaths, and Feasts, and Sieges, and
Adventures, and Elopements, and Slaughters.

—*The Book of Leinster*

There were 250 Prime Stories and 100 Secondary Stories, but in
The Book of Leinster, fewer than 200 of the Prime Stories and none of
the Secondary Stories are listed. One could assume that the stories are
simply missing from the canon. One could also assume, however, that
certain stories were joined with other stories to provide a more complete story. A section of *Táin Bó Cuailnge* is devoted to the *Macgnímartha* (youthful exploits) of Cúchulainn and in the Fenian Cycle, there
is a tale simply called *Macgnímartha Finn*.

The listing of the tales in this fashion by the bards provided a loose
system of categories that restricted the telling of certain stories at certain times. For example, certain poems would be recited for people
going off on a voyage, before going to a court of law, or going out on a
hunt. It would appear that the telling of these stories in accordance with
Brehon Law formed a system of censure. Apparently the ancient storytellers realized the power of their stories in the effect that the stories
had upon those who listened to them.

Myths belong to the world of symbols, but there are no definitive
exegeses. The *dramatis personae* from tales in one cycle often refer to
tales in another cycle as well. In the so-called Mythological Cycle, the
chief characters belong to the Tuatha Dé Danann, "The People of the
Goddess Danu," who were the inhabitants of Ireland before the Sons of
Míl came on "the ninth wave" (that which comes from the outermost
limits of the cosmos) to overthrow the Tuatha and take control of the
land. According to legend, the Tuatha and the Mílesians held a confer-
ence in which the Tuatha said that it was senseless to be fighting over
the land since it was big enough for all and suggested that the land be
divided between the two peoples. The Mílesians agreed, saying that

they would take the land above ground and the Tuatha could have the land below.

The Mílesians were being metaphorical here, telling the Tuatha that they intended to do battle, but the Tuatha took them literally and melted away into the ground, becoming residents of *sídhes,* which can roughly be explained as "portals" into the Otherworld.

The Tuatha are the forerunners of today's fairies and sprites (the famous fairy-rings are sites where they hold their dances on special days such as harvest days) while the Mílesians are the ancestors of today's Irish.

The Tuatha, however, were also involved in conquering another race that inhabited Ireland before the Tuatha arrived. The Fir Bolgs were overthrown by the Tuatha, who then were forced to fight off the Fomorians, a race of giants who apparently were the forerunners of the Vikings. These stories are found in the medieval pseudo-historical tract *Lebor Gabála (The Book of Invasions).*

For our purposes, The Mythological Cycle is simply a collective term that applies to stories dealing *for the most part* with characters from the Otherworld, a type of sixth dimension, if you will. Many of these characters are Irish manifestations of the Celtic pantheon of divine beings. Lugh, however, who appears as a major participant in *Oidheadh Cloinne Tuireann (The Fate of the Children of Tuirenn* also known as *Iuchar agus Iucharba)* in the Mythological Cycle also plays a major role in *Táin Bó Cuailnge (Cattle-raid of Cooley)* in the Ulster Cycle.

We find references to other characters as well in some of the stories from the Mythological Cycle that are also in the Ulster Cycle. Characters from *Togail Brhuidne Dá Dérga (The Destruction of Da Derga's Hostel)* are also found or referenced in Ulster Tales such as Táin Bó Cuailnge *(Cattle-raid of Cooley),* the central tale of the Ulster Cycle and often referred to as the "national epic" of Ireland for its metaphorical alignment with modern Irish culture and society. Maeve's father, Eochaid Feidlech, is synonymous with Eochaid Airem in *The Hostel.* Cormac, the king of Ulster (referred to in several Ulster or Red Branch Tales), is married to étain in *Tochmarc étaíne (The Wooing of Étain).* Consequently, we have to be careful not to be too didactic when consigning a tale to a single category.

Actually, the ancient tales are arranged in a loose chronological sequence that extends from the time of the Great Flood to the Viking raids in Ireland. Events in the Mythological Cycle seem to be synchronized, for the most part, with main events in ancient world history. Conchobor, king of Ulster in most of the Ulster Cycle, usually is found in tales that bridge the time just before and after the birth of Christ, while the Fenian Cycle is named after the tales in which Finn and his *fiana* (brotherhood) served Cormac Mac Airt, believed to have been king in Ireland in A.D. 3.

"The Three Sorrows of Storytelling" (*Trí Truagha Na Scéaluidheachta*) bridge the Mythological Cycle and Ulster Cycle with two of the tales, *Oidheadh Cloinne Tuireann* (*The Fate of the Children of Tuirenn*, also known as *Iuchar agus Iucharba*) and *Oidheadh Cloinne Lir* (*The Fate of the Children of Lir*) appearing in the Mythological Cycle while *Loinges Mac nUislenn* (*The Exile of the Sons of Uisliu*, also known as *Oidheadh Cloinne Uisneach*) appears in the Ulster Cycle. This is a rather strange arrangement, yet each of the tales provides us metaphorical insight into tradition. The tales exist in several recensions, the earliest appearing in the latter half of the eleventh century in *Lebor Na hUidre* (*The Book of the Dun Cow*) followed roughly fifty years later with inclusions in *Leabhar Na Huachongbála* also known as *Lebar Na Núachongbála* or *The Book of Leinster*. The stories existed much earlier, however, as a part of the bardic tradition, being handed down through the ages through "bardic schools" in which they became required memorization by aspiring bards or poets. Although the first instinct of a scholar is to follow such a line warily, I must point out that the Ancient Irish bard schools were very strict with their scholarship and demanded *exact* renditions from what we can tell through the *Senchus Mór* and Brehon Law. Individual interpretation was not allowed, and the purity of the recitation was graded sternly by a judge from another school.

The Fate of the Children of Tuirenn, the oldest chronologically of "the three sorrows," can be seen as a metaphorical allusion to one of the basic sorrows of the Irish people: civil war, although several other allusions are attributed to it as well. The work seems to be a parallel to the Greek story of Jason and the Argonauts, which would also suggest a lineage link between the Ancient Irish and the Ancient Greeks through the goddess Danu. Indeed, in many of the sagas and tales of the Ancient Irish, one can find a sort of "transient myth" at work that might be useful for sociolinguists in tracing ethnic movement and development or stagnation in early history. The story is mentioned by Cormac in his

Glossary (ninth or tenth century) and by Flann of Monasterboice (c. 1056). We find the story partially told in the *The Yellow Book of Lecan* (1416) and snippets of it in several manuscripts in the Scottish collection, notably No. LVI.

This story is the one least familiar among "the three sorrows." Lugh, a Tuatha hero, discovers that his father, Cian, has been murdered by three brothers, the children of Tuirenn, as the result of an old family/clan feud. He places an *éric* or "blood-penalty/fine" upon the three brothers that sends them around the world to collect magical weapons and trophies that he intends to use in later battles. But after they complete the tasks set before them, Lugh refuses to forgive them.

Many of the labors the brothers perform to gain the needed trophies have a parallel in other stories in the Mythological Cycle. It appears that an Ancient Irish storyteller wished to provide a story about how the Gaelic gods obtained their legendary possessions. The spear of Pisear, king of Persia, is obviously the same (as elsewhere) weapon as the lance of Lugh, which another tradition describes as having been brought by the Tuatha Dé Danann from their original home in the city of Gorias (Greece). It could also be the inspiration for the famous *gae bulga*[1] that Cúchulainn uses so effectively as a weapon in the Ulster Cycle. Failinis, the puppy of the king of Ioruaidhe, is Lugh's "hound of mightiest deeds" (and, perhaps, the famous "hound of Culaun" that Sétanta kills to become Cúchulainn) while the seven swine of Asal, king of the Golden Pillars, reflects the famous pigs of Manannán Mac Lir, who uses them in the "Feast of Age" which he establishes to preserve the eternal youth of the gods in the Irish pantheon. The two horses and magical chariot seem to be a parallel to those obtained by Cúchulainn (the Black of Saingliu, Gray of Macha, and his magnificent chariot *Carbad Searadha*, a scythed chariot with wheels bristling with knives). The Golden Apples reflect those golden apples that Herakles must bring back as one of his famous Twelve Labors. But we also find apple imagery in other Gaelic tales, most notably in the Arthurian Cycle. Avalon, the legendary isle to which Arthur is taken after the final battle, is the "Isle of Apples."

One of the major problems that exists in *The Fate of the Children of Tuirenn* is the question of the two Battles of Mag Tuired. Some of the tales suggest that this story precedes *The Second Battle of Mag Tuired* (either the Plain of Reckoning, Plain of Weeping, or Plain of the Stone

Pillars), where Nuada and Lugh make their plans for the battle. Nuada and Lugh call the magician, the cupbearers, the Druid, the craftsmen, the poet, and the various physicians of the Tuatha Dé Danann together and ask what each will contribute to the struggle. Still, the Tuatha need some magical weapons to aid them in the coming battle, and this is the reason for Lugh picking the particular labors for Brian, Iuchar, and Iucharba, the sons of Tuirenn.

I believe however, that the original story was corrupted and that both battles are an integral part of *The Fate of the Children of Tuirenn* and the weapons that were obtained by the brothers in their labors for Lugh were for future use *after* the second battle. The second battle was probably removed from *The Fate of the Children of Tuirenn* to provide an explanation for the acquisition of certain magical weapons by the Tuatha. This does cause some linear problems in the text, and to correct that I have emended the text and merged the second battle with the translation of *The Fate of the Children of Tuirenn* here to provide a more complete story.

The Fate of the Children of Lir is the second oldest chronologically of "the three sorrows." Although the setting is in the earliest cycle, it is not represented in any of the ancient manuscripts. The oldest manuscript in which one can find it appears to be No. XXXVIII of the Scottish collection, composed in the early seventeenth century. There is a copy in MS.LVI as well. All the other manuscript copies in which this story appears seem to belong to the eighteenth or nineteenth centuries. It appears to be a Gaelic version of the "Seven Swans" *märchen* that was once a common folktale. This particular tale appears to have been put together by a sixteenth-century monk. The Lir of the title is also the Lear of Shakespeare, although the Irish story appears to have little resemblance to *King Lear*. The Ancient Irish word for "taboo" is *geis*, it appears to have been taken from *géis*, which means "swan." This might suggest that the word used for something forbidden, a spell, or witchery (note that Fergus has a *geis* upon him in *The Fate of the Children of Uisliu* that ultimately brings about the death of Naisi, his brothers, and Deirdre) is taken directly from this tale after the children have been shape-shifted into swans by their evil stepmother.

The story line is a familiar one to those aware of the many fables in which a stepmother becomes jealous of her husband's children by a previous marriage and changes them into various animals. Here, the jealous stepmother changes Lir's children from a previous marriage (to her sister, no less) into swans, cursing them for a period of nine hundred years, divided into three-hundred-year segments which they must spend in different parts of the country. The metaphorical allusions here are many, including the naming of certain parts of the country. We can also make a metaphorical reference to Cromwell and his bloody-handed dealings with the Irish in the seventeenth century as well, with Ireland being the child of the monstrous stepmother England.

A problem exists with *The Fate of the Children of Lir*: Two separate endings appear to exist. I have given both, marking them Recension I and Recension II for the reader. We observe that the older tale, Recension I, was probably intruded upon by a monk (as mentioned earlier) with the result that the children are released from their barbaric and pagan curse through the advent of Christianity, most notably through St. Kemoc (Cemoc), who baptizes the children just before they die. One could see this as a celebration of Christianity over paganism, or one might interpret this story (as well as *The Fate of the Children of Tuirenn*) as the necessity of the Irish to leave their homeland in bad times, returning to it as soon as possible. Each of the main characters in these stories reflects the tragedy of the Irish, who are victimized by forces over which they have no control.

By far the most familiar of "the three sorrows" is *The Fate of the Children of Uisliu,* known informally as *The Tale of Deirdre.* Deirdre's name suggests a mixture of *"deirir"* [conflict] and *"dáir"* [a desire for copulation] and *"dré"* [cart] along with *"dreić"* [as in *dreić na talman,* "a darkness spreading over the earth"]. This is the story that William Butler Yeats used as inspiration for some of his poetry and his play *Deirdre* (1907). George William Russell (Æ) used the story for his poetic drama *Deirdre* (1902), as did John Millington Synge in his *Deirdre of the Sorrows* (1910). Deirdre is seen as the personification of Ireland in the time of its Troubles. She is also the epitome of the woman being a victim of man, the object of lust and possession. This is the only one of the three stories that does not belong (strictly speaking) to the Mythological Cycle as the characters are firmly entrenched in other tales of the Ulster Cycle. It is devoid of the fantastical and absurd elements of the other two tales, and may have come from one of the early Indo-European *romans* of the

Aryan family that once spread from India to Ireland.

This tale is actually the oldest of the three although chronologically it is the youngest. It is mentioned in the twelfth-century *The Book of Leinster* and *The Book of the Dun Cow* as one of the *primscela* that the bards or poet/singers were required to know. The shortest version of the story appears in *The Book of Leinster*, although a fuller version exists in *The Yellow Book of Lecain* (fourteenth century) which is in the Egerton MS. in the British Museum. The *best* version (and most complete) is in a fifteenth century vellum found in MSS.LIII. and LVI. of the Scottish collection. The complete story, however, must be pieced together from several documents and manuscripts that contain snippets and references to it.

Of the three stories, *The Fate of the Children of Uisliu* is the most popular. Deirdre, the most beautiful woman in Ireland, is the cause of a rift between factions of the heroes in the Red Branch. The familiar story of "one woman and two men," Deirdre is the object of a king's lust and, although forbidden by him to follow her heart and marry another, does so anyway. This is in strange contradiction to the Celtic tradition that one sees in stories of elopements and wooings in that in wooings man is normally the suitor while the role of the maiden is largely passive, while in elopements it is the woman who chooses the man and compels him to do her will. Deirdre conforms well with the latter, selecting her mate herself, but it is the *attempt* at wooing by Conchobor that provides the catharsis for the story. There is a strange polarity at work here in that we have age, symbolized by Conchobor the King, at odds with youth, symbolized by Deirdre and Naisi, her Chosen One. We understand that Conchobor's selection of Deirdre for his wife on the day of her birth is hardly an expression of love, yet his sensual lust becomes evident when Deirdre matures. This lust, contrasted with the simplicity of Naisi's devotion, places Conchobor in an unfavorable position. Symbolically, we can see a parallel in this story in the relationship of Ireland and England with Ireland being seen as the beautiful Deirdre while England is symbolized by the grizzled king, Conchobor, who is unreasonable and, although he can have anything he wants including *almost* any woman, refuses to leave Deirdre alone. What he cannot have, he destroys.

The story of Deirdre's thrilling defiance of her self-appointed lord and master seems strangely current today, especially in the Feminist school of criticism, but equally as important to humanity, for Deirdre gives hope and strength to all those who are willing to defy *ex cathedra imperium*—those supreme dictators who disdain human rights to satisfy their own lusts for power. Deirdre is not only a symbol of womanhood and the right of equality in a male-dominated world, she is the symbol of an unflagging spirit that refuses to accept enslavement. Although she triumphs over Conchobor, her triumph, together with that of Naisi, the man she loves, provide us with contrasted sorrows. As such, she becomes the embodiment of Divine Woman.

These stories were very important to the Ancient Irish in that they reflected a tragedy that normally wasn't seen or felt in the happiness of their lives. Still, it was necessary for them to be reminded of tragedy, so they could be prepared for it when it came their way. Consequently, tragedies were required recitations of the bards who, in accordance with Brehon Law, had to keep careful count of when each tragic tale was told in order to keep tragedy from becoming an unnecessary part of their lives.

In addition, the sorrows performed another function in that it reminded those in the present of their past, much in the same way that we today learn about the past by examining the literature of the past. It is also necessary, however, for one to look into the stories of the past in order to understand what has contributed to the present societal structure. To do that, one must understand the intricacies of that daily life. I have tried to provide that with this translation.

In scél fodessin is ní and fodechtsa.

—Randy Lee Eickhoff

Ireland of the Sorrows

Come ye sons and come ye daughters
Of Erin's bright and holy land.
Hear ye now who came before us
Of the tribe of Danu's band.

Learn ye now of pain and sadness
Learn ye now of coming death
Of the glory and the brightness
In every single human breath.

What is life but a short trial?
What is dying but one long rest?
What is gained with each denial
Is the company of the blessed.

The green fields and the singing plover
Are interlaced with peace and love
And when your fleeting grief is over
Ye will know it and be beloved.

Listen closely, my children aching.
Learn to accept what you must endure.
The past is yours for the taking.
Hold it tight and your quest is sure.

—Mícheál O'Ciardha

The Fate of the Children of Tuirenn

*Rachad a haithle searc
na laoch don chill.*[1]

The Defense of the Sons of Cuireann

A sin, was it a sin? We are warriors too.
We did what all warriors do.
We met in battle at Brugh na Boinne,
And a warrior we slew.

Now far and wide we have gone for you
To pick foreign apples from where they grew,
To steal the skin of a Grecian pig
To heal your wounds and your strength renew.

We have met a king and the spear he threw,
The chariot of Dubhar and his whole retinue
Fail-miz and eazal and the spit
Of Finchory and its bubbling stew.

We have stood on *cnoc na mochaen* and shouted our "ballyhoo."
It has taken us years to do what you've asked us to
But sore and broken we have returned
And kneel before you, good Prince Lugh.

We beg mercy for breaking an old taboo.
If God will not forgive us who will? Will you?
Quickly now, lay upon us
The healing skin in the mountain dew.

We are soldiers only, and soldiers true.
We have made every deadly rendezvous.
All we ask is what is our due.
Yet you turn your royal cheek in the morning.

—Mícheál O'Ciardha

i.

AH, BUT WHAT A STORY it is to tell, this one of the Tuirenn children! There is much to it, but one cannot simply begin at the beginning of such a tale. No, it is far too complex a thing to do that and cheapen the story by leaping into it like a dancer playing among the dappled shadows of the willows along the Boyne River. No, no. That won't do at all. Instead, we shall have to begin a little before that story and peek into the dregs of another story first in order to see how this one connects with the next and the next with the one after that and—

But one can play word games only too long. Enough. Here, then, is the tale at the proper beginning.

Oh, but the Battle of Mag Tuired—the first one—was magnificient! The Tuatha Dé Danann[2] sent many of the Fir Bolg to their deaths in that one! Blood washed the ground and a great stench rose up from the battlefield for days after. Crows and ravens feasted well, I tell you! For four days, the battle raged back-and-forth over that plain until at last the Tuatha rallied behind the great warrior Nuada[3] and pushed the Fir Bolg back into the rocky recesses of the northwest, where the great king and magician Conn ruled. Perhaps the Tuatha would have ended it for all time then, for the battle-rage was full upon them, but Conn did not want his country wasted by war and performed great magic, laying a thick field of snow over the entire province in one day. Slowed by having to slog through the great drifts, the Tuatha pulled back and away from the battle, leaving the Fir Bolg in that province they called Conn-snechta.[4]

But the Tuatha had grown weary of battle by then and their great king, Nuada, had nearly been killed in a duel with the Fir Bolg champion Sreng,[5] a great hairy monster who wielded a huge, two-handed sword that split Nuada's shield in twain and sliced Nuada's arm from his shoulder. He might have even killed Nuada had not the great Tuatha warrior Oghma[6] driven Sreng away from the fallen Nuada.

Then did Diancécht[7] work his magic by forming for Nuada, a silver hand, and setting it in place against the stump so that from that time on, Nuada was called Nuada Argatlam.[8] But since the king of the Tuathas was to have no blemish, he was forced to step aside for another man to rule.

"Aye," one of them said in council when the question of Nuada's replacement came up. "There are many to chose from, but who among them can do what Nuada can. Perhaps we should—"

"Tch. Tch. Tch," another said, wagging his forefinger in objection. "I know what you are up to, you rascal! You would have us step away from the ancient laws and let Nuada rule despite his blemish. Well, I say no! Step once away from a law, you step away from others later, and then you have anarchy! No, no, no! We shall have a new king!"

"I agree," a third chimed in. "But who? And we had better be quick about it. The Fomorians[9] have been watching to see how the battle went with the Fir Bolg, and I have a hunch they know how weak we have become."

"And your point?" the first asked, snapping his fingers impatiently. "Get to it before an oak grows from an acorn! You could talk the water to dust!"

"Very well," the former said icily. "I suggest we cast our lot in with the Fomorians. Only temporarily," he hastened to add, raising a hand to stave off argument. "I say let's send an ambassador to Elotha[10] and ask to let his son Bres to be our ruler. That would keep the Fomorians from raiding our lands until we can rebuild our strength."

"A Formorian as a king over the Tuatha Dé Danann?" the first said indignantly. "What stuff and nonsense! Better to let Nuada continue, I say, than to bring the wolf into the fold!"

"His mother is Ériu," the former said pointedly. "Who is, I'm certain you recall, a Tuatha Dé Danann. That gives him a foot in both kingdoms, eh?"

"I'm for it," the second speaker said. "Great balls! We'll be at it until the sun turns to cinder if we don't settle this fast. Besides, what harm can be done? If he's no good, we get rid of him"—he snapped his fingers—"like that!"

"A wolf in the fold can kill a lot of sheep before he's driven out," the first said. "But I'm ruled against—I can see that! But don't throw my words to the winds! I still say you're wrong!"

And so ambassadors were sent to Elotha, who listened to the proposal, scarcely able to hide his glee. He willingly gave up his son to be king of the Tuatha Dé Danann, thinking that he had won the battle without dipping a single spearblade in Tuatha blood.

But politics seldom agree with logic. Had Bres been an honorable man, perhaps peace would have existed between the Fomorians and the Tuathas. But Bres had inherited only his mother's beauty, while from his father he inherited the ruthlessness of the Fomorians. He quickly imposed a heavy tax of an ounce of gold upon each man of the Tuatha Dé Danaan, enforcing the tax with soldiers from his father's army. The Tuatha were quickly made slaves, and there was nothing that Nuada could do to help his people.

And then Bres imposed another tax upon kneading bowls, another on querns, and yet another on baking stones. Each year, the Tuatha were to gather on Balor's Hill,[11] which would soon be called The Hill of Usneach,[12] and there pay their taxes. Any who refused to pay the taxes would have his nose cut off. Year after year, the unhappy Tuathas gathered at the hill to await the tax gatherers sent by Elotha.

ii.

ONE DAY, THE STEWARD OF Nuada's house, a one-eyed grizzled warrior who had lost an eye the day his master lost his arm, stood on the wall of the Tara house, facing the sun, feeling its warmth soak into his bones. He held a cat in his arms and toyed with its ears, taking comfort in the rumble of its purring against his breast. Idly, he looked across the green plain at the foot of the hill to where a field of grain shone palely gold in the setting light. Two dots appeared in the distance, and he watched as they grew larger into young men, crossing the thick sedge, past clumps of skullcap and monkshood.

"And who might you be?" he called as they paused at the gate. They looked up at him and smiled.

"Well," one said in a musical voice, "I am Miach and this is Omiach. We are the sons of Diancécht."

"The doctor?" the steward asked.

"Yes. As are we. And not bad ones either, if I may say so," Omiach answered.

"We have a few healer's tricks," Miach said cautiously, giving his brother a reproving look.

The steward snorted. "That's as here as now. I can't tell you how many of you young sports come to this here gate bragging on how they have the gift of the hazel wand. But there's the difference between berries and turnips as 'tween them and Diancécht. Sons you may be, but do you have the magic of the old man? There's a difference between taking a splinter out from 'twixt the toes and closing a wound so it don't fester."

"We've been known to heal a bit," Miach said. He elbowed his brother in his ribs as the latter opened his mouth to speak.

"Umph!" Omiach grunted. He rubbed his side. "Now, what would you be doing that for? Eh? And why hide our skills under an whortleberry bush? When you're good, you're good, and there's no two ways about it!"

The steward laughed. "Well, if you're that good, then maybe you could put an eye in this hollow where my own good eye once was? Damn nuisance it is, looking at the world through one window when two were meant to be a man's use."

"Easy," Omiach said, ignoring Miach's vain attempt to hush him. "How about one of that cat's eyes? Would that serve you?"

The steward glared suspiciously at him, but the young man met his stare calmly. "Huh," the steward said. "If you ain't a sassy cockleburr. Very well, let's give you a try."

And no sooner were the words from his mouth than the cat leaped up in his arms, raking its claws down his arm, squawking, "Rrrrowrrrr!" It leaped upon the wall, looked wildly around for a moment, then streaked down from the wall and ran into the barn and hid under a sheaf of straw.

The steward suddenly looked out at the world from two eyes, blinking wonderingly at what suddenly had depth and a strange mixture of color. He raised his fingers and lightly touched the hollow where the lid had once been stitched down against his cheek. He saw his fingers coming toward the hollow and flinched away.

"Damme, if you don't have the whisper of the gods in your ears!" he exclaimed. He looked around wonderingly, enjoying the sudden beauty and strangeness that he had missed for so many years.

"I'm happy for you," Omiach said. He glanced at Miach, who shrugged.

"It's done, and once the milk's spilt, you can't put it back in the pail," Miach said. He looked up at the steward. "Would you be so kind as to tell your master that we wait outside his gate for his permission to enter?"

"Right back," the steward said. He climbed down from the wall and hurried across the yard. Suddenly he stumbled as a sparrow slipped across the edge of his sight and the new eye leaped in its socket, following the sparrow's flight. "Damme, if this won't take some getting used to," he muttered to himself. "But there's a bit of bad to all gifts, I'm thinking."

As he hurried through the hall, he heard a tiny rustle, and again the eye leaped to focus on a mouse scurrying along the wall to disappear in a crack beside a center beam. He closed the eye and stepped into the warm hall where Nuada lounged on his chair, nursing a cup of honeyed ale.

"What is it?" Nuada asked crossly as the steward came close to him. He had been cross since rising with new pains where his silver arm joined the stump, and now it seemed to have spread across his shoulders, making the other ache as well.

"Beg pardon," the steward said, "but two physicians wait outside your gate for permission to enter."

"I'm not in the mood for company," Nuada said sulkily. He buried his nose in his ale cup, drinking deeply. "But don't let it be said that we don't pay attention to the laws of hospitality.[13] Take them to the guest house and make my apologies. Say I'm ill and crave their pardon for my seeming rudeness. I'll greet them properly in the morning. If," he grunted as a stab of pain washed up from his shoulder, "if this cursed arm stops giving me trouble!"

The steward fidgeted for a moment, then said, "I really think it would be best if you saw them now. They ain't your run-of-the-mill quacksalver. Look!" He opened the new eye and stared at Nuada. "How many you know could put the eye of a cat in place of me old eye that's long been jelly dessert for a battle-crow? Eh?"

Nuada stared with sudden interest at the new eye meeting his. "Hmm," he said. "That's truly a gift that one of them has, I'd say. Well, don't just stand there like a stool, bring them in!"

The steward scurried away, limping as a stab of arthritis hit him in a hip. "Drat and mouse turds!" he grumbled, swinging one leg shorter than the other in a truncated gait. "Must be a storm gathering!" He cast an eye over the sky as he ordered the bar slipped from the gate and the doors swung wide.

"My master bids you welcome and to take you to the Great Hall," he said. Something rustled in the grass beside the gatepost. His new eye jerked down and around, seeking the source of the noise. "Damn," he muttered, holding his hand over it. "Becoming a bit of a nuisance, this is. Just takes some getting used to, I suppose."

"Thank you," Miach said politely as he and his brother entered and followed the steward to the house. As they entered the Great Hall, they heard a deep groan, then a long sigh, as from someone in great pain.

"There's a warrior here who is injured," Miach said. "That sigh seemed to come from deep within him."

"Hmm. Maybe," Omiach said cautiously. The sigh came again. He cocked his head, listening. "Of course, it could be the sigh of a warrior with a *darb-dóel*[14] working within him."

"You could be right," Miach said seriously. "I believe we have a bit more work to do before we'll be able to rest tonight. Steward!"

The steward turned toward him, staring with one blue eye and one yellow. Miach smiled as the yellow eye turned reflexively toward the wall and a fly buzzing by.

"It takes a little getting used to," he said solicitously. The steward nodded and sighed.

"Making me head swim, it is," he muttered. He pressed the heel of his palm against the yellow eye. "But beggars can't be choosers, and it has its blessings as well. What is it?"

"We heard a groaning and sighing as if someone was in pain when we entered the hall," Miach said. "Tell me: is there a warrior here with some difficulty?"

"Ah," the steward said, nodding. "That would Nuada. Ever since Diancécht gave him that silver arm, he's been bothered with aches and pains. Getting worse, it is, though he won't admit it." Miach and Omiach exchanged glances.

"Well, bring us to him," Omiach said. "Perhaps we can help."

"I dunno," the steward said, scratching his head with a long nail. He hawked and spat, rubbing the spittle away with the toe of his shoe. "Nuada said to bring you to him, but I reckoned to give him a bit more time to get rid of the bogles if that's what's bothering him."

"Oh, I think he'll want to see us," Omiach said breezily. "Lead us to him, then. There's a good lad."

"Lad? Old enough to have been a grin on your mother's lips," the steward muttered. "And you ladding me about, are you? Well, then, on your head it is, then."

He took the two brothers into the king's room where Nuada lay back against his couch, rubbing his shoulder softly. His face was white with pain, tiny beads of perspiration dotting his upper lip. The brothers' noses wrinkled at the sour smell of the sickroom. They looked at each other and nodded.

"A *darb-dóel*," they said in unison.

Nuada's eyes opened. He stared through pain-dulled eyes at them. "Ah, excuse my bad manners, please," he said softly. He grimaced and grabbed his shoulder. "I seem to be having difficulties here."

"Your shoulder?" Miacht came forward, and touched Nuada's shoulder gently; Nuada flinched away, growing paler. He grabbed his ale-cup, draining it.

"Hurts, doesn't it?" Omiach said. He looked over at the steward. "Call a few servants, will you?"

"What for?" the steward said suspiciously.

"Well, if it is what we think it is, we will want to kill it when we release it," Miacht said. "A *darb-dóel* is a tricky devil. Very fast and elusive. You stomp on it, and it's not there."

"A *darb-dóel?*" the steward said, shaking his head. "What's that?"

"You'll see. You'll see. Now, get a few others in here. With shoes on," he called, as the steward turned away. "We don't want to have to go after the creature more than once."

When the others had gathered around Nuada's chair, Miacht gently took the silver arm in his hand.

"Now, this is going to hurt a bit," he said quietly to Nuada. "But there's nothing for it. Ready?"

Nuada gritted his teeth, nodding. Miacht took the silver arm, then suddenly wrenched it up and out away from Nuada's body, ripping it away. "Ye—ow!" yelled Nuada. A great stench of putrefying flesh rose from the wound. Within it, a large black beetle, the size of an adult cockroach appeared. The *darb-dóel* hesitated, then bounded away from the stump and scurried through the Great Hall.

"There it goes!" yelled the steward. "Filthy beast!"

He stamped at it with his good foot, but the *darb-dóel* slipped away, heading for the door. The servants leaped after it, their feet slapping like thunder as they tried to kill it. The *darb-dóel* swerved and dashed into the cooking room. The steward leaped over it and raced ahead to the door, grabbing a meat mallet as he raced past the cook's table. He knelt on the floor, and when the *darb-dóel* came close, smashed it quickly, spattering it over the floor. He rose with satisfaction and handed the meat mallet to one of the servants.

"Here. Clean up the mess, now," he ordered. The servant looked with disgust at the splotch before the threshold and left to get a bucket of water. The steward walked back into the Great Hall, pausing to straighten his tunic, before approaching the dais where Nuada slumped pale-faced on his couch.

"Got the bloody thing," he grunted. Nuada nodded, the color already beginning to return to his cheeks. He glanced at the silver arm in Miach's hands. He shuddered.

"It was good while it lasted," he said. "But I don't think that I want it back."

Miach smiled gently and handed the arm to the steward, who took it gingerly. "Yes, I can understand that. But, all things are possible if you believe in them. Of course, one must be careful with what one wishes to believe as there can be problems unforeseen that come from wishes." He frowned. "More harm has been done in the name of good than you would expect. Good is evanescent. One must remember that."

"As should you," Omiach pointed out. He shook his head. "I know what you're thinking, Miach. There's danger in being a meddler."

Miach smiled again. "Well, shouldn't one always follow one's beliefs?" He turned back to Nuada. "Would you like a real arm in place of that silver thing?"

"Here we go," growled Omiach. Miach ignored him.

"It is possible. Not"—he held up his hand—"completely certain, you understand. But possible."

"Of course," Nuada said.

And that began Miach's search for an arm to match the arm of the former king. But that was no easy task. The arm had to be equally as long and muscular and flexible. But among all the Tuatha, none could be found that would match Nuada's—except that of Modhan the Swineherd. But this simply wouldn't do, you see, for a man of Nuada's stature simply could not carry a swineherd's arm with him into polite company. Besides, what would the swineherd do without it? No, no, there was, as Miach had put it, possible, but not certain.

Nuada was crestfallen.

"I warned you," Miach said softly.

"Yes, but warnings like that are seldom heeded as warnings," Nuada sighed. "Children do not think of the possibility of failure, and what are we but grown children?"

"Men," a passing wench muttered to another, "are grown children, perhaps. But who does the washing and cleaning around here, I would ask you? Eh? And then, we're to look sensuous[15] for them when they're in their cups! I tell you—"

"Would the bones of the man's own arm be of any help to you?" Omiach asked.

Miach frowned, pursing his lips, musing. "Well, now, 'tisn't a thought I've given to it, but there is that which can be done. *If*," he emphasized, "we had the true bones."

"We can only try," Omiach said.

A man was dispatched to the battlefield of Mag Tuired. There he discovered where Nuada's arm had been buried and uncovered it. He brought the bones back to Tara, where Miach examined them closely.[16] Then, he looked at Omiach and said, "Would you prefer to place the arm or go for the herbs?"

"I'd rather do the arm," Omiach said. "You are much more successful grubbing around the dirt for herbs than I."

And so Miach left to gather the herbs. When he returned, Omiach had the arm placed and Miach made a paste of some of the herbs and bound the arm straight down Nuada's side. He chanted an incantation:

> "Joint to joint I join you.
> To the joints, I join the sinew.
> After that, we will bend
> The joint and after that tend
> To making the flesh that I'll bid
> To grow under which all will be hid."

After three days had passed, the arm had joined once again at the shoulder. Then Miach bent the arm at the elbow, covered it again with herbs, and bound it for three more days across Nuada's stomach. After those three days were up, he made a paste out of charred bulrushes and cattails and covered the arm and wrapped it for three more days.

On the tenth day, he took off the bandage. A great shout went up over the land, for Nuada's arm once again hung from his shoulder and he could again be king. Word quickly spread and reached the ear of Diancécht, who left immediately for Tara to see for himself. When he entered Nuada's hall, Nuada rose from his couch and flexed the arm, saying, "You have a marvelous son there, Diancécht! I daresay that in time his fame will surpass your own."

Diancécht grew red with rage, and when Miach entered the room, he drew his sword and slashed his son across the head, slicing the flesh.

"Father! Why did you do that?" Miacht asked, healing himself immediately. Again, Diancécht slashed at Miacht, cutting his son to the bone. And again, Miacht healed himself.

"Father! Why did you do that?" he asked again. But Diancécht did not answer and swung his sword a third time at Miach, cutting through the skull to the brain. But again, Miacht healed himself. Enraged, Diancécht trepanned his son. When Miacht's brain fell out upon the floor, Miacht fell dead.

Diancécht took his son's body and buried it secretly in a glade deep in the forest. Three hundred sixty-five herbs grew up from his grave, one for each part of the body. His sister, Airmed,[17] who had skills as great as her father, gathered the herbs, carefully sorting them upon her cloak. But when Diancécht learned what she was doing, he went to the clearing, grabbed her cloak, and shook the herbs into the air, mixing them. Airmed was unable to sort them again, and Man lost his chance at immortality.

Seven years had passed, however, since Bres had taken the throne from which Nuada had once ruled; and during that time, Bres had grown very strong, and the Fomorians ruled them ruthlessly.

When the Tuatha went to Bres and told him that they no longer wanted him as their king, Bres laughed at them and laid even heavier taxes upon them, having grown too strong for Nuada to do anything to upset his rule.

One day, Cairpré, the chief poet of the Tuatha, came to the court, expecting to be greatly honored as all poets were, but Bres laughed when he heard that Cairpré had entered his house and ordered the poet to be placed in a small, dingy room without fire, bed, or chair for the table upon which tiny cakes without seeds, burnt from the oven, were left for him to eat. When Cairpré rose the next morning to take his leave, he delivered the first magical satire ever spoken in Ireland against his host, saying:

> "I received no meat upon the plate
> Given to me. No milk from a cow,
> Either. So, now I pronounce the fate
> Of Bres who has the honor of a sow:
> May he likewise receive the honor
> That he cheerfully has given to another!"

Upon hearing the poet's words, red splotches broke out upon Bres's face, which caused the Tuatha to heave a sigh of relief since no one who had a blemish could be their king. Bres was forced to leave and Nuada stepped upon the throne. But Bres's strength was so great that Nuada could do nothing to ease the heavy taxes that had been placed upon his people.

iii.

ONE DAY AS NUADA SAT in a feast, a stranger dressed as a prince came to the door of his house and demanded of the gatekeepers, Gamal and Camall, that his presence be announced to the king. Gamal looked at Camall and winked, then turned to the young man, saying:

"Aye, that we'll be certain to do. But tell us, youth, what reason does the king have for seeing you?"

"Tell him that I am Lugh, the grandson of Diancécht by Cian, my father, and Balor's grandson by Ethniu, my mother," the youth replied.

"Uh-huh," grunted Camall. "But that tells us little, as Balor has many grandsons from dallying his tallywhacker in so many honey-wells. So, young one, tell us what it is that you do. This is the master's feast, and one must be a master to gain entrance."

"Then, tell your king that I am a carpenter."

Gamal spat. "That may be well and good, but we already got the best of them: Luchtainé's his name. Doubt you see many that can mortise joints like him."

"I'm also a very good smith," Lugh said again.

"Got one of them, too," Camall said. "No one turns iron like Goibniu."

"And I am a champion among warriors," Lugh said.

"Uh-huh," Gamal said doubtfully. "Well, we have the king's own brother, Oghama in there. One of them's enough."

"And I am a harper," Lugh continued.

"Can you play as well as Abcan?"

"I'm as good with my wits as I am my strength," Lugh said.

"So is Bresal," Gamal said.

"I have many stories to tell."

"We already got a poet," Camall yawned.

"I am no stranger to magic."

"And we got a lot of sorcerers and Druids," Gamal said.

"I am a healer."

"We got the best: Diancécht."

"I bear cups."

"Got nine of them. That's more than enough."

"I work well in bronze."

"Well, if you could best Credné, then you might be worth the coal for the forge. But I doubt it," Camall said.

Lugh smiled. "But," he asked gently, "do you have one man who can do all these things? Take this to your king, and if he has, I will shake Tara's dust from my heels."

"Best go and see about it," Gamal said to Camall. He eyed Lugh carefully. " 'Tis a good brag and if he's half as good with his hands as he is his words, he might be of use to the king."

Camall sighed and trudged away from the gate, making his way into the banquet hall. There, he approached Nuada and told him about the boastful youth at the gate.

"We got a young one, dressed like a prince, who claims to be an *ioldánac*,"[18] he said. He shrugged. "Thought it best to let you know. Might be a bit of amusement in it for you."

Nuada laughed. "Well, then, let the young man in! And bring the *fidchell*[19] board and our best players. If he beats them, why, then, bring him to us!"

Camall sighed and went off to do Nuada's bidding. But Lugh beat all of the players, inventing a move that came to be known as "Lugh's Enclosure" as he did. When he saw this, Camal brought the youth into the banquet hall. There was a seat vacant beside Nuada that was known as the "Sage's Seat," and Lugh went straight to the seat and took it. Eyebrows rose at his brashness as the four great leaders of the Tuatha—Dagda, the chief Druid; Diancécht, the physician; Oghma, the champion; and Goibniu, the smith—all exchanged glances.

"Well, now," Oghma said quietly to the others, "let's see about this young rooster."

He rose and went to a huge stone that four teams of oxen had brought in. He spat on his hands, bent, and lifted it, then hurled it through the thick wall of the fort.

"Always with the theatrics," Nuada sighed. "Now we'll have to have it brought back in again. I really wish you would find something else to amuse yourself with."

Lugh smiled and rose, and walked through the hole in the wall where he picked up the stone and tossed it negligently back through the hole in the wall where it landed in the exact same place from which Oghma had plucked it. Oghma shook his head as he retook his seat. "Boy has a set of shoulders on him under that tunic, I'm thinking," he said.

Then Lugh took a harp off the wall and smiled gently at the court as he plucked the strings. Golden notes rang softly through the room as Lugh played the "Sleeping Lullaby," and Nuada and his court fell fast asleep. They awoke the next day at the same hour, bewildered. Then Lugh played the "Song of Sorrow," and Nuada and his court wept buckets of tears.

" 'Tis a fine hand you have with the strings," Nuada blubbered.

Lugh smiled and his fingers danced faster and faster across the strings, playing tune after tune, and the Tuatha laughed and began dancing wildly as music rose and soared around the room. At last he stopped, and Nuada smiled and stepped down from the throne.

"A better man you are than any here," he declared. "You must be the king of the Tuatha, not I."

And so Lugh reigned for thirteen days among the Tuatha Dé Danaan. Then he took Nuada aside along with his advisors and spoke with them about doing battle with the Fomorians. Then, he disappeared, promising to return when the Tuatha needed him the most.

Nuada and his advisors went back to the halls of Tara, and again Nuada took the throne. But nothing was done about the heavy taxes laid upon the Tuatha and for three years, they languished under the Fomorian rule while memory of the magical youth slowly disappeared.

iv.

NOW, ONE DAY WHEN THE time rolled around for the new collection of taxes, Nuada and the rest of the Tuatha Dé Danaan assembled at the Hill of Usneach, waiting for the Fomorian tax collectors the duties imposed upon them by Bres. A cold wind blew that day, stinging the eyes of the Tuatha as they stared across the plain, waiting.

" 'Tis an evil day," remarked Aengus, staring across the plain. His nose began to run, and he wiped it absently with the back of his hand, then heeled the tears from his eyes, drying his hands upon his scarlet cloak. He turned to face Nuada. "What I don't understand is why we put up with them. You're whole again."

Nuada moved his new arm uneasily, feeling it leap to his command. He felt the temptation to once again place his sword, the great sword brought by the Tuatha from Findias in Greece that no one could escape and whose injury no one could heal. He shook his head. "We left Bres on the throne too long," he said at last. "He has grown very strong over the past seven years while we have not prepared ourselves for battle."

"Speak for yourself," growled Lir. He fingered his sword, then hawked and spat. The wind drew his spittle and splattered the face of Ogham, who frowned angrily at Lir, but the great warrior ignored him. "As for me, I'd give anything to cross swords with that Bres. Why, I'd—"

"—cause all of us a great deal of harm," Aengus finished for him. Lir glared at him. "No, Lir, we must be a bit tactful on this. Nuada is right; we must bide our time until we can down them. Remember the last battle with the Fir Bolg? The Fomorians will be worse."

"Better the dust than the bended knee, you ask me," Lir said. Forgetting the wind blowing from the east, he turned and spat and swore when his spittle blew back upon him. He wiped his paw across his tunic, then frowned and stared hard at a small cloud of dust coming toward them across the plain.

"Now, who's this, you suppose?" he asked.

Nuada and Aengus turned, looking where he pointed. A stately band of warriors rode toward them upon white horses, with a young man leading them. Bright sunlight seemed to gleam from his figure, his forehead. They blinked as the brightness burned their eyes, then tried to make out his features with quick flicks of their eyes.

"I don't know about this," Aengus said doubtfully. "What more can happen to us?"

"Ah, shut your gob," Lir said. Aengus gave him an indignant look, but Lir ignored him. "From the looks of this group, they know which end of the sword to use. I say we make ready." He glanced over his shoulder at the Fomorians still riding toward them in their groups of nines. "We could be caught between two stones like grain in a gristmill."

"Hold your sword," Nuada said quietly, placing his hand on Lir's arm to keep him from drawing his weapon. "Diplomacy, my friend. Let us see what they want before we do anything."

Lir hawked, then remembered the wind, and swallowed. He

glared at Nuada. "It's the fine words of people like you that got us in this mess in the first place. Bres as king. Phaw! A cold blade's what we should have given him instead of the crown!"

"And who else should we have placed upon the throne," Aengus asked. "You?"

"And what would be wrong with that?" Lir asked, glowering at the fair-faced youth whose beauty caused all women to sigh and conspire to meet with him in the dark.

"Enough," Nuada commanded quietly as the riders came up the hill to them. "Greetings!" he called. He blinked at the brightness burning from the forehead of the leader. "I bid you good day! I am Nuada of the Tuatha Dé Danaan."

The leader reined in and lowered his head, removing his helmet that had a precious stone set behind it and two more in front. For the first time, they saw fully his comely countenance as bright and glorious as the setting sun. He looked over the people, still sitting or squatting on their haunches. He frowned; then a small smile crept over his face and many a maiden there felt her heart flutter in her breast and her breath come in shallow gasps.

"I am Lugh Lamfada[20] from the Tír Tairnmigiri.[21] These"—he turned to indicate the warriors behind him—"are my foster-brothers, the sons of Manannán Mac Lir.[22] Sgoith Glegeal and Rabach Slaitin, Gleigal Garb, Goithne Gormsuileach, Sine Sinderg, Domnall Donruad, and Aed, the son of Eathall." His mare moved restlessly beneath him, shuffling her feet daintly. He smiled and smoothed her brightly flowing mane. "And this is Enbarr," he added. He laughed, and the notes of his laughter tinkled over the crowd like a bell tone rung from clear glass. The others stared admiringly at the beautiful horse, recalling the legend of the mare of Manannán who was as fast as the naked cold wind of spring and so swift that she could run equally over land and water and so quick that no rider upon her back was ever harmed in battle.

"We know her," Lir said gruffly. He nodded at the breastplate and mail Lugh wore. "And I see your foster-father gave you the loan of his armor as well."

Lugh laughed again and touched the sword hanging from his left side. "And his sword, Fregartach, 'The Answerer,' from whose wound no one recovers. I would draw it, but all who gaze upon it become so frightened that they become as weak as a woman in the arms of a deadly disease or childbirth." He grinned at Lir. "Even you, Grandfather," he said teasingly.

Lir flushed, his face growing dark with suppressed anger. He fingered the hilt of his sword. "For an acorn, I'd teach you a bit of respect," he said.

Lugh held up his hands. "Is this a greeting or an invitation to battle?" he said. He shook his head, laughing merrily. Then, he noticed the Formorians drawing nearer to the bottom of the hill. "But I see you are expecting other company."

Nuada glanced over his shoulder at the Fomorians. The others stood as the tax gatherers rode up the hill toward them. Nine times nine groups of them, they were, each as dirty as the other, greasy hair hanging in half-ringlets beneath their helmets, the smell of rotting flesh following them. Nuada recognized four of the riders, the cruelest and fiercest of the Fomorians: Eine, Eithfaith, Coron, and Compar, who inspired such fear in the Tuatha that none dared punish their children or foster-children without begging their permission first.

Lugh frowned at the honor paid the Fomorians. "Now, what are these *rógaires* who bring you to your feet when you stayed seated when we came, eh? From the looks of them, they could stand a good wash and currying."

"Sh," Nuada said nervously. "Don't anger them. If anyone—even the smallest child—a month-old babe, even—had stayed on the ground when they came up, that would have given them the excuse they want for killing us. Especially, those four in front. Why, they would rather drink blood than honeyed-beer."

Lugh glared at them for a moment, then said, "Why for a hickory nut or acorn, I'm half-minded to put them down myself."

"I'm telling you—" Nuada began nervously, but Lugh spoke loudly over him.

"Why, these rascals should be killed themselves. I'm half-minded to do it now."

"We would meet our own deaths and destruction would follow across our fair land if you did," Nuada said.

"At least, we'd be men," Lir muttered darkly.

Lugh shook his head and gathered his reins. He looked down at the group and said, "You have been under the thumb of the Fomorians long enough, I'm thinking." A bright smile flashed across his comely face. He clamped the helmet on his head, controlling the dancing Enbarr with his knees. "I say let's see how thin their blood runs!"

"Lugh!" Nuada said sharply, but Lugh only laughed again and took Enbarr down the hill in a gallop toward the group. Manannán's sons followed, loosening their weapons in their sheaths. Lugh slid to a stop, brazenly barring the path up the hill from the Fomorians. Eine frowned at this behavior.

"What's this, puppy?" he asked. He bared his long yellow teeth. "You're a handsome one, I'll give you that. Not very smart, though, to stand in the way of your betters."

"Oh?" Lugh asked carelessly. "And who might they be?"

"Let me take his head," Compar growled. He pulled his sword, the blade well-blooded. "A little chop-chop, and we'll be done with this mosquito."

Coron gave Lugh a careful look, then shook his head. "Don't look like there's much sting to him. Swat him and be done with it, I say!"

Compar nudged his lathered horse forward, but never saw Lugh's hand move as Fregartach leaped from its scabbard and sliced cleanly through Compar's neck. Compar's eyes twitched. "An accident!" he mumbled. "Blind, mindless accident!" Then his head toppled from his shoulders and rolled across the dusty grass.

The others stared dumbly at Compar's head rolling like an agate among the hooves of their horses, then Enbarr reared, lashing out with her hooves and striking Eithfaith's horse between the eyes, stoning him dead instantly.

"What the—*waa!?*" Eithfaith exclaimed as he found himself thrown sideways. "Trickery!" he howled. "Watch yourselves!" A blinding flash exploded in his eyes. He blinked. Felt a tug at his neck. Then looked stupidly up at his body, staggering and falling. "Arm yourselves!" he roared, but the words came out in a squeak.

Then Lugh's battle-cry roared over the plain and his foster-brothers fell upon the Fomorians from the flanks. Fregartach leaped and danced in the bright sunlight, deadly rays like rainbows flying from its edge as Lugh boldly carved his way through the troop, slaughtering and disfiguring all who stood in his way.

"Mercy!" howled one, but Lugh ignored his plea as he dealt red slaughter to all until only nine of the nine times nine remained standing in a tiny, bewildered knot, staring in dismay at the carnage around them.

"Sanctuary!" Eine exclaimed, tossing his sword aside. He held his bare hands up beseechingly. Lugh frowned at the grimed wrinkles in the hairy knuckles then relented.

"All right," he said. He reached down and ripped a section from Eine's tunic, grimaced at its filth, then wiped the blood from Fregartach's blade. He sheathed it and said, "I suppose it's only good form to spare some of you. Besides," he added thoughtfully, "I want you to take word of this slaughter back to your king and tell him and the rest of the foreigners that they are no longer welcome in the land of the Tuatha Dé Danaan. Better he should kill you as the messengers than my own men."

He turned Enbarr and rode up the hill as the Fomorians whipped their horses away from the red slaughter, galloping back to the coast, where their long ships waited to take them and the taxes they had gathered back to Balor of the Evil Eye.

"By the great balls, but that was something!" Lir exclaimed as Lugh rode up to them. He slapped Lugh's knee. "It's no knitting boy you are, I can see! That's as fine a blade dancing as I've ever seen!"

"Now you've done it for certain," Aengus sighed mournfully, watching the Fomorians disappear in the distance. "We're in it for sure, now! Balor will not take this lightly."

Lugh smiled at him. "We can only hope that he doesn't."

"Hope? Hope?" Nuada shook his head. "There's little hope for us, I'm thinking."

"Isn't it better to live like men, then die and be done with it, instead of starving and wasting away little by little?" Lugh demanded. He shook his head. "Why men prefer to live on their knees instead of their feet is beyond me."

Lir slapped Nuada on the shoulder, staggering him. "The boy speaks truth! I say we make ready!"

"Yes, of course," Nuada said, rubbing his shoulder. "We have little choice in the matter, now. That's all been decided for us."

And then memory of the youth who had come to the halls of Tara three years before returned and he smiled.

"But," he said, "I believe the time has come for us to make plans."

And so they returned to the halls of Tara and went into council, planning for the battle they knew was coming.

V.

BALOR FROWNED AS HE LISTENED to the tale Eine told, his hands dancing nervously in the air as he described the rack and ruin Lugh had carved through their ranks.

"Monstrous!" Eine finished, beads of perspiration dotting his forehead. "Monstrous, I say. Gave no warning that he was going to be carving on our hides. Uncivilized, you ask me!" He snarkled, hawked, and spat to the side, wiping his nose with a dirty forefinger. "And there was poor Eithfaith, head rolling among the hooves of our horses like a rock being kicked this way and that, still yelling. A sight I won't forget for a long time, I tell you that!"

Balor sucked the end of his long mustache into his mouth, chewing. He glared at the others. "Well?" he demanded. "Anyone know who this upstart is?"

The others stirred uneasily, looking away from the angry Balor, hoping that he wouldn't part his hair in the back and release the beams and dyes of venom from his evil eye that could fry men's courage and drop them dead in their tracks.[23]

"Your grandson," said Cathleann the Crooked-Toothed, his wife. His good eye clicked toward her like agate stones in a cold stream.

"What's this?" he asked suspiciously, his brow lowering like a dark thundercloud. "What's this you say?"

"Oh, stuff and nonsense!" she said exasperatedly. "He's Lugh Il-Dana,[24] the son of Ethniu, our daughter, the grandson known as Lugh the Long-Armed. The one of the prophecy."

A hard look settled over Balor's face. His cheeks grew dark with anger. A strange grinding noise seemed to come from his direction, and it took a moment before all there realized he was grinding his teeth in fury. They stirred uneasily, moving slowly toward the door, for all knew Balor's fury and what might happen when reason left him like leaves leaving the branches of oak trees in autumn.

"Yes," she said grimly. "That one. The one who's coming will end our power over the Tuatha. And stop grinding your teeth. It's most unseemly."

"Quiet, woman!" he growled. "There's enough of your yammering! I know that it cannot be our grandson. It must be somebody else. All right, enough of your sniveling!" he said to the others, raising his voice. "All of you leave except for the council. We'll give weight to the words we have heard and decide what to do."

"How do you know—" Cathleann began, but fell silent as Balor glared at her.

"Women," Balor growled. He leaned back in his chair, tugging his fingers through his gnarled beard, glowering into the center of the room. *Now, how could it be the one of the prophecy? Did I not have him killed? Did I not send Ethniu's son out onto the cold gray sea?*

And indeed he had after Cian, a Tuatha nobleman, disguised himself and made his way to the crystal tower on Tory Island where Balor had imprisoned his daughter after hearing a prophecy from a rogue Druid who warned the king of the Fomorians that his grandson would slay him in a last great battle, and there Cian had made love to the lonely Ethniu. After the child was born, Balor had given the baby boy to one of his minor rulers by the sea and ordered the infant to be drowned. But because Balor did not say why he wanted such a terrible thing done, the retainer hesitated and looked at the glowing face of the gurgling babe and his heart went out to the infant. As he stood beside the shore of the cold gray sea, torn between his duty and his desire, word came to him that his wife had given birth to a stillborn child. With that, the retainer wrapped the child in his cloak and smuggled the baby into his house and to his wife's side, taking the dead child away and giving it to the sea in place of Balor's grandson. When it came time for the fostering of the child, Manannán Mac Lir, the god of the waves, took the child for his own and raised it carefully in the old ways.

But all of this Balor did not know as he waited for the council to settle: Eab, the grandson of Nét,[25] Senchab, the grandson of Nét; Sotal Salmor, Luath Leborcham, Tinne Mor of Triscadal, Loisginn Lomgluineach, Luath Lineach, Lobais the Druid, Liathlabar, the son of Lobais; the nine wise poets and prophets of the Fomorians; the twelve white-mouthed sons of Balor; and Cathleann.

"Well," he asked when the great oaken door had been swung shut, leaving them alone. "Well?"

"Well, yourself," Cathleann said grouchily. "First you tell people to hold their lip, then you want them to banter about like fishwives. Make up your mind, husband!"

Balor sighed and dug his knuckles furiously into his temples. "Woman, if you have something to be adding that will help us here, say so! Otherwise, stop your gob!"

"A mouth at rest offers nothing," she said stoutly, then fell silent, folding her arms across her heavy breasts, glaring defiantly back at him.

"We'll get nowhere at this," Senchab said. "Remember that a wedge from an oak tree splits itself."

"Enough homilies," Balor said. He glanced around the table. "Well? There's an upstart standing tall in Ireland, now, defying us. Will no one rid us of this man?"

The council members exchanged quick looks with each other, holding caution on their tongues, for none knew more than the other about the man who had sent the nine tax collectors packing with their tails between their legs like tick-filled dogs. That he was a man to be reckoned with was obvious: The heads of Compar and Eithfaith had been solidly attached to their broad shoulders, and many a man had tried to separate them before, only to be cleaved from gob to stopper by the warriors themselves. 'Twas a mighty man, indeed, who could send those two kicking their way through the dark to the land of Donn.[26]

"Not one man?" Balor asked again, his words cutting through their thoughts like a pruning knife. "Is there not a one of you who drinks real beer and not watered wine?"

"Enough," growled Balor's son Bres, whose authority had been flouted by the Tuatha and Lugh. "Give me seven brigades of brave men and I'll bring Lugh's head to the green of Berva in Lochlann."[27]

"That makes sense," Eab said. The others looked at him. "Well, he's the one who lost his place in Ireland. Only right that he should take it back." He looked at Bres. "And it would be good for your name that you do so. After all"—he shrugged—"what else does a man have? A sword is only temporal. But victories, ah, yes, victories leave a man immortal."

Bres nodded and, drawing himself up straight, said, "Then it is settled. Make ready the warships and the barks and let them be filled with food and stores."

The council closed quickly before he could change his mind and Luath Leborcham scuttled down to the docks to give orders to have the best warships and deeply prowed barks hauled up and their sides freshly caulked with pitch. Luath Lineach hurried to the warehouses and ordered the supplies to be taken down to the docks while Sotal Salmor ordered the smiths to grind fresh edges upon the blades of all warriors. Then they went throughout Lochlann, bringing the warriors from their hearts and homes.

At last, all was made ready, and the ships were filled with frankincense[28] and myrrh.[29] Bres made his way down to the docks with Balor. There, he clapped Bres upon the shoulder and cried loudly so that all could hear: "Go now, then! Go to Ireland and lop the head of Lugh Il-Dana from his shoulders and bring it back to Berva. And for good measure, tie that island to the sterns of your ships with stout cables and yank it from those green waters and drag it north of bitter-cold Lochlann. None of the Tuatha Dé Danaan will follow it there. And if they do," he added grimly, " 'tis cold enough to freeze a bear's balls. Their magic won't work in that wasteland!"

The warriors gave a mighty shout and pushed away from the port, raising their sails. A sudden wind from the south caught the red and black and yellow sails and sped them away from the untilled land and out upon the blue-gray sea that flowed over the formidable abyss, upon the ridge-backed flood, over the high, cold-venomed mountains of the fathomless ocean. Straight did the pilots set their courses, never varying until they rounded the Skellig Rocks and made hard for the harbor at Es Dara.[30]

There the warriors stormed from their ships, laying waste to the land of Connacht, burning fields and villages, slaying men who tried to stand against them, raping women where they found them.

vi.

NOW THE KING OF CONNACHT at the time was Bodb Dearg, the son of The Dagda.[31] Who quickly sent word to Tara[32] where Nuada was entertaining Lugh after the Long Arm had slain a pocket of Fomorians who had remained behind as spies at Es Dara, while the others fled back to Balor's court. The red spearpoints of dawn struck the palace when the news reached them. Immediately Lugh prepared Enbarr of the Flowing Mane to ride over Ireland and draw the Tuatha together to drive the Fomorians from the land.

When Lugh reentered the palace, he went to Nuada and said, "Well, friend, I will ride to Connacht and gather the men as I go. We will hold the Fomorians there until you can bring your army up to support us. Together, we'll rid this land of those rogues once and for all."[33]

"Ah, yes, that," Nuada said. He refused to meet Lugh's eye and pretended to admire the curving hip of a serving wench as she hip-slinked her way past, casting a saucy glance over her shoulder. Lugh frowned.

"Explain, what you mean by that," he said, toying with the pommel of Manannán's sword hanging by his side.

"Well, what's happening is happening in Connacht, not here in Tara," Nuada said. He sipped from his cup of spiced wine. "Yes, that is very good," he said. He glanced at Lugh, who looked at him in disbelief. "Oh, I mean no harm to Bodb Derg and his people," he said quickly. "But really, I don't think the affairs of Connacht should become the affairs of Tara."

Lugh shook his head. "They could become the affairs of Tara if Bodb Derg cannot hold the Fomorians at Connacht. The country is like a loaf of bread. As a slice is taken off, the rest becomes easier to handle."

"Ha, ha. Yes, very humorous." Nuada laughed politely. "But nevertheless, I don't think we should dive into that briar patch just now. Why, it was only a few weeks ago that we managed to drive the Fomorians out of our own country."

"*I* drove the Fomorians out of your country while you sat sniveling with others on top of Usneach's Hill, fawning over the filth that came to tax you," Lugh said hotly. "I gave you help. Now you must return the favor by going to the aid of Bodb Dearg."

"I won't give it," Nuada said. "I will not lift a hand against someone who hasn't done anything against me. There is no deed there that calls for me to avenge it. Now, there's an end to it. I don't want to talk about it any more."

"It isn't talking that will be done with the flapping lips of politicians if the Fomorians get past the Connacht borders," growled Lugh. "But I'll leave you to your sweetmeats and wine and"—he glanced at the serving wench batting her long eyelashes at Nuada from the end of the room—"a saucy wench's hips. You'll fit that saddle better than a warhorse."

"Now, there's no reason to be insulting," Nuada complained, but Lugh ignored him and, turning on his heel, walked angrily from the room. He leaped onto his horse and galloped westward.

The sun had risen nearly to merdian height when he saw three men loping toward him. He reined in Enbarr and waited on the crest of a hill until they neared and he recognized his father Cian[34] and his two uncles Cu and Ceithen. Then his face broke into a wide grin, and he rode down the hill to greet them.

"Greetings, Father!" Lugh called as he neared the others. He drew in Enbarr who danced and shuffled her feet, snorting impatiently. Automatically, he ran his hand down under the flowing mane, soothing her.

"Good morning, Lugh!" called his father. They drew up beside

Lugh. "And what brings you out on this fine morning before the dew is gone from the long grass?"

"Bad news." Lugh shook his head. "The Fomorians have landed in Connacht. Even as we speak, they lay waste to the country. 'Tis said they burn what they cannot use, scorching the land, and that grass doesn't grow where the hooves of their horses strike. I ride to give them a taste of my sword, but I don't know for how long I can hold them there."

"Well," said Cu, brightening. "Sure, and we'll ride with you for a bit of carving on Fomorians hide. Each of us is easily the worth of a hundred Fomorians. Eh, what say you, Ceithen?"

"Only a hundred? I suppose that's enough for a woman's arm, but a man will take another hundred for himself," Ceithen said.

"A wager!" Cu cried happily. He clapped his hands together, the sound like thunder. Their horses danced uneasily. "A fingerlength of white gold for every warrior over the other's count!"

"Hate to make a pauper out of my own brother, but beggars get the pelf they seek," he said. He looked at Lugh. "So, let's ride to the sound of swords against shields! Each of us will easily keep a hundred or so of the Fomorians off your back."

Lugh laughed, the notes of his laughter putting the songs of the birds on the meadow to shame. "And I accept! But first, each of you must ride throughout Ireland where the Tuatha gather in their *Sídhes* and bid them to join me at Mag Mor over the mountain of Keshcorran. There, we will find the Fomorians and there we shall drive them from the land."

"Rather go with you now and carve a bit of their dirty hides," growled Cu, fingering his sword. Lugh laughed and shook his head.

"No, there'll be more than enough to go around and enough blood to bathe your blade. Now, go! Time's wasting!"

"Perhaps it would be better if you brought Nuada from Tara," Cian suggested, putting out his hand to stay Enbarr. Lugh's face clouded.

"Nuada would rather stay behind and play the king rather than *be* the king," he said.

Cian shook his head. "Perhaps you should try again," he said.

"Even the wisest king often needs pause to consider. He may have changed his mind."

Lugh hesitated, then shrugged. "It will make little difference, but we'll see." He nudged Enbarr with his heels and the great horse shook himself and turned and galloped back toward Tara. Cu and Ceithen watched him ride away, sunlight breaking radiantly off him, and shook their heads.

" 'Tis a fine lad you sired there, Cian," Ceithen said. "I'm surprised you got him with only one night of romping."

Cian laughed and gathered the reins of his horse. "Well, there's loving as a man gives a woman and loving that a lad wishes for," he chided. "You and Cu head south. I'm for Muirthemne."[35] The others watched as he galloped off toward the north.

Cu sighed and turned to Ceithen. "Well, brother, there's a hard day and night of riding ahead of us if we are to do our nephew's bidding."

"Aye," Ceithen said, grinning. "And let's get to it before that bloodthirsty youth robs us of the battlefield."

They touched their heels to their horses and galloped away to the south.

Meanwhile, Cian had reached the Plain of Muirthemne and reined in as he saw the three sons of Tuirenn riding toward him. He bit his lip, pondering what to do, for a great hatred existed between the sons of Cainte and the sons of Tuirenn. When they met, fighting broke out. Now, Cian was no coward, but he quickly realized that he was no match for the three sons by himself. He glanced around and saw a herd of pigs rooting for acorns beneath an oak tree nearby.

"Well," he said to himself. "If Cu and Ceithen were with me, we'd have a brave fight of it all. But alone, well, there is little I could do. Ah, well. Discretion is the better part at this time." He pulled a hazel wand from his cloak and dismounted. He muttered a magic spell and touched himself with the wand, changing instantly into the shape of a pig. He fell down upon all fours and quickly ran in the middle of the pigs and joined them in rooting for the acorn mast.

The riders reined in, Iuchar and Iucharba looking curiously at their brother, Brian, tall, bronzed from the sun, his blond hair bleached almost white, his blue-gray eyes flashing curiously, watchfully.

"Well?" Iuchar asked impatiently. "What is it? What do you see?" He turned and stared out over the land, searching for riders or walkers, but all he saw was a herd of pigs rooting for acorns beneath an oak tree at the edge of a forest.

"I thought I saw a rider," Iucharba, his twin, said from beside him. They were both dark-haired and black-eyed, so dark that many did not think they were brothers with Brian. But a closer look would see the similarity in them in the planes of their faces: high foreheads, hard chins, and shoulders broad enough to bear the weight of an oxen yoke.

"Is that what you are looking for?" Iuchar said.

Brian nodded, his eyes still scanning. "Yes, it is. But now, I don't see him anywhere. Why do you suppose that is?"

Iuchar shrugged. "Maybe it was an illusion."

"Or a wizard. Or an enemy with magic," Brain said dryly. "You really should be more watchful riding in the open country when war is upon the land. This is damned careless of you." His eyes fell upon the pigs rooting. "But," he added thoughtfully, "I think I know what has happened here. The rider must have been a Druid who changed himself into one of those pigs. And whoever he is, you can bet your walnuts that he's no friend of ours."

"Mere speculation," Iuchar grumbled. "Maybe he just didn't want to have any truck with us, eh? Did you think of that?"

"Yes," Iucharba echoed. "Did you think of that? Always seeing weasels when cats are around. You've got a suspicious mind."

"And a good thing, too. Otherwise, we would have been in a tanner's pool many times if things had been left up to the two of you."

Iuchar shook his head, gesturing toward the pigs. "Words, words, words. A lot of good they do us now. Those pigs belong to one of the Tuatha. Even if we killed all of them, there's no certainty that we would get the right one. He could shape-shift into something else while we slaughtering the others. Logic, brother. Logic," he added loftily, for he was very proud of his schooling.

"Logic, is it?" Brian said dryly, pulling a wand out from under his cloak. " 'Tis a sad state when you play pithy word games and cannot tell a Druidical beast from a natural beast. If you had attended to other learning instead of concentrating on pretty songs and phrasing, you might know that."

"What are you going to do?" Iuchar asked nervously, trying to edge away from Brian.

"Root out the right pig," Brian said, and quickly struck both of his brothers with his wand, changing each into a fast-hunting hound.

They fell from their horses, rolling in the heather. Iuchar was first up and sat immediately upon his haunches, scratching vigorously behind his ear with his hind foot.

"Ah well," sighed Iucharba, shaking himself. "He's at playing games again."

"Get the pig!" Brian commanded.

And the two hounds bayed and ran after the pigs, scattering them hither and thither, sniffing at their heels, until finally the Druidical pig slipped out the back of the herd and scrambled toward the protection of the forest. But Brian had been watching this and when the pig separated itself, he cast his long spear at it, striking the pig in the chest.

"AHHH!!" cried the pig and fell to the ground. " 'Tis an evil thing you have done to stick me with your spear! More so since you know me!"

Brian laughed grimly as he rode up beside the pig. He leaned over, striking the hounds with his wand, changing them back once again into his brothers.

"Ow!" Ichubar said, glaring at Brian. He rubbed his head. "You were a bit hard with that blow!" But Brian ignored him.

"And what kind of a pig would speak the language of men?" he asked.

"One who is a human," the pig said in anguish. "I am Cian, the son of Cainte.[36] Give me quarter!"

"Of course," Iuchar said, shaking himself and settling again into his human form.

"Indeed," Iucharba said. "And sorry we are for the ill that has befallen you."

"In a pig's arse," Brian said firmly. He glared at his brothers.

"There's no quarter I'll be giving to you. I swear this by the gods of the air."[37]

" 'Tis a hard man, you are," the pig said painfully. It coughed and a great gout of blood gushed from its mouth. "Well, then, if that be the way of things, at least do me the decency of letting me die in my own form. I was in it far longer than in this disguise."

"A man should die as a man, a pig as a pig," Brian said.

"I take that as a yes," the pig said. The air shimmered for a moment over the pig, and Cian emerged from the pig form and lay gasping on the green.

"Now, then, since you wouldn't give quarter to the pig, I ask for quarter for the man you see before you now," Cian gasped. Blood pulsed gently from a huge gash in his chest.

"Not by your chinny hair," Brian growled.

Cian laughed painfully. "That is the mark of a hard man. But, 'tis the last laugh that I'll be having upon you now! You should have killed me as a pig! It would have been far cheaper for you! You would have had the fine only for a pig to be paid. But killing a noble person such as myself will bring the greatest of all blood-fines to be paid by rogues such as yourselves! Aye! Listen closely to me, now! You will not keep the secret of my death to yourselves and get away with it! The very weapons you use will sing my death to my son and to him will you be forced to pay the greatest *éric*[38] that will ever be granted to a man's family!"

"Now this," Iuchar said uneasily, "is a different matter. Be listening closely to him, Brian! There's many a slip made between a man's head and his sword arm!"

"Talking swords?" Brian laughed. "Then we won't kill him with our arms. Let the earth do it!"

"The earth?" Iucharba asked, puzzled.

In answer, Brian picked up a huge stone in both hands and heaved it upon Cian with all his strength. Iuchar and Iucharba grabbed stones, and soon Cian's body was a bloody, crushed mass, unrecognizable from the man who had lain before them, wounded, asking that quarter be granted to him.

"There," Brian panted grimly. "That should be enough to keep him quiet."

"We can't leave him here for the wolves," Iuchar said. Brian paused on his way to his horse to look at his brother. Iuchar raised his chin. "You know as well as I that there are those Druids among the Tuatha who can speak with the animals of the forest. We have to keep him from the wolves who might consider him to be a tasty dish and brag about it to their brothers. Word gets around, you know. Birds sing, wolves howl, even the trees—"

"Enough." Brian raised a blood-spattered hand and pinched the bridge of his nose and dug his knuckles into his temples to stop their pounding. "Let's bury him, then."

"And deeply," growled Iucharba. "Don't want nothing digging him up and scattering his bones around." They set to, digging a hole down to a man's height.

"There," Iuchar said, pausing and panting from the effort of throwing dirt up out of the hole. He looked around in satisfaction, then craned his head, staring up at his brothers waiting patiently at the edge. "I wonder if this ain't deep enough to bury a cow, let alone a man. Here"—he held up his hand—"be giving us a hand up. This is deep enough to be knocking on the door of the hall of Cernunnos[39] himself, and I'm fairly short."

They hauled him up from the grave and, without ceremony, dumped Cian's body in and pushed the dirt in. Then, stomping the last of the dirt down hard, Brian said, "Now, then, let's be off. There's a battle to be fought and won."

They walked to their horses and mounted. Suddenly the earth heaved and their horses reared and bucked so that the brothers were hard-pressed to be kept from tumbling ass-over-heels over the heads of their nervous steeds.

"Here, now! What's this? Whoa, damn you!" Iucharba yelled. He pulled hard on the halter, yanking the head of his horse up. The mount stood trembling, walleyed with fear as the earth beneath its hooves grumbled and rumbled.

"I don't like this," Iuchar began, but then his words caught hard in this throat as Cian's body was thrust up from its grave.

"Magic!" howled Iucharba, yanking his horse's head to gallop away. "Black magic!"

But Brian reached out and seized the reins from his brother's hands. "Stop that!" he said crossly. "It's only an accident. The heaving of the earth. We'll bury him again."

And so they did. And again the earth belched forth Cian's body. And again. And again. And again. And again. But the seventh time, Brian heaped a cairn of stones over the grave, and this time, the earth kept his body within its mouldy grip. A great sigh seemed to rise from the ground around them, raising the hackles upon their necks.

"I don't know," Iuchar said, gazing fearfully around him. " 'Tisn't right that his body don't stay in the earth. I say we get away from this witchy place while we can."

Brian laughed and leaped lightly upon his horse. He turned its head to the west. "Then, let's be riding to battle before all the glory is taken from it!" he said. He clapped his heels to his horse's ribs and galloped away from the grave with his brothers in hot pursuit, each secretly goading his horse to greater and greater speed.

Behind them, a cold black shadow settled over the stone-marked grave and a deep chill fell over the land. Slowly, the leaves turned brown and russet and fell from the limbs and branches. And from the wind soughing through the branches came the words of Cian:

> "My blood lies darkly upon the ground.
> My son will search until he has found
> Where you have killed Cian, the Hero,
> And buried his body beneath this barrow.
> Do not think that you escaped your fate
> For he will follow and upon that date
> When he finds your dark secret, you
> Will find your doom. You will do
> Terrible deeds to remove the stain
> From your name. Here, I will remain
> Until my son searches for me.
> And then, he will find you three."

vii.

MEANWHILE, LUGH REINED ENBARR IN at Nuada's gate and leaped down. He strode determinedly through the gate into the Great Hall where Nuada sat, musing over what had transpired earlier between himself and Lugh.

"Nuada!" Lugh called as he entered the hall.

"Ah, there you are!" Nuada said. He scrubbed his hands furiously over his face for a moment, then sighed and leaned back in his chair. "I have given some thought to what you said before and have concluded that you are right. *All* the Tuatha need to be in this battle, or else we shall be fighting another and another. It is time," he said grimly, "for us to put an end to the Fomorian threat once and for all."

Lugh paused, uncertain for a long moment, then grinned and walked forward, stretching out his hand. Nuada rose and took it solemnly. Tired lines hooked deeply through his cheeks and under his eyes, but his grip was firm and strength shone from his eyes.

"We don't have much time," he said. "If I know the Fomorians, and I do, they are hacking their way across Connacht as we speak."

"Then," Lugh said, "let us begin. Call your people together."

And Nuada called forth the magician, the cupbearers, the Druid and craftsmen, the poet and physicians of the Tuatha Dé Danann together—all those with special skills. Lugh questioned each one closely, asking what each would contribute to the Tuatha to help them in their struggle against the Fomorians.

The magician said that he would topple the mountains of Ireland and have them roll on the ground to crush the Fomorian army. Yet, these same mountains would shelter the Tuatha during the battle.

The cupbearers promised to bring a great thirst upon the Fomorian army, but then drain the rivers and lakes so that there would be no water for the Fomorians to drink. Yet, water would be provided for the Tuatha even if the war should last seven years.

The Druid said he would send a shower of fire to fall on the heads of the Fomorians and make them fearful and rob them of their strength. Yet, each breath the Tuatha drew would make them stronger.

Goibniu, the clever smith, would make swords and spears that would never miss their mark.

Credné, the clever worker in brass, would provide rivets and sockets for the spears and swords and magical rims for shields that would never allow a harmful blow to land to those who carried them.

"And what," Lugh asked Cairpré, the poet who had cursed Bres, "will you contribute to our struggle?"

"I will use weapons that are invisible," Cairpré replied. "I will attack the mind by composing satirical poems at daybreak and sing them before battle to cause the Fomorians great shame. Then they will lose their desire for battle."

Last of all, Lugh spoke to Diancécht, the great physician and asked him what he would bring to the battle.

"My daughter Airmed and I will bring the wounded back from the battlefield each day and bathe them in our magic well, where they will be cured of all hurts unless they have suffered mortal wounds. There is no magic that can bring them back from Donn's Hall. In the morning, they will be even more eager for battle and fight more fiercely than ever."

At that moment, the Mórrígan appeared in the shape of a crow and promised that she would be there in the hour of their greatest need to lead them to victory.

"But you must ready yourselves now," she said. "For even as I speak, I see Balor's army streaming off their ships at Scetne. Some have already begun their march over Ireland toward Tara."

Lugh encouraged all to ready themselves for battle, but Nuada had determined that Lugh was so vital to the success of the Tuatha that he commanded Lugh be kept behind the lines with nine champions to make certain that he didn't join the battle.

As the two armies marched across the Plain of Mag Tuired, Bres rose, yawned, and stretched, then stared wonderingly into the west. Mystified at what he saw, he called his Druid to him, saying, "There is a wonder placed upon this day. Look!" He pointed at the bright light moving steadily across the Great Plain of the Assembly. "It appears the sun has decided to give us an omen by rising in the west."

The Druid shook his head grimly. "Better it would be for your army if that were so," he said. Bres looked at him curiously.

"Then how would you explain what we are seeing?"

The Druid laughed, but there was no mirth in his laughter. "Ah, would-be prophet! Nature does not alter herself to play to the whims of man! That light is from the face and the arms of Lugh, the man who slew your taxmen." He dug a long finger into his ear and screwed it vigorously. "Ah, me! Expect the worst, now. You have dilly-dallied long enough to allow Lugh to rally the Tuatha! Now, there will be a heavy penalty extracted. I dreamed last night of acorns falling from the oak," he said solemnly.

"And what is that to mean?" Bres asked.

"Time will tell," the Druid said, smiling secretively and placing a finger alongside his nose. "For now, I think Lugh plans a parley." He nodded at the approaching figure who rode quietly up the hill upon dancing Enbarr. He reined in and saluted them respectfully, then sat easily, waiting for them to speak.[40]

"Well?" Bres demanded. He glanced up the hill to where Balor camped in the center of a ring of warriors. No one stirred around the cookfires, yet. He glanced back at Lugh. "Now, why do you salute us with such niceties of manners when you know full well what we want here?"

Lugh smiled gently and shook his head. "I greet you in the old way for I'm partly you, partly Tuatha. I belong in both camps. My mother was the daughter of Balor of the Mighty Blows. Yes," he added as Bres raised his eyebrows in disbelief, "my mother was Ethlenn." He glanced around at the great herd of cows that the Formorians had gathered as they moved across the rich land, scorching it as they rode. "Now, I asked you peaceably to please return all the milch cows to their rightful owners, the men of Connacht, and leave in peace."

Bres stared openmouthed at Lugh, then laughed. "Hee-awk! Hee-awk! Hee-awk! Why, you puny rascal! Do you think that your wee army can stand against our might?" He turned contemptuously and spat. Enbarr danced away daintly from the Formorian's streaming spittle.

"I ask again—" Lugh began, but Bres cut him off short.

"Ah, little cricket! You're done with your chirping! Off with you, now, before we splatter you upon the hillside!"

The Druid shook his head at this and turned away silently from the meeting. A crow flew cawing high overhead. His eyes narrowed. He fingered his oaken staff, well-polished from much handling.

"This, then, is your last word?" Lugh asked quietly.

"And your last warning," growled Bres.

Lugh turned Enbarr silently and rode away.

"Now, can you figure that upstart—" Bres said, turning toward the Druid. He paused, looking around, puzzled. The Druid had disappeared. He glanced up half-fearfully, but saw only the crow circling slowly over the Great Plain.

"Apples and acorns!" he exclaimed. "What do you suppose got into him?"

He yawned and scratched himself through his tunic as he turned reluctantly toward the camp of Balor, certain that he had better tell Balor about the meeting before he heard about it from someone else. And there were many who would be scurrying to earn favor by being the first to say something against him. There are always those who build another's misfortune into their fortune, even if they have to bend a word or two here and there.

That night, Lugh cast a spell over the Fomorian army so the soldiers saw only shadows and not the milch cows moving slowly down the hill, back toward ravaged Connacht and their own home fields. But the dry cows stayed behind, munching the grass, forcing the Fomorians to care for them, slowing their march across the land until the entire Tuatha army could assemble.

For three days and nights, Lugh stayed close to the army, harrying them with his tiny minor spells, sending a flood down a river to keep them from crossing, a host of mites into the blankets of the army, keeping the men scratching and turning restlessly instead of sleeping soundly, making their fires burn hotter than planned so their meat became scorched and their bread twice-baked and burnt to iron-hard crust.

Then Bodb Dearg moved up on Lugh's flank with twenty-nine hundred men. On that day, Lugh began to dress for the battle. First, he donned Manannán's mail and breastplate. Then he placed Cannbarr, his helmet, upon his head where it caught the sun's rays and glittered with a bright rainbow of colors that danced bedazzling in the still air. He placed his blue-black, cleverly engraved shield,[41] the color of the ocean's depths, its edge rimmed in bright red the color of lung's blood, over his back and hung his great sword upon his muscular thigh. Then he hefted his two great spears, the shafts hewed from the trunk of an ash, the points dipped in adder's blood, testing their balance. Satisfied, he studied the army at his back as the kings and chiefs rode among their men. Spearpoints bristled like a blackthorn hedge. Their shields touched rim like a fence.

Lugh nodded in satisfaction, then took a deep breath and sounded his battle-cry that curdled the blood of the Fomorians with its gruesome challenge, and charged their ranks. But the Fomorians rallied quickly and drove the Tuatha back brutally, slaughtering them left and right, leaving the wounded groaning upon the field so that Diancécht and his men were kept busy.

First, a bristling cloud of spears flew across the field from army to army. Then the warriors drew their gold-hilted swords from their sky-blue sheaths and clashed together, shield upon shield, sword upon sword. Sparks soared skyward from metal clashing against metal in forests of flame. Blood flowed upon the ground like a red river, so deep that it choked all grass. Even today, only stones grow upon that plain.

But Nuada's army could not overcome the many men that the Fomorians threw at them. Slowly, the Tuatha were driven back, then rallied and drove the Fomorians back. Day after day the battle raged, and night after night the wounded were brought to Diancécht who bathed them in his magical well. But the battle seesawed back and forth without either side gaining the upper hand long enough to bring victory.

Finally, Balor, with Bres and Cathleann (his wife) at his side, went to lead the Fomorian horde in one great assault. At this moment, Lugh could bear watching no longer. He broke free from his guards and raced to the front of the line to lead the Tuatha against the Fomorians. Nuada, The Dagda, and the other champions raced after him while the Mórrígan soared overhead to watch the battle. Lugh glanced up and, noticing her, cried, "Now! Now, you must fight to the death! If we lose this battle, we shall all be slaves forever!"

The two armies came together with much shouting and clanging of spears and swords. There was no time for the physicians to heal wounds, no time for smiths to repair weapons. The screams of the wounded and roaring of the warriors rolled over the plain that quickly became soaked and slippery with blood. Still, the armies fought on, each trying grimly to drive the other back. The river carried away the dead, friends and enemies.

Cathleann of the Crooked Teeth hurled her spear at The Dagda, causing a terrible wound that forced him from the field. But Nuada rallied the army and led them in another charge. Suddenly he came face-to-face with Balor and raised his shield immediately, but he was too late. Balor swung his mighty sword and killed Nuada with one blow.

When they saw their king fall, the Tuatha lost heart and great despair rose within their ranks. At that moment, the Mórrígan appeared above them and let out a terrible scream that drove a shaft of fear into the hearts of the Fomorians. They hesitated. Lugh rushed forward to stand over Nuada, taunting Balor.

"Oh, One-eye! Where is your mighty strength? Come, fight with me, filthy one! Or are you One-balled as well as One-eyed?"

Furious, Balor cried to his attendants. "Lift up my eyelid so I might see this upstart!" he roared.

Immediately, a great hush fell over the battlefield, for all there knew the power of his hidden eye. Ten Fomorian champions raced forward and seized the ring to raise the heavy lid of the Evil Eye. Those nearest fell to the ground, hoping that the venomous gaze would not fall upon them. As the lid opened slowly, Lugh placed a stone in his sling and threw it at Balor. The stone pierced his eye, driving it backward and out of his head. It landed in the middle of the Fomorian army, where twenty-seven fell from its venomous rays until life seeped from it.

Lugh raced forward and cut off Balor's head, holding it high in the air. The Tuatha gave a great shout and fell upon the Fomorians, slaughtering them. The Fomorians turned and raced back to the sea and their ships. They boarded them and raised the sails quickly sailing away from Ireland, never to return.

Bres was captured and brought before Lugh, who had assumed Nuada's throne. "Quarter!" he begged as he was thrown at Lugh's feet. "Let me live and I will bring the Fomorians to side with you in the great Battle of Mag Tuired, which is coming soon. I promise by the sun and the moon, the sea and the land, to never draw a blade against you again if you should let me live."

The Tuatha called for him to be killed, but Lugh refused, demanding Bres's secrets of husbandry and farming in exchange for his life. Bres agreed and taught the Tuatha how to plow and sow and harvest the fields before he left Ireland for good.

Then the Mórrígan proclaimed peace, saying:

> "Peace will reign in this land, I
> Say, from the earth up to the blue sky
> And back down again. Let the bees
> Bring forth from their hives the honey
> For the mead and let everyone
> Enjoy happiness. It is done."[42]

viii.

As soon as the battle ended, the Tuatha withdrew to the home of Bodb Dearg for a feast, but Lugh, who had missed Cian, his father, went among his army, searching for him. He found two of his friends sitting quietly beneath an oak tree, sharing a wineskin.

"Have you seen my father?" he asked.

They shook their heads. "No, perhaps he joined the battle late and was caught in that ambush by the bend of the river," one answered. "He might have been slain there.

"I searched the dead there and did not see him," Lugh answered. "I asked for him with Diancécht, but he had not taken him to the well for wounds, either. I fear, however, that he is dead. A darkness lies over my spirit that wouldn't be there otherwise."

"Would you care for some wine?" the other asked politely. Lugh shook his head.

"No, neither food nor drink shall pass my lips until I find his body and discover how he has met his death. I fear," he said, dark lights brooding deeply in his eyes, "that it was an ignoble death at the hands of one of our enemies."

The others exchanged glances and shrugged. They tossed the wineskin aside, belched, and rose. "We'll go with you," they said quietly. "A man shouldn't have to bear that search alone."

Lugh clasped their hands gratefully, then set off, retracing his steps to the hill where he had last seen his father. Once there, he brooded for a long moment, then said, "Well, I think that we should follow the direction in which he rode. There's not much else to do, but we might get lucky and find someone along the way who has seen him."

They rode down the hill and soon came to the place where Cian had taken the form and shape of the pig when he recognized the children of Tuirenn. Lugh dismounted and squatted upon his haunches, brooding, feeling a deeper darkness move upon his spirit. His companions noticed the change in him and waited watchfully, their eyes flickering around the edges of the forest in case a roving band of Fomorians waited to leap out upon them from ambush. It was then that Lugh felt the whisper of the earth in his mind.

"*Lugh.*"

It seemed more a sigh of the wind than words, but Lugh felt his blood quicken within him. He raised his head, listening.

"*Lugh.*"

He cocked his head, and a thought leaped from him like lightning: *Speak!*

"Great danger awaited your father here. He saw the children of Tuirenn—Brian, Iuchar, and Iucharba—approaching and took care to disguise himself as a pig. But they slew him after he changed back into his own form."

Tears leaped to Lugh's eyes. He rose and turned to face his friends. They looked away from him, embarrassed to let him see that they had seen his sadness before he could tell them what had happened.

"Here, my friends," he said. "Somewhere near here, my father lies buried. The earth speaks out against his bloodletting. It was a foul death, I fear. Help me search."

They dismounted and spread out, each going in a different direction. Then, when Lugh approached a pile of stones, he felt a strange prickling sensation upon his skin. He cupped his hands and called the others to him. When they came up, he pointed wordlessly to the pile of stones.

The others fell to, throwing the stones away until they came to the grave. Then they dug, and soon came to the body and lifted it from the earth. But he had been so battered that Lugh could only recognize him by the golden torque around his neck.

"Murderous death!" Lugh exclaimed bitterly. "See what the sons of Tuirenn have done to my father? A pig should not have died this death, let alone a man!"

And he kissed his father's lips three times, promising between each kiss: "Your death has taken away words and music from my ears, beauty from my eyes, the pulse of my heart! By the gods, I wish I was here when this happened to have fought with you against them!" He struck his breast three times. "This is a terrible thing when brother kills brother and Tuatha kills Tuatha. This evil shall not be lost to memory."

And then he spoke a lament:

> "At evening, Cian met his terrible fate.
> And now my body feels this pain late
> After the deed was done. The tearing
> Of this hero's flesh, the burying
> Of his body in earth, the road eastward
> That he rode for me, the dirt westward,
> All shall lock the land in evil until
> This is avenged. Cian's filthy death
> By Tuirenn's sons through stealth

Has overpowered my will. Blackness
Covers my face, my spirit. Blackness
Covers my senses. This dirty deed
Will split the Tuatha until the seed
Of revenge is satisfied. No longer
Will the Tuatha be aided by me. Longer
Will the children of Tuirenn wait
Until I have decided upon their fate."

Gently, reverently, he washed his father's body and placed him back into the earth. Over this, he again raised a barrow of stone and capped the barrow with a tombstone upon which he carved his father's name in *ogham*. Then, he held great funeral games[43] and after these had finished, Lugh said:

"This hill shall now be called Cian's Mound[44]
Though Cian himself is no longer sound
Enough to care what is called after him.
The deed that was committed here dims.
The Tuatha Dé Danann glory. Fratricide
Does not lead to glory by shame. Besides,
This was an ignoble death by Tuirenn's sons.
And now, I shall speak the truth. Their grandsons
And their great-grandsons shall all pay
For this deed. This I promise, this I say!
The three sons of Cainte—brave company!—
And Tuirenn Begrenn's sons shall see
The depth of my revenge. My heart aches
Within my breast, for this death breaks
The Tuatha brotherhood. Cian lives not.
The sons of Delbaeth, however, shall not
Grieve alone! Tuirenn's children will see
How great my vengeance shall be!
It begins here in the shadow of this tomb
That drapes the entire world in gloom!"

Then Lugh turned to his people who had waited patiently and said, "Go, now, back to the king of Ireland's place and wait for me there. I shall come shortly. Do not speak of this to anyone until I return."[45]

They returned to Tara, but said nothing of where they had been and the others, after questioning them and getting evasions instead of answers, forgot that they had been missing and turned their attention again to the feast of celebration.

Not long after this, Lugh came and made his way silently into the Great Hall where he took his seat, appearing calm and composed to those who knew the angry Lugh who had stood over his father's grave, speaking of black revenge. They shuffled uneasily, as they watched him, but he ate and drank as if nothing had happened while he looked around the hall until he saw the sons of Tuirenn playing in the games. None were as fast as they; none could stand up to their strength in arms; and from the hungry looks the maidens threw in their directions, it was easy to tell that few there were as handsome. The poet-singers sang songs of their bravery in battle and no one came close to their great deeds except Lugh himself, who still sat quietly, waiting until the games had finished and a lull fell over the festivities. Then, he asked that the chain of silence[46] be shaken. Golden notes tinkled in the air and all sat back, looking at Lugh who stood and spoke, saying, "Are you all listening to me now?"

"We are!"

"Speak!"

"Good," Lugh answered. He took a deep breath to calm himself, then said, "I have a question for you to consider: What vengeance should be taken on one among you who kills the father of another?"

A sudden rush of talk sped around the room. Bodb Dearg leaned forward, frowning as he said, "Is it your father, Cian, then, Lugh, who has been slain?"

" 'Tis," Lugh said. His lips thinned into a straight line, his eyes hardened, and all glanced away from the death that showed there. "And I see in this very hall, the killers who eat meat and drink wine and honeyed beer as if they have not slain him in as dark a deed that has ever been done. All murder is foul, but fouler still is the murder of one's own."

Bodb Dearg shook his head, leaning back upon his couch. He waved away a preferred goblet of wine. "Many days would pass before my father's killer would die. I would cut off one of his hands or arms or feet or legs each day until he begged for death from my own hands," he said grimly.

The others shouted their agreement with Bodb Dearg's words. Lugh's eyes never left the sons of Tuirenn who led the shouting, each asserting that he would do the same as the king to the slayer of their father. Lugh waited until quiet again reigned in the Great Hall, then said, "I notice that the murderers here have also agreed with your words, my king. But I will not let their own judgment be their deaths, for they have been drinking and there is much to be said for drink addling one's thoughts and loosening tongues that would better have been kept quiet. But since they have passed judgment, and by this agree that they deserve to be punished, I claim the right—as you all are my witnesses—to lay an *éric* upon them for the death of my father. If they refuse, well, I won't bloody this hall with their deaths, but I will wait for them in the courtyard with my blade and settle the account of Cian there."

Puzzled looks were exchanged as each one there tried to ferret out the murderers, then Bodb Dearg spoke, saying " 'Tis a fair reckoning you have asked for, Lugh. If I were the one who had done this, I would agree to an *éric* of your choosing as that owed by me."

The others shouted their agreement, but by now, the sons of Tuirenn recognized themselves in Lugh's words and whispered quietly among themselves.

"It's us he's talking about," Brian said, tugging at an earlock.

"Then," said Iuchar, "the best thing for us is to fess up and take the blame. Let us take his accounting before we lose face among all here."

"I don't know," Brian answered, frowning. "Suppose he's only playing with us and is waiting until we confess and then refuses to let us pay an *éric*? If we admit we are the ones he wants in front of everyone here, then we have thrown ourselves into his hands. He can do with us what he wants."

"He can do that anyway," Iucharba said, watching Lugh carefully. He wiped his greasy fingers on his tunic and spat a piece of gristle onto the floor. "I say let's salvage what honor we can by admitting to it rather than have it thrown in our faces like a slap to a gullyboy's face." He looked at Brian. "You're the eldest. You do our talking for us."

"If you don't, I will," Iuchar said as Brian hesitated.

Brian shrugged. "All right, I'll do it," he said, and stood, standing tall. He faced Lugh across the room as a wave of shock rolled over the others at the feast when they saw what he was doing.

"It is us you are seeking, Lugh," he said. A wry smile twisted his lips. "But I think you knew that before you spoke. All right. We are the ones you *think*," he emphasized, "rode against your father. That may be or it may be not. But, if it's a compensation you are looking for, we shall give it to you, as if we were indeed the ones who had killed your father."

Iuchar struck Brian on his thigh, saying, "Damn it, don't play twisting words with him! Tell him the truth, man! It'll be all the worse for us if you deny the truth and we're found out!"

Brian pushed away from him and stood, legs slightly spread, his strong hands cupped near his thighs. "Well?" he challenged. "What is it you wish?"

Lugh studied him, a faint line of contempt appearing between his brows. "Well, then, so that's the way it is to be, is it? Very well. I'll give you my demands. And if you think it is too great for such strong warriors as yourselves, then"—his lips curled derisively—"well, we shall reduce part of it so it won't be too much for fine warriors such as yourselves."

Brian's face flushed hotly as snickers rose around him from the others. He drew himself up as Iuchar and Iucharba leaped to their feet, eyes flashing angrily. "Let's hear it, then," Brian said.

"Sure of yourselves, are you? Well, then," Lugh said. "First, gather three apples. Then, bring a skin of a pig, a spear, two horses, a chariot, seven pigs, a wee puppy, a cooking-spit, all after you shout three times from a hill. Now, are you thinking that might be too much from three warriors such as yourselves who fight one man? That is the compensation I demand. *But,* if you think it is too much, why, I'll be happy to take some of it back," he said carelessly. "I really wouldn't want you to overtax yourselves. Fine warriors such as yourselves."

Laughter greeted his last words, and the brothers spun angrily on their heels to stare at the bold eyes staring contemptuously at them.

"Done," Brian said. "And a hundredfold of that upon it, if you wish. But," he added, as Iuchar whispered quickly in his ear, "it's wondering I am if there isn't something else behind such a small compensation as this. What murderous design have you in reserve for us after we do this?"

"Oh, nothing," Lugh said innocently, spreading his hands. "I have delivered my asking, and that's all. By the guarantee of the Tuatha and the trees and the land and the sea and the sky, that is all that I wish."

"Very well. We accept," Brian said boldly. " 'Tis a pity, though. It doesn't seem as if that is much of a challenge to provide."

"Good," Lugh said, clapping his hands. The smile disappeared from his face. "But, 'tis often people of your ways give promises then back away from them like a weasel out of a henhouse, slinking away in the soft of the night. I'll be asking your pledges to all here against that."

"Well and good, if our word isn't enough," Iuchar said hotly.

"It isn't," Lugh answered coolly. "And what word would you accept from three warriors who attack and kill one old man alone in the middle of nowhere without a friend to guard his back? It would not be the first time that you and your brothers had gone back on the promise of a fine."

Brian placed his hands on the forearms of his brothers, restraining them from leaping across the room at Lugh for this insult. "All right, then we pledge ourselves to the compensation that has been given unto us this day in the Hall of Micorta[47] and that we shall not rest until the account is paid in full. To this we pledge our name, our homeland, and our lives as surety. *Provided*"—he fixed Lugh with an angry eye—"that you do not increase your claims." The brothers growled their agreement. Brian gave Lugh a hard look. "Now, is that good enough for you?"

"Depends upon how great your honor is. To me, it's nothing, but"—he held up his hand to keep the brothers at bay—"enough men here have heard your word given and taken. So." He grinned at them, but there was death in his smile and a shudder seemed to shake convulsively through the room. "You'll be wanting to know the details?"

"We would," Brian answered.

"Then hear them," Lugh said harshly. "The three apples I wish are three from the Garden of the Hesperides to the east of the world.[48] I will take no other apples other than these which are the most rare and beautiful apples in the world. They are the color of burnished gold, the size of the head of a month-old child, and taste of honey. They heal all bloody wounds and malignant disease when eaten, yet each bite is never seen in them, and they can be eaten forever. One may throw them at a target, and they will return to his hand. The owners guard them well, for a story is told of three young warriors who will come from the western world to steal them. Brave as you are, or *think* you are, I doubt if any of you is strong enough to bring them back."

He paused a moment and looked around him. The faces of everyone in the room were grim for all knew now the clever trap that Lugh had set. He continued, "Next, the pig's skin must come from the skin of the pig owned by Tuis, a king in Greece. When the pig lived, every stream she stepped in turned to wine for nine days. All the sick and wounded who touched her hide were cured at once, even if only the barest breath remained in their bodies. Now, it seems that the king's Druids told him that such virtue the pig had lay in her skin, so the king had her killed and skinned, and now keeps the skin for himself against his own mortal day. I don't think you will wrest it easily from him. Now, would you be knowing what spear it is that I want?"

"Let's hear it," Brian said, white-faced. His brothers stood silent beside him. The room was quiet as the others looked with something approaching pity upon them.

"The spear is the one that belongs to Pisear, the king of Persia. It is called Aredbair.[49] It has never lost a battle, and its head must be kept always in a cauldron of water to keep it from melting itself by its fiery heat and the entire city where it is kept. It will be no easy matter to take it away from the king, for whoever possesses it can never be defeated. Now, would you be knowing about the horses and chariot?"

"We would," Brian said.

"They belong to Dobhar, the king of Sicily. They do not know the difference between sea and land and there are no others as fast or as strong as they. The chariot is the strongest and most beautiful in all the world. Would you be guessing the seven pigs I want?"

"We wouldn't," Brian answered.

"Well, they would be those who belong to Asal, king of the Golden Pillars. They are killed every night for a grand feast, but when the light of morning strikes the land"—he snapped his fingers—"there they are, alive again. Their flesh cures any who eats it.

"Now, the puppy I want belongs to the king of Iruad.[50] Her name is Failinis, and not even the sun shines as splendidly as does her fine coat. All the wild beasts who see her fall dead instantly.

"The cooking-spit belongs to the women of Inis Findcuire, the sunken island. They are three times fifty who live there, each the better of any three warriors who come to their island.[51] One must defeat them in battle before they will surrender the spit."

He looked at them contemptuously. "If you should survive all that, then the last for you, which seems the easiest, is to give three shouts upon Cnoc Midcain in the north of Lochlann.[52] That may seem simple enough for you, but the hill is guarded well by Midkena and his sons, who are under a *gesa* to keep people from shouting upon it. They taught my father how to use arms and warfare and loved him very much." A catch seemed to hang words in his throat for a minute, but he cleared it and continued. "Even if I were willing to forgive you for his death, 'tis sure I am that they are not. Even if you should be so lucky as to escape with the first of the *éric,* you will not come away from that hill without his death being avenged by them. This, then, is the compensation I demand."

A great silence fell upon the sons of Tuirenn, as they walked slowly from the Hall of Micorta. The warriors around them watched them go, and each felt within his own heart the black despair that filled the hearts of the children of Tuirenn as they left to their fate.

ix.

ASTONISHMENT AND DESPAIR SETTLED ON the children of Tuirenn as they left the Great Hall and stood outside in the gloaming. Iucharba ran his fingers desperately through his hair and looked at Iuchar and Brian. "Well, what do we do now? That Lugh was a clever fellow to taunt and tease us into this trouble." His lips trembled for a moment. Then anger came to him, and he turned and spat hard against the side of the building. "So that for you." He turned back to Brian and Iuchar. "Well?" he demanded. His neck swelled like an adder's and he glared at Brian. " 'Tis your fine words and ideas have gotten us this far. So, what's your reckoning now? Eh?" His eyes burned darker, fuliginous.

"We must be objective about this," Brian started, but Iuchar interrupted him.

" 'Tis enough of your fine words and philosophical games," he said. "I'm a *feeling* creature, and I *feel* that you have just committed us to an impossible task. Tasks," he corrected himself. "Even if we succeed, we'll still have the stigma of our actions upon us. We'll be squatters—mere tinkers in society—for the rest of our lives." His face became gloomy. He farted. The smell of onions filled the air. Brian and Iucharba backed away from him hastily.

"The law—" Brian began.

"—gives justice, but it doesn't control people's thoughts," Iuchar finished for him. "Order has become chaos. Mindless, meaningless."

"We have the tasks," Iucharba reminded him.

"Ah yes, the tasks. And when we have completed them, what remains of order?" Iuchar fulminated. "Anarchy!"

"I suggest we go to see Father," Brian said firmly. "We need a clearer head than any here now to see what has to be done."

Iuchar shook his head sorrowfully. "Father! Ah, me! I don't think I can take another lecture right now." He hunched his shoulders and glowered from beneath bushy brows, drawing his lips in tightly as if he had just bitten bitter lemons. He lowered his voice harshly, imitating: "The trouble with you young whippersnappers today is you have no sense of responsibility! None! Your life is all action, but the wee bit of difficulty comes your way, you deny your responsibility for the actions that you have done. Rascals! Whelps! You should have spent more time with the Druids than the armorer and brewer and tickling your fancies with the dancing girls in the inns and hostels around the country! But, that's youth today!"

"It won't be like that," Brian said soothingly.

But Iuchar shook his head. "Mark my words," he said darkly.

And together, they left gloomily, making their way back to their horses for the long ride back to their father's house.

X.

TUIRENN GLOWERED AT HIS CHILDREN standing in front of him. "Responsibility!" he roared. Iuchar exchanged a glance with Brian; both shrugged. Tuirenn failed to notice. "How many times have I told you? Think!" (*Think!* mouthed the three automatically.) "Well, not for a moment am I going to take the blame for your actions this time! No, by Donn's great balls! You've made your bed, plowed your fields, now reap the whirlwind!"

"Mixed metaphors," mumbled Brian. His father glared at him.

"What's that?" he asked suspiciously.

"Oh, nothing. Just . . . words," Brian finished hastily, lamely.

"Men *live* by words!" Tuirenn roared again. "How many times have I to tell you that? Open your yaw and let your tongue flap, and you'll find yourself neck-deep in horse shit! They're not to be tossed like baubles to girls at the harvest dances! Or singing those nonsensical songs!" He stuck his fingers in his belt, rolled his shaggy head back on his shoulders, and bellowed:

> "There's some take delight in walking
> And others take delight in talking.
> But I take delight
> In the wee gloaming light
> And in the maids I'm stalking!"

He shook his shaggy head. " 'Tis fine to sow those wild oats, but how many times have I told you that you must reap the harvest as well? And now, now, this *éric* you let be posed upon you—" He paused, drawing deep breaths to calm himself. The anger suddenly went out of his eyes, and the flesh of his face sagged into bags and wrinkles. "Lads, lads, what am I going to do with you now?"

Brian exchanged quick glances at his brothers, then cleared his throat. "Well, Father, that's what brought us to you. The benefit of your years, your wisdom, your—"

"Doom!" his father interjected. Brian fell silent. They exchanged looks again and heaved silent sighs, waiting resignedly. "Doom! Bad tidings! 'Tis death and destruction that will be visited upon you in seeking to pay that fine!"

"Damned unfair," muttered Iucharba.

"Unfair? Unfair?" bellowed Tuirenn. His eyes bulged; his face grew fiery red. "Unfair, is it? 'Tis just, that's what it is! Oh, that Lugh is a smart one, he is! Even if he allowed it to happen that you could work out the compensation with others, not all the men in the world could pay that fine! At least," he said, pausing, a thought flickering like dawn light to him, "unless you have the help of Lugh himself or Manannán mac Lir. Hmm." He fell silent, his eyes wandering as he looked into his thoughts. His sons held their breath, waiting, hoping. Then Tuirenn shook his head. "Improbable," he sighed. He raised a horny palm and rubbed it across his heavy cheeks, knuckling his tired eyes. "But, possible. Depends on how much Lugh wants you dead and how much he wants the fine. Which is more important to him? He might—*might*, mind you—give you a bit of help. But you must play it right when you go to him. First, ask him for the lending of Enbarr, Manannán's mare. He won't give her, but that doesn't matter—we know he won't give her. But then that he's refused you the one gift, he'll have to grant you another—it's forbidden to deny the second request—the one you really want: Manannán's boat, the Scuabtinne.[53] The horse is prettier, but the boat is more practical."

He shook his head and raised his hands, palm out, in despair. " 'Tis the best I can do for you, lads!" Tears glinted in his eyes as he embraced each son. "Go and good luck!"

xi.

LUGH STARED SUSPICIOUSLY AT THEM. "Enbarr, you want, is it?" He grinned suddenly. "The answer, then, is no. Enbarr is only a loan to me. I won't give away the gift of a loan."

"I see," Brian said. He pretended to think. Then he sighed and shook his head despairingly. "This is a fine place of briars and brambles that we are in! Of course," he continued in an injured tone, "I really don't blame you for it. 'Tis a time of our own making! But, as things are, we have as much chance of finishing the task you've given us as we have of bringing words back out of air!"

"The deed is yours; you must live with it," Lugh said. "But you are leading up to something else. What is it? Stop running around the bush like a weasel and come out with it!"

"Well, we can't have the horse, but 'tisn't right that you refuse us a second request," Brian said. Lugh's face hardened, his eyes narrowed. "So, give us a loan of Manannán's curragh."

Lugh nodded slowly. "Ah! Now, we come to the gist of your wants. 'Twasn't Enbarr you wanted in the first place. Well, played, Brian! But remember: Wine is very pleasant to drink, but the price is often hard. You shall have Scuabtinne. But nothing else from me. Do not come back and play more ducks and drakes with me!"

"Fair enough," Brian said. "And where will we be finding this Wave-Sweeper?"

"At Brugh na Boinne,[54]" Lugh answered. "Mind you: It's only a loan."

When they returned to their father to tell him about their success, they discovered that Ethne was with their father, having heard about

Lugh's demands on her brothers. Her eyes filled with tears as they came into the room.

"Well, Father," Brian said, clasping his hands together. "It went as you said. Lugh wouldn't give us Enbarr, but we have Scuabtinne. Now, I expect we should be getting on with the quest. It's showing to be a long enough chore without putting more days on the end of it."

"That is as it must be," Tuirenn said, tears springing to his eyes. He embraced each of his sons, giving his blessing to them. "You will be facing much danger, but Lugh has a need for much of what he has demanded. But I can see no value for him for the cooking-spit and the three shouts on the hill. Malicious assignment, those. Do not expect much help from him on those."

"I don't expect any further help from him at all," Brian said. "He was as hard as oak about that."

"As it should be," Ethne said. "You've hoed the ground, now reap the crops."

Iuchar smiled bleakly at her. "Surely there are other metaphors you can use. That one is becoming extremely tiresome."

She gave him a sharp look, then smiled sadly and shook her head. "I use metaphors, so I don't have to explain myself to you, Iuchar.

> "You've done a dark deed,
> My brothers, with the seed
> Of hatred you planted when you killed
> Lugh's father as a man. You stilled
> A tongue that might have brought
> Peace to a people who have sought
> Peace for so long. Now you must
> Pay the blood-fine before you are dust."

And her brothers answered:

> "Enough, dear sister! Your cries
> Of doom and gloom now tries
> Our patience. This will become a tale
> For poets forever once we set sail.

What more can a warrior ask
But glorious words about his task?"

And Ethne answered:

"Then search, my brothers, for immortality
Across the land and the sea. You will soon see
That cruel Ildánach decree is not a game
To be played. You will never be the same
For having played along with this quest
Of his. Death does not bring out one's best.
Others have been where you are now
And preferred Achilles's sword to his plow.
But even lofty Achilles was wont to say
That he preferred life to death any day
After he had foolishly selected his way
When the gods granted him a say
In his fate. I fear I will never see
You alive again. Only my salty
Tears will splatter your tombs
Once you have met your doom."

"And that," Brian said quietly, "is where you are wrong. We can only live by the myths that are imposed upon us like actors in a play. The play may be bad, but we must still play our part in it."

"You are as clever as a buckle," she said sharply. "Be careful that you don't become as intransigent as a mountain."

And the brothers left, thinking quietly about her black words that cast a shadow over the quest and the glory that they thought they would win.

xii.

WHEN THEY CAME TO BRUGH na Boinne, Iucharba looked disdainfully at the small boat, a shell dancing lightly on the lightly lapping waves licking the shore. He shook his head.

"Is this a boat or an eggshell?" he asked. He glanced at the size of his brothers and laughed. "Why, 'tisn't enough to hold one of us let alone three and our weapons. You've made a bad bargain with your words," he said to Brian. "It's a poor man who seals a deal without looking at the property first."

"I don't know," Iuchar said dubiously, frowning at the boat. "There must be something more to this than meets the eye."

"And why do you say that?" Iucharba demanded angrily. "Maybe this is all that it is. Maybe in this whole world this is all there is. Why must there always be something more than what there is?"

"Because it is Manannán's," Brian said, breaking into the conversation. "He is more than we are. Things that he has are more than the things we have." He shrugged. "Logic."

"Logic?" Iuchar's eyebrows closed in a deep frown.

"Philosophical objectivity," Brian answered. His eyes burned darker. "What we see as witchcraft may be witchcraft, but it could also be only the workings of our minds. But the boat is there, and that is all that is important now. We must attempt to use it as we wish to use it and then—and only then, mind you!—will we determine its usefulness to us. Before we use it, we can only speculate on its purpose. By using it, we perform an act of unity and completion."

Iuchar shrugged his massive shoulders and gathered his weapons. "Whatever," he said. "You still begin the journey with a first step. We spend enough time munching words." Cautiously, he stepped into the boat and sat. It wobbled for a moment, then relaxed, the sides easing away from him to give him room.

"Magic!" Brian crowed. He slapped Iucharba across the shoulders, and stepped into the boat, his bulk causing the craft to sway wildly back-and-forth on a wave before it settled and stretched to accommodate him.

"Uh-huh," grunted Iucharba, looking suspiciously at the boat. "It still seems too small for all of us. And who's to say that it won't decide that it has had enough of us when we're in the middle of the sea? That isn't a pond we'll be crossing, you know. None of us can walk on water if it decides to become what it was when we first saw it."

"Will you get in and stop being the doomsayer?" Brian demanded.

Iucharba took a deep breath and placed a foot in the curragh and waited, holding his breath suspiciously. The craft bobbed on the waves, waiting. He shook his head and suddenly stepped in, squatting on his heels and crouching, holding hard to the gunnals as he waited for the craft to stop its pitching and yawing.

"There, you see?" Brian said, smiling. Iucharba grunted, looking around suspiciously as the craft expanded to hold him and the others comfortably.

"Now it begins," Iuchar said. "What should we do first?"

"I say we follow the order given," Brian answered. "Let's not tempt fate by abandoning the natural order given to us by Lugh. The apples were requested first. I say we seek them first."

Iucharba shrugged. "Apples or puppies. Doesn't matter to me."

"All right by me," Iuchar echoed.

Brian looked around at the curragh bobbing patiently on the waves. He cleared his throat, saying:

> "Scuabtinne, mighty Wave-Sweeper,
> Voyager to distant lands, keeper
> Of wave secrets, we ask that you
> Take us to the Hesperides Garden. Do
> Not tarry along the way, we humbly
> Ask, and fly quickly across the sea."

Scarce were the words out of his mouth than the small craft seemed to gather itself and rise up onto the waves. Without delay, it flew across the deep sea-chasms, soaring up the gray-green waves and sliding down the other glassy sides as quickly as the clear, cold March wind. Its course was direct, flying into the wind, tearing the eyes of the brothers as they strained fearfully to see what lay ahead, not tarrying until it entered the harbor. Then it slowed and slipped gracefully next to the land of the fabled garden.

xiii.

BRIAN ROSE CAUTIOUSLY AND STEPPED ashore. The ground seemed to lurch and sway under his feet. He bent forward at the waist, waiting until the dizziness passed, then called to his brothers, "Come! Let us sit and make our plans until we gather our land-legs under us!"

Iuchar and Iucharba, both looking a bit green around the gills, stepped from the curragh. Iuchar sank to his knees while Iucharba turned, leaned upon the gunwale of the curragh, and vomited.

"Ah, me!" he sighed. " 'Tis not something I'll be willing to do again!"

"You'll have to," Brian said grimly. "Best you be getting used to it."

"I didn't say I wouldn't," Iucharba declared. "I said I wasn't willing. I know necessity as well as you, so shut your gob!"

Brian grinned. He drew a deep breath, tasting the salt and dampness deep in his lungs. His nose twitched, and he turned into the land breeze. What was that? Apples? A happiness leaped up within him, and he clutched the hilt of his sword, slipping it experimentally in and out of its scabbard.

"Smell that, lads?" he said. They looked at him questioningly. He nodded inland. "The apples? Ah, 'tis a rich orchard indeed, I'm thinking."

Cautiously, Iuchar and Iucharba took deep breaths, then again greedily.

"Ripe for picking," Iucharba said. He bent and took a handful of seawater and rinsed his mouth, spitting onto the fine white sand at his feet. A strange singing swept through him. He felt invigorated and marveled at the sudden change within him. He glanced at Iuchar who nodded.

"Yes, I feel it, too," Iuchar said.

Brian grinned deeper, feeling himself growing closer to his brothers than ever before. "Well, lads, what do you think our strategy should be? Remember that we have many more deeds to do before Lugh will be satisfied. I think we should be prudent."

"I'm good for a dozen or two," Iucharba growled happily. He drew his sword and swung it high overhead.

Brian grimaced and frowned. "You call that prudent? Dash in like a Fomorian, swinging and stabbing and slashing?"

"Why not?" Iuchar slapped his sword by his side. "And since when did you become a cautious rabbit?"

"Since I realized what men will be saying after we are finished with all this," Brian said. "We must be careful that our deeds reflect greatly upon us, not only in valor, but wisely as well. We want the future men to say, 'Those sons of Tuirenn were brave men, champions.' Not: 'Those scoundrels don't deserve anything more than what they got. Senseless, rash youths! Their deaths came from their own folly!' "

"No man will say that to me face," Iucharba said, growling and frowning as he fingered the edge of his sword.

Brian closed his eyes and pinched the bridge of his nose between thumb and forefinger. "Ah, me!" he sighed. "That's just what I meant. Do you think that you will live forever to be giving everyone the lie back in their teeth? Your flesh is only temporal, lads! Soon it will be dust, but the earth will still be here! And so will those whose sons will be born long after the flesh has rotted from our bones! So, I say we take care how we act! Remember that at times discretion is needed!"

"Is this more of your philosophical ruminating?" Iuchar asked suspiciously.

"No. Pragmatism," Brian said firmly.

Iucharba groaned. "Philosophy! Pragmatism! Phooey! Give me a few heads to crack!"

"Soon, soon," Brian said soothingly. He brushed his fine blond hair back off his high forehead with a sweep of his hand. "Let us use our brains instead of brawn here, I say. Let us take the shape of swift falcons. Then, we should be able to approach the garden quietly, for I'm certain that birds are as common here as strangers are rare."

"Makes sense," Iuchar said grudgingly. "Swoop in and out with the apples clutched in our talons, eh?"

"Yes," Brian said, but wagged his finger cautiously. "Take care, though. There will undoubtedly be guards there with long, sharp lances. Maybe even arrows and darts, and sling-stones. They will certainly throw at us. Be active, cunning. Swoop in and out, pretending to gather the apples, but dash back before you come into range. Make the guards waste their throws. Then, when they are empty-handed, we'll swoop in and gather an apple each."

"Or two," Iucharba said, flexing the mighty muscles in his arms. Huge knots bulged.

"Don't be greedy!" Brian said sharply. "One apple will be enough. Remember: We still have to be away before the alarm is answered. The more you carry, the slower you will fly. Speed, my brothers! Speed!"

They nodded at his sage counsel, and Brian took his hazel wand from his cloak and struck his brothers lightly upon the forehead (if truth be known, he knocked Iucharba a little harder than Iuchar in an attempt to drum wisdom into his thick forehead) and then himself. Instantly, they turned into three beautiful falcons with high, proud heads and strong, curving talons.

Brian lifted up and away from the ground first, but his brothers, clumsy at first with the awkward lifting of their wings, came quickly at his heels. They flew to the garden and began to descend in long, swooping gyres.

"Blast and blazes!" a guard yelled. "Scavengers! Have at them, men! Shoo! Get away!" He launched a spear at Brian, but the son of Tuirenn easily dodged the missile and banked sharply to avoid an arrow shot from another's bow.

Iuchar and Iucharba whistled shrilly and swung down from their widening gyres, flickering tantalizingly in and out of the guards' range as a shower of spears and shafts flew toward them.

"Dirty buggers!" howled one guard, trying to sight on Iuchar. He didn't see Iucharba swinging by from behind. Suddenly a warm *splat!*

spattered against his forehead and splashed into his eyes. The guard cursed and dropped his bow, digging knuckles deeply into his burning eyes to wipe limy stool away.

Within moments, the eager guards had thrown their light weapons and stood empty-handed, staring as the two younger brothers stooped down into the trees, grabbing a golden apple each before climbing rapidly out of range. Forgetting his warning to his brothers, Brian grabbed one with his talons and another with his beak before rising rapidly high into the air and drawing a bead back to where Scuabtinne waited by the beach.

"Awk! The alarm! You bastards!" howled the head guardsman, shaking a heavy fist at the sky. "Bring those back! The alarm! The alarm, you whoremothers! Sound the alarm, you rascally yeaforsooth knaves, you foulmouthed, calumnious whoresons!"

News spread quickly through the city about how three swift falcons had slipped through the shower of spears thrown by the guardsmen and made away with the precious apples of the king.

"What?" cried the king angrily. A large purple vein began to pulse like a thick worm in the middle of his forehead. His face grew dark like liver. "Bring the headsman! I want the heads of all those guards on pikes by evening! Where are my daughters? Playing lickerish games with goatish guardsmen, I'll bet! Daughters!" he roared angrily.

Hearing their father, the daughters (who had indeed been playing pandering pareunia with willing partners) slipped away, leaving groaning paramours in the cool shadows of grape arbors, and slipped quickly into the throne room, where their father waited, tiny bubbles of angry foam forming at the corners of his mouth.

"Where have you been, you . . . you . . . never mind!" he snapped. "Three hawks—I suspect Druids—have stolen our apples! Get them back!"

Now, these daughters were cunning cunnies gifted with magic. Swiftly, they changed themselves into three sharp-taloned ospreys. They rose swiftly into the air and soon overtook the apple-laden brothers. Rising high, banking into the wind, the daughters unleashed shafts of brimstone burning lightning at them. One bolt charred Iuchar's tailfeathers.

"Awk!" he squawked, nearly dropping the apple he clutched. "Me arse is on fire!"

Another bolt passed between Iucharba's legs, nearly womanizing him with its blast of heat. "EEEeeeYOW!" he howled. "Help! Help!"

"Down!" shrilled Brian, diving toward the sea. His brothers came hard on his tail, clinging desperately to their spoils. When they came close to the sea, Brian shuffled the apple into one talon and slipped the hazel wand from beneath a wing and whacked himself and his two brothers, turning them into two swans. They slipped into the waves, hiding among the whitecaps of Fand's flowing hair.[55]

"Ahhh!" sighed Iuchar, wiggling his seat in the cooling water.

"Yesss," Iucharba echoed, splashing happily.

Brian watched as the ospreys searched vainly for them, then gave up and swept up high, angling back inland.

"Back to the curragh!" Brian ordered.

"A minute more," Iuchar said. "That's all I ask."

"And have them come back as sea-demons?" Brian asked, for he had recognized the three ospreys as magic, illusions only. "We escaped their lightning bolts, but what other magic will they have?"

"A point," grumbled Iucharba, turning reluctantly towards shore where Scuabtinne floated daintily upon the waves.

"Yes, I suppose," Iuchar said, sighing.

They swam back to the waiting curragh. Brian immediately changed them back into men and stowed the apples away carefully. Then he took his place in the stern and spoke softly to Scuabtinne. The curragh raised itself and flowed swiftly out to sea and away from the Garden of the Hesperides.

xiv.

AFTER RESTING FOR A DAY at Tír Na mBeo[56] the brothers
sailed to Greece to seek the skin of the pig. When they entered
Scuabtinne, Brian chanted softly:

> "O vessel of Mannanán, mighty Wave-Sweeper
> We ask you to take us to Greece and the keeper
> Of the magic pigskin. Do not dawdle along the way
> But take us to that far land without delay."

"Here we go again," Iucharba muttered, already turning white as
he seized the gunwales when Scuabtinne gathered itself and hurtled
forward, skimming along the green-gray waves.

"We'll be there in no time!" shouted Brian gleefully.

"Uh-huh," grunted Iuchar, unconvinced. He swallowed heavily
against his rising gorge. "What—what do you think we should do this
time?"

Brian frowned, sitting comfortably in the stern. Unlike many who
could work magic, he did not suffer badly from water travel. "I don't
know. Perhaps as hounds?"

"Nonsense," gulped Iucharba as the curragh skimmed down a deep
wave then back up the other side. "Last time, when we tried to be birds,
we nearly met with disaster. I say we go as men this time. That way, we
at least can die as men and not a roasting pigeon in someone's gullet!"

"I agree," Iuchar said gamely. "Let us go as bold champions and
make our demands. When he refuses, we'll simply carry it off. You
have the magic in that stick of yours. You can dust up a cloud or fog or
something to hide us while we slip away after seizing the pigskin."

"Hm," Brian said, furrowing his brow and gently tapping his lips
with the tips of his fingers. "Much to be said about that, but that is
magic again. And who's to say that the good king doesn't have another

around who can whistle up a wind to blow the fog away? Then where would we be? Hacking and slicing our way out. We're certain to be outnumbered. Probably killed, if it came to that."

"Better than drowning in this blasted water!" moaned Iucharba, clinging so hard to the sides of Scuabtinne that his knuckles showed whitely.

"You say that now, but it's better to be a plowman among the living than a hero among the dead," Brian said.

"You don't know that," Iuchar accused. "You just made it up."

"I know!" Brian said. He sat forward excitedly, the sudden change in his weight making Scuabtinne wobbled alarmingly from side-to-side.

"I knew it," moaned Iucharba. "He's going to turn turtle us. No hero's death for us! We'll drown here as ignominiously as a fat purse-stringed merchant!"

"Oh be quiet," Brian said, annoyed. "You sound like a fishwife damning the storm that keeps her husband from the kelp beds! Now, here's what we'll do: We'll go to the court as famous poets. Poets from grand Erin, *learned* poets," he corrected. "Bards are greatly admired by the nobles of Greece."

Iuchar and Iucharba exchanged glances, then sighed. "And just when," Iuchar said slowly, "did you become an expert upon Greece? Eh? Or, is this more of that you heard from the singers in our own land?"

Brian gave him a hard, disdainful look. "And better off we'd be if the two of you might have spent more time with the *seanchaís*[57] than with *striapachs*."[58]

"Maybe so," Iuchar said. "But there's no use of playing the king after the battle's fought. None of us has a song or poem upon our lips, and our tongues are not wily with words. If we go in as poets, sure as heather is on the hills and the gloaming in the west, we'll be asked to give the court a sampling of our work."

"We'll ford that stream when we come to it," Brian said firmly. "In the meantime, turn your backs to the other and let's rebraid our hair."

Resigned, Iucharba turned to Iuchar, who backed himself to Brian, who backed himself to Iucharba and, with warriors' fingers, they plaited poet-knots in each other's hair.

Soon Scuabtinne nestled into shore, and the three brothers stepped out, making their way to the palace gates. When the guards asked what they wanted, Brian smiled, gestured simply with his hand, and said, "Visitors who would pay their respects to your king."

The guard eyed them narrowly and said, "We get a lot of visitors here, and some who mean mischief and some who look for handouts. So which are you?"

"Mere poets from Erin," Brian said modestly. He indicated his brothers and himself. "Singers of fate and adventure, of heroes and tragedy, we are poets of the highest order, well-versed in divination and philosophical maunderings and—"

"Do you ken the stories dear to a soldier's heart?" the guardsman interrupted. "Battles and wars and"—here he winked vulgarly—"a tale about a saucy tart or two?"

"My brothers," Brian said, casting a disdainful eye upon Iucar and Iucharba, "specialize in the latter. Although I fear they aren't for the delicate ear or *polite* company such as those lingering in the king's court."

"We can split a tun over good saucy stories without bothering his worship about it all," the guardsman said. He leaned down, hollering at the gatekeeper. "Open those doors for poets with a fine sense of order."

Slowly, the ponderous doors slid open and Brian and his brothers entered, shuffling confidently, but with a poet's step. The guardsman came down to greet them, saying, "I sent a messenger with word to the king. If you will wait a moment, we'll have word directly what to do with you."

The words were barely passed his lips when the young messenger scurried up to him, saying, "The king waits eagerly for them."

"Does he, now?" the guardsman said. "And what were his words? Precisely now," he warned. "None of that pantywaisted paraphrasing. That may be good for the jesters and the courtiers—though truth be known, you can't tell one from the other if you're listening to their jabber—a soldier gets the meat with the bone."

The young messenger closed his eyes, composing his thoughts, then said, " 'Bring them to me. If they're from Erin, they've come a goodly distance to find a decent and generous master who is worthy of their faith. I'm just the one for them. We could use new tales around here. The old ones are wearing a bit thin.'" He looked sternly at the singers sitting in the shadows who pretended not to hear him. "'It seems that most of the new ones these days are turning out thin satires and whining whimsies in the name of art. No mystery to them. Paltry playings with words, words, words. Bring them here so they can see that our court is as grand as any they have found in their travels.'" He opened his eyes, nodding. The gatekeeper looked at him suspiciously.

"Seems to me there's a bit of yourself there playing the critic. But no mind. There's truth to the words." He nodded at Brian and his brothers. "Off with you, then. Mustn't keep the king awaiting. He gets a little cranky when he's stayed on fishhooks."

The sons of Tuirenn nodded politely and fell in behind the young messenger who brought them—still disguised as poets of the seventh order—before the king. They were greeted gladly by the king, who ordered food and wine be laid out for them. They fell to drinking and eating merrily, exchanging pleasantries with the others in the court. Iuchar muttered to Brian that he had never seen a household so numerous and so friendly. The women eyed the brothers boldly, the serving wenches leaning low over the brothers' table to show their breasts, black eyes smoldering as they considered the brothers' frames.

" 'Tis a shame we're here to rob him blind," Iuchar said softly. "He seems like a good sort, friendly to guests and travelers."

"Aye," Iucharba said, grinning at the big-breasted woman standing over him. He winked boldly at her. A high flush came to her cheeks. She licked her lips saucily. "And there seems to be a great promise here as well."

"Perhaps," Brian said, taking a bite of honeyed meat. He smacked his lips. "I'll say this for him: he keeps a fine table. But"—he rolled his eyes significantly—"remember that the rules of hospitality would not let him do otherwise."[59]

"Always the cautious one," grumbled Iucharba, staring frankly and appreciatively at a young black-haired woman who blushed prettily at his open gaze.

"And well for you, I am," Brian retorted. "Enough. We're supposed to be guests here. Shh. I think the king's bards are going to entertain us."

"Yes, but then we will have to respond," Iuchar said urgently. "And Elada[60] hasn't touched me with his wand. It's up to you."

"We'll see what happens when it happens," Brian said. "Now, be quiet before we appear to be rude."

They listened unhappily as the king's poets sang their lays and poetry for those at the feast. And when they had finished, they took their seats, gazing expectantly at Brian and his brothers.

"I knew it," moaned Iucharba. "I just knew it! Now, we're in for it!" He reached beneath his cloak, fingering his sword, loosening it in its sheath. But Brian put his hand upon his shoulder, staying him, as he rose to face the king.

"Your singers appear well-versed and gifted," he said.

The bards exchanged self-satisfied smirks that hung limply on their faces like smoke as the king said impatiently, "Yes, yes. Though I have heard them so many times that I could very well sing them myself. Not much originality anymore! The new copy the old, change characters here and there, and call it new!"

Brian leaned over, shielding his words with his hands as he spoke to his brothers. "Now's the time. We have to make a poem for the king. The old ones won't do, I'm afraid."

Iucharba shrugged. "Makes no difference to me. I can't remember the old ones. Not," he added acidly, "that that would make much difference. I sing like pigs grunting."

"Well, I can remember 'The Lass from Tara,'" Iuchar said, but fell silent as Brian glared at him.

"We can't be singing those here," Brian growled.

"The proprieties must be observed," Iucharba said. "You do it."

"Me?"

"What was all that you were yammering about back at the curragh with the *striapachs* and all?" Iucharba said. Iuchar nodded agreement. "We ain't got a poem to recite for a king. You want us to fight like warriors should, why, then we're for you. But to make a poem for these ears . . ." He let his voice trail away as he shook his head. Brian gave him a look of disgust and rose, gathering his cloak around him as he faced the king.

"My lord," he began. "Our poems are most unworthy of such an august body—"

"Here's an out if I ever heard one," a poet said loudly. The others snickered, then fell quiet, looking at the offender in accusation as the king stared in their direction.

"But," Brian said, "in so much as there is the shadow of Aengus upon us, I will attempt to grace you with a modest verse or two."

"Such a trifling that one would sing only to oysters and cockleshells," muttered one of the bards. The others stuffed cloaks into their mouths to hide their mirth.

Brian took a breath, and sang:

> "In honor of your grace and fame
> O Tuis, we will play a poet's game.
> Like a great oak among bushes you stand
> As king among kings to lead any band.
>
> We ask little for our song, but the bard
> Must be paid and so I ask a little reward:
> Namely that an *Imnocta-fessa*[61] be given
> For our words that may be short-shriven.
>
> "As to this game we pretend to play
> While guests in your land we stay,
> Let us play the riddling-game
> And tease your bards to play the same!
>
> "Two neighbors meet upon a raging sea
> One a bard unrequited—a dreadful foe he—
> While the other meets an O to an O.
> Which, would you say, is the deadlier foe?
>
> "Now, if your bards, with all their art,
> Can play the ass to my common cart,

Then let them speak or else hold their din
As I collect my payment: a simple pigskin!"

"Well done!" Iucharba said loudly.

The king's poets looked at each other. "Well," one sniffed. "That isn't bad, although I think he strained the meter a bit, and the rhyme is only a modest one at that."

"Enough playing with syntax," Tuis said, glaring at them. "Well? Which of you has it? The answer, I mean?"

"Your Majesty," began one. "This is not a simple task that is set before us. One must be careful to measure each nuance, the exact connotation, if you will, not only of rhyme, but of meter as well. One suggests one thing, the other another. That is to say—"

"—that you have no idea what you are talking about," Tuis finished. He frowned darkly at them, then turned to Brian, smiling uncertainly. "A fine poem, by my reckoning. But I must confess that I cannot make sense of it. Although," he added hastily, "it is pleasing upon the ear."

Brian smiled tolerantly. "If I may be so bold—"

"Yes, yes," Tuis said eagerly. "By all means. Elucidate."

"As the oak rules over the other trees of the forest, so do you stand, firm and resolute, a king among other kings, renowned for your generosity. My words, however, cannot do justice to you. As words are only air, they cannot compare—"

"Ah, another rhyme," muttered a bard.

"—to your glory and are worthy of only a pigskin for their composition. Now, as for the O, why that simply refers to 'ear,' which you will lend to my song—unless you refuse. Then we shall be fighting ear-to-ear for the pigskin."

The others fell silent as Brian's words dropped among them, holding their breath as they watched to see what Tuis would do with Brian's demand of his magic pigskin. The king's face had tightened at Brian's words. Now he nodded thoughtfully and said, "Well, enough. I really would have given your poem the praise it deserved *if* you had not made an issue of my pigskin." He wagged his finger admonishingly at Brian. "That was not very wise or gracious of you, man of verse. Even if all the poets and scholars of Erin *and* all the nobles and chiefs of the whirling world should request it of me, I would not give it up." He held up his hand, staying the babble that threatened to come from the poets who, despite their animosity toward Brian, recognized that a poet must be paid his due. "But I recognize the tradition that must be upheld between a singer and his patron. To that end, I will give you enough red gold to fill that same pigskin three times over if it were made into a bag as the price of your poem. Although," he added warningly, "I would not compose another quite in that same, ah, style."

Brian bowed and smiled at the king. "It is a goodly ransom that you offer in place of the pigskin, Tuis. And, given the reputation of the pigskin, only a fair one, I would say."

"Then, you accept?" Tuis asked, smiling, secretly relieved, for he knew that an angry poet could tatter a person's reputation with a few well-chosen words.

"Oh, yes, of course," Brian said. "In fact, you are being more than generous. It is, after all, when one considers it carefully, only a pigskin. But, I am—how shall I put it—"

"He knows well how to put it," grumpily grunted one of the king's bards. "A plague on false modesty."

Again, Brian smiled engagingly (and the ladies present felt their hearts lurch and their loins grow weak at that) and said, "I hope Your Majesty won't take this badly, but"—he indicated the poets and bards in the shadows—"if your servants are no better mannered than your poets, I should like to watch the measuring. That may seem to be ill-mannered—for which I apologize—but for a man who hasn't an ounce of white gold, that much red gold is more than mere imagination can suggest."

Tuis looked admiringly at him. "If only my ambassadors could speak so prettily politically. No offense is taken, man of verse."

He turned and ordered that Brian and his brothers be taken to the treasure room, where the pigskin was to be held by a servant while another measured it full three times with red gold.

"Please be good enough to measure the first two for each of my brothers. The last will be for me," Brian said.

The servants shrugged and brought the pigskin out. Brian looked at it. "Is that it? The magical pigskin that has become so famous?"

"It is," one of the servants said. But they were his last words, for with one quick move, Brian snatched the pigskin with one hand while his other flashed from beneath his cloak, holding his sword. With one clean sweep, he cleaved the servant from crown to groin, halving him neatly. Blood spouted like a fountain, washing the room redly as the servant fell twice to the floor. The second servant dashed from the room, yelling shrilly, "Help! Oh, help! Murder! Murder!"

Quickly, Brian wrapped the skin around himself as his brothers drew their weapons, stepping from the treasure room to stand shoulder to shoulder in the hall. In this array, they met the guardsmen running with drawn weapons.

Iuchar raised his battle-cry, decapitating the first while beside him, Iucharba roared an echo, hacking his way through the guardsmen until the floor washed red with blood. Together, they pushed the guardsmen back into the throne room. By this time, Tuis had managed to arm himself, and when the brothers came out, he stood waiting for them.

"So," he said grimly. "This is the true poet, eh? A singer of blades?"

"I regret the deception," Brian said, advancing toward him with his drawn blade dripping gore. "But, we have a great need for this pigskin. There is an *éric* upon us that must be satisfied."

" 'Tis a pity that it won't," Tuis said. He lashed out suddenly, his sword slipping beneath Brian's guard, slicing his arm open to the bone.

Brian gasped, then his blade danced in and out as Tuis and he fought back-and-forth across the throne room. So fierce was their battle that all others stopped to watch the duel. Brian's sword sliced through the breast of Tuis, severing his nipple, while Tuis returned the stroke to Brian's collarbone, nearly cleaving his shoulder, but the pigskin quickly healed him. Furious, Brian stormed like a winter torrent upon Tuis, forcing the king to use all his wiles to defend himself. Then, he seemed to gather strength and like a raging wind among oak branches, he battered Brian back across the room, knicking him first here on the cheek, then there upon the thigh, as Brian fought gamely to keep the blade away from his breast and neck, for the weakness in the pigskin was that a man's head needed to stay firmly attached to his shoulders. And then his mighty battle-cry leaped from his lips like the screech of an eagle, the cry of a hawk, and Brian swooped forward, darting like a bird of prey as he slipped beneath the guard of Tuis and spitted him from shoulder to ham. Tuis's sword clattered to the floor as the king swayed, trying to push his intestines back inside. Then he fell forward, dead.

At that, Iuchar and Iucharba roared again their battle-cries and fell upon the guardsmen, slaughtering all until the throne room was awash in blood and limbs. Then, they rested, panting, their arms and breasts sliced to ribbons.

"Ah," Iucharba grinned painfully. "Now, that's better than trying to bandy words, if you ask me."

"Nobody did," Brian said. He heaved a great sigh, looking ruefully at each of them. "But now we have hurts that must be healed."

And so they remained for three days and three nights, healing themselves with the pigskin and the apples, rebuilding their strength. At night, their beds were visited by the most beautiful of the kingdom's ladies, who romped wildly in the brothers' beds, nearly finishing in pleasure where the swords of the nobles had failed in battle.

XV.

ON THE FOURTH DAY, BRIAN rose, stretching, gazing fondly at the naked woman sleeping soundly beside him, her dark nipples rising like ripe olives from the brown mountains of her breasts, her wide hips, the thick black bush, the strong thighs that had threatened to crush the breath from his lungs in the night. He felt himself move, then reluctantly turned and sat up, stepping from the bed. He seized a pitcher of water and poured it over him, gasping from the cold of the morning's breath upon the water.

He dressed quickly, then slipped from his bedchamber and made his way to each of his brothers, gathering them to him. Together, they crept from the palace and made their way to where Scuabtinne bobbed patiently upon the waves, waiting for them.

"Where to now?" Iucharba asked. He rubbed his neck, where teeth marks showed, and grinned. "I hope somewhere where the women are as anxious as these."

"Well, we have a good start," Iuchar said. "We have the apples and the pigskin. Things could be worse." He grinned at his brother. "And you haven't come out too worse the wear for it all."

"Persia," Brian said firmly. "We must stay to the natural order of things."

Iuchar sighed. "Always the order. 'Twill be the death of you yet."

"We owe a death for the life," Brian said, stepping into the curragh.

Within minutes, they had left the deep blue streams of Greece far behind, skimming over the wine-dark sea toward Persia, their pulses quickening with the thoughts of the exotic and the adventure ahead.

XVI.

AS MANANNÁN'S CRAFT NEARED THE rocky Persian shore, Iuchar stirred himself, sighed, and looked at Brian. "I think I could stay here," he said, looking around contentedly at the crashing seas and the squawking birds wheeling high overhead. " 'Tis a great peace here, I'm thinking."

"Looks are deceiving," Brian said. "Remember how Cian disguised himself as a pig?"

"I remember how *you* got us into this mess," Iuchar said, anger flashing hotly for a moment. "It would have been fine enough to leave him rooting in that acorn mast. But, you had to be playing that game with him. What good has the blood-feud done for us, now? Eh?"

"Easy," Iucharba said, placing a restraining hand upon Iuchar's thick forearm. His brother flung it off, glaring at him. "We're all in this together, now. That's our strength. Together. Separately, we don't have a chance of completing this *éric*."

"We don't have a chance anyway," Iuchar said darkly, turning to stare at the waiting headland. Scuabtinne waited patiently, measuring the waves as they rose and moved toward the land. Then, Scuabtinne caught a wave, slipping down the face, turning to avoid the jagged rocks, sliding deftly between two others, to coast to idle water in a small cove sheltered by thick-limbed tamarind trees.

"Don't think about that," Iucharba said, punching his brother gently upon the shoulder. "There's not much use and need in thinking about the obvious."

"We must walk the road given us," Brian said soberly. "And make the best of a servant's supper." He shrugged. "Who remembers the cowherd and who remembers the warrior?"

"But," Iuchar said unhappily, "which one is happier? And what do we care after we're dead and gone?"

"Enough!" Brian said. "How should we approach this task?"

Iucharba shrugged and spread his hands. His eyes met Brian's. "And how else but what we are? We cannot be kings."

"No," Brian said. "We cannot be kings. But I think we should try again our ruse as poets. It worked before," he added sharply as Iuchar rose up to argue.

Iuchar started to argue, then shrugged his shoulders and glanced at his brother. Iucharba spat over the side of the curragh and shook his head resignedly.

"Why interfere with success?" he said. " 'Tisn't easy to be what you're not, but sometimes one can fool the others into thinking that what they are looking at is grain and not chaff."

So once again they put the poet-knots in their hair and made their way to the palace of Pisear, king of Persia, passing through the outer gate to the inner one where Brian raised his fist and banged on it.

"Knock, knock, knock! Who's there?" cried the gatekeeper.

"Three poets from Erin," Brian announced. "We come with a poem for the king."

"Poets, eh?" said the gatekeeper, drawing the bolts and throwing the gate wide. " 'Tis a warrior's fist that banged at the gate, not a poet's." He peered out and, noticing the poet-knots in their hair, threw the gate wide. "Methinks you've chosen the wrong profession, sar. With an arm like that, you could carve a name for yourself on the battlefield."

"Thank you," Brian said politely, stepping in through the gate. "And if you would be so kind as to take us to the king—Pisear, isn't it?—we'll be giving him a bit of entertaining."

"Yes, that's his name," the gatekeeper said, staring with rheumy eyes at the three standing before them. "They certainly make poets differently in Erin than we do here in Persia. Ain't a one of them got an ax-handle's width to his shoulders in our king's court."

"The king?" Brian repeated, smiling gently.

Startled the gatekeeper rattled his keys and gestured for them to follow him as he turned and hobbled on arthritic legs up the stairs. "Bunch of limp-wristed queens looking for a king, if you get my meaning." He paused to stare back, winking lewdly. "Or a knight." He cackled at his own ribaldry as he led them to the throne room, where Pisear rose to greet them.

"Ah, grand, grand!" he said, clapping his hands when told they were poets from far beyond the ninth wave. "We shall have a feast and a fest! And to the winner, a grand prize for him to claim."

"If that pleases Your Majesty," Brian said. He glanced at the young princess, Pisear's daughter, sitting beside her father, her young breasts pressing like ripe pomegranates against her dress, her lips smiling seductively at Brian, eyes wide in open invitation. Brian grinned at her, and her pink tongue darted out to lick her full lower lip.

"Yes, yes," Pisear said, ignoring the teasing of his daughter. "That would please me greatly. Greatly."

The king's poets sniffed and drew their fine dress around them, taking great pains that the shoulders draped well. Then, one-by-one, they stood and sang their lays, their songs, their fine poems until the last harp note slipped away into silence and they all looked expectantly at the brothers.

"Now, my brothers, arise and sing softly for the good king," Brian whispered to his brothers. They looked at him with surprise.

"We've been through this before, remember?" Iuchar whispered back. " 'Tisn't the sound of grackles cackling that he wants to hear, but one whose voice is sweet and pure. Like that catamite simpering over there against the pillar," he added, nodding at a youth with rosy cheeks who looked back at him with great admiration shining from his black, limpid eyes.

"Don't ask us for that which we can't do," Iucharba said. He poked his brother in the ribs with a hard forefinger, stiff as a blacksmith's poker. Iuchar looked back at him. "I think you're getting strange ideas," Iucharba said. He glanced at Brian. "It's up to you again, brother. But, if you wish it, why, I'll crack a few heads for you and split a couple from whistle to woozle if you like."

"That would be a strange poetry—to hear blades singing in this room, I'm thinking," Brian whispered back, then rose and said loudly. "As it is, Your Majesty, I have a poem for the ears of a king. If it be your pleasure, I'll give it song."

The king nodded and leaned forward on his throne, rapt attention shining from his face as Brian positioned himself carefully. Then he raised his voice in his fine tenor, singing:

> "May the great King Pisear ever reign
> Across Persia's great mountains and plain.
> And may his great spear continue to break
> The backs of his enemies for his country's sake.
>
> " 'Tis a great weapon, this magical spear,
> Yew-handled of the finest wood, dear
> To all who would stand before it. King
> Itself when compared with others. It brings
>
> "Death to all who oppose it. None withstands
> That blazing spear wielded by Pisear's hand.
> Mighty armies and heroes quake in fear
> When Pisear is near with his spear."

When he had finished, he remained standing, staring into Pisear's eyes as the king frowned in puzzlement. Idly, Brian reached into a pouch hanging by his side and removed one of the golden apples, rubbing it absently against his tunic.

"I must confess," sighed Pisear, leaning back in his chair and throwing his hands up. "I do not understand what my spear has to do with your poem. Although," he added hastily, "it is a good poem for all of that. None here would reckon otherwise."

And the other poets nodded in agreement, for although none there could understand the poem, none wanted to be accused of being simple if pressed for a critique.

"It's not that hard," said Brian, son of Tuirenn. "In fact it is very simple. I give you the poem and within the poem itself, name the reward I would have for the poem."

Pisear's mouth dropped open in astonishment at the youth's rashness. Then he laughed and said, "Ah, but that is a foolish request, man of verse! No man who ever requested that spear from me walked away from the spot where you are now standing."

"Your Majesty," one of his nobles interjected quickly. "He is a poet, and there are many of those here. Remember the danger of the satire."

Pisear gestured his advisor away, saying, "But I will give you a greater reward than that spear." His eyes crinkled merrily and he tugged at his carefully curled beard. "I'll give you your life!" He looked around at his nobles who all nodded in satisfaction at the king's decision.

Brian pursed his lips as he tossed the golden apple up and down in his hand for a minute. "Well, a life is a grand gift. That I will admit," he said. "But I already own my life, so it really isn't a gift so much as a threat to be taking it from me."

Pisear shrugged, the humor disappearing from his eyes. "Then have it that way, if you will," he said ominously.

Brian sighed. "And that's your final word on the subject?" He looked over his shoulder at his brothers, eyeing them significantly. They rose and casually slipped their hands beneath their cloaks, grasping the hilts of their swords. He glanced back at the king. "Well?"

Pisear's face darkened with anger. "Base insolence!" he snapped. "Who do you think you are to speak to me in this way?"

At that, Brian pitched the apple at the king's head. So rapid was his throw and so true to the mark, that Pisear had time to blink only once wonderingly, as the apple blasted his forehead apart, driving his brain out the back of his skull where it splattered against the back of his throne like a squashed spider. Then the apple flew back to Brian's hand.

He dropped it in his pouch, then whirled, drawing his sword from beneath his cloak. Then, roaring his battle-cry that would cause lesser men to piddle their britches, he fell upon the nobles and warriors of the court, hewing and hacking his way through them like a scythe through fall-ripened wheat. His brothers' cries came as a terrifying echo of his own as they stepped to his side, each slashing his blade through flesh and bone, bright blood fountaining in the air and spraying in a fine mist that covered all there.

All too soon, the battle was won, and the brothers leaned against each other, staring at the carnage they had left on the floor behind them.

"Well," Iuchar said, licking at a slice across the back of his hand. "So much for that." He heard a rustle from behind a curtain and stepped quickly to it, pulling it down and away from its rings. Young women, small and full-breasted, stared wonderingly from the brothers to the blood-soaked floor.

"Well, now," Iucharba said, grinning. "It seems as if there's still a use for our swords after all."

For four days, the brothers slept with the women of the court. Brian spent the days and nights with the princess, and so grateful was she with his swordsmanship that she led him to the chamber where the great spear stood upended in a great cauldron of water so that its heat would not scorch the people of the court.

And then it was time for the children of Tuirenn to leave, and Iucharba carefully gathered the cauldron and heavily venomed spear and carried it back to where Scuabtinne waited, dancing patiently on the waves of the wine-dark sea.

xvii.

"Sicily," Brian said when his brothers asked him in what direction they should next travel. "To Dobhar's court to collect the two horses and chariot that Lugh Idlánach has demanded."

Iuchar sighed and scratched his arse before stepping into Scuabtinne's prow and settling himself. "You know," he reflected, "I'm becoming a bit fond of this travel." Scuabtinne lifted itself, wriggling like a puppy in pleasure at Iuchar's words. "Yes, I'm beginning to take to this."

Iucharba sighed and stretched out in the bottom of the curragh. "It's pleasant—after a fashion," he added. Then he rolled his head back, squinting up at Brian, who carefully stored the treasures they had gathered before stepping into Scuabtinne. "Tell me, brother: Are you beginning to feel that Lugh has demanded a bit much for his blood-fine? Seems to me that we have paid enough blood to make half-a-dozen Cians if we only had the wizardry to do so."

Brian shrugged. "It doesn't matter what we think. It only matters what Lugh asked for and we agreed to. Don't blame him for his request. We were quick enough to accept when we thought it little enough to do."

Iuchar sighed and rubbed his nose with the heel of his hand. "Damn him for his golden words. 'Tis a poet's soul he has beneath that good strong arm of his. Who would have thought to find a poet's tongue in a warrior's mouth?"

"Speaking of which," Iucharba said, rolling his great head on his shoulders until it rested comfortably against the side of Scuabtinne. "I think we've played enough of these poet games, Brian. Word's bound to be getting out about three brothers masquerading as what they aren't. We got away with it twice; only fools will try the same trick three times."

"I've been giving some thought to that," Brian said. "Let's take a page from your book, Iucharba."

Iucharba sat up, his brow furrowing in puzzlement. *"My* book? What's that?"

"Why pretend to be something we aren't?" Brian answered. "Let us go to Dobhar's court as mercenaries from Erin, seeking a good king to pledge our blades to. That way, we'll be among soldiers and warriors—where the horses and chariots are certain to be—instead of poets and players. I think we'd have better luck seeing the lay of the ground from a soldier's eyes than a bard's."

"Ah, a familiar role to play!" Iuchar said, clapping his hands. "I'm for it."

"And me. Or I. Whatever," Iucharba said.

"Then it's done," Brian said. He leaned forward, speaking softly to Scuabtinne. The brave craft leaped forward, skimming the waves, as it set its course toward the sunny shores of Sicily.

Soon it slipped into a narrow cove and ran itself up on a sandy beach, allowing Iuchar to step out without wetting his heels as he had before. He patted the brave craft's gunwales. "Thank you, Scuabtinne," he said. " 'Tis a fine job you've been doing for us."

"Come on," Brian said, settling his sword at his waist. "Let's be off to the palace and see what we can find out."

Now, as it happened, Dobhar was holding court on the broad, level green in front of his palace, idily away the time with wine and olives and cheese and oranges when the brothers came upon him.

"What's this we have?" Dobhar said laconically, staring at the brothers whose dress was salt-wrinkled although their arms glittered brightly, dangerously. "Surely these are warriors? Or crow men?"[62]

Giggles from the scantily clad young women sprawled upon the green floated up into the cobalt-blue air behind his words. Iucharba flushed and fingered the haft of his sword, but Brian laid a cool hand on his elbow, staying him.

"We apologize for our appearance, Your Majesty," he said smoothly. "But we have come a long distance from Erin to offer our blades to your service and are fair famished from the effort."

"Hmm," Dobhar said. "Is then your intention to remain here awhile in my service?"

"Yes," Brian said, smiling disarmingly. "It is that." Not a few of the young women there felt their hearts lurch and bang wildly in their chests at his bright smile.

"I see," Dobhar said thoughtfully. He sipped from a glass of resin wine. "Then I take it that you are handy with those swords hanging by your side and they are not simply there to help you balance?"

"We've been known to carve a duckling or two," Brian said, grinning.

"Ah, a warrior with a sense of humor. Good, good," said Dobhar.

And so it was that the children of Tuirenn entered the service of the king of Sicily in a post of honor, for the king loved a jest with his warriors when the mood was upon him. And it was often after the brothers took their posts. They stayed with him in the palace for a month and a fortnight, slowly discovering the information that they needed. But during that time, they not once saw the steeds or the famed chariot they would pull.

One rainy day, as they sat in their room, pondering the gray mist outside their window, Brian cleared his throat, saying, "I don't think this was such a good idea, my brothers. We are no further along with our *éric* than we were the day before we came. That is, we haven't learned anything at all about whereabouts of the king's fine horses or his chariot."

"No," Iuchar grinned, "but we have ridden some fine mares in his stable."

"Always the man with the *striapachs*, eh?" Brian said

"I don't see you pushing any out of your bed, except early in the morning before the lark sings, so she can slip back to her husband's room," Iuchar said pointedly.

"That," Brian said loftily, "is research. Sometimes women always know more than they are willing to tell. Especially in bed. Men have a habit of flapping their lips to impress the women with how good and how important they are. Chances were that they spoke about Dobhar's horses while frolicking in bed with certain ladies."

"And did you find out anything?" Iucharba said. Iuchar grinned and nudged him with his elbow.

"No, but it isn't for lack of searching for the right mare."

"Enough!" Brian said as his brothers snickered. "The fact is we know nothing more than the day we came to this court."

"So, what should we do?" Iucharba said, sighing. He could tell that Brian's restless spirit was upon him, and there would be no more tarrying until they had finished what they came to Sicily to accomplish.

"I say we arm ourselves, put on our traveling clothes, go to the king, and tell him that we are planning on leaving his service and this sunny isle unless he shows us the famous horses," Brian said.

"Oh, that is certain to win us friends, indeed," Iucharba said sourly. "We simply march up to the king and say, 'Give us a glimpse of your horses, or we'll be leaving your place.' " He looked sourly at Brian. "And you expect him to believe that we don't have other ideas in mind at that?"

"Do you have a better idea?" Brian asked.

"No," Iucharba said, "but that doesn't make yours any better. Just the only one."

"And?" Brian asked gently.

Iucharba sighed. "Come on, Iuchar. There's no reasoning with him when he's got a thistle up his arse or next to his *bod*."

They went forth that day to see the king, finding him at lunch with goat cheese and resin wine, surrounded by poets and players and scantily dressed women. "Ah," he cried, upon seeing the brothers finely dressed. "I see you are off to an adventure." He frowned, worrying a piece of meat out from between his teeth. "But, don't you think you should have asked me first? I'm really fairly informal, except on formal occasions."

"We are sorry, Your Majesty, but my brothers and I must leave your service. Regretfully," he added.

The king's eyebrows flew up. He sat erect, spilling wine over his hand. A steward hastened forward with a cloth to blot it away from the royal hand.

"Leave my service?" he exclaimed. "Why? Have you been mistreated in any way?"

"It is a minor thing, but very important to men such as ourselves,

Your Majesty," Brian said smoothly. "You see, we are from Erin, and as such, our martial gifts naturally draw us close to those whom we would serve. We are always the guards and confidants of kings. We have guarded their rarest jewels, been the champions of the virtue of the queens, their gifted arms of victory. We are accustomed to being the repositories of the innermost secrets and desires of those whom we serve. But you have not treated us as such. It may seem a minor thing, but it is a matter of honor with us."

The king's brow furrowed in puzzlement. "But, how have I not treated you in this manner?"

"It has come to our attention that you possess two fine and won-drous horses and a magnificent chariot the likes of which have never seen elsewhere in the world. Such wondrous things surely must be guarded by the best warriors a king has. Yet, you have not posted us to them. Indeed, you haven't even told us about them. We had to learn of their existence elsewhere."

"I see," the king said. He shook his head as a steward tried to hand him another cup filled with wine. "But this is most unseemly of you to leave my employ in this matter. Especially since this is the first time I have heard that you would like to see them. Had I known that, I would have shown them to you on the first day. But if that is all it will take to keep you in my service, why, then, you shall certainly be allowed to see them. I have never had soldiers in this court from Erin who have earned greater confidence from me and my people."

He clapped his hands and called for the master of horses. When the man appeared, the king ordered that the steeds be yoked to the chariot and brought forth so that Brian and his brothers could see them.

They came, and the children of Tuirenn marveled at the horses. As fleet they were as the clear cold wind of early spring that travels equally over land and sea. Brian walked around them slowly, admiring the fine turn of their legs, the sheen of their coats, the magnificent chariot. Suddenly he seized the charioteer, stripped the reins from his hand, and lifted him high overhead, smashing him against a standing rock carved as a tribute to Dobhar. He leaped into the chariot, taking up the

reins himself, then cast the great spear of Pisear straight at the aston-
ished king, destroying his heart as the venom point cleaved his breastbone.

Iucharba roared his battle-cry and, with his brother, drew his
sword, and fell upon the warriors and host of the court. Together, the
three brothers brought red slaughter to the famous court. But they
were sorely wounded in this battle, as Dobhar had many champion
warriors in his service. They were forced to rest for a week while their
wounds healed.

" 'Tis great luck we're having," Iucharba said as they finally made
their way back to where Scuabtinne waited.

"Don't be tempting fate with your words!" Iuchar said curtly.
" 'Tis a cautious and wise man who keeps his fortune secret from others. Many a warrior's been laid low with a slip from his lip." He glanced
at Brian. "And where will we go from here?" he asked.

XViii.

BRIAN SHOOK HIS HEAD. "AS always," he said. "Disturb the
natural order, and we may bring disaster down upon our heads. We
shall go to Asal, the king of the Golden Pillars, and ask him for the
seven pigs that Lugh Ildánach has demanded from us as a part of the
éric that we must pay before we may be again the masters of our own
destiny."

Iuchar gave him a strange look. "I think we were too long at
Dobhar's court," he said. "You're beginning to talk like a courtier
instead of a warrior."

"And a good thing for us, too," Iucharba said. *"One* of us needs a
silver tongue. Otherwise, I doubt if we would have gotten this far on
our own."

"Donn's great balls!" Iuchar swore. "Fine words didn't get us
our trophies. 'Twas our good strong sword arms that brought us this
far."

"Only," Iucharba said firmly, "after Brian's fair speeches and fine poems bought us the time to get close. Do you think we could have hacked our way through an army to get to the palace? No. A bit of subterfuge was needed. Squirrels don't hide all their acorns in their nests."

"Stuff and nonsense," Iuchar scoffed. "I'm not belittling Brian's fine words."

"See then that you don't," growled Iucharba. "I'm as much for fighting as another, but the odds must be shortened."

By this time, they had settled in Scuabtinne, and Brian had given the sturdy craft its directions. When they came close to the harbor of the Golden Pillars, they noticed the shoreline with armed men waiting for the sons of Tuirenn; for while they rested, their fame rushed on ahead of them. Stories varied, but all had heard of their strength with the sword and how they had been forced to leave Erin by the hard words of Lugh and how they were wandering the world, collecting the fine trophies needed to pay the price of their blood-fine.

"What's this?" Iucharba asked, looking at the spears bristling above the heads of the army.

"It looks like word has come about us," Iuchar said resignedly. "Ah, me! Now things will be getting more difficult for us, I'm afraid."

"Shh," Brian said soothingly. "Land us, Scuabtinne," he ordered. Obediently, the craft edged up to the port. The brothers stepped ashore, their weapons close by their hands as they stared at the unfriendly faces around them. Then the ranks parted and Asal, king of the Golden Pillars, came forward to greet them. His face was hostile, his words harsh as he ignored the proprieties.

"So, what has brought you to my land?" he asked bluntly. "Mind you, we have heard how you have slaughtered the other kings of the world. We'll not be having that nonsense here."

"As if you could stop us," Iucharba growled, half-drawing his sword. But Iuchar stayed his hand as Brian stepped forward, light glimmering from his arms, a hero's halo hovering above his fine golden hair.

"We have come for your pigs," he said simply. "We know that word of Lugh's demands upon us has come before us, so you should already know this without asking why we have come. Do you play us for fools by pretending to be ignorant of our travels, our odyssey?"

"Hmm. Boldly and bluntly spoken," Asal said. He placed his hands on his hips, his chin jutting forward ominously. "And just how did you think you would be managing this?"

Brian shrugged. "If possible, we would like to get them with your goodwill. We would thank you greatly for your hospitality and good faith. But"—he shrugged and his eyes glinted dangerously— "if it must be, why, then, we will be forced to fight for them. If we do, many will die—maybe ourselves, but that is fate, and who knows the whimsical turnings of Fate? Perhaps yourself, Your Majesty," he said pointedly.

"Hmm. So you would fight us to get the pigs, eh?"

"Yes," Brian answered.

The king nodded and studied the sons of Tuirenn carefully, then turned and looked at his own preparations. Although his army was a fine one, he could see that the sons of Tuirenn would collect a heavy score before they could be placed under the sod. *If*, he reminded himself, they could be. Men with their success so far had to be very skilled in the arts of war.

"Well, if it is to be a gift or a triumph, it would seem to be very ignoble of us to fight with you for the sake of a few pigs."

"Very," Brian said cautiously.

The king nodded and waved his councilors close. After much whispering and arguing, the king held up his hands and stepped away from them, studying the brothers. "All right. You may have the pigs," he said.

"That is most gracious of you," Brian said, bowing his head.

"I smell a pig in a poke," Iuchar growled quietly to Brian and Iucharba. "No one gives up a prize like that without a bit of a struggle."

"I agree," Iucharba said. "There's treachery here somewhere. I can smell it."

"Maybe. Maybe not," Brian said. "But we have two choices: Go along with the king and play the game as the rules become known, or strike out now. Either way, there's going to be a bit of bloodshed, I think. The odds may improve later. We've left a lot of blood in other places. Let us see if we can do this peaceably."

They followed Asal to his palace, where he entertained them with fine food and drink and serving wenches to share their beds at night. When they arose the following day and came to the king's presence, the pigs were already waiting for them with their swinekeeper glowering beside them.

"We thank Your Majesty for your fine gifts," Brian said. "It is the first of our requirements that we have been able to gain without battle. If we have seemed a bit suspicious, it is only because of the battles we have had to fight to get the others before we came to your fine court and generous ways."

"You have pretty words about you," Asal said. He smiled. "But, in reality, they are only pigs—even if there is a bit of magic about them."

And Brian composed a poem for the king, honoring him by saying:

> "The prizes we have brought with us here
> Have been won with blood spilled most dear.
> You have given us these pigs as we depart.
> For that, we thank you with all our heart.
>
> "Other kings have not been so noble as you.
> We had to fight with Pisear and to gain the yew-
> Shafted spear that he held most dear. The steeds
> And chariot of Dobhar we also took with our deeds.
>
> "We should all have fallen in that battle
> Where champions fell like slaughtered cattle.
> And we might have died there without the skin
> Of the great pig that healed us after the battle-din.
>
> "Now, Asal, we thank you for these most happy days
> And promise that we will always sing your praise
> For giving up your pigs to us
> Without a battle, without a fuss!"

"You are quite welcome," Asal said, overwhelmed with Brian's extemporized poetry. "It's most unusual to find a silver tongue in the mouth of such a formidable warrior. Where are you off to next?"

"To Iruad," Brian said firmly. "To collect Failinis, the king's puppy."

"Would you do me a favor, sons of Tuirenn?" Asal asked. "I would travel with you and, perhaps, I might intercede on your behalf. You see, my daughter is the wife of that king." He frowned. "He's not as willing to listen to reason as I am. But perhaps tactful words will keep you from having to bloody your weapons again."

"That would be very good of Your Majesty," Brian said, grateful for the king's generosity.

"Oh, posh," Asal said modestly. "It will give me a chance to visit with my daughter and see how things fare with her."

xix.

SO KING ASAL'S SHIP WAS made ready for him, and the brothers carried their wealth aboard to travel with him. No further adventures claimed their attention as they sailed peacefully over the seas to the borders of Iruad.[63] Again the shores were lined with fierce men well-armed with spears and swords as the ship of Asal sailed into the harbor. The warriors shouted crudely at the sons of Tuirenn and Asal, warning them not to come nearer.

"Not very hospitable, are they?" Iuchar grinned, fingering his sword. He laughed with delight at the anticipated fight. "I don't think your fine words are going to win us this one, brother," he teased Brian.

"Let me see if I can reason with the king," Asal said cautiously. "You wait for me here, and I'll see if he's willing to listen to my words."

"We'll wait," Brian said, studying the army assembled before him. "But it looks as if he's already made up his mind."

Asal hurried from the ship and made his way to where his son-in-law waited on a hill overlooking the harbor. When he arrived, he told the king about the adventures of the sons of Tuirenn. The king studied him and the brothers, then said, "So what brings them to my country?"

"For your puppy," Asal said.

The king laughed and shook his head. "You shouldn't have meddled in this," he said. "I'll deal with you after we are finished with these upstarts. You really overstepped your boundaries, Asal. You may be my father-in-law, but you should not be taking sides against me."

"Taking sides? Why, you fool, I'm trying to save your life!" Asal gestured toward the ship where the brothers waited. "These are far better champions than any you have in your employ."

"Maybe," the king said smugly. "But the numbers, Asal, the numbers. Do you think that the gods have smiled so favorably upon those champions that they can fight an entire army successfully to gain my puppy? I'll give them the chance to sail away, though. Take that back with you."

"Many another king thought the same as you," Asal said warningly. "And now they lie in the dust."

"Asal, do not tempt my good will. I haven't forgotten that you have taken up sides with them," the king answered.

And Asal went back to where the children of Tuirenn waited and told them what the king had said. Brian grinned and rubbed his nose with the heel of his hand as he turned toward his brothers.

"Well, it looks like we'll get to use the apples and pigskin again, brothers!" he said.

Iuchar drew his sword, shouting gleefully as he charged toward the waiting army, with Brian and Iucharba bringing up the rear. They fought throughout the day, and then Iuchar and Iucharba became separated from Brian, who found himself surrounded. But he wielded the dreadful spear of Pisear, and when its hateful burning point appeared, his enemies fell away from him. Iuchar and Iucharba began to hack and slash their way to him, blood streaming from their swordblades and many wounds, but Brian did not wait. Immediately he surged forward toward the king, striking down swords and spears as he charged recklessly. And then the two warriors came face-to-face.

"Well?" Brian panted, halting before the king. "I'll give you a last chance."

But the king ignored Brian's words and, drawing his sword, fell upon the champion. They fought, bloody, venomously, striking each other with swift and terrible blows, until at last Brian closed upon the king, shattering his sword with a mighty blow that stunned the king. Brian seized the king, lifting him high off the ground, and bound him with strips of supple cowhide. Then he took him to where Asal waited.

"Here," he said, throwing Asal's son-in-law at his feet. "Here is your son-in-law. It would have been easier to kill him three times than to bring him to you once. But for your kindness, your daughter would have been a widow by now!"

He turned, facing the army that threatened to surge forward, saying, "Hold! Your king is now our prisoner. Lay down your weapons."

"Do it," the king said resignedly.

The army stood back and away, watching. Brian turned with satisfaction to the king.

"What is it you want?" the king asked.

"You know what I want," Brian answered.

"I know," the king said. "But I want to hear it from your lips."

And so Brian told him about the *éric* laid upon the children of Tuirenn and how they needed his puppy to fill a part of the blood-fine. And the king, realizing that it was far better to be friends with warriors like the sons of Tuirenn than enemies, gave up the puppy willingly.

Brian ordered the king to be untied, and after the puppy was turned over to them, the brothers left the shores of Iurad, leaving Asal and his son-in-law poorer, but wiser and friends behind them.

XX.

BY NOW, HOWEVER, THE CHILDREN of Tuirenn were weary with their world travels and with the battles they had to face and wanted to take what trophies they had captured back home to Lugh.

But they knew that he would not forgive the rest of the blood-price that had been laid upon them for killing his father.

But Lugh already knew the successes the brothers had had, although they had not gained the cooking-spit or given the three shouts from the Hill of Midkena. He also knew that the odds were gaining on the sons of Tuirenn and that the next battle could be their last. They were, he reflected, earning a great reputation for their honor and ability as warriors, which did not settle well with Lugh, who desperately wanted them dishonored for having killed his father, Cian. He knew as well that the remaining duties of the *éric* they had to perform were also the most dangerous, and that the Golden Apples and the magic pigskin they had would help heal them of their wounds. So, he sent a Druid's spell after the sons, making them forget the rest of the *éric* they had to pay. Thinking that they had finished that which had been set before them, the brothers entered Scuabtinne and ordered Manannán's craft to take them home.

When they came ashore at Brugh na Boinne, Lugh left secretly and went to Cathair Crobaing, that became Tara. He closed the gate behind him and dressed himself for battle, donning the smooth Greek armor of Manannán and the enchanted cloak of the daughter of Flidais.[64] Then, he took up his arms, waiting patiently for the children of Tuirenn to come to him.

Brian and his brothers went straight to the king of the Tuatha Dé Danann, where they were made welcome for they had become heroes through their exploits. Every one of the Tuatha could recite at least one of the tales of daring that the brothers had performed.

"Have you fulfilled the *éric* that Lugh placed upon you?" inquired the king after the celebration had abated.

"Yes, we have," Brian replied. "But we have not been able to find Lugh to deliver it to him. We have searched high and low, but he is nowhere to be found."

The king frowned. "That's strange. He was here not long ago." And he ordered the entire assembly to search for Lugh. But Long-Arms was nowhere to be found.

Then a vision came to Brian and he said, "I think I know where he is. He heard of our return and went to Tara to avoid us. I do not think he wants us to finish the quest that he demanded we fulfill before we could receive forgiveness for having killed his father. Perhaps he fears that we shall use these weapons upon him. But that would be dishonorable."

"Hmm," Bodb Dearg said. "That is very strange. It's almost as if he doesn't want you to fulfill the éric. This is most unseemingly."

He immediately sent messengers to Tara, ordering them to find Lugh and return to Brugh na Boinne to receive what he had demanded from the sons of Tuirenn. But Lugh refused to return, ordering the messengers to have the brothers deliver their trophies to the king of Erin.

And so the sons of Tuirenn gave Bodb Dearg the trophies that they had won on their long and arduous journey to fulfill Lugh's blood-fine.

"This is very strange," the king frowned, as Brian delivered the trophies into his hands. "I'm not certain why Lugh would want this done in this fashion, but it is done. Now, let us go to Tara together so the Long-Armed one can release you from your oath."

They traveled to Tara and Lugh came out upon the green to receive them, still wearing his magnificent armor. Bodb Dearg gave him the trophies that the brothers had earned. Lugh received the items silently and ordered them to be taken into Tara.

"And now," Bodb Dearg said, "it is time for you to release them from the éric, for they have fulfilled that which you placed upon them and now there will be no more bad blood between the sons of Tuirenn and the son of Cian."

"Of course," Lugh said. "That is the law. No one who has returned full compensation of the éric is to be harmed, and forgiveness will indeed be granted." He frowned, pretending to look around him. "But where is the great cooking-spit? And when did you give the three shouts from the Hill of Midkena?"

At that moment, he caused the Druid spell to be lifted from the brothers, and a great faintness came upon them as the joy they felt at having fulfilled Lugh's éric left them.

"This is most unseemly," Bodb Dearg said sternly to Lugh. "You have behaved most dishonorably in this matter."

"Have I?" Lugh said. "Perhaps. But nevertheless, the éric has not been fulfilled; and until it is, I am under no obligation to lift the ban upon them."

"You could forgive the remainder of it," Bodb Dearg said.

"I could," Lugh acknowledged, "but I won't."

A great bitterness filled the children of Tuirenn as they realized the trick that Lugh had placed upon them, and they left and went to the house of their father where they told him of the deception Lugh had played upon them.

"He has behaved badly," Tuirenn said as gloom and grief fell upon him. "But he is within the law. You shall have to fulfill the rest of the *éric*. I know that you are disappointed, but you must do what has been laid out for you or live in dishonor the rest of your lives."

And so they passed the night, not in the triumphant way that they had planned, but quietly, suddenly aware of the black mantle that had been thrown over them. The next day, they went back down to the shore with their father and sister Ethne. As they put out once again upon the gray-green sea, she spoke a lay:

> "I grieve for this, O Brian of my heart
> As you make ready the boat to depart.
> Despite all that has befallen you,
> To your quest you have remained true.
>
> "You are like the salmon of the silent Boyne
> And the salmon of the Liffey. Lugh's toying
> With you is dishonorable. Still, I cannot detain
> You and to go with you would be insane.
>
> "You are like the horseman of Tuaid's Wave[65]
> For in combat you and my brothers rave
> Wildly among the foe. If you should return
> As I hope, Lugh's revenge will burn
>
> "To ashes and he will become despised
> For these tricks that he has contrived.
> Oh, all should pity the sons of Tuirenn
> Who once again carry their shield of green.

"The matter of Lugh disturbs my mind
For when looking into his heart I cannot find
Any intention of forgiving you. I fear
That he means to kill my brothers dear.

"I pity your journey from Tara and
From Tailltiu[66] on the pleasant plain.
And from great Usneach Hill[67]
The leaving of which is sadder still."

XXI.

A GREAT FOREBODING CAME UPON the little party as
Manannán's craft took the brothers once again out upon the great green
sea, where they wandered for a quarter of a year, inquiring of all for the
Island of Fincara, but no one knew where the island was.

At last, they found an old man who recited an old legend that
proclaimed the island lay at the bottom of the sea[68] after it was sunk
beneath the waves by a spell. Brian put on his water-dress with a helmet of crystal and made a water-leap, staying for a full fortnight
beneath the waves of the salty sea, seeking the island. At last he found
it and was amazed to find the court composed of only a troop of
women who seemed to be engaged in embroidery and needlework
around a large table. In its middle lay a brightly polished cooking-
spit.

He spoke not a word, but walked straight to the table, seized the
cooking-spit, and started back toward the door. The women paused in
their labors, each admiring his handsome form, feeling her heart lurch
with desire within her. But when he neared the door, peals of laughter
halted him. He turned to them, frowning at their laughter.

"Boldly done, son of Tuirenn!" a magnificent red-haired woman
cried. She put aside her sewing and rose, her great breasts bare and
bouncing, dark tips like ripe plums beckoning to him. He frowned.

"And how do you know my name?" he asked.

She shrugged, her breasts wobbling seductively. "All here know of your triumphs!" She laughed. "But tell me: Did you think that you would get away with that freely?" His hand stole to grab the hilt of his sword. She laughed again. "Why, puny man! There are a hundred and fifty women here who have been trained in war far better than you. The weakest of us would be more than a match for you *and* your two brothers if we were not willing to let that cooking-spit go. You take much upon you by trying to leave without payment."

"And what payment would that be?" he asked, gripping his sword tightly, and looking warily around him.

"Why," she said, walking toward him, hips switching like a cat's tail, " 'tis certain I am that we can think of something."

And when she came close so that her breasts brushed his chest, he smelled her perfume and felt faint. Then a great desire came upon him as her eye ran raunchily over him. A great heat seemed to rise from her like a lava flow. And he smiled and placed his arm around her.

"Perhaps we can think of something," he said.

Much later, he stumbled from the room, content and tired, the woman's voice calling to him, "For your bold ways and valor and handsome bearing, we will let you have that cooking-spit, for we have many others that will suit our purpose as well."

Brian turned and waved a farewell to her, happy in the different duel he had fought. He made his way back to the curragh, where his brothers waited anxiously, fearing that he had been lost in the depths of the great sea. When they spied his crystal helmet glittering beneath the dark waves, they hauled him aboard. When they saw he had the cooking-spit and was unharmed, a great joy lifted the black burden from their heart.

XXii.

THE THREE BROTHERS THEN COMMANDED the craft to take them to Lochlann, where they moored the boat near the Hill of Midkena, which rose tall and smooth and green over the shore. They walked to the hill, gripping their weapons nervously, for they could see no danger. And because could see no danger, they were more fearful than ever.

As they mounted the hill, they saw Midkena, the guardian, walking toward them. They looked around and, seeing no others near them, Brian said, "There seems to be one only. I will deal with him."

Midkena paused as he neared them and, drawing his sword, spoke his challenge, saying, "Well, it's taken you a while, but you have finally managed to make your way here, have you?"

"You know us, then?" Brian asked, walking slowly toward him.

Midkena nodded. "And who doesn't know the children of Tuirenn and how they killed Cian, my friend and student?"

"That was in answer to a long feud," Brian said narrowly, watching him, his eyes flickering around the rest of the country uneasily. He was wary because he thought Midkena should have had others with him.

"Well, now you have another on your hands," Midkena declared, lifting his weapons. "For you shall not leave here until you have answered for his death."

And the two heroes came together like two boars, their weapons clashing with a din that echoed around the countryside. Midkena struck swiftly, but Brian turned his cut with his shield and delivered an answering blow that was equally met by Midkena. They fought back and forth along the hill, blood flowing like water from the many wounds they laid upon each other until, at last, Brian let loose his battle-cry and swung a hard blow that cleaved Midkena through the brainpan and he fell dead at Brian's feet.

Meanwhile, the din of battle had alerted the three sons of Midkena, Corc, Con, and Aod, who donned their armor quickly and rushed headlong to the aid of their father. But they arrived too late to save their father. Enraged, they sped forward, carrying their long spears in hand, joining the three brothers in battle. So fierce and great was the battle that all men in the world, from the Hesperides in the east to the frozen north should have gathered to watch the great champions close in battle for not until much later in the annals of the Red Branch did such a battle occur. No man could have withstood the great blows rained upon each other, no man had a spirit that could have burned as fiercely and brightly as did those spirits, and no man had the courage of those great champions as they fought grimly against each other.

Then the sons of Midkena took their great spears and lanced the sons of Tuirenn through their bodies, but the sons of Tuirenn drove their own spears deeply into the bodies of the Midkena brothers and Corc, Con, and Aod fell together to the blood-soaked ground, dying.

Brian leaned heavily upon the spear that that been driven through his body, holding his wounds closed. He glanced at Iuchar and Iucharba, kneeling in great pain beside the bodies of the champions they had slain.

"How are you?" he asked.

"Dying, if you must know," Iuchar panted. He smiled feebly at Brian. "But it has been a good run for us, hasn't it?"

"Aye," Iucharba echoed, grinning painfully. "That it has. We have fulfilled that blasted *éric* at last."

"Not quite," Brian said. "I, too, feel Death coming upon us. Come, let us give the shouts from this hill and be done with it for certain. Can you stand?"

They tried, but were unable, and so Brian stumbled to their sides and, gaining strength from within that he had never before marshaled, he lifted them to their feet and together, they gave three feeble shouts from the hill while their blood sluiced like streams from their bodies.

Then Brian took them with him back to the curragh and commanded the craft to return them to their home. As they sailed, Brian studied the gray water slipping past like lead and, looking forward said, "I can see Benn Etair, Dun Tuirenn, and Tara, the home of the kings. Hold on, my brothers, we are nearly there."

Iuchar groaned, trying to rise, and said, "Alas, if only we could be sound in body and see Benn Etair one more time! But we cannot. Brian, raise our heads so that we might gaze upon Erin one last time. Then, we shall welcome life or death—whichever Fate has for us."

And from them came a lay:

> "Brian, take our heads to your breast
> And give us the moment to rest,

You mighty, red-armed son of Tuirenn,
That we might see our land of Erin.

"Hold our heads upon your shoulder,
You mighty champion! None is bolder
Than you. Allow us once again to see
Where Usneach, Tailltiu, and Tara might be!

"Ah, Ath Cliath, and smooth Brugh! I see
Fremann and Tlachtga and I also see
Mag Breg, and the gentle Plain of Liffey
And also Tailltiu's greenery.

"Ah, if only we could once again see
Dun Tuirinn, the home for me
And my brothers. We would welcome
Black Death's arms. We are home!

"A pity the brave sons of Tuirenn
Should fall like this. A bird can
Fly through the hole in my side.
I think soon all of us will have died.

"Now, let Death come and take us,
Brother Brian, before he does
Take you. Those wounds on your body
Cannot be cured by Diancécht's study!

"Cursed be Lugh who took the pigskin
From us by guile and left us to battle's din
And the wounds we cannot heal.
We do not think this was a fair deal.

"Let us once again see our home
Or even Tara's magnificent dome.

And then we shall in death's arms lie
And give up life and willingly die."

By now, they had reached Benn Etair, still clinging to life. Brian
had a cart readied and together, they traveled to their home, where they
were greeted by their father, who cried salty tears when he saw the
great wounds upon their bodies. Brian took his arm and pressed the
cooking-spit into his hands, saying, "Go, Father, to Tara and give this
to Lugh. Tell him that we have given the three shouts upon the hill he
wanted. Then ask him to give us the pigskin to heal our hurts."

And then he spoke a lay:

"Father, do not tarry! Depart without a fuss
Quickly or soon Black Death will be upon us.
Travel quickly to Lugh in the south. Crave
The pigskin from him if our lives you would save.

"We have traveled around the world to the lands
To get the trophies he wanted. We fought many bands
Of men and suffered greatly for his trophies
That we brought home to him from across the seas.

"The least he could do, I would say, would be
To forgive us now. But I do not think that he
Is of like mind. Tell him we have paid his due
For killing his father. I fear he wants our lives, too!

"Dear Father, be swift and fly quickly to Lugh
And for our lives his forgiveness sue.
Bring back the pigskin or you will find
Death has left only cold bodies behind!"

Tuirenn called for his chariot and swiftest horse and rode fast to
Tara, where he delivered the cooking-spit to Lugh.

Lugh took the cooking-spit and turned it over in his hands and shook his head, smiling. "I did not think that your sons could do this, Tuirenn. Tell me truthfully: Did they deliver the three shouts from the Hill of Midkena?"

"That they did," Tuirenn answered. "But they are sorely hurt and need the pigskin to cure their wounds."

"Badly hurt, are they?" Lugh said, smiling, and Tuirenn's heart sank for he could see that Lugh had no intention of giving up the pigskin. Yet, he tried one more time.

"Yes. And soon they will die unless I can return with the pigskin and heal their wounds."

"Then," Lugh said diffidently, "let them die. They *did* kill my father, Cian, and now let them lie in the dust where he lies."

"This is not seemly," Tuirenn said hotly. "They have paid the *éric*. There is no reason to let them die."

"My reasons are reasons enough." Lugh laughed. "They gave the pigskin to me. Now, it is mine to do with as I wish. And I do not wish to give it to them."

And so Tuirenn left to return home without the skin. When he told his sons what Lugh had said, Brian raised himself up with a mighty effort and said, "Take me back with you to Lugh. Let me see if I can convince him."

Tuirenn did as his son requested. Lugh knew they were coming and waited for them in Tara's Great Hall. When Brian made his way painfully to Lugh and requested the pigskin to heal his brothers, Lugh laughed at him and said grimly, "Even if you were to give me the earth's weight in gold, I would not give up the pigskin to you."

"This is a foul deed you have done," Brian said.

"As foul as you committed when you murdered my father," Lugh answered.

"We have paid the *éric* that you demanded. That cleans the slate."

"Perhaps." Lugh shrugged. "The law absolves you. I do not. And, according to the same law, I do not have to give up any of my possessions to you. And the pigskin belongs to me."

"Even if it means our deaths?"

"For the blood you willingly spilled
From my father's body and killed
I now take my final revenge. Your deed
Is finally punished. As is your seed,
Tuirenn! I do not have any desire
To let your sons sons sire!"

And Brian and his father left sadly to return home. Brian lay down between his two brothers, and the life departed out of all three at the same time. When he saw this, Tuirenn wailed and beat his breast, saying:

"Ah! How my heart does break
Over the sight of your deaths! I ache
To the core of my spirit, my soul!
Yet, I admire you all for your toils!

"You have the honor of any king
Of Erin, Iuchar and Iucharba. You bring
Honor to our name, Brian! No one
Can question what you have done!

"But now I, Tuirenn, your unhappy sire,
Cannot any more this life desire.
I will not mourn above your grave
But join you. 'Tis Death I crave!"

And with that, Tuirenn lay down beside his sons and willed his soul to depart from him. When Ethne saw what had happened, she demanded mournfully that one grave be made and into that, the father and the children of Tuirenn were lain.

This ends the Tragical Fate of the Children of Tuirenn.

The Fate of the Children of Lir

taillte is nås laighean na learg,
oileach is eamhaim Fhindearg
—gan teacht tuirseach uatha d'Fhior—
uisneach is cruacha is caisou[1]

The Lay of Fionnuala

Be still, oh, be still
My brothers and sing.
Let your hearts be as light
As the dew on your wing.

Though the moyle be stormy and cold
Dear Aodh, Fiachra and Conn
Even the shadows you see on the ground
Have the power to right all wrong.

For nine hundred years, o nine hundred years
We are doomed the good children of Lir
And though our limbs must yet beat
Shed not a single tear.

For beneath this tattered beastly attire
Lives something bright and sacred and strong
And there is naught so wanted in this dank world
Than to fill the heavens with song.

—Mícheál O'Ciardha

i.

LONG, LONG AGO BEFORE THE setting of the new ways and the making of the féth fiadha,[2] many battles were fought between the Tuatha Dé Danann[3] and the Fomorians.[4] When the Battle of Tailltin[5] was over, and it was time for the warriors of the Tuatha Dé Danann to choose a new king for the five provinces of Ireland after the three great kings and their queens were slain in that battle, many were suggested for the throne. Now, such choices were not meant to be taken lightly; but, even so, Lir of Sidhe Fionnachaidh—the cairn on Deadman's Hill of the White Field—was certain that he would be named the new king of all Ireland.

"Who," he asked defiantly from his home on Deadman's Hill, "has fought as strongly as I? Whose name causes his enemies to quail and foul themselves when they hear it? Whose name is used to frighten the children?"

"Yours, mighty King Lir," always came the tired response from his badgered warriors and servants.

And King Lir would *haa-rrumph* grumpily at this and call for more wine that he had brought over from Iberia, rich and red like old blood.

But the nobles of the Tuatha knew that Lir was a warrior, and when his blood heated up, he would roar recklessly into battle, slashing away at any who came into reach of his great sword and mighty arm, and they were very tired of war.

The nobles met finally at Tara in the *Teach Midchuarta*,[6] which had been built by Nuada the Silver-Armed. They paused at Nemnach, the well at the elf-mound from which Nith flows, and then paused at the *Fáil*[7] for guidance before moving into council. The men were dressed in their finest for the choosing, wearing purple robes with white tunics, and around their necks were golden torques, heavily engraved with mystical spirals.

"Better the acorn than the stick," they said, after they went into council to select their new king. " 'Tis a time for building rather than beating."

"What's this?" Lir said suspiciously, rising before the council and fixing each in turn with a hard eye. He fingered a golden brooch set with amethyst upon his breast and cocked his head, considering the others. "Why, there's not a one of you milksops who don't owe your lands and cattle to me!" He lifted a massive hairy fist and shook it. "Whose battle-cry turned the bowels of the Fomorians to ice and caused them to puddle their breeches? Eh? And now you sit here like brainless brattling birds and say you want to do away with the battler?"

"Yes," Aengus Mac Ind Óg[8] said. "Yes. It is time for us to put such things behind us. We need to seek the finer things of life." He toyed with his fingers, drawing mystical shapes of varying hues in the air that disappeared with the blink of an eye.

"Ahh," Lir said disgustedly. He pulled at his frosted beard. "You talk of making green fields out of a stand of blackthorn and briars. Do you think the Fomorians are finished with us and all? Or the Fir Bolg, for that matter? And what of others who might be coming across our fine land while on a wandering sail? Do you think they'd be coming ashore with a polite *ceiliúr* or song? And who will stand before them while you're off mooning over some woman or the other?"

Aengus's face flushed deep red. "Is there any here, yourself included, who casts doubt upon my sword-skills?" He looked around the council, daring the others to give him the lie.

"There's none here challenging your bravery," Bodb Dearg said kindly. He looked over at Lir. "And you have no right in this council to be suggesting otherwise, Lir. We could likely say that you have little use for anything but your sword."

Lir's face darkened. "Aye, and what else has a man in this day?" he asked bitterly.

"The question, I think," Aengus said softly, but sternly, looking pointedly at Lir, "is what does a warrior do when there is no war? You must remember that there are three candles that shine into every dark corner: truth, nature, and knowledge. And there are three sounds of peace: a cow lowing for milking, the happy clang of metal in a smithy, and the swish of a plow cutting deeply in the land."

For once, Lir remained speechless, his jaw moving up and down as if cracking walnuts, but no words slipping through his thin lips.

"I think we have spoken enough on this," Mac Cécht[9] said. "We can argue this until the sea changes to dust, but there'll be no berries on the holly when we finish." He fumbled his fingers in the air, dusting them. "Enough, I say, of privity and cant. You can't substitute movement for thought or the other way around—"

"Any more than you can motion for movement," Aengus said gently. "Enough metaphors, Mac Cécht. What are you proposing?"

"Proposing? Yes. What am I proposing?" A look of bewilderment crossed his face momentarily. He was one of the old Tuathas who set their minds on a port tack and became confused when logic interfered with their elaborate circafustigating, often losing the train of thought in metaphoric embellishments. He tugged at his beards, squinting up at the lead-gray clouds scudding by overhead. A tiny sunbeam bolted down and skewered him between the eyes.

"Ah, yes!" he cried, clapping his hands wildly. "The election! Enough puff, I say. Let's select our king!"[10]

"Thistles and thorns!" swore Lir. "Haven't I been saying that for the past couple of moon turnings? Let's do away with the yammering and yawping and get on with it."

"Aye," growled Midir the proud, giving Lir a baleful look. "You've been batting your gums about that for a while, now. Everyone would think that you are the only one standing for this election."

"And who better suited?" challenged Lir.

"Me, for one," Midir said, jutting his chin out like Ben Bulben. "My feats easily match yours."

"Why, you . . . you . . . *mucaire!*"[11] he snarled, clapping his hand on his sword. Instantly Midir leaped to his feet, his hand flashing down for his weapon.

"Enough!" roared Bodb Dearg. "You rascals would carve a man over barren words?"

"Words can rob the hive and leave it honeyless," Aengus said quietly. "And cast a heavier stone than the mightiest sling."

"And what does that mean?" Midir said, glaring suspiciously at Aengus.

"Oh, that? Nothing. Foot-and-a-half words only. I don't expect you to understand. They're called metaphors," Aengus said innocently. "A poor offering for your alms-basket." Smiles quivered on the lips of the others gathered to watch the exchange before voting.

"Har-har-har," chortled Lir, slapping Midir across his shoulders. "He's got you there."

"Words!" Midir spat darkly. "Only wind."

"But some winds are gales that topple oaks," Aengus said. He smiled. "Really, Midir, word-dueling with you is like fighting with an unarmed man."

"Let's vote," Lir said abruptly. "This wind-exchange will give someone a cold before long."

And the *cáinteacs*[12] cleared their throats, gargling and coughing like magpies, as they rose to their feet, clamoring for attention to laud the virtues of choice by calling scornful attention to the faults of the others.

Lir closed his eyes and rubbed his temples furiously against the raucous cawing of the *cáinteacs* then let loose a soldier's oath and rose to his feet, roaring, "Enough! By Dagda's balls, enough! You heard the call to the polls! Your speechifying is over! The vote's to be taken!"

"A pompous puddling poltroon—" droned one, but Lir's glare

froze the alliterative phrasing half-spoken. Silence fell.

"Better. That's better," Lir said quietly. "Now, let's be getting this foolishness done. We all know who the best man is, don't we?"

And so Bodb Dearg, son of The Dagda,[13] was elected.

Midir rose and looked around the assembly, his thick brow lowered like a thundercloud. "Fools!" he snapped. "Bodb Dearg can do nothing for you. He'll play hazelnut games with our enemies when cold iron is needed! But you've made your choice! For now." He glared at Bodb Dearg. "Do not rest easily on your throne, Bodb Dearg! Words may have put you there, but iron can take you off it!"

He turned and strode angrily away, his heels gouging deep holes in the green turf. The others watched them go, then turned to look at Lir. He hawked and spat insolently in the middle of the assembly.

"Trickery," he said, scowling. "You got this seat through some sort of witchery. No doubt about it. There can't be this many fools in this assembly. But you're the king for all of that." He glanced down the hill at Midir's dwindling back. "Midir's thick noggin gets the better of him: rest wary on your throne. And as for the rest of you, you dunderheads! Take what comes your way without sending for Lir to rescue you!"

He spat again, hitched his belt, and left, his heavy sword swinging angrily like the tail of a mad dog. Mac Cécht watched him go, digging a long nail thoughtfully into his ear. He grimaced.

"I think that this went badly," he said. "Oh, yes. Very badly. *Tsk. Tsk.* Now we have our bread cut for us. And a cut loaf can never be made whole again, I'm afraid. No, no. Never be made whole again. Not even with a potter's clay and kiln."

"The best thing for it is to destroy their houses," one growled. "I say let's rid ourselves of them."

"No," Bodb Dearg said thoughtfully. "No, that wouldn't help us. We don't cross gorges and gullies by throwing stones in them. We build bridges."

"Won't build many bridges across that rift," Aengus said dubiously. "Midir isn't a logical man. Words defeat him too easily."

"Maybe not in Midir's case," Bodb Dearg said. "But we can bring Lir into our camp, I'm thinking."

"How?" Aengus asked, wrinkling his fine brow.

Bodb Dearg smiled gently, his dark eyes dancing merrily. "You of all people should know that, Aengus. Lir's about to become a lonely man, shutting himself off from us in this way. And what does a lonely man want more than anything?"

"Ah," Aengus said, his eyes brightening. "Of course. A slender thread over the hand of a lovely women, the song from her lips as she sings to her baby, the softness of her arms in the dark."

"Why," Mac Cécht said crossly, "must you always speak in threes?"

And Aengus laughed and sang:

> "There is no short year in love
> When a man hears the dove
> Cooing softly in the dawn
> While he stands and yawns
> The night away. No ghostly battles
> Remain for him. No war cry rattles
> From his throat. He feels the arms
> Of his woman and her charms
> And peace falls, dropping softly
> Through morning's veils. Softly
> Folding both in the arms of love
> While listening to a cooing dove."

"Precisely." Bodb Dearg smiled. "You do that well."

"Practice." Aengus smiled.

11.

AND SO, BODB DEARG sent a messenger to Lir's home at the Sídhe Fionnachaidh. He found Lir sitting in the sun by a grinding wheel, sharping his sword that was already sharp enough to split a hair if a light breeze blew it against its edge. Lir looked up as a shadow fell across his work and, recognizing the messenger, growled, "And what brings you out here? You know I'll have no dealings with the rest of them. They can keep their fine words for wooing women. About all they are good for anyway."

The messenger cleared his throat. "Well, in a way, that's what brings me to your fine home," he said. "I notice there's not the hand of a woman about the place."

Lir leaned back away from the whirring wheel. He tested the edge of the sword with his callused thumb, nodded, and slid it into its sheath. "And why would you notice that?"

"Because," the messenger said tactfully, "I've been standing here in the hot sun for a good while without the offer of shade and drink to cool my thirsty throat."

"Ah," Lir said, nodding, clapping his hands and rising. "So, it's thirsty you are. Well, then, come on up to house. The milking wench has fresh milk cooling in the spring there."

"Milk?" The messenger shuddered gently. "Ah, well. 'Tis a poor house for all of your mighty battle-arm, I'm thinking."

"Be battering your lip like that, and you'll be eating mashed grubworms," Lir said grumpily. "I know the rules. Hanged if I can see why you can't see a joke in the offering when it's made."

"And when was it you last made one?" the messenger countered. "Sure, and if we know when you're serious or laughing. Words pickle in your mouth before you release them."

When they arrived at the house, Lir called for honey beer and slabs of meat and bread, and when they had eaten their fill and leaned back away from the table, contented stomachs pushing hard against their wide belts, Lir belched and said, "Well, now, you've slacked your thirst and stuffed your maw, so what brings you to my home?"

"As I said, there appears to be no hand of a woman about the place," the messenger said. "And that's a shame, for a man needs a woman around to ease his days and warm his nights. 'Tis a bad thing for a man to go lonely through the weeks and months."

"Humph," Lir said, looking closely at him. "You've got the gift of gab, that's for certain. Well, out with it. Stop walking around the bramble bush and cut through it."

"My master, Bodb Dearg, the king—"

"I know who your master is, numbwit! Out with it while there's still light in the day."

The messenger stared at him for a moment. "By the hawberry, but you are a cranky man! I'm given to turning around and heading back to his place and telling the king that to send one of his stepdaughters here—"

"What's this?" Lir said suspiciously, leaning forward. "A woman? Here? What for?"

"Now, what," the messenger said, exasperated, "would you be thinking a woman would come to this fine home for? To be a wife."

"A wife?" Lir flopped back in his chair, his thick eyebrows snapping together like a beetle's click. "What would I have with a wife?"

The messenger closed his eyes for a moment, a hot retort trembling on his lips, but then he remembered Lir's temper and forced a smile. He opened his eyes and said, "Well you should ask. 'Tis a woman a man needs when the warring's done and he's rambling around alone in his great empty house. And where are the children who will brighten his day, without a wife? A sad life, I say. A sad life."

Lir pursed his lips and looked thoughtfully around his house. It was neat enough—the serving wenches kept it that way—but there was a sparsity to it that suddenly closed in on him and left him feeling lonely.

"There's truth to those words," he said slowly, and the messenger heaved a quiet sigh.

"So, out of the greatness of his heart and his feelings for his old friend, Bodb Dearg makes the offer of one of his stepdaughters to be your wife. They are the three daughters of Ailill of Aran, the fairest of form in all the land: Aebh, Aoife, and Ailbhe. The choice is yours to make. *If,*" he emphasized, "you will be friends with Bodb Dearg."

"I already called him the king," Lir growled. "A man's word given once is enough unless there are those who doubt it." A war light flashed from his eyes, and the messenger held up his hands.

"Oh, no, no, no! There's none that will give the lie to your words," he said.

"Well," Lir said, unconvinced. "There's a Formorian's logic, I'm thinking."

"Ah, now," the messenger protested. "Surely you can see that it would be only stark foolishness for me to be coming to your house and eating your meat and drinking your beer only to throw a lie into your teeth. Why, aren't you the mightiest warrior among the Tuatha?"

"I am," Lir said stoutly.

"And a fine figure of a man?"

"I am that," Lir said.

"Then why would I be sent to insult such a man when there's great need of unity in the land? The day of the warrior is gone, now. It is a time for healing."

Lir shook his head. "I'm all of that you say, but I am a plain-speaking man without your fine flair for words. You're welcome for the night, and I'll be giving you my word in the morning."

That night, while he lay awake in his bed, Lir felt the emptiness of the room, and a great loneliness came over him. The next morning, when he appeared at the table with the messenger, he gnawed at his lower lip for a moment, then said, "There is truth to your words. I can see now that the day of the warrior is numbered—although I still think there's a value to us, yet—and I accept Bodb Dearg's offer. Today we'll make ready, and tomorrow leave for your master's house."

The messenger heaved a sigh of relief. He had been worried for his safety, knowing the hot temper of Lir could bubble over at any moment. He wondered briefly what had happened in the night to change the bull to a sheep, but decided to swallow his curiosity and not to test those waters by wading in them.

The next day, Lir left with fifty chariots from *Sídhe Fionnachaidh*, for he was still wary enough of the others not to travel without his bodyguard. But such was his mind when it was finally made up that Lir took every shortcut he could find as he wended his way across the land to Bruig na Bóinne, where he was greeted with great honors and a great feast that lasted for three days for all were relieved that the rift between Lir and Bodb Dearg had been bridged.

The next day, Bodb Dearg took Lir into the great hall where the three daughters, dressed in their finery woven by the most skilled fingers in *Sídhe ar Femen*, waited demurely. Lir's mouth dropped open at their great beauty. Aobh wore a shift of pale gold like ripe oats that hugged her breasts closely and a golden torque around her neck. Aoife wore a deep purple shift like late gloaming, cut up the side to show her alabaster thighs and falling far away from her throat to show the deep valley between her breasts, and a jeweled belt around her waist. Ailbhe was dressed in white like the foam of the ninth wave and had a golden belt around her waist.

Bodb Dearg saw the change in Lir, then, and smiled gently. "The choice is yours, my friend. Take the one you want."

But Lir shook his head, overcome at the beauty before him. "I'm only a simple warrior," he said. "I have nothing that would help me make my choice. I don't have the gift of Aengus to know which one would be a good wife for an old warrior."

"I cannot make the choice for you," Bodb Dearg said gently. "The choice should come from your heart."

"My heart," Lir mumbled. "What do I know of that? A sword and a shield, yes. Good horses, yes. A fine smithy who can work magic with a hammer and tongs, yes. But the heart?" He shook his head. "That has never been possible. No, I cannot make a choice. But she who is the oldest has to be the noblest, and that would do for me."

Bodb Dearg grinned and patted Lir gently upon his shoulder. "Then, you have made your choice." He raised his eyes and beckoned. "Aobh."

She rose, a deep blush rolling up the ivory column of her neck to grace her cheeks. She stepped forward demurely, keeping her eyes downcast until Bodb Dearg told her to look upon her husband. Then, she raised her eyes, and when Lir peered into their deep blue he felt his heart lurch in his chest and begin hammering as if it would smash its way through his breastbone.

"My lord," she said softly. Her voice trilled like a wren,[14] and at that moment, Lir's warrior heart melted. A great contented warmth seeped through him, warming his limbs, and a soft golden glow seemed to rise from his cheeks and forehead.

He took her hands in his, marveling at their softness beneath the calluses of his palms. "My lady," he said, and a small smile curved deeply into dimples in her cheeks, and for the first time in his life, Lir felt happiness.

The wedding feast lasted two weeks as Bodb Dearg had bullock after bullock turned on roasting spits beside carcasses of sheep and deer. Apples were roasted along with pork loins and great barrels of honey beer and tuns of rich wine brought from Iberia were opened for drinking. Salmon and trout wrapped in watercress baked in the coals of the fire. Wild leeks, sorrel, and nettles seasoned the meats and bowls of wild cherries, raspberries, blackberries, rowans, and elderberries were scattered among the tables. The guests sat on cushions of dried grass and in the corners, harpists played merry melodies.

At the end of the second week, Lir took Aobh away to *Sídhe Fionnachaidh*, and there they lived happily for many years. First, they were blessed with twins, a girl and a boy whom they named Fionnuala[15] and Aed. And so happy were they with these children that when Aobh came full with child again, they looked forward with great anticipation for the birth. But the birth was a difficult one and when at last Aobh gave birth to twin sons, Fiachra and Conn, she died, and Lir fell into a deep grief that was lightened only by the joy of his children when they played around him.

And such was his grief that a sadness spread over the land and the Tuatha mourned for the loss of Aobh as well, and a darkness settled over the land for many years.

iii.

THE DAYS, THE MONTHS, THE years passed, dragging slowly for Lir who saw sadness in the changing of the seasons and when his children looked at the setting sun and the soft golden light bathed their faces and he saw the face of Aobh reflected in them. At times like these, his heart ached and he would walk down by the river, listening to the evening breeze sough through the rushes, hearing the bullfrogs croak, and the trout jump after night flies.

The Tuatha, too, mourned Aodh's death, for they feared that Lir would become half-crazed with grief and all had seen him when the madness came over him in battle and how the enemy fell before his flashing sword like reeds to the scythe. But Lir seemed to have little interest in war now. His sword hung rusting on the wall of his house, the blacksmith's forge gathered cold ash, and his horses grew sleek and fat from the lush grass they grazed upon.

Lir ordered the beds of his children to be placed at the foot of his so that he could watch them sleep and guard against the coming of Donn[16] or any of the nighttime demons that roamed freely once the limiting rays of the sun had sunk below the horizon.

At last, Bodb Dearg sent word to Lir, asking the grieving warrior to come to his home. Lir first sent his regrets, but when Bodb Dearg insisted, he ordered his chariot hitched and with his guard of fifty warriors, he made the long trip to Brugh na Boinne.

The grasses were greening as Lir rode across the land and the tiny jaws of crocuses were pushing up through the rich black earth. With pain-filled squeaks, small birds lay eggs. But Lir noted only the dust and the seeming mindless spinning of the sun overhead casting long, walking shadows on the road.

At Brugh na Boinne, Bodb Dearg greeted the melancholic man, reflecting silently how the great warrior had aged in the time that had passed since the death of Aobh.

"Ah, Lir!" he said when the sad-faced man came into the Great

Hall. "It is good that you decided to join us!" He gestured at a serving wench, who hip-slung her way over to the warrior, carrying a jar of ale that she offered him. She curtsied low so the warrior had a good look at her saucy pear-shaped breasts, but Lir ignored her.

"What do you want?" he asked bluntly. Bodb Dearg frowned.

"Still brusque, I see," Bodb Dearg said. Lir frowned.

"You knew long ago that I didn't have the poet's tongue. I'm a plain-spoken man. The warrior needs no fancy words to do his carving. Indeed, they get in the way more often than not."

"There are the amenities," Bodb Dearg reminded him gently. The serving wench pouted and flounced away, buddies bouncing indignantly. Lir didn't see her go.

"I have no use for them," Lir said. He shrugged. "Now, what was so important that you'd draw me away from home?"

"Straight to the point like always, eh, Lir?" Bodb Dearg sighed. He took a swallow of wine from a goblet he took from the small table beside him. He shook his head. "You've grieved long enough, I'm thinking. You need to let Aodb go. Your grieving is keeping all of our people at twelves and sixes."[17]

"I don't ask them to water my horses or wear my black," Lir said darkly. "Fact is, I'd rather they just left me to my business and minded their own. Best for all around, you ask me."

A slight twinge of pain jerked at Bodb Dearg's eyelid. A tic twitched his cheek. *Blast this man and his stoic ways!* he thought. Then aloud he said, "Well, right you may be, but nevertheless you can't fault the Tuatha for grieving when such as Aodb dies. She was well thought of by all of our people. You must allow them to mourn what, when, and where they will."

A lump came into Lir's throat, and a fine mist settled over his eyes. "Ah, well! If they have their wants and needs, who am I to deny them? But, leave me be, I say!"

"Most gracious of you," Bodb Dearg said dryly. "But for your sake and the sake of our people, it is time to put this grieving behind us. So, to that purpose, I offer you her sister, Aoife, the next oldest, for your wife."

"No," Lir said bluntly.

"Hear me out," Bodb Dearg began, but Lir interrupted him.

"No, I said, and there's all I'm going to say on the matter. No."

Bodb Dearg sighed and took a deeper draught of wine. He coughed and cleared his throat, then looked tiredly at the stolid Lir in front of him. "Might one ask why?"

"Might," Lir said.

Bodb Dearg waited, but Lir stared straight at him with brooding black eyes. "Well? Why, then?" he asked finally.

"It's too hard," Lir said bluntly.

Bodb Dearg frowned. "What?"

"Saying good-bye," Lir answered.

And then Bodb Dearg understood the depth of Lir's despair and he shook his head, saying, "Ah, man! That's part of the life plan, didn't you know that? There's no guarantee to any of us. We take what we are given, and are to be thankful for that. Who said you would ever have complete happiness? For all of that, who said that you should have complete sadness? 'Tis man's nature to remember the good times and forget the bad."

"Easy to say," Lir grunted. "But words are only air. Pain is real."

Bodb Dearg closed his eyes, slowly willing himself to relax. He took a deep breath, then opened his eyes and looked at Lir. "But," he said gently, "it is my will that you take Aoife as your wife. At least," he added as a deep frown pulled Lir's bushy white eyebrows together, "look at her. That's all I'm asking. Just look at her and then decide."

So it was that Lir walked out into Bodb Dearg's garden, more to put an end to the whole affair than to consider a wife. But then he saw Aoife standing in the shade of a willow tree, her alabaster form showing through the sheer black she wore, the gold chain around her naked waist beneath the black, her heavy breasts with nipples like ripe plums.

"Hello," she said throatily. A deep smile curved its way into her high cheeks. Her green eyes, tilted like a cat's, gleamed. A soft mist seemed to rise around her and spread out, touching him lightly like the scent of spring flowers. Lilac seemed to wash over him, followed by an earthy musk scent.

"I am pleased that you came to visit me," she said softly. She laughed, and her breasts shook with her humor. A light breeze came through, lifting her gown, blowing her nipples to rose-hip buds. She held out her hand. He took it automatically and felt the heat like a brand flow through him.

And so they were married. But afterwards, when he was alone and watching the ducks and drakes on the small pond beside *Sídhe Fionnachaidh*, Lir wondered what magic had been wrought that made him forget Aobh when he was close to Aoife. The mystery of being nagged at him, but whenever he resolved to look closely when Aoife was near him, to look beyond her beauty, that same mist seemed to rise up and gently enfold them, and he forgot his resolve when she wrapped him in her white arms and shapely thighs.

iv.

AT FIRST, AOIFE HELD HER sister's children close to her heart, playing with them when they were young, comforting them when they scraped their shins and knees on the flints in the ground around Lir's house, laughing with them when they pretended to be Bodb Dearg and gave each other funny orders, cheering them on in their mock battles when they pretended to be Lir. Everyone who met them remarked what a kind person Aoife was for taking over her sister's family and providing a home for the beautiful children.

Gifts came for the children with every visitor to the house, for all who saw the wee ones fell in love with their grace and beauty. Aoife's love for them grew each day. When Lir rose in the morning, he stepped from their bed and touched the head of each of his children, sleeping in their own beds at the foot of his, and Aoife felt his tenderness for his children and waited for their own. But none came.

Now, Bodb Dearg came often to Lir's house for, as the children grew older, they grew more and more beautiful. With him came his court, and the Tuatha whispered among themselves that never had such beauty been seen in children. Although mothers protested this, they secretly knew that compared to the children of Lir, their own off-spring were as common as clover. For a few years, they were happy together, as Bodb Dearg visited often and just as often took the children to his own home.

Perhaps things would have remained happy and idyllic forever had not Lir and Aoife impulsively decided to celebrate the Feast of the Ancients at *Sídhe Fionnachaidh* that year and invited the Tuatha to join them. Aoife was pleased with this, as it would be the first time since their marriage that they had entertained in such a way. For weeks, Aoife ordered the servants around, sweeping out the Great Hall time and time again with fresh rush brooms, scrubbing the gray smoke stains from the walls with fresh lime, ordering mattresses stuffed with fresh straw, preparing sheep and goats and bullocks for the many feasts, raiding hives for their honey, having fresh tunics and cloaks woven for the children and Lir and herself.

At last, the day came and their guests began to arrive. Lir and Aoife stood at the door along with the children Fionnuala and Aed and Fiachra and Conn, welcoming everyone. Aoife had taken special pains with her clothes and had risen early that morning to have her hair washed and plaited, dressing carefully in a green gown edged with gold that plunged deeply in front and rose high upon her shoulders to touch her ears. Yet it was the children who drew everyone's attention. They barely glanced at Aoife and Lir before exclaiming over the children's beauty and giving them presents.

Lir beamed and welcomed everyone, laughing and joking with the men, flirting modestly with the women, but whenever the children were complimented, his joy ran over like rich wine poured by a careless serving wench. Slowly, Aoife was edged out of the circle as her husband and the others laughed and played with the children.

"And how was the journey?" she asked one of Bodb Dearg's women, when there was a lull in the merrymaking and the musicians were tuning their harps and readying their flutes.

"Oh," the young woman responded carelessly, "you know how dusty and filthy that road is and how the men love to race their chariots across the flats! I thought many times that we were going to take a bad spill, and that I would not have the chance to see how your sister's lovely children had grown! I'll bet they keep you very busy, don't they? Why, I can see the mischief in those eyes of Conn!"

Aoife laughed politely when the topic quickly changed to the children, but slowly, a great jealousy began to build up inside of her and when the Feast of the Ancients was finally over and all had left, she heaved a sigh of relief.

"Well," she said to Lir, "that's over. What a relief!"

Lir looked at her curiously. "I thought you were looking forward to seeing everyone and having a good time."

"I was," she said. "But it seems that everyone was more interested in your children than anything else. Why, I never even had a moment when I could find out what marriages are being planned and where the feasts are going to be held in the spring."

"Yes, the children were quite wonderful, weren't they?" Lir said. He looked around. "And speaking of them, where do you suppose they have gotten off to?" He strode away from her, calling for the children, and Aoife felt a rage begin to burn within her.

That night, when Lir came to bed, Aoife pretended to be sick. And for the next night after that and again for every night for a whole year, giving no name for the strange sickness, but locking herself away from everyone, brooding over her unhappiness. Each day, Lir would rise and go first to his children before turning to ask her how she felt. Each night, he would go to bed with them and tuck them in before lying down beside Aoife. Day-by-day, Aoife's anger grew until, at last, she began to plan ways to get rid of the children. As her husband's attention strayed, she took Cian,[18] the leader of her husband's guards, to bed, casting a spell upon him with her white arms and round breasts and eager white thighs.

One day, an invitation came from Bodb Derg for them to visit at Brugh na Boinne, but Lir could not go. A complaint had come from the far side of the Sídhe about raiders and outlaws and such. He told Aoife that she should take the children and go on before him, and he would follow as soon as he had set things right among the people on his lands.

Aoife ordered the chariots yoked and took the children with her. At first, though, Fionnuala refused to go as she had had a bad dream the night before and did not like the strange look in her stepmother's eyes.

"But, why can't we wait for Father?" she asked.

"I have told you that many times, now," Aoife said, exasperation making her voice sharp. "Your father has to take care of a little trouble on the border of his land. He told us to go on ahead of him. Do you want to disobey your father?"

"But there's no hurry to go to Bodb Dearg's house, is there? I mean, there's no feast day or state occasion that's calling us there right away, is there?"

"Can't we just go somewhere for a quiet visit without all these questions? Do we need a reason to visit your grandfather, who loves you very much? Must you always be such a selfish child?"

At that, Fionnuala burst into tears, for she could see that their step-mother was angry with them although she did not know what had caused her rage. She had no doubt that evil would come from such a visit, but she could not make her brothers see the value of dreams. They had not yet cast aside the warrior-play that all boys spent time at before they became men.

"Come on, Fionnuala!" Conn said, pulling her hair. "There's enough of your foolishness! We have made that trip dozens of times—"

"Hundreds," chimed in Fiachra.

"Thousands," added Aed, not to be undone.

"—and nothing has happened to us, has it? And it's boring to take because of that. You'd think we'd see a giant or a *bachlach* or something to make it more interesting, but it goes on and on until I don't think we'll ever get there."

"Not even Father's shortcuts make it shorter," Fiachra claimed.

"But, when we get there, it's all worthwhile," Aed said. "The singers have new songs for us—"

"Always with the songs!" Conn muttered, then yelped when Aed cuffed his head.

"You always like them when they sing about the Battle of Tailltin," he said accusingly. "And it won't hurt you to listen to a few other stories as well."

But Fionnuala simply shook her head and went off by herself to make ready as Lir's warriors and guards made ready for the trip. Lir kissed the children and Aoife good-bye and drove off in his chariot along with his warriors to the north to see if there was truth to the raiding, or if a few cattle had simply wandered off and the wagging tongues of doomsayers had invented the rest. As the dust settled around the Cairn on Deadman's Hill, Aoife took aside Cian, the leader of the men assigned to escort them to Brugh na Boinne, and said, "Now is your chance. Take the children up into the hills and kill them."

"What?" Cian asked, frowning. "What's this you say?"

She smiled and leaned close to him, letting the fine mist wrap gently around them. She pressed her breasts against his chest and felt his spear rise quickly. She smiled. "Ask of me what you will—you've already had most that you've wanted—or choose what else you will have from all the good things within the world. It shall all be yours for the asking after you have done my bidding."

"Well," Cian said, feeling himself weakening under the magic of her nearness.

She pressed her fingers to his lips. "No, let's wait. It would be better if it were done on the way after we have crossed the great plain Mag Mór. The children can disappear quietly along the way. We'll claim they are lost and can't be found. We'll say they were spirited away by the old followers of Crom Dubh[19] and taken to Mag Slecht."

Cian nodded agreement, although he felt faint misgivings. After she had pressed her lips against his and walked away, rich hips swinging saucily in promise, the darkness of his promise came upon him, and he resolved to refuse to do her bidding. "After all," he argued to himself, "you've ridden that mare enough to know the fit of the saddle. And there's the magic of Bodb Dearg—no mean man to be trifling with, I'm thinking. No, better for you to graze in other pastures!"

The next day was lead-gray, with a dirty fog rolling across the land when they set out for Brugh na Boinne.

"A foul day," grumbled the chariot driver. "Can't see the bridle at the end of the reins. Could run off a cliff and be coasting on air before we knew the ground had left the wheels."

"It's Mag Mór," Aoife said sharply. "Flat as a plate. No cliffs to be found there."

They continued their cautious way until they were across Mag Mór. Then the sun broke through the gray clouds and before long, heat waves rolled up in front of the horses and sweat gleamed from their sides. At last, Aoife's driver called a halt by Lough Dairbhreach[20]—the Lake of the Oaks—to give the horses a rest and to let the children swim in the lake to cool.

"Now's the time and this is the place," Aoife said in a low voice to Cian after they had walked away from the others beneath the shade of the oaks. "Take your sword and kill them, then sink their bodies in the lake."

"Yes," Cian said, fiddling with his earlocks. "Well, now, you see, I've been thinking about that and, well, I'd rather not."

"What's this?" she asked crossly. Her eyes narrowed, flintlike.

"No," Cian said. "There's too much evil in the slaying of a child. Especially the children of Lir. You've never seen that madman with a sword. Carve a person to chum before you could cry 'winkle!' If that's not enough for you, then think of Bodb Dearg!"

"I see," Aoife said. She took a deep breath and slipped out of her gown. Cian swallowed hard as he gazed upon her full breasts, her beard, the white columns of her thighs. The familiar mist began to rise up around her, but he stepped back hastily, away from it.

"Ah! No, I don't think so! Not like this!" he protested.

Her lips thinned into a hard line. She stepped forward and, seizing his sword, drew it sharply from its sheath. "Then I'll do it myself!" she snapped.

Holding the sword beside her, she slipped through the shadows of the oaks to the lake. But when she saw the children laughing and frolicking naked in the lake, her womanhood overcame her and her courage left her.

" 'Tis needing the hand of a man, not a woman," she muttered to herself. She turned to go and saw a small hazel growing by the lake. She stepped to it and, using the sword, cut a limber branch and shaved it clean. She threw the sword aside and stepped into the shallows of the lake.

"Come, children!" she called.

Obediently, they swam over to her, as sleek as otters, and when they gathered in front of her, she raised the wand and sang:

"Powers of the air,
Powers of the sea,
Come, and to me bare
The secrets that let me
Work this magic. There!"

And she struck each child upon the shoulder, chanting.

"Feathers for skin!
Music for the din
Of a child's voice!
This is my choice
To let the children ride
Forever upon the wild
Waves of the sea!
Let there never be
Children of the king
Any more. Now, bring
Them out among all
The flocks of birds. Fall
Into swanlike shape
And be feather draped!"

Slowly, the children's forms folded in upon themselves. Their feet
became webbed, their necks curved gracefully, and feathers grew
sleekly from their skins.

And Fionnuala answered her.

"Foul witch! Now we know your name!
What witchery you witched, may the same
Follow you on your evil path! The sea
May become our home, but you will be
Cursed forever! At times we will rest
Upon the land, but within our breasts

Will remain the warm memory
Of our homes. However, your territory
Will be forever changing. I do not know
Which way that wind shall blow, though.
But this I do know: Your evil ways
Will be over within a few days."

And Aoife laughed as she stepped from the lake and tossed the wand aside. She brushed the water from her shapely legs languidly, catching her breath as a cool breeze pebbled her flesh, caused her nipples to rise, and she wished Cian had followed her to the lake.

"Aoife!"

She paused and looked toward the lake, where four swans swam sadly around in the shallows.

"Yes? Which one are you?"

"I am Fionnuala," the middle one said.

"What do you want?"

"Let us know how long we shall be
Snow-white swans, my brothers and me.
You are evil! That we all can see,
But how long will we swim upon the sea?"

And Aoife laughed hard at the plaintive voice. She placed her hands upon her naked hips and said:

"The worse is yet to come for three
Hundred years I say you will be
Here on Lough Dairbhreach. And three
Hundred years on the Moyle Sea
Between Ireland and Scotland. Three
Hundred more between Erris and the Isle
of Glora you will swim. But meanwhile,
I will enjoy my time in your father's arms.
Or"—she shrugged—"give my charms
To other men who intrigue me.

Who knows the morrow? We shall see.
Never shall the four of you be free
Until a woman from the south shall be
Married to a man from the north. In
The meantime, I will relent: the sole din
Of a swan's song will not be your own.
You may keep your tongue and own
Language. You will be able to sing
The softest and sweetest songs and bring
Sadness to all who hear your woeful tale
On sunny shores or within tempest's gale."

And then she left them, singing this lay:

"Away from me, now, you snow-white swans.
The water's edge will be your home. The dawn
Will come when you'll return. But my spell
Will not be broken before then. Now, dwell
Within the reeds and sedge of this lake. Sing
Your sweet music to the men who will bring
You news of what happens. The calm and still
Waters of this lake, the squalid northern bay,
The cold Sea of Moyle, you will swim. The day
Will come when Lir will call and hear no reply
And then his veins will chill and he will die.
His heart will become a flagon filled
With frozen red wine. His flesh chilled
With death's touch. And as for me, I think
I have erred with this spell. But I sink
Or rise with my deeds as all do. I regret
That my jealousy caused this and I fret
That Lir's fury will fall upon my head!
I shall never be free! I have been led
Into this evil day. May black want
Follow you! This is not what I want
after all. My victory cuts my heart!
I have driven a sword into Lir's heart!"

She ran back to her gown and dressed quickly, then made her way to where the others waited, horses harnessed to the chariots. She handed his sword back to Cian, who glanced closely at the blade and, seeing no blood, heaved a sigh of relief.

"Where are the children?" he asked.

"Drowned," she answered and mounted the chariot, staring off into the setting sun. Tiny colors glinted from the tears sprinkling her eyes. The others turned to run back to the lake, but she called them off, saying, "Their bodies sank. There's nothing that can be done. Let us continue on with our journey."

They looked at her strangely, but she was the wife of Lir and to be obeyed. Sadly, they mounted their chariots and rode away.

V.

WHEN THEY ARRIVED AT DEARG'S Great Hall, the son of The Dagda came running out to meet them, clapping his hands in delightful anticipation of seeing the children. He had presents for all: a fine gown woven of gossamer for Fionnuala, a golden harp for Aed, a chestnut mare for Fiachra, and a finely made ash bow for Conn. He pulled up short, puzzled, as Aoife stepped wearily from her chariot, brushing the dust from her cloak. He glanced at the drawn faces of the others and felt the blackness drape over them.

"What's wrong?" he asked. "Where are the children? I thought you were bringing them for a visit."

"Alas," she said, her eyes shifting away from his and giving the others a warning look to the others behind her. "I cannot bring them. Lir has become very jealous of your love for them. He is afraid that you will not let them return to his house if they come here anymore." She spread her hands, shaking her head. "He is beyond reason, I'm afraid."

"What?" Bodb Dearg exclaimed angrily. "Why would he think that? Have I not always honored him, stayed by him when others wanted to assassinate him? Brought him into my family not once, but twice—first with his marriage to Aobh, and then to you? Stuff and nonsense!"

"I know," she sighed. She glanced into his eyes, then looked down, pretending to brush more dust from her cloak. "But what can I do? I am only a woman."

He stormed away from her, marching through his house, his face a mask of blackness. Servants scurried away from his anger, leaving him to his foul mood. At last he calmed down, and then he began to wonder about Lir and why Lir would behave in this fashion. Then he remembered how Aoife avoided looking into his eyes when she spoke.

"Hmm," he mused. "There's more to this than Lir's jealousy, I'm thinking. And what woman can't bend a man to her own will when she wishes? Especially Aoife, who has never had trouble getting her way before."

He called a messenger and instructed him to leave quietly and go to *Sídhe Fionnachaidh* and there ask Lir why he refused to allow the children to come to the home of their grandfather.

"Be tactful," he warned the messenger. "Do not anger him. When the red rage falls upon him, he cannot control himself. You might return to me with your head tucked under your arm!"

The messenger blanched at this, but bowed and left alone quietly, driving his chariot himself. As he crossed the great plain of Mag Mór, he composed over and over again the words he would deliver to Lir. At last, he came to Lir's gatepost. He left his horses with one of the stablehands and entered the Great Hall, where Lir greeted him warmly.

"Greetings! I was just making ready to leave and come to visit Bodb Dearg myself. But we can wait until you refresh yourself. There's no great hurry," he said, playing the host perfectly. "One of my servants has just brought a large basket of eels that we can have for dinner."

The messenger frowned, this pleasant greeting was not what he had expected. Lir noticed the frown and said, "What is it? There is something troubling you. You have only to name it, and I will take care of it for you. Have you been insulted by one of my servants? Someone accosted you on the road across my lands? What?"

"Well," the messenger said, "my master would like to know what he has done to anger you so that you refuse to allow his grandchildren to visit. He means this most respectfully," he added hastily as he saw the frown settling over Lir's face. "He wishes to make amends and sends his apologies even though his is quite mystified as to what has happened between you."

"Not send the children? But they left with their stepmother three days ago for the House of Dearg. I don't understand! Didn't Aoife arrive yet?"

"Oh, she arrived," the messenger said. "But not with the children. When my master asked why she came alone, she said it was because you had refused to let the children make the journey as you were afraid Bodb Dearg's love for them was too strong, and he would not allow them to return to your home."

"Brambles and thorns!" Lir swore. He rose and walked to a window, staring out at the west. The messenger shifted his feet uneasily as a gray cloud began to whirl slowly around Lir's feet. His eyebrows seemed to become thick with ice, his nose pinched white. "There's wickedness brewing here! Enough to fill The Dagda's cauldron! Poor children! What has happened?"

He tore at his beard with his fingers as he pondered the messenger's words. Tactfully, the messenger backed away, then found a servant who brought him bread and fresh cheese and a cup of beer to wash it down. Meanwhile, Lir paced urgently back-and-forth, forth-and-back, in the room, pausing to peer into a cauldron set upon a tripod in which a small fire burned. But he could find no answer in the glowing coals, nor in the candles with the wax melting and veining down the sides in their sconces along the walls.

The next morning, he rose early and left in his chariot, following the road across the plain of Mag Mór, driving slowly as he searched for anything that would give him a clue to the great mystery. At last, he came to the shore of Lough Dairbhreach, and since the day was hot and the horses wet with sweat, he pulled up in the shade of an oak to rest.

From the middle of the lake, Fionnuala saw the horses and recognized Lir's chariot. She cried:

"Look! Those are father's horses! He has come
Searching for us! But what has been done
Is done. This is now the Lake of the Red Eye.
The dreaded black magic of Aoife can by
No means be undone, but surely he will
Avenge the wrong done to us. Now, be still
Until we get closer. Fiachra, Conn,
Aed! Come! We know what must be done!"

Eagerly they rose in the air and flew toward Lir, landing with a great clattering of wings.

"Father!" they called together. Then, separately.

"Lir!"

"Lir!"

"Lir!"

"Lir!"

He heard their voices and looked around for them. "Children!" he cried. "Where are you hiding? What magic keeps you hidden from me?"

Fionnuala reached out and caught his cloak in her beak, tugging at it. Lir turned, looking down.

Then Aed spoke. "We are your children, Father!"

"What?" Lir reeled and nearly fell. Fiachra danced out of the way. "What evil magic has done this to you?"

"It is your wife, our stepmother," Aed answered.

"She changed us into swans," Fiachra said.

"He can see that," Conn growled. "He's not blind!"

Lir fell to his knees, stretching out his hands toward them. "My children! Ah, my children! What can I do to help you? Tell me! Can this evil spell be reversed?"

Fionnuala lifted her head on her shapely neck and said.

"We are doomed by her jealousy
To stay in this shape for three
Times three hundred years. No one
Can reverse the spell that she has done!"

And Lir cried:

> "Then, stay ashore with us, my dears,
> So that we can protect you from your fears.
> At least, you can live on dry land with us
> And we'll keep you safe from evil fuss!"

And Fionnuala said:

> "Alas, poor Father! We cannot stay
> On dry land or live for long far away
> From the waters to which we are confined.
> We know the love and goodness in your mind.
> But on these waters for three hundred years
> We must swim. Now, do away with your tears.
> They serve no purpose. We can still sing
> To you and talk to you and perhaps bring
> Comfort to you. Our music is enchanted,
> You see. Like a fine wine that's decanted.
> In time you may be able to forget
> And perhaps other children you'll beget."

Lir and those that had followed in his chariot's dust gave three groans of deep despair. They began to keen their sorrow, and cries of deep lamentation spread throughout the dusty afternoon and into the gloaming. That night, as they lay beside the lake, the swans sang sweet *Sídhe* songs, and the pain and grief began to ease from Lir's heart.

The next morning, Lir rose and, stretching his arms across the water, cried:

> "Oh, Fionnuala and handsome Conn
> And Aed and Fiachra of wondrous arms!
> The time has come and now, I must leave.
> Although with my parting I also grieve
> At leaving you to your fate. I lie down
> At night, but I cannot sleep. The ground

Is cold and will not warm despite the sun.
My house will no longer be filled with fun.
To be parted from you torments my heart.
I did not know that Aoife's love would part
Us. Jealousy has brought about this fate
For you. Bodb Dearg will now decide her fate."

And Lir mounted his chariot and drove furiously to the great home of Bodb Dearg. The king came out to greet Lir when he heard the clatter of his horse's hooves. Lir did not wait to be greeted. There, in the courtyard, he blurted out his tale of woe. The son of Dagda flew into a rage that scorched the walls of the Great Hall and sent the servants cowering in fear beneath willow trees. He called Aoife to him and when she arrived, he fixed her with a hard glare, saying, "Well, now, daughter! Where again are the children of Lir?"

She moved uneasily under his stare. Her eyes shifted away, flickering around the room like hummingbirds. "I told you," she said sullenly.

"And you lied, didn't you?" Bodb Dearg said. "He is here."

Her eyes widened with alarm. She spun and saw the tall figure of her husband standing in the shadows in the corner of the room. His white beard and hair glowed softly. She gave a little cry of despair and turned back to Bodb Dearg.

"Mercy!" she pleaded.

"As much as you gave those innocent children," Bodb Dearg said. "Tell me: What is it that you fear the most?"

She shook her head, refusing to answer.

"Very well," he said. "Then, since you punished the children by shape-changing them, then you, too, shall lose your fair form. But, what shall I change you to? A horse? A cow? A fish? Perhaps a demon of the air—"

"No!" she cried, then bit her lip as she realized her mistake.

"So," Bodb Dearg said grimly. "That is what you fear, eh? Then, that shall be your fate!"

She turned and tried to run from the room, but Lir stepped forward. She skidded to a stop and turned, trying to run to the other end of the Great Hall, but the son of Dagda took a hazel wand banded with silver and struck her on the shoulder as she ran past. A bitter blast of cold wind whipped through the Great Hall. Her feet folded under her into a faint wisp. Something seized her and threw her into the air like a withered leaf. She cried out in great fear, her words mingling with the shrieking of the wind. Then her limbs turned to gray shadow, and she became an air-demon and in that shape, rode away on the wind.

And still on a stormy night, when the moon tosses like a barque upon cloudy seas, people say her despair can be heard in the sobbing of the wind.[21]

vi.

THE ROAD TO THE LAKE of the Red Eye became quite well-traveled over the years as clan after clan of the Tuatha Dé Dannan came to camp beside its shores and listen to the sweet and sad songs of the enchanted swans. The ground became strewn with antler combs, pone pins,[22] scale-pans,[23] ashes from bone-fires, the refuse that falls beside the byway of netted routes. Sun-bleached white bones, porous to the touch, lay in the grass and among exotic wildflowers. A few wattle-roofed huts went up, the roof-beams turning black from the fires of hundreds of families who took lodgings there, the lovers who found their secret dens, dream-bowers for the harpers and singers. Even through the seeps of winter, visitors tarried by the shores to visit the swans, and none departed without tears spilled at least once during their stopover. The men gathered to make their stories, and teachers taught their pupils by day and listened to the sweet music at night. All who heard that music slept the peaceful sleep free from trouble and the sickness that fell upon the rest of mankind.

But soon the three hundred years passed, and the appointed day for their leaving dawned. The children of Lir were saddened, for they had become quite fond of the lake where they could speak sweet Irish. The thought of swimming in Sruth na Maoile, the cold Sea of Moyle, in the north, with its huge white-capped waves, saddened them. But the spell cast by Aoife could not be undone by any magic or witchery. Then Finnuala sang her lay:

"Farewell, our friends! Farewell Bodb Dearg, Master
Of all the Tuatha lore! Farewell, Father,
Dear Lir of the Hill of the White Field! We
Must leave now and fly north to frigid seas!

"We must leave, now, to pass the appointed
Time set aside for us. Disappointed
Latecomers to the Lake of the Red Eye
Will have to travel to briny Moyle. I

"Hope they come to visit us. We shall be
Alone otherwise upon that deep sea.
Then, we shall fly to Irrus Domhnann.
For now, farewell! Our time here is done."

They lifted their snow-white wings and flew away, soaring high
on gentle winds toward the cold north. The people of Ireland were so
saddened to see them leave that, for all time, they forbade the killing of
a swan. Behind them, the children of Lir left only the stones of silence.
The Lake of the Red Eye became known once again as the Lake of the
Oaks, for seldom did people gather by its shores to weep over the children's fate once the swans had left.

Aoife's curse chased them north until they reached the Sea of
Moyle, that stormy band of water between Ireland and Scotland
lashed by fierce storms in the spring and hail and ice in winter. Here,
the children did not sing for there were none to hear them but seals
and terns and seagulls. Huge waves tossed high by gales forced them
to struggle constantly to stay together until at last Fionnuala said,
"Brothers, we must be careful! These storms may toss us apart. The
winds are unpredictable. Let us decide where to meet if we should
become separated."

"I agree," Aed panted, straining against a huge whitecap that
threatened to dash him against a rock. "But where?"

"How about at Carraignarone, the Rock of the Seals?" Fiachra
said. He paddled furiously with his webbed feet as a backwave threatened to wash him away from the others.

"Good enough for me," Conn answered.

At that moment, a huge storm roared up from the south, battering them. A mighty wind blew hard against them, scattering them over the storm-tossed seas. For eight days, the great tempest blew. Lightning cracked and flashed like sea-snakes among them. Fionnuala screamed in terror, but although her brothers beat hard against the waves, they could not overcome the storm.

But then a great calm fell upon the sea on the ninth day, and the great waters rolled like thin sheets of lead. Wearily, Fionnuala rose into the air and flew to the Rock of the Seals. There she waited for two days. On the third day, afraid that she would not see her brothers again, she sang:

> "Alas! Alas! I feel a great sorrow
> Has fallen upon me. If by tomorrow
> I do not find my brothers, I shall die.
> My wings are frozen to my sides. I
> Fear we shall never meet again. The dead
> Are far more happier than me. I dread
> The long day even through the warming sun.
> This is the cruelest thing Aoife has done."

She sank down upon a rock in despair, lamenting her loss and loneliness. Suddenly she heard a familiar cry and, looking up, saw Conn flying toward her wearily, his feathers soaking wet. Behind him came Fiachra, so exhausted that he could barely move his wings. They glided in close to her and huddled beneath her wings, snuggling tight, seeking warmth.

During the night, the weather changed. Their feathers became frozen together, and the webs of their feet stuck fast to the icy rock. They struggled to free themselves and at last, with a mighty effort, tore themselves away, leaving feathers, wingtips, and the skin of their feet stuck tightly to the rock. Fionnuala sang:

> "What evil Aoife has played upon us!
> The salt water stings our wounds. Alas!

I wonder if our suffering will end
With our starvation, for who will tend

"To feeding us? We cannot enter the sea
To gather our food. I cannot see
How we will survive until we can heal.
I am afraid we are finished. This I feel."

At that moment, however, Aed heaved in view, head and feathers dry. He had been blown far to the south, where he waited out the storm on a dry island before flying north to find his sister and brothers. He landed upon the rock, took one look at their wounds, and said, "Stay here where it is dry. I will bring food to you."

For weeks, he flew tirelessly back-and-forth, bringing food to them while the skin grew back upon their feet and their feathers again filled their wings. Then, together, they entered the sea and drifted with the blowing winds upon the mournful waves.

One day, as they were swimming near the mouth of the River Bann on the northern coast of Ireland, they noticed a group of horsemen galloping on white horses along the shore.

"Those riders look very familiar," Fiachra said.

Conn gave him a cross look, shaking a wing irritably. "And how would you know what horsemen they could be? We've been out on this infernal sea so long, the brine's about pickled my feet."

"Too bad it wasn't your brain," Aed murmured.

"What's that? What's that?" Conn said suspiciously, cocking his head to one side.

"Nothing, nothing," Fionnuala said soothingly. "But Fiachra's right; they do look familiar."

The leader of the horsemen drew rein as he heard the children speaking and looked down at them, knowing them as the children of Lir.

"Hold it," he called to the others. He rode closer to the swans and leaned over, looking at Fionnuala.

"You are the magical swans I've heard about—*all* of us have heard about," he amended, sweeping his hand to indicate the others.

"Why, yes," Fionnuala said. She preened her feathers anxiously, trying to make a good impression on the rider. He was quite handsome, and there was something about him that suggested another person in the brambles of memory. "And who, pray tell, might you be, sir?"

The rider drew himself up and said, "We are the sons of Bodb Dearg. Your cousins, I should say. Although your mother was not a blood relation, she was close enough as the stepdaughter of Bodb Dearg to earn you the right of blood and all. We have been looking for you to see if you are well. I am Fergus, the Fidchell Player. The younger one is Aed of the Great Wit."

"As well as can be expected confined to this confounded brine," Conn said grumpily. He swam to the shoreline and waddled up out of the water, craning his head to look up at Fergus. "And it's been a while since anyone cared if we were alive or filling a fish's belly. Damn inconsiderate, you ask me."

"Hush, now," Fionnuala said. "You're being rude."

"What difference—*ow!*" he yelped as Aed nipped him on the tail. He leaped aside, craning his head around to inspect the damage. "What did you do that for?"

"To remind you of yourself," Aed said. "You have a tendency of forgetting what you are. Remember that you could be a feast as easily as a bird."

"Not really," laughed Fergus. "Bodb Dearg has forbidden the slaying of swans out of respect for you."

"What's that?" Fiachra said. He came ashore and flapped his wings, flinging droplets from him. "What's that you say?"

Fergus smiled. "After you left the Lake of Oaks—"

"Red Eye," Conn grunted. "The Lake of the Red Eye."

"—Lake of the Oaks, now, since few go there anymore and the huts have nearly all fallen in—Where was I?"—he frowned—"Oh, yes, after you left and Bodb Dearg returned to his Great Hall, he made a pronouncement throughout the land that there would be no more killing of swans."

"A good man," Conn said. "Now, if he could find a way of lifting this eternal curse—"

"—which, alas, he cannot," Fionnuala said. "You have been told that enough to know that once a hazel wand is used, only the person who laid the curse can lift it."

"Aye," Aed said, stabbing Conn again in the rump with his beak. "Stop grumping about and let's get the news. How is Father? And Bodb Dearg, our grandfather?"

Fergus looked sadly down upon them. "Old, they are. As you can expect. They are together while we speak at *Sídhe Fionnachaidh*, celebrating the Feast of the Ancients. Time, though, has been kind to them. The aches and pains of age are little for them and, except for your loss and not knowing what has happened to you since leaving the Lake of the Oaks, they are quite content."

Fionnuala's eyes became moist and she spoke, saying:

"Happy is Father Lir at his great home.
While we are forced upon the sea to roam
The world, he eats well-cooked meat and rich wine.
As for his children, we search bitter brine
For our food. Once we dressed in purple and
Drank the rich mead that gave us laughter and
Slept well in our warm beds. Now, Conn and
Fiachra take refuge under my wing and,
While we swim upon the Moyle, we think
About Manannán's teaching, and we think
About the sweet kisses of Aengus. I
Swim now upon the Moyle. Good-bye."

Her sorrow too heavy to bear, Fionnuala swam away. Her brothers looked sadly upon the sons of Bodb Dearg and slowly followed after her. The tears of Fergus sprinkled the dust beneath his horse's hooves. Sadly, he turned away from the shore and led the troop back to *Sídhe Fionnachaidh*, where he told his father and Lir that the children were well, but lonely and miserable upon the Sea of Moyle. And all wept at this story as sadness crept in upon the Feast of the Ancients.

vii.

SWIFTLY THE TIME PASSED, AND then the children of Lir
visited one more time at Carraignarone before leaving for Irrus
Domhnann. Fionnuala sang:

> "Come, my brothers, and fly away with me.
> Let us take wing toward the western sea.
> Three more centuries and then we'll be free.
> For now, we are through with Moyle's cold sea."

On the way west, they flew over *Sídhe Fionnachaidh*, hoping for a
glimpse of their former home. But when they came to the Hill of the
White Field, they were bewildered to see nothing of the fine home that
had been Lir's.

They dropped lower and lower through the azure sky, until at last
they saw nothing but green hillocks and bramble thickets. Nettles grew
down the slope where once they romped on the green sward, but there
was no house. Even the hearthstone had disappeared.[24] They raised
their voices in lamentation and Fionnuala sang:

> "*Uchone!* Bitter, bitter is this sight
> To our hearts! Where is our fine house? A blight
> Has fallen upon our father's place! I
> See no packs of dogs romping merrily
> Upon the green. I see no hounds guarding
> The door. I see no women weaving
> In the sun. I see no drinking horns, no
> Cups by the well, I see no horses, no
> Riders. Green grass grows over the ruins.
> *Uchone!* Our entire lives are now ruins
> As well. There is no one left who knows us.
> But more suffering is ahead for us."

Sadly, they rose into the air and flew to Irrus Domhnann by the Western Ocean.[25] There they lived through bitter cold and gale-tossed years. But they could take shelter in several inlets, and on Innis Gluaire, there was a small lake where they could find shelter and sing their enchanted songs. During the day, they flew as far as the Isle of Achill to gather food, but always returned to Irrus Domhnann by night. On Innis Gluaire, other birds flocked to the lake to hear them singing, settling in the ash trees around the lake to listen to the music of the swans which was far sweeter than any other bird could make. When the air was clear and a light breeze came from the south, their songs would carry to the people who lived on the island. The people living there would pause in their labors to listen and remember the ancient story about the children of Lir.[26]

Recension I

And so time passed and the swans became melancholy, barely marking the passing of the days, weeks, months, and years. So it was that the three hundred years came to an end on Irrus Domhnann and the swans made their home on Innis Gluaire, where they felt welcome and comforted by the other swans.

At last came the day for which they were waiting. Lairgnéan, the king of Connacht, fell in love with Deoch, the daughter of the king of Munster. He pressed his suit upon her, but before she would consent to marry, she insisted that she hear the songs of the enchanted swans and that they always be near her.

Lairgnéan traveled to Innis Gluaire to bring back the swans, but they would not return with him. He ordered them to be captured, and when they were brought to him, Fionnuala sang such a wonderful and sad song to him that he stretched out his hand to comfort her. When he touched her, the spell was broken. But instead of the young Fionnuala, there appeared before him an old woman. Her brothers appeared as old men, ancient, withered.

Sadly, Lairgnéan returned to Connacht and told Deoch what

had happened. They married, and the children of Lir lived out their lives upon Innis Gluaire. They died on the same day and are buried together on the island with Fionnuala lying in the center, her three brothers buried around her to protect her in death as they did in life.

Recension II

And so time passed and the swans became melancholy, barely marking the passing of the days, weeks, months, and years. So it was that the three hundred years came to an end on Irrus Domhnann and the swans made their home on Innis Gluaire, where they felt welcome and comforted by the other swans.

The day came when the Tuatha Dé Danann slipped into the ground and disappeared from the earth. And upon the shores of Ireland came Patrick, who brought a new religion with him, bringing a new God that took the place of the old gods who went underground with the Tuatha Dé Danann, slipping into legend along with the story of the children of Lir.

One day, Kemoc,[27] a holy man, came to the Lake of the Birds on Innis Gluaire and heard the swans speaking in human voices. It was then that he remembered the legend of the fate of the children of Lir. Their song was so beautiful that he built a small church upon the island near the lake, so that he could hear the songs while he prayed.

The children of Lir were comforted by the church and the kindness of Kemoc. The day came when the church was finished, and Kemoc rang a brass bell to celebrate and announce matins. The deep, mellow note rang out over the island, frightening the swans. Kemoc saw how frightened they were and called out to them, saying, "Do not be frightened. Remember that I came to this isle for your sake. For hundreds of years, you have brought pleasure to people with your beautiful singing. This is the time of love, though, and not hate. You will be free. It is only a matter of time."

The children took comfort from his words and swam closer to

him. He had a light silver chain made and linked them together so they would never be separated by storm or wind. They lived with him in his simple hut with oaken beams and wattle roof, praying with him, and singing their wondrous songs to comfort him while he rested. Fionnuala sang:

> "Listen to this wondrous bell
> That with its golden knell
> Will soon free us from our pain.
> God will free us from the rain
> And the rocks and the stones
> And return us to human bones."

Then came the day when Lairgnéan, the king of Connacht, traveled south to Munster to take Deoch, the daughter of the king, for his wife. He asked her what she wanted the most for a wedding present.

"I have long heard about the enchanted songs of the swans on the Lake of the Birds. I would have them as a present from you," she said.

"The swans? That is one thing I cannot give you," he said regretfully. "They belong to Kemoc, the saint of the island, and he will not give them up, for he believes them to be the children of Lir."

"That old legend?" scoffed Deoch. "That is only the stuff of poets and singers. If you love me and want me to stay in your house, you will bring those swans to me and make them at home here, so I may hear them when I wish. If not, well, then I shall return to my father in Munster."

Now, Lairgnéan could not let her return to her father, for that would have thrown him into disgrace. So he sent a message to Saint Kemoc, ordering him to have the swans brought to his house as a gift for his new bride.

But Kemoc refused to do as Lairgnéan ordered, and Lairgnéan grew furious and called his guards to him. He journeyed to Innis Gluaire, and when he arrived there, Kemoc saw him coming and took the swans and locked them in the church for safety.

"Is it true that you refused to allow my messenger to bring the swans back to Connacht?" Lairgnéan asked Kemoc when the saint met him on the shore.

"It is," the holy man said calmly. "I refused the messenger, and I will refuse you as well. The children of Lir have suffered enough. They have found sanctuary in my church. They will stay there as long as they wish."

"You would refuse the king?" Lairgnéan roared. He shoved Kemoc aside. The holy man staggered, protesting as the king stormed into the church. He saw the swans together by the altar and seized the silver chain binding them together.

"My lady waits for your singing," he said.

He pulled them from the church, ignoring their struggles as they beat the air with their wings and tried vainly to escape. He took them only three paces from the door of the church when their struggles ceased. He glanced behind him and stopped, amazed at what he saw. The swans had disappeared. Lying in the dust, chained together, were three ancient men and one withered woman.

"Witchcraft!" Lairgnéan howled. He flung the silver chain away from him and ran for his boat, ordering the men to row him back to the mainland.

"May God's curses land upon you and yours!" Kemoc shouted angrily. "May your children and their children know the pain of the children of Lir!"[28]

Kemoc hurried to the side of the four frightened ancient ones, lying helpless upon the ground. "What may I do to help you?" he asked.

> "Sprinkle us with holy water, I pray,
> To cleanse us of our sinful ways. Then stay
> Beside us, if you will, for we are dying.
> Bless this ground upon which we are lying
> Then bury us here. Fiachra and Conn
> Shall lie on each side of me. When that's done,
> Place Aed beside my breast within our grave.
> Here we shall find peace. Here we shall be saved."

Kemoc baptized the children of Lir and gave them the peace for which they craved. He held their hands as first Fionnuala died, then Aod Fiachra followed shortly after, a smile upon his face. Conn wept to see the others lying lifeless around him. Then slowly the breath left his body, and he lay quietly beside them.

And Kemoc wept bitter tears over the tragic fate of the children of Lir. He buried them there after first consecrating the ground. He placed Conn on Fionnuala's right side and Fiachra on her left. Her twin brother, Aed, he lay upon her breast.

That night, a great wailing was heard across the land as news of their deaths traveled rapidly, as if a gathering wind blew news of the end to their tragic fate to all who lived, but the children of Lir did not hear the great lamentation raised for them. Over their grave, the saint raised a stone upon which, in the ancient *ogham* script, he carved their names.

This ends the Tragical Fate of the Children of Lir.

The Exile of the Sons of Usnech

fir ar se ingen fil and agus bid Derdriu a
hainm, agus biaid olc impe. cid dia mboi
longes mac nusnig. ni handsa[1]

The Last Words of Deirdre to the Sons of Uisliu

"Quickly bolt and bar the shutters,"
Said Deirdre to Ardán.
"Conchobor's army has come to get us
Still Naoise's better than any man.

"Let all Erin descend upon us,
Let us go where all love goes
When cold winds swirl around us
Let us turn to frost and snow.

"No man who quests true beauty
Will hold my sad and defiant hand.
If tender Naoise cannot have me
Then neither will any mortal man.

"The king's gold exceeds all others'
He is mighty just like Prince Eoghan
And though they both will say they love me
I'd rather dash my head against a stone."

Mícheál O'Ciardha

i.

RAGGED SONGS BOUNCED MERRILY FROM the rafters as the warriors of the Red Branch sang lustily, drunkenly.

"More ale!"

The cry rang from the smoke-blackened beams and rafters of the house of Fedlimid,[2] the son of Dall,[3] who was the teller of tales to Conchobor,[4] the king of Ulster. He watched the boisterous party with satisfaction. Not many bards enjoyed such privileges to entertain the king in their own homes. Or, he reflected, casting an eye around the rich furnishings of the feasting hall, enjoy such favors from the king. But it was his due as the king's storyteller, a post he had earned well, spending long hours memorizing stories at a *seanchaí's* knee.

The serving wenches cast saucy eyes upon the warriors as they sling-hipped their way around the low tables, swaying just out of reach of the groping men as they filled drinking horns with the rich nut-brown ale. The women moved from left to right, north to south,[5] and the Ulster heroes from the Red Branch laughed and fondled a ripe hip when one came within their reach, or weighed a pear-shaped breast with a practiced eye.

"More ale!"

Conchobor laughed and shouted taunts when one of his heroes came up empty-handed. He took a long drink from his gem-encrusted goblet and belched and sighed. He looked fondly at Fedlimid, who smiled and shook his head.

"Your men have their wits befuddled with drink," Fedlimid said, laughing.

"That they do," Conchobor said fondly, watching his men as they ate and drank. "But they have earned it, I think. They have guarded Ulster's borders well, and it is time they were allowed a little leeway before winter sets in. A hound always on the leash becomes a lazy hound."

The wenches laughed and danced their way among the tables while the wife of Fedlimid,[6] who was great with child, stood next to a red oak pillar, watching the merrymaking. Her feet ached and a dull pain throbbed at her lower back. She looked down at her swollen belly and sighed. Not long now, she reflected. She winced from a sharp kick. That was a warrior's kick, but the Druid[7] had said the baby would be a girl. She frowned and rubbed her belly uneasily, trying to soothe the restless babe waiting to be born. A raven[8] had landed in the oak tree above his head when the Druid had made his prediction. He had cast an uneasy eye at the unblinking coal-black bird. That had been a very ominous sign. Very ominous and—

"More ale!"

She sighed and caught a passing wench by her saucy shoulder and ordered another jar to be brought to the feasting hall from the storeroom. Again she rubbed her back and tried to straighten her shoulders. The men were in fair fettle tonight. A faint smile formed on her lips. The women would be hollow-eyed and bandy-legged by tomorrow morning for certain if the men kept up their drinking at this rate.

The woman returned with the jar of ale and passed away to her right. Fedlimid's wife reached out and grabbed the wench hard by the shoulder, spinning her around.

"Fool! The glass always passes from left to right, from north to south. Do you want to bring disaster upon the house by going widder-shins?"

The wench blanched and scurried off to her right, slopping ale from the jar as she hurried away from her mistress's wrath. Fedlimid's wife sighed and shook her head. Lately, they were coming to her dumber and dumber. But in the end it was all twigs and sticks; old wives' tales told as wisdom.

She glanced out the window and saw a black storm approaching, lightning cracking among the thunderheads. Rain slanted down like a curtain, sweeping toward the house. The wind was cool against her flushed face, and she breathed deeply as the first fat drops of rain hammered against the roof.

"You should turn your back to the storm."

She looked at the speaker, Cathbad[9] the Druid. He smiled at her. "A woman carrying a child should face the sun and turn her back to the storm. Bad *geis* otherwise."

"Foolish words," she said irritably. Her skin felt flushed and she faced the storm again. "Superstitious nonsense. Old wives' tales. I've had my fill of them, mark my words."

Then a bright flash scorched the air with the smell of brimstone burning, and a loud crack of thunder silenced the merriment.

"By Donn's balls,"[10] Cathbad the Druid said, looking blearily at the thunderhead. "That was close enough to singe a cat's whiskers!"

A deep moaning filled the air and the warriors looked nervously from each other. Rain drummed against the roof like nails driven by a god's hammer.

"I don't like this," one warrior said to another. He hiccuped and covered his mouth with a huge hand. "Hmm. Feels like the *Sídhe* devils are riding out."

"Aye," another said uneasily. "I saw a water-wagtail coming to the house as we entered and when I went to the ditch to piss, a red and white cat bounced across my path."

"Ballocks," Sencha mac Ailella[11] said scornfully. "A bit of rain and thunder boomers and you all look to the Otherworld crying 'Doom! Doom!' Next thing you'll be doing is crying the sky is falling or some other such nonsense. Mark my—*brrraaacccchhhh*—'cuse me—words, crying wolf too much will only kill the sheep eventually."

"A natural phenomena," Cathbad agreed. He raised a buttock from his cushion, farting gently. Pfft! A raw odor of onions hung in the air. Those near him drew away hastily. He leaned forward, wagging his finger, pushing a small leather bag containing four spiders he wore against the ague, back inside his robe. "This puts me in mind of—"

"Now, now," Conchobor said hastily, cutting in on the Druid's words before Cathbad could launch into one of his old memories. "Is this a party or a wake? Fedlimid! How about a little music to sweeten the hour?"

Fedlimid took down his harp and, grinning, made himself comfortable on a cushion as the men shouted out their drunken requests. Some of the women snuggled down beside them to listen as Fedlimid's fingers plucked the harp-strings and lifted his voice in song.

"Never saw I a woman like Maeve,[12]
Whose breasts cause grown men to rave—"

Shouts of laughter met his words. All knew the legend of Maeve, the wife of the Connacht king Ailill, who needed thirty men a night to satisfy her lust. Many there who had seen her leaned back on their cushions and listened with half-slitted eyes as they fondly recalled her red-haired beauty.

Thunder boomed again, nearly drowning out Fedlimid's words, but the crystal notes of his harp hung in the air long after the thunder rolled away. The merriment grew and more than one warrior rose to his feet, threw a shrieking serving wench over his shoulder, and carried the laughing woman into the sleeping shadows at the back shadows of the Great Hall. Fedlimid sang song after song until the warriors' eyes grew heavy-lidded with drink and they stumbled off to bed, brawny arms wrapped around willing wenches.

At last, the Great Hall fell silent, and Fedlimid's wife passed slowly in the house toward her own sleeping couch. Suddenly the child in her womb gave a huge kick that drove her to her knees. She pressed her hands hard against her swollen belly, trying to soothe the babe. And then the child shrieked, an eerie cry that raised hackles on the backs of necks and sent dogs howling. The men scrambled from their sleeping rooms, looking bleary-eyed in alarm. Some ran to gather their weapons.

"Arms!"

"We're attacked!"

"Arms! Arms!"

Then Sencha Mac Ailella shouted, "Silence! Fools! You rattle words like Druids' stones! Useless till thrown! Stand where you are!" He stood spraddle-legged in the middle of the room, his eyebrows drawn down in a heavy frown as he stared around the room. He spied Fedlimid's wife kneeling on the floor, her hands clutching her belly.

"Woman!"

She raised her head. Pain flickered across her eyes. She humped her shoulders against it.

"Did you make that cry like the *Sídhe* riding their long-maned horses among us?"

She shook her head, rocking back and forth, her arms cradling her swollen belly. " 'Twas the child," she gasped.

"Bring her forward! *Wumpf!*" Sencha demanded sternly, then staggered as her husband Fedlimid pushed his way through the crowd. He raised her gently to her feet saying:[13]

> "What is this scream that rages
> From your womb, the fleshy cage
> Between your swollen sides?
> What is this child that cried
> In a voice so filled with woe
> And terror that my heart is so
> Filled with grief that I fear
> It will break and great tears
> Will flood this huge hall,
> Rising high and drowning all."

He tried to hold her, but she pushed away strongly and ran to the side of Cathbad, tears filling her eyes, words pouring from her lips, saying:

"Lend me your ears, Cathbad,
Exalted among all white-robed Druids,
Whose great words of wisdom can tell
The secret that no woman can foretell—
Namely what her womb bears. My
Husband demands to know why
This cry has come from my womb
With its dreadful hint of the tomb!"

Cathbad drew his bushy brows together, hooding his eyes, then widened slowly as a brilliant glow descended over him. His eyes shined with an intensity, bringing forth a rainbow of colors. Then he spoke slowly and solemnly:

"In the cradle of your womb rocks
A baby, fair of face with golden locks
That shall flow around her. Her eyes
Are gray-green and men will sigh
Over her cheeks, pink like foxglove,
And all who see her will love
The snow-white softness of her skin
And all will hear a mighty battle din
Over her flame-red lips. Great slaughter
Will follow the birth of this daughter
For whom our chariot-warriors will ride
To their doom. A woman shrieks, a bride
Sought by many chiefs. Tall and beautiful,
Men will scamper around her heels. A fool
Will demand her love and others will flee
To the west from which a great army
Will come in time to battle the Red Branch
And the land will be covered by the stench
Of death. Her lips will frame teeth like pearls
And great queens will want her form and curls
For she will be faultless, her beauty unflawed.
But for that beauty, men will become outlawed."

Cathbad stepped close to the woman and gently laid his hand upon her rolling belly.[14] The child screamed again beneath his hand. He smiled gently and said, "Yes. I am not mistaken. You carry a woman-child. Her name shall be Deirdre[15] and a great darkness shall fall upon the land and Evil will ride black horses across the scorched earth following her birth."

The glow left him and his hand fell away from the woman's belly. He shook his head, looking around at the men standing silently in the great hall. He glanced at the frowning Conchobor.

"Mark my words," he said crankily. "Great sorrow will fall upon Ulster through the birth of this child."

"What shall we do?" Conchobor asked, frowning.

Cathbad scratched his rump vigorously. "Do? Why, nothing. Yet. Time to decide that when the time comes. The day of the storm is not the day for thatching."

He walked away, muttering to himself. Fedlimid's wife followed meekly in his path, cradling the child in her womb gently with her arms. Folly, she thought. You should have turned your back to the storm. This is what comes of tufthunting vanity. Old saws have wisdom hidden in them. She had been a fool to have thrown taunts to the *Sídhe*.

ii.

AUTUMN DAYS COME QUICKLY WHEN disaster looms, like the running of a hound on the moor, and Cathbad's words hung like a dark cloud over the heads of those who waited in nervous dread for the birth of Fedlimid's child. So it was that the days passed swiftly until Fedlimid's wife lay in labor in his house, and when word reached the Red Branch of Fedlimid's wife's lying-in, chariots were quickly harnessed and Conchobor led his warriors to Fedlimid's house to attend the birthing of the child that had already been named by Cathbad.

It was on the third day that the child came forth from the womb of Fedlimid's exhausted wife. Cathbad took the tiny babe wrapped in white swaddling and closely studied her tiny face, seeing with his Druid's eyes, the passing of time, the growing of the babe into a child and the child into a woman. He lifted the child in his arms toward Lugh's[16] rays and sang:

> "Ah, Deirdre! You will be famous, fair and pale
> But you will cause great pain and ruin. Your tale
> Will cause all Ulster to wail its role
> In causing your death bell to toll.
>
> "A jealous man will dog your steps
> Until evil into his heart has crept.
> On your account Usnech's three sons
> Will be banished from Ulster's sun.
>
> "The Red Branch will be dealt a bitter blow
> That will divide the house and hate will glow
> Between them. Yet will they mourn the loss
> Of Roich's great son, the mighty Fergus.
>
> "It will be your fault that Fergus leaves
> The Red Branch hall to try and retrieve
> His honor after Conchobor's son Fiachna
> Dies. A deadly curse lies upon Emain Macha.
>
> "Noble woman, your guilt will be great
> When Gerrce, Illadan's son, finds his fate
> And when Éogan Mac Dubthach's great life
> Is ended and we hear the wails of his wife.
>
> "This shall be a grim deed of yours. Our king
> Shall find his honor gone. Poets will sing
> Over your lonely grave and all will wail
> The loss of our ways 'cross hill and dale."

"Kill her!" cried a grizzled warrior, raising a huge scarred fist in horror. "Kill the child and put an end to this curse upon the House of the Red

Branch. Crabapples and goblins! We have enough *geasa* upon us now without adding more! And what is this shame that we will have to bear because of our king? I say we cut her throat like a goat and leave the sin to the air!"

"Aye!" another shouted. "I agree. Why should we let a babe reshape our world? Eh? Answer that, if you can, Druid!"

"Stuff and ballocks! This is the way of those who stare into the mindless world and change brittle twigs into gold! I say enough of this prattering! Kill the child and let's get on with it."

"Aye, but who's to do it? You?" Cathbad, shrewdly eyed the last speaker, a warrior with a scar down one eye. He turned away, pretending interest in a lark flying high in the sky. "I thought not. You? You?" Cathbad turned from one to the other.

"Well? Here she is. Not much of a warrior's challenge. So, who's to take the knife to the wee throat and cut it? Eh? Easy talk, nattering among yourselves like fishwives! Will you draw straws and treat her life as chaff?"

"Enough," Conchobor roared. All fell silent and turned to stare at him from glowering eyes. He rose from his couch and crossed over to the child and drew a fold of her swaddling clothes down from the tiny face. He peered at it. She looked up boldly at him and waved her tiny fists in the air. He chucked her under the chin with a broad forefinger, and she gurgled with pleasure and kicked her tiny feet against the restraining blanket.

"Be careful!" Cathbad cautioned. Conchobor looked up at him. "The innocence of this child will bring the end to joy and prosperity for the Red Branch."

"Will her death cancel Fate, then? The child is already born. Forces have been set in motion. Should the king of the Red Branch quail before a child who has yet to pull at her second teat?" he scoffed. He shook his head scornfully. "And what would Ailill and that horny bitch Maeve say if they knew this? Secrets are like honey; they draw busy bees. Connacht would cross our borders in a minute if they knew the Ulaids' king now made war on newborn babes. The baby's death will strip the Red Branch of all its honor."

"The baby will strip the Red Branch of its honor if she lives," Cathbad said. "There is no virtue like necessity."

"And if the baby dies? What then? What honor will we find in the baby's death?" He laughed brittlely. "Come, Druid! Speak! What can you see with those Druid eyes in the dark future and the abyss of time? Slip aside the curtains of time and tell me more."

Cathbad sighed and shook his head. "Either way, it is a trim reckoning now. As you say: Forces have been set in motion, and it is easier to stop the wind and the sea to put a pause in Fate's gallop. It isn't your fault; men are only gilded clay. But many men will feast upon the bitter bread of banishment if this child lives."

"A Druid's tongue demands attention. But even the wind has harmony when it rustles the hazel-tree branches. Enough talking now, of graves and worms and epitaphs. If earth's breast is to have sorrow written across it, then so be it!"

"As you say," Cathbad sighed. "So be it. The past is only a prologue now." He glanced at the warriors watching them. He chuckled grimly. "Well, you'll have no help from them. They'll follow any suggestion like a cat laps milk! Not an idea flickering like marsh gas in a single noggin. Blind faith!"

Conchobor placed his hands on his hips and threw his head back, laughing. "Haw-haw-haw!" His laughter boomed off the rafters. His men looked at each other, sniggered, then broke out in laughter to match his.

"Then it's done!" he cried. "Take her to the nurse's teat; then bring her to me in the morning.[17] She will be reared according to my will, and then she will be my wife!"

The laughter stilled quickly as if a knife had sliced the throats of the warriors.

"Wife?" sputtered one. "This little bitch is to be the ruin of us all, and you're going to marry her? Take a viper into your bed! Be quicker that way!"

"Aye! Sleep on a bed of swords!"

"Have a cup of hemlock!"

"Jump—"

"Dolts!" Conchobor roared. "Think, cabbage heads! If she is my companion, then what harm will she do?"

"I dunno," Dubthach[18] said, pulling at his earlobe. He scratched in his beard with a dirty fingernail. "Many's a dam put her backside to a strange stallion. A wife's no guarantee. Besides, you've got a wife with hips and buddies to make any man's stalk a wooden stake. No offense," he added hastily at a frown from Conchobor. "I know you can have a second wife. What I'm saying is what about Mugain?[19] What will she say about you plowing new fields, eh?"

"She'll have fourteen years to prepare for it," Conchobor said. He nodded at the babe still nestled in Cathbad's arms. "Take another look, Dubthach! Do you think she's ready for the marriage bed?"

"I dunno," the former said, digging furiously at his beard. "I mean, no, of course not! But if Mugain was my wife, I'd think twice about bringing another woman into her house. Two women in one house and one of them a redhead with a fondness for bedding! Asking for trouble, if you ask me!"

"Nobody's asking you," Conchobor said. "And I have spoken." He looked back at the child and chucked her again under the chin. She gurgled. "Name her, Druid."

"I already have," Cathbad said quietly. "She shall be called Deirdre."

And so it was done.

iii.

NOW, FEDLIMID AND HIS WIFE were greatly honored by Conchobor's insistence that he be given fostering care of the child; for a king rarely took a child to foster and, when he did, only from the most important families. But they were also secretly relieved, as they were worried about Cathbad's gloomy prediction.

" 'Tis enough to bring about the snubbing, it is," Fedlimid remarked to her one day. "And you know well what that means."

But Conchobor had relieved them of that possibility by taking the child under his fostering. No one of the Red Branch would have had anything to do with them as long as the child was with them which meant, in these turbulent times, that they would have been fair game for any poacher or raider and would not have been allowed to trade with their neighbors or at any of the fairs. They would have been isolated. Yet, it was hard to give up the child. When Fedlimid's wife handed the baby over to Conchobor the next morning, she wept bitter tears and clung to her husband's mantle watching through a veil of tears as the Red Branch warriors returned to Emain Macha.[20]

"There, there," Fedlimid said, patting her shoulder awkwardly with his hand. " 'Tis for the best. She'll be well-kept in Conchobor's house, of that you can be certain."

But his words failed to halt her tears, and she shed them for a year and a day.

Conchobor, however, did not dismiss Cathbad's words lightly. When the Red Branch warriors arrived back at Emain Macha, he gave the babe to Mugain to care for the night, then commanded that a house be readied for her well away from the Red Branch Hall, deep in the forest where no eyes would see her save those whom Conchobor sent to serve her. After the house was built, Conchobor commanded the child be given over to Leborcham, a middle-aged nurse with a pleasant disposition and kindly ways. There was strength as well in Conchobor's choice for Leborcham was a satirist,[21] a poet with a tongue that could cut as thinly as the sharpest blade. No one save Conchobor and Mugain was permitted to enter that part of the forest. And no one wished to, with watchful Leborcham womaning the house, for no one wishes to come to odds with a satirist whose scathing poetry could lift the wattles from a house and cause them to dance down to the sea.

And so Deirdre grew, loving the forests and the wild, but feeling lonely for others to play with. Even children had to be kept away from her, lest stories of her beauty would be carried back to the grizzled warriors of the Red Branch by innocent children who would grow to adulthood, remembering the beauty in the woods. In the summer, she spent her time gathering the fruits of the thickets and hidden beds: sloe, wild cherry, raspberry, blackberry, strawberry, rowan, crabapple, and elderberries.

Leborcham was patient in teaching Deirdre how to sew and spin wool that was brought to the forest house by Conchobor, who always had his chariot stopped a goodly distance away so that Ibar, his charioteer, would not see Deirdre and bring back stories of her loveliness. Still, Ibar was questioned closely by the warriors when he and Conchobor returned from one of their forest visits.

"Aye, a careful man, he is, to never let me catch a glimmer of that fine girl," Ibar said.

"Do you not want to?" one of the younger members asked him. Ibar fixed the speaker with a scathing eye.

"Aye, I'm not made of stone, you know, but Conchobor's not a man to be taken lightly and when he says 'stay,' I stays. I'm not needing his sword through my gizzard."

And so he drank quietly the wheaten beer sweetened with honey that was brought to him by Mugain's servants upon their return while others spoke quietly among themselves, vowing that if the opportunity came their way, they would sneak through briars and brambles for a glimpse of the legendary beauty of Deirdre. But the talk was only the chattering of squirrels, for none there wanted to bring down the wrath of Conchobor.

One day, Conchobor trailed a calf behind his chariot into the forest. He commanded Ibar to stop at his usual spot, a glade surrounded by large, twisted oaks where fairies danced at night under the full moon. Rich grass grew thickly here, and Conchobor's horses grazed contentedly while Ibar stretched out upon its softness and dozed, listening to the singing of the birds and the trickle of a small spring not far away, contented to laze away the warm afternoons. But this day, snow had fallen in the night and the bare limbs of the oaks looked wet-black in the gray light; so Ibar huddled on the chariot floor, wrapped in a warm robe of fleece while Conchobor led the calf down a path to a grove of hazelwood where Deirdre's house had been built beside a running stream. Snow began falling gently, dusting his shoulders with a light covering. There he drew his knife and cut the throat of the calf, tilting the head away from him so the blood wouldn't spatter his clothes.

He lay the calf down on a bed of snow and went to skinning it. Steam rose from the warm body, and the blood lay like a scarlet blanket upon the white snow. A raven, black as the bottom of a well, dropped down beside the blood and began to drink it. Deirdre stood by with a bowl to receive the tenderloin after Conchobor had cut it from the carcass, watching in fascination.

"Leborcham," she called. The good woman came to the doorway and stood, looking at her. Deirdre placed the bowl beside Conchobor's heels and backed away from the raven and stood beside the door. She pulled her cloak tightly around her, shivering in the cold air that made her cheeks ruddy. Snowflakes had caught in her hair and sparkled there like tiny crystals.

"What is it, child?" Leborcham asked affectionately. She placed a heavy arm around Deirdre, hugging her. With her other hand, she gave Deirdre a wooden bowl filled with warm stirabout made from oats. A thin dripping of honey had been added to it.

"The colors," Deirdre said. She spooned a mouthful of stirabout, relishing the taste of honey. "See the colors? White, black, and red? Such beauty! I wonder, do men have those colors to them?"

"Aye, I know of one not far from here," Leborcham said. "He is at Emain Macha, one of Conchobor's warriors."

Deirdre turned her head to look at her. "What is his name?"

"Naisi," Leborcham said. "One of Usnech's sons. Oh, but they are a charm to watch. Experts they are in all that they do. None attack the goal as fiercely as Naisi. And his brothers Ardan and Ainlé have cracked a pate or two to help him, I tell you!"

"Naisi," Deirdre breathed. Leborcham looked closely at her, then rapped her gently with her knuckle on top of her head.

"Here, now! We'll have none of that moonglowing! The one for you is yonder. Conchobor!"

Hearing his name, Conchobor paused and raised his head, smiling at Deirdre. Her beauty made his throat tighten. She smiled back gently, noting the streaks of gray in his hair, the tired wrinkles around his eyes.

"Are all men like those colors? Or do they all look like Conchobor?" Deirdre asked.

"You need to pay attention to that man," Leborcham said, chiding her gently. "Forget others. There's danger in such talk. Your king is not a man to trifle with."

Deirdre studied Conchobor thoughtfully for a long moment, then laughed and said, "But he is only a man when you take away the crown, is he not?"

Leborcham sighed and stroked Deirdre's long hair. "Aye, my dear. He's a man. And that is what makes him dangerous. You have much to learn about men."

Deirdre laughed again, the notes dancing through the air like a sparrow's chirping. Conchobor paused and smiled at her, the smile touching his eyes warmly. "Oh," she said carelessly, "I don't think there is much mystery there. All you have to do, Leborcham, is to look into his eyes. Can't you tell what he is thinking? I can."

"You were born too wise," Leborcham said, shaking her head.

"Perhaps," Deirdre said. Her eyes became distant as she slumped against the door frame. "But I don't think that I will ever be whole until I see this Naisi."

She turned and went back into the house, crossing to the fire where a cauldron of stew bubbled cheerfully. She used a wooden paddle to turn the thick brown gravy. Then she sat on a three-legged stool and carefully settled the stones holding the strands of wool to her loom made from stout oak. She studied the nubbing carefully, then tightened the last run again.

Leborcham glanced into the coals and paused as heat rose and turned slowly, forming images. She studied them carefully, feeling a dread tighten around her breast like an iron band. A lump grew in her throat as she remembered the words of Cathbad the Druid, for she had been there when Deirdre had screamed from her mother's womb and again when Cathbad had named.

> "On your account Usnech's three sons
> Will be banished from Ulster's sun."

Stupid old woman! she told herself. What have you done now with your pattering and nattering? Now you have given a name to her dream, when it could have become nothing but air, forgotten after the moment.

And sorrow welled up in her until tears formed and dripped down the heavy seams in her face to fall heavily onto her lap.

Meanwhile, Deirdre watched Conchobor fold the hide carefully back away from the calf. With a curved knife, he began slicing roasts from the carcass, dropping them into the bowl by his feet. As he worked, the snow around him became packed and the raven left off drinking the blood-soaked snow, seized a piece of suet in its beak and, turning, it fixed Deirdre with a hard stare from its black eyes. Then the raven lifted its wings and rose silently into the air and disappeared into the dark reaches of the forest.

And Deirdre felt a thrill like terror rush through her veins.

iv.

DAYS PASSED SWIFTLY AS DEIRDRE neared the marrying age. Then one day, on La-Bel-Taine,[22] when the snow had sunk into the rich black loam and spring flowers leaped into bloom in the meadows and glades, Deirdre crept out in the early morning before the lark sang dawn into day and made her way through the forest to Emain Macha. She had been forbidden to do this, but as with most young ladies, the forbidden is more exciting than common sense.

When she arrived at the path leading around the earthwork of Emain Macha, she paused as she caught sight of Naisi, who had been appointed to walk the ramparts of the earth bank beneath the west oak wall of Emain Macha in the dawn watch. When the red fingers of dawn stroked the hills of Ulster, he filled his lungs and gave forth with his warrior's cry to mark the time. All stopped to listen to the melodious medley that came from his throat. Women felt their hearts catch in their throats at the honeyed notes, men nodded in satisfaction, and even the cows lowed softly in appreciation and gave a third more milk to the milkmaids pulling on their udders. Dogs whined pleasurably, cats purred, and even the birds twittered joyfully at his musical bent. He was answered by his brothers from the east and south walls, and women wondered if any among the *Sídhe* could have matched that music and thought longingly of bed. Men remembered battles and fingered their weapons with pleasure, remembering the three sons of

Usnech in battle. So skilled were the brothers that had all Ulster formed battle-ranks against them, if the brothers stood back-to-back, their skill at parrying blows would still have sent the warriors on their heels, and when the three chased game, they scorned the use of horses and chariots, choosing to run down deer with their own fleet feet.

Deirdre heard his cry and her heart hammered hard in her breast. She threw her hair back over her shoulders and stepped out boldly on the path, angling her walk to take her by Naisi. He heard her light step on the path and turned quickly. He drew in a quick breath as he saw her beauty. She pretended not to see him and lifted her dress above her ankles and ran past him so that her white calves twinkled in the dawn.

" 'Tis a beautiful heifer that runs past me!" he called, grinning at her.

She paused, tossing her hair, and his throat caught, nearly strangling him, with her beauty. "Heifer, is it? Well, 'tis a fine heifer indeed when there are no bulls to keep her company!" she said saucily. She pretended to glance around at the grassy meadow stretching down away from them. "And I see no bull here worthy of this heifer."

Naisi leaped down, landing lightly on the balls of his feet. He leaned on his spear and looked down at her. By Donn's balls, but she is a beauty! he thought. I have never—. But he didn't complete the thought. Suddenly he remembered the prophecy of Cathbad and knew her name. He drew back and cast a great look around to see if any around had seen them.

"Aye, you may think that, but 'tis well-known that you have the Bull of Ulster to watch over you. Conchobor has marked you for his herd, and I have no doubt that he will tame your wilding ways."

"He's an old bull." She eyed him up and down boldly. "But if I had to choose between him and a young bull, I would choose you—though it's sure I am that a young bullock like you has much to learn."

"Wisht! Be careful of your words!" he said lowly. He looked anxiously around them again. "Ears are where you least expect them."

"And what brave bull are you to be afraid of ears?" she teased.

"One who has heard the prophecy of Cathbad the Druid and knows when to draw his sword or leave it in the scabbard."

"I heard that young bullocks were always willing to test their horns." She placed her hands on her hips and swayed back-and-forth so that her dress brushed across her white feet.

"Then your ears betray you," he answered.

"You reject me, then?"

"I'm a prudent man," he answered.

She frowned, then leaped forward suddenly, wrapping her legs tightly around his waist. Startled, he dropped his spear and tried to push her away. His hands cupped around her breasts, and he threw them wide, away from her, stumbling to catch his balance. She grabbed his ears and pulled them hard, rocking his head back and forth.

"Then you have two ears filled with shame and mockery! 'Tis a bold man I want, not one creaking with age and smelling like a wet dog!"

"Help! er . . . No! . . . uh . . . Release me, woman!" he roared, trying to pry her off him.

"No!" she yelled. She leaned forward and bit him hard on the neck below his ear. He roared again, and his war-cry echoed across the rathfort of Emain Macha.[23]

The Red Branch warriors heard his cry and leaped to their feet, running to gather their weapons, certain that they were under attack.

Naisi's brothers bounded away from their posts, racing across the yard to help their brother. They paused on top of the rampart and looked down at the odd sight of Naisi, stumbling around, trying to peel a woman off him.

"What's this? What's this?" Ardan laughed merrily as he grounded his spear and leaned upon it. "I had heard you had to beat the women off with a stick, but never did I think that one would be bold enough to ambush you in daylight."

"*Haw, haw, haw!*" Ainlé chortled, joining his brother. "Well, Naisi! What have you to say for yourself? Eh? What game is this you're playing? If Conchobor catches you diddling when you should be on watch, 'tis a fine example he'll make of you!"

" 'Tis a fine example he'll make if he finds out who," Naisi grumbled, finally pulling Deirdre off him. She spun away from him, falling to the ground on her rump.

"Oomph!" she grunted. Her hair fell forward over her eyes. She tossed it back and glared up at Naisi. " 'Tis certain that you have the manners of a bullock! Is this a way to treat a lady?"

"Is it a lady who throws herself on a man like a *striapach*? Even Maeve has more manners than to maul a man before she beds him."

"As if you would be knowing Maeve's manners!" she sneered. "Why, I've heard about her: thirty men a night she needs, not a puppy with a thumb for a tail."

"By Donn's balls—" Naisi growled.

"Uh, brother," Ardan said. "Aren't you going to introduce us?"

Deirdre rose and faced them, placing her hands on her hips. "And which one are you? Ardan or Ainlé?" she asked.

"Where have you been hiding yourself, woman, if you have to ask our names?" Ardan asked. *"Huh?"* he grunted as Ainlé struck him with a sharp elbow in the side. He glowered at his brother, rubbing his smarting ribs.

"What's this?" he demanded. "Why'd you—"

"Dolt!" Ainlé snapped. "Don't you know her? 'Tis Conchobor's ward."

Ardan straightened, looking closely at Deirdre, noting her beauty. His heart sank within him. "Aw, Naisi! Now what were you not thinking about when you decided to pluck this one, eh? You know that this will bring down Conchobor's wrath. No old man likes to find a young bull sampling the heifers in his pasture, let alone Conchobor!"

"That's all and well," Naisi said, rubbing his ears softly with his fingertips. "But this isn't any heifer. This is one worthy of the Dáire's Brown Bull himself.[24] There isn't a man in Ireland that wouldn't take the chance to draw her as his wife."

"Do you want war between us and the men of Ulster?" Ainlé demanded.

"Of course not," Naisi answered. "No one would want that."

"But you do want the girl?"

Naisi remained silent, refusing to look at Deirdre as his brow furrowed in thought.

"And is that what you want, brother?" Ardan asked gently.

Taken aback, Naisi looked hard at Deirdre. A slight wind blew from behind, gently lifting her hair, bringing with it a scent of blossoms. He felt his heart quicken, and then a hollowness in the pit of his stomach. She smiled suddenly at him, and he was dazzled by the whiteness of her teeth, the lift of her cheeks into dimples. And then he became conscious of the fine woman's body beneath her dress.

"Yes," he heard himself saying. "Yes, it is what I want."

She leaned in closer to him, placing her arms around his waist. "And you," she said softly, "are what I want."

"Ah, me!" Ainlé sighed. He scrubbed his hand vigorously through his hair. "Nothing good will come of this, I'm telling you! You'll bring shame down upon your head and our father's house as well. But," he said resolutely, nodding at Ardan, "we'll support you, if that's what you want. And I'm certain that we'll not be lacking for a place to stay elsewhere in the land, for there are plenty of kings who hate Conchobor and his raiding ways. No, we'll not be at a loss for a welcome anywhere we go; that's for certain! For a while, at least, until Conchobor brings enough threat against their borders. But, if this is what you want, then I'm for it."

"And me," Ardan said. He cast a quick look over his shoulder. "But it's in a hurry we'd better be. It won't be long before the others will be coming out to see what caused you to raise the alarm." He turned to Deirdre. "Do you see the stand of hazel down at the edge of the meadow?" She looked and nodded. "Well, you wait for us there. Hide yourself well, and we'll come to you in a bit. Then, we're off."

"To where?" Naisi asked.

"To the west," Ainlé said. "But we need to gather a few things. Carefully. We must make the others think that we are going to the east, to the sea. Maybe to visit Dubthach's son Éogan. That should do it."

And so it was that that night, the three brothers left with a hundred and fifty warriors who followed them, a hundred and fifty women and a hundred and fifty dogs and servants. When they moved past the hazelwood, Deirdre slipped out and mingled among them, pulling her shawl around her face like a veil that her beauty might be hidden.

And when Conchobor found she was missing, his rage was great, blaming at first mauraders and raiders who might have slipped across the border from the north. But then he remembered Cathbad's words and knew that the truth of the prophecy had blossomed like the wild hedge rose.

V.

YEARS PASSED, AND THEY LIVED like vagabonds, roaming here and there, serving one king, then another as the sons of Usnech sought to avoid the vengeance of Conchobor. Yet the enraged Ulster king sent warrior after warrior to find them and kill them. But the wily sons of Usnech avoided the ambushes and the secret assassins sent to slay them in the friendly courts. Still, great sadness came with their victories as they slew friend after friend who came to serve Conchobor's wrath.

And so they moved frequently around the country, searching constantly for a place where they could live in peace. They tried Es Ruad near Ballyshannon in the west, but Conchobor found them there eventually; for the legend of Deirdre's beauty was meant for poets' songs and those songs eventually found their way to the Great Hall of the Red Branch. Then Conchobor sent out his warriors to slay the sons of Usnech and bring Deirdre back to him.

They traveled to Benn Etar in the northeast near the Hill of Howth, and for a while, they lived there in peace when the king sternly forbade the singing of songs celebrating Deirdre's beauty. But by now, the story of the trick played upon Conchobor had become the source of humor. The story of an old man seeking the love of a young woman is always fodder for those who envy the old man or who were victims of the old man when he was in his youth. And always there was Deirdre's beauty, that was irresistible to the bards. More stories and songs were composed celebrating the victory of youth over age and love over desire. The sons of Usnech quickly became the source of inspiration and were sought frequently by young women, who found romance in their daring and dreamed of lying in their arms at night when the moon rose high over the dark hills and when *La-samnah* came and *Lughnasa* and the fire-festivals; but it was mainly at *Lughnasa*, when the hay harvest had finished and the wheat and barely harvest loomed and marriages and love-matches were arranged and lovers would hunt for whortleberries and make love on beds of fragrant ferns that young women would feel an ache in their breasts and a weakness in their loins when they dreamed about the sons of Usnech.[25]

And during this time, too, the rage of Conchobor would grow even more fierce, and he would hunker down on his throne with a cup of mulled wine, his burning eyes fixed on memory of Deirdre dancing among the forest flowers, bathing in the stream beside the forest house, her laughter, her bold, teasing words, her hair and sparkling eyes and pearly teeth, and black bile would rise up in his throat, and red fury would cloud his mind.[26]

But after years had passed, the brothers and Deirdre found other forts being closed to them. Then the crannogs[27] also became well-known to Conchobor until finally they took to hiding under dolmens and in caves among the high rocks, in huts hastily build deep in the woods. There was no shortage of food, for the brothers were all expert hunters; and when the game fled, the brothers raided the herds of nearby clans.

Slowly, Conchobor's knot tightened around Ériu[28] until, at last, the four decided that they had little choice but to leave the land and travel to another place. One day in early fall, when acorns began to appear on the oaks, they took a curragh[29] across the sea to the Island of Shadows.[30] There the great woman warrior, Scáthach[31] held her school for warriors. So famous was she that kings from all over the world sent their champions to her to be trained. The brothers worked hard on the skills Scáthach taught while Deirdre was heavy with child. After the child was born, she sent it to Manannán, son of Lir, to foster, as she knew the child would have little hope if it fell into the hands of Conchobor. And then she was heavy with another child and this, too, she sent to Manannán. She named them Gaiar and Aebreine and Manannán took them willingingly and cared for them in Emahin, the place of the apple trees, and he brought the famed poet Bobaras to teach them and when they were full grown, he gave Aebreine, whose face shone with the brilliance of the sun, in marriage to Rinn, son of Eochaidh Juil in the Land of Promise.[32]

After the birth of their second child, Scáthach taught Deirdre some of the warrior skills as well, and she learned to perform the salmon leap[33] and hunting tricks that would aid them greatly in their future life.

They were happy there with Scáthach, but soon they learned that some of Conchobor's warriors were being sent to the Island of Shadows for training and so they took a curragh to Alba[34] and moved into the mountainous wilderness there.

A long time passed before Conchobor learned where they had gone. While he waited for word about them from the warriors he sent out to search for them, the black and yellow bile rose up greatly within him until all shunned him whenever possible, leaving him in melancholy. His skin tightened around his eyes that looked suspiciously out at the world, and his tongue became as sharp as an adder's.

Meanwhile, the sons of Usnech and Deirdre had moved deep into the wild mountains of Alba, where they built crude cottages to shelter them from the cold and snow and rain. They fed upon the wild beasts, and when the beasts became wily, they took to raiding the cattle herds of the Alba men. At first, the herdsmen thought that wolves had been taking their cattle, then that other clans had been building up their herds through nightly raids. But then they discovered the brothers and sought to kill them.

At last, the four went to the king of Alba and swore allegiance to him as warriors. The king was pleased to have them in his army, for they had trained with Scáthach, and warriors who had survived training with her were in great demand. He generously gave them space upon the greensward and servants to help them build houses. The brothers were careful, however, to arrange their houses so that they formed a tiny compound, where Deirdre would be safe from the eyes of the men, for they feared they would be slain by treachery if other eyes feasted upon her beauty.

Early one morning, the king's steward was stretching his legs and clearing his head after a night of feasting and happened to take a turn around the compound the sons of Usnech had created. As he passed the home of Deirdre and Naisi, a wren landed on a windowsill and chirruped madly at him.

"Begone!" he demanded crossly, but the wren ignored him and preened its breast with its beak. Irritated, he crossed to it and took a swipe at it with his hand, but the wren danced aside. Suddenly a bright shaft of sunlight shone through the window and reflected off Deirdre's hair as she lay sleeping next to Naisi. The steward's breath caught in his throat, and he turned and ran back to the king's bedroom."

"Wake up! Wake up!" he crowed, pulling on the king's bare foot sticking out of the covers.

"Humph! What? Who?" the king sputtered, coming awake. He fixed a red-rimmed eye on his steward. "You'd better have a damned good reason for waking me!"

"What is it?" a sleepy voice asked. A young woman pushed her way out from beneath the covers. She stretched and yawned, her large breasts popping free like melons.

"Er," the steward stammered, "that is, I have found what could not be found."

"Great balls! What are you talking about?" the king demanded.

"Well." The steward took a deep breath. "We have been searching and searching for a wife worthy of you, and have had no luck. But I have found one. Naisi, the son of Usnech, is married to a woman worthy of being the wife to the king of the world. Indeed, she is enough to stop any warrior in his tracks and put wood in the oldest man's goad."

"Oh?" The king furrowed his brow for a moment, then shook his head. "But she is already married to Naisi, you say?"

"Pittling problem for pattering boobs!" the steward said airly, waving his hands in dismissal. "We simply send someone around in the dead of the night and have him stick a knife between Naisi's ribs and *poof!* she's a widow pining for pleasuring."

"And have you forgotten the rules of hospitality? Eh?" the king growled.

"Rules are for the weak; the strong make their own," the steward said.

"Better a hawk than a vulture, though," the king said. "And what would happen to her love if she found out I had her husband killed? Eh? Answer that, foolish man!"

"But—"

"But-but-but-but nothing! Leave Naisi be! That is my wish, that is my command! *But* each day take a gift to her and, with your oily tongue, woo her in my name. Tell her about my virtues, my riches, and my gentle ways"—the steward's eyebrow raised at this—"and do it in secret. Don't let the devil Naisi hear your words, though! He'll thump your ribs good and proper!"

"Wouldn't it be better if—I'm going! I'm going!" the steward whined, beating a fast exit from his king's bedchamber.

"Why me?" he muttered, making his way from the hall, searching for a poet. "I fetch his drink and fetch his food, and now I have to woo a wench for him! Nuts and thistles!"

But the steward was no gamecock and knew better than to pretend otherwise when it came to his king's commands. He dressed himself in a jackdaw's manner and took the paltering poems prepared by the poet with him, waiting patiently outside Naisi's house until the son of Usnech left. Then he knocked on the door and, in his most fawning manner, made the brag of his king for Deirdre's dainty ears.

But Deirdre saw through his weasling ways, often biting her cheek to keep from laughing at his pretensions. At night, she regaled her husband and his brothers with the steward's latest offering. And since Deirdre had the mimic's gift, she soon had everyone rolling on the floor in helpless laughter.

After a couple of months of this, the steward approached his king, admitting his failure.

"She has the heart of a stone except for her husband," he said. "Why, there's not another woman around who wouldn't strip naked and leap into bed with you after hearing the stories I've strung together about you. Of course," he said, lowering his voice so that only the king could hear, "if I had a better poet to work with, maybe that would have made a difference. But that's neither here nor there. I'm afraid we're back to what I suggested at first: a quick knife in the dark, and everything is fine and dandy."

"Enough of that knife business," the king growled. "Let me think on this a bit! There are other ways to skin a calf than gutting it where it stands. Let me see. . . ."

"Well," the steward said absently. "Too bad there isn't a war—"

"What's that?" the king asked leaning forward. The steward was taken aback for a minute.

"Too bad there isn't a war?" he repeated.

"That's it!" the king said triumphantly. "All we need is a war. We'll send those sons of Usnech into the front lines. All matter of things happen in battle, you know. Who can tell where the spear or sword thrust comes from? Eh?"

"But . . . but . . . We're not at war!" the steward said.

"A minor muddle," the king said. "Simply a question of rhetoric. The question is not that there is no war, but determining with whom we should war."

The steward scratched his head at this, but decided matters were royal concerns, and not his. Besides, he was thinking that Deirdre had been getting a little bored with his daily declarations and it was time that he moved back into the shadows before Naisi planted his big foot up the steward's arse.

That night a herdsman casually mentioned that he found a bull missing from one of the pastures and, since that pasture was shared by a neighboring king, our king quickly fell upon it as an excuse to go to war.

The sons of Usnech were sent alone deep into the country to raid the flocks and herds of the suspected marauding king. They returned, driving a whole herd in front of them. Despite every trial, every mission the king devised for them, Naisi and his brothers returned unharmed.

At last the men of Alba decided to take matters in their own hands before their king alienated all the other kings so that they rose up against him. But Deirdre overheard a couple of wives talking about their husbands' plotting in the bathhouse and quickly brought the news to Naisi. She found him honing his blade while sitting comfortably in the warm sun.

"Now, my husband, I daresay
That we should leave before another day
Shines upon us. Tomorrow will bring
Troubles to us in an assassin's sting,
For that lustful king has grown mad
With his failure. He has found many bad
Men to lie in wait and kill you on the morrow
And take me into his bed despite my sorrow
At your death. A foul king he's turned out to be!
But now it's time for all of us to flee!"

At first, Naisi felt his stubborn pride rise up within him, but common sense soon crept through his red rage. He sent Deirdre to tell his brothers to ready themselves and that night when the pale moon was bright, they crept out and away from their homes and made their way down to the sea. There they packed two curraghs with supplies and put out into the rolling waves, making their way to a small island, still called Oilean na Rón, the Island of Seals, that lay midway between Eriu and Alba. From there, they could look on yearningly toward both countries and remember how their love had made them outcasts. There they made their new home, and when warm days fell upon them, they would laze away in the sun and dream about the bright green hills of their homeland and wistfully wish ways had been different for them.

vi.

TIME PASSED LAZILY FOR THE exiles, but even more slowly for Conchobor, who frequently flew into black rages when someone innocently mentioned Usnech's sons or the whereabouts of Deirdre, whose beauty by now had become a legend. Since none had seen her for years, her beauty became even more renowned in the minds of the people. Her beauty had become part of their own dreams, and in their dreams, she became plenary perfection.

Soon enough the bards learned where the sons of Usnech and Deirdre lived. As more songs came from their harps, Conchobor's anger grew like a festering wound.

One day, the sun rose, bathing the green meadow stretching down from Emain Macha with a soft golden glow and a romantic youth sighed and said, "Ah! Surely that must be as beautiful as Deirdre!"

Unfortunately for the youth, he had been standing in the doorway to the hall of the Red Branch at the time. Conchobor seized a short three-legged stool and threw it angrily at the youth, braining him, knocking him arse-over-head out the door where he sprawled unconscious in the dust.

"A very kindly manner you have about you," Fergus said sarcastically, sprawling against a cushion, one hand clutching a cup of must, the other fondling a maiden's ripe breast.

Conchobor turned towards him, saying crossly, "You're a fine one to talk! Didn't you give up the crown for my mother's friendly thighs?"[35]

"Aye," Fergus said. He belched. *Braaach!* "But don't be wishing me into your shadow. You've become shatterpated, jugging around like a muddleheaded mooncalf! 'Tis enough to push a starving man away from a feast!" He leered at the maiden. She giggled and sighed as his hand slyly stroked lower. "Find another wench, if Mugain isn't enough to wilt your wand! Though," he added, remembering when she had stripped naked to distract Cúchulainn so the Red Branch warriors could calm his fury, "why you'd want to bounce against another's buddies when you have that one seems foolish to me!

"Ahhh!" Conchobor said disgustedly, scrubbing his hands furiously through his tangled hair. "I'll hear no more of this! *Hmmmm!*" He cupped his hands around his ears, screwing his eyes tightly shut in anger.

"And this," Fergus sighed, pausing to drain his cup, "is our king." He threw his cup at Conchobor, hitting him in the chest. Conchobor stopped and glared at Fergus.

"Why, you—"

"Oh, be quiet!" Fergus said, annoyed. "A right mess you've made of our lives with your muddling about! Take my advice and forget her! Make a feast for our nobles and gadlings! A long feast! At least a sennight long! You'll need that time to mend the many walls you've shafted through your wooding! There's talk of changing the crown!"

Conchobor paused and glared at Fergus, pulling thoughtfully at his lower lip. "That bad, is it?"

"Worse," Fergus answered. "They're right drubbed!"

"A feast, you think?"

"Aye."

"Hmm," Conchobor said. He turned and wandered away, wrapping an earlock absently around a busy forefinger.

Fergus waited until he disappeared behind a column, then glanced around surreptitiously and, not seeing Nessa nearby, tossed the cup from him and rose, cradling the maiden in his arms, and slipped out the back of the Great Hall and into the milk barn where he tumbled her into a hayrick and leaped in after her. Soon the air was filled with sighs and moans and stalks of straw.

Meanwhile, Conchobor mulled over the words of Fergus as he wandered around Emain Macha, pausing on the ramparts where Deirdre had found Naisi, staring off into the purple woods towards the hidden house. Slowly, an idea came to him. He seized upon it, twisting and turning it, then suddenly a sharp grin sprang to his lips. He slapped his hands together in one thunderous clap and, turning, made his way back to his house, calling for his servants.

"Donn's balls!" one swore, hearing his master's voice. "What's got his goad now?"

"As if you didn't know," another grumbled. "For a briar apple, I'd go the other way and pretend I didn't hear him!"

"There's that to consider," a third said. "Don't turn your head away, or you may get a rap around the pate to muddle your wits!"

"By Lugh's spear! Where is everyone?" roared Conchobor, coming through the doorway. He paused, blinking away the sun's brightness in the room's gloom. "Ah! There you are! Bring the cooks and the ale-makers to me! And send for Mugain! 'Tis a feast that needs planning! A grand one!"

The servants exchanged frowning glances, but sped away to do his bidding. Yet, each wondered what had brought about the sudden change in their master's manner.

"Ah, yes, my little thrush," Conchobor muttered, looking with relish at the row of enemy heads mounted on the beams below the thatched roof of the great hall. "Now, we'll see if we can't bring you back to our nest!"

vii.

EARLY ON THE MORNING OF the feast day, the burnished halls of the Red Branch once again rang with merriment as musicians played their harps and pipes and flutes and bards made ready to shout their newest creations. First Cathbad the Druid gave his offering; then Conall, son of Rudraige followed by Geanann Bright-Face, the son of Cathbad; Ferceirtne, Geanann Black-Knee, and Sencha, Ailill's son.

Honey-beer flowed like water in a swift-moving creek as the warriors drank deeply in relief that their king had apparently cast aside his black cloak of melancholy and ate and laughed with relish, slapping the saucy backside of serving wenches as they flipped a hip in his direction.

At last, Conchobor struck his silver scepter against an oaken column, and all fell silent, waiting to hear what he had to say. He laughed and waved a broad hand around, indicating the Great Hall.

"Tell me!" he shouted. "Has Emain Macha ever been merrier? Has there ever been a house as fine as this?"

They all roared their agreement, lifting brimming cups and draining them as pledge to their words.

"Well, then!" Conchobor said. "I can assume that none of you have found anything wanting? That is"—he paused to hiccup—"you all have enough to eat and drink and the songs and merriment has tickled your fancy?"

"It has!" Dubthach said blearily. He pulled a serving wench down onto his lap and nuzzled her breasts as she shrieked with laughter, her bare white heels twinkling as she kicked against his tickling.

"Alas," Conchobor said, the smile suddenly slipping from his lips. "I wish that were true. But—" He heaved a sigh and drank from the gem-encrusted goblet in his hand.

"Ah, now," Fiodcha said, wrinkling his scarred brow. "Now, what is it that we are missing?"

"Why," Conchobor said, looking around in pretended amazement. "Has it been so long that you can't tell?"

"Tell what?" Cathbad asked, suddenly nervous at the turn of the conversation. "What is it that we are supposed to know? What whimsy?"

" 'Tis the saddest of all things," Conchobor said. A tear trickled down his seamed cheek. "Why, it's the singing of the sons of Usnech; that's what is missing! Who here doesn't feel the loss of their voices that would put a lark to shame? The three brightest lights in all of Ulster, that's what they are! And where are they? Gone for the love of a woman! Now, I ask you: Is any woman worth the loss of Naisi, Ainlé and Ardan? Hmm?"

"If you recall," Cathbad said dryly, "I and many others have tried to tell you this over the past years. But you were moping around as if you wore a cuckold's horns, leching after a young girl a third your age! A third? More like a sixth!"

"Yes, yes," Conchobor said hastily. "I know I've been difficult to live with—"

"Difficult?" Fergus growled. "Like grabbing a mad dog by the balls!"

"*And,*" Cathbad said severely, wagging a finger in admonishment, "I warned you before about that girl-child—"

"We all heard your words," Conchobor said, interrupting the Druid. "And you were right!" He spread his hands and shook his head sorrowfully. "I have behaved badly. But even the sorest wound is healed by time—metaphorically speaking, of course! So, I say that it is time that we bring back those three lions. What say the rest of you?"

They remained silent, looking uneasily around at each other, for all remembered the black rages that had left Conchobor nearly foaming at the mouth at the mention of Deirdre's name or any of the sons on of Usnech. Why, just last week, had he not brained a youth for comparing a sunrise to Deirdre's hair?

"Well," Cathbad said cautiously, "it's all very well and good that you should feel that way about them. That is, that you should no longer feel like a nutted dog at the mention of Deirdre's name."

"*But?*" Conchobor said, raising his eyebrows. "I know you, Cathbad. When you speak like that there is always a qualifier lurking around the corner. Out with it!"

"I think it's a bit too soon to be bringing them back to Emain Macha," he said firmly. "A freshly healed wound is easily reopened. No, no. Best leave them where they are. They're happy there."

"But they'd be happier back here among their friends, wouldn't you say?" Conchobor insisted.

"Aye, that's only common sense speaking, now," Dubthach said. "But I agree with Cathbad: leave well enough alone, I says. I miss the rascals around here as much as any man, but why yoke a wild horse to a chariot without breaking him? Eh? Only a fool does that."

Conchobor laughed and drank deeply from his cup. "Stuff and nonsense!" he said. "I say let's send a messenger to Alba and bring them back to Emain Macha, where they belong. Now, who will take the journey for us?" He looked around the room, but none met his nervous eye.

"Something seems wrong here," Froech muttered, burying his nose in his mug. "Ain't all night and day, you ask me."

"Aye," Cormac agreed, pretending to worry a chunk of meat from between his teeth. "I've smelled sweeter stables than those words!"

"Come, come!" Conchobor shouted merrily. "How about you Conall Cernach? What say you to this journey?"

"No," the brawny, blunt-spoken warrior said. He shrugged his heavy shoulders. "Why bother? The only way they'll come back is if I give them my guarantee. I bring them back, you change your mind and kill them, I would have to kill you. Or," he said, glowering around the room, "any Ulsterman who would harm a hair on their fine heads! There's the meat of it all. No."

"Well," Conchobor said, his eyes narrowing slightly, "so it's no friend of mine, you are then."

"Wouldn't say that," Conall grunted, lifting a huge joint of meat in both hands. "Just saved your life, I think, by refusing to go." Grease ran down his chin as he sank his teeth into the meat.

"Well, then! I should thank you for your wisdom!" Conchobor

said. He chuckled and shook his head. "Ah me! I suppose I can't blame you for having your doubts! So, what about you, Cúchlainn? What says my brave hound, eh? Would you take this journey for me?"

Cúchulainn leaned back against the cushions and stared into Conchobor's eyes. The three pupils in his eyes[36] pulsed from the intensity of his stare and Conchobor shifted his gaze as he felt heat at the back of his brain.

"No, I think not," Cúchulainn said gently.

"You doubt my word?" Conchobor said sharply.

Cúchulainn shook his head, his heavy mane moving gently across his shoulders. "I don't know. And because I don't, it would be foolhardy for me to pledge my word, then have to kill you or any other Ulsterman who might betray it. All of you know me well: The sorrow of death will fall upon any who causes me to lose honor, and what has a man but the honor of his word? No, Conchobor, I won't go to Alba for you."

"And this is the thanks I get for putting you under my protection and bringing you into the Red Branch? I gave you my own chariot, my own spear, my own driver and horses until you found your own! 'Tis certain you're no friend of mine!" Conchobor snapped. He looked over at Fergus, lounging on the cushions. Five maidens lay around him. He grinned. "Well, Fergus? How about you?"

Fergus shook his head, annoyed by the question. "What Conall and the Hound have said goes doubly for me."

Conchobor cast a quick eye around the room again, then shrugged. "By Lugh's spear! So that's the way the grain grows, is it? So be it! Fergus, go after them and take your sons with you. Tell them that they have my pledge, the pledge of a king. That should be good enough for them or anyone here!"

Fergus shrugged. "All right. You've heard me word upon it, and knowing that, you still want me to go! I'll make the trip. But you see to your word!" He grinned wolfishly and many there shuddered at the darkening of his brow. "You know the nut of it if you lie!"

"I know," Conchobor said quietly. He leaned back with satisfaction in his chair and slapped his hand hard upon his knee. "And, why does it suddenly seem like a death-house in here? Eh? Music, I say! Sencha! Give us another song! By Dagda's balls, is this a wake or a feast?"

Obediently the musicians broke into a rollicking air, but many there quietly put their cups aside, and Conchobor pretended not to notice how they rested politely but did not join in with the rest of the celebration. He called his wife Mugain to him and when she came, big breasts moving like melons beneath her shift, sloe-eyes gleaming blackly, he pulled her down onto his lap and kissed her noisily, then rose and took her into his sleeping quarters.

Then—and only then—did the Red Branch take up their cups again.

viii.

"EEEAH!" THE SHARP CRY ESCAPED from Deirdre's lips as she awoke with a start and sat up sharply in the tousled bed. Naisi leaped up from her side immediately reaching for his sword that he kept always near him.

"What is it?" he said. "What did you hear?"

"A bad dream," she said shakily. She tried to laugh, but her voice cracked and she reached for the jug of water she kept beside the bed. She drank thirstily as Naisi lowered his sword and sat down beside her. He took her in his arms.

"Tell me," he said gently.

The door to their room flew open as Naisi's brothers rushed in, swords raised threateningly. They noticed Deirdre's naked pear-shaped breasts tipped with ripe plums, and turned their backs immediately as she gasped and automatically scrambled to pull a cover up over her.

"We heard—" Ardan began. But Naisi interrupted him. "It is only a bad dream," he said. "Please leave us."

"Been getting more and more of them lately," Ainlé noted sourly. He peeked over his shoulder and, seeing Deirdre modestly covered, turned around. He scratched his nose with a thumbnail. "I thought I heard the *Sídhe* in the late night wind. And the black horse of Donn riding from Tech Donn.[37] Is it the same dream as the last, lass?"

Deirdre nodded miserably and tucked her head between Naisi's chin and broad shoulder. " 'Tis that. All of that. The three of you buried beneath a red oak in blood-soaked ground, and snow falling over the houses of Emain Macha. I see the Great Hall broken apart like two eggshells, and I hear the women keening over dead sons and husbands." She raised her eyes and looked deeply into Naisi's. "Oh, my husband! I fear our happiness has run its race like Macha."[38]

"We haven't heard much from Conchobor," Ainlé said thoughtfully. "I cannot believe he has forgotten the hurt we did him."

"*I* did him, you mean," Deirdre said. Tears welled in her eyes. "He's a hard and ruthless old man!"

"Wisha!" Naisi said, chucking her chin gently. "There'll be no more of that. He's still the king of Ulster, and for that we must honor him."

"Honor him!" Deirdre said sharply. She pushed away from him, forgetting the cover that fell to her naked lap. Her bare breasts bobbled prettily in the light. "After all that he has done? Forcing us away from our homes? And knowing full well that I had the right to choose for myself the man who would share my bed? 'Tis a right all freeborn have! When I turned fourteen I was free to choose! And he being three, no four, times my age!"

"Enough! And cover yourself before my brothers, before they think you're a *striapach*. We'll have no more talk like that, woman! A man's king is his king; and although he may not be in his land, he is still bound to the man. Would you have me live with more dishonor than—" He brought himself up shortly. Deirdre pulled away from him.

"And that is all I am to you? Dishonor to your king?"

"Ah, no! No!" He tried to take her in his arms, but she pulled away. He glanced over at his brothers. "Please?"

"Aye, we should be leaving you, now. 'Tis not long before the sun is up and Lugh's rays burn away the fog of the night. Things always look better then. The night-hag will be tucked in her barrow for certain!" Ardan said. He nudged his brother and the two of them turned and left, pulling the wooden door shut tightly on his leather hinges.

Naisi sighed and poured a bit of water from the jug into his cupped hand. He rubbed it over his face, then slipped onto the bed and pulled Deirdre into his arms. "Now, surely you know by now that I love you. I would not have come away with you had I not. But a man must always belong somewhere, and although we are here now, it is not our home."

"Why? Why can't it be our home," Deirdre asked. She relaxed, slumping into his arms, laying her head upon his chest and listening to its slow, steady beat.

"To go back is to go into darkness
Deep, a cold bed devoid of lightness,
No joy, and women's tears in floods
That wash across the land. Black clouds
Cover the sun. Here we have light
And our few discomforts are slight.
The sun warms us during the day
And the nights keep our fears at bay.
I fear Conchobor and his warrior men
Who hunt across Ulster's wild fen.
I think our happiness comes to an end
Soon for Conchobor's hate will not end.
A man we trust will soon come to bring
Us back and our death chants will ring
Across the land. I see two oaks twine
Their branches together.[39] Our time,
I know has come, but Conchobor's crime
Will split the Red Branch. I see
Coming from the west a mighty
Army and in its ranks Ulster men
Will scorch Ulster fields. I see ten
Times ten times ten days will pass
Before Ulster will be able to amass
Its army and defeat the western foe.
Alas! We shall become a tale of woe!"[40]

At a loss for words, Naisi held her gently while hot tears fell upon his naked breast, searing his flesh with her prophecy as the cold morning breeze that rises from the sea at first light caressed them gently with its damp fingers.

ix.

EARLY IN THE MORNING, FERGUS rolled naked from his warm bed and Nessa's arms. He crossed to the window and looked blearily out at the gray morning with the cold, cold rain falling in a slanting curtain. His head throbbing, his mouth dry, and his tongue furred from the honeyed ale he had drunk the night before as he had a *geis*[41] on him that would not allow him to refuse any feast-offer. He scratched his hairy chest gently and swore. Nessa rolled over to stare at him with sleepy eyes.

"What is it?" she asked crossly.

"Rain," he said gloomily. "I've got a bad feeling about starting out on a journey in the rain. Nothing good comes of this, I'm telling you."

She sniffed. " 'Tis the night of drink that brings that out in you."

"Enough, woman!" Fergus said. He pressed his knuckles hard against his throbbing temples. " 'Tisn't my fault that Conchobor invited me to rounds at the ale-feast. You know the *geis* upon me. Would you have me death upon your conscience?"

"A handy excuse for getting drunk, you ask me," Nessa grunted, pulling the covers over her head and snuggling into the warmth left by Fergus upon rising.

"Ahh," Fergus said disgustedly. He stared despondently out into the gray morning, wishing that he could put the trip off a day and spend the time playing *fidchell*[42] with other warriors in the great hall of the Red Branch instead of traveling in that cold wetness.

He sighed. "And if wishes were gold, there wouldn't be a poor man in all of Ulster," he said resignedly. He grabbed a cloak and threw it over his shoulders and walked naked to the bathhouse to scrub away the night before setting out on the journey. He ignored the women who watched covertly (and men with admiration) as his mighty bod swung gently against his thighs with his every step.

He didn't know that while he drank at the ale-feast, Conchobor had sent a messenger to Borach,[43] a chieftain who had the ring-fort that lay near Emain Macha and was directly in the path that Fergus would have to take home, informing the eager-to-please chieftain that he would consider it a great favor if Borach would invite Fergus and his company to a feasting day when he chanced to pass on the way back to Emain Macha with the sons of Usnech. But he had also charged Fergus to tell Naisi and his brothers that he would consider it a great honor if they would pledge not to eat or drink in another's house until they reached the Great Hall of the Red Branch once they set foot on Ulster's shores.

"And take with you as my promise that I will not harm a hair on the head of either Naisi or his brothers, your sons, Fiacha, Iollan, and Buinne," Conchobor said. "And as security, Dubthach and Cormac, my own son."

Fergus had frowned and tried to look into Conchobor's eyes, but Conchobor had averted them, turning instead to a passing serving wench whose big bare buddies, intricately outlined with whorls and swirls of blue paint, had drawn his attention. He reached out a broad thumb and forefinger and pinched her rump, causing her to yelp and jump, the bowl filled with brimming honeyed-beer she was carrying, flying from her hands and upending over the head of Rómit Rígoinmit, his jester.

Howls of laughter arose from the Red Branch warriors taking their ease with bowls of beer and bouncing bawds. Rómit rose, blinking owlishly in confusion and stumbled over a trivet, falling over a low table. His elbow hit a wine strainer that flipped up and threw its dregs in the face of Dubthach, who rose, roaring curses, kicking over a cauldron of bubbling stew that spilled into the lap of Cormac who howled and rose, frantically stripped his sodden tunic from him and cradling his beet-red *bod* and *magarlac* in his cupped hands.

"Boiled balls!" crowed Fachtna[44] and received a slap along the head with a stone cup that crossed his eyes and knocked him backward into Loegaire.[45]

Conall Cernach rose and dumped a bowl of beer over Cormac's *magarlac* and reached down one mighty hand to pull Fachtna off Loegaire. *"Haw, haw, haw!"* he laughed, then grunted as Loegaire, striking out blindly, caught him in the stomach, bending him over. He gagged and sour beer gushed forth from his mouth, spattering Loegaire full in the face. Loegaire rose, swinging and Conall grappled with him, and the two of them fell over a low table into a group of laughing warriors.

"Ah, me!" sighed Cathbad, eyeing the confusion. "What has become of dignity?"

He turned away, looking into the fire below a trivet. Suddenly his face went blank, his eyes narrowed, and warm shapes began to move slowly in faint flames from the glowing coals. Fergus noted the change and leaned forward, speaking softly in his ear.

"What is it? What do you see?"

"Wintery times," Cathbad said lowly. "The road from the coast slick with ice and people moving slowly, blindly muffled against the cold. Two shadows; they could be trees, they could be people. Hard to tell."

A bowl of beer splashed over the fire, dousing it.

Cathbad blinked and looked into the square face of Fergus, whose scowling brows drew a straight line over his eyes.

"I don't like the feel of that," Fergus said. He glanced quickly at Conchobor. "Especially when I have to ride that road."

Cathbad shrugged and sipped from a goblet of red wine. "Be careful not to think too much. Probably nothing. All human feeling is an exaggeration."

"Well," Fergus muttered, unconvinced. He leaned back, nibbling hard on his lower lip. Cathbad took another sip.

"Then again," he said, "that's all humans have."

"Aargh," Fergus grunted. "Damn you Druids and your pattering pundits. What's a man to believe?"

Cathbad shrugged again. "Whatever you wish. Eat an apple. Maybe it will clear your mind."

"Ahh," Fergus said disgustedly. He reached for a huge bowl of beer and, holding it in both hands, raised it to his lips, draining it in one long draught. He threw it from him, belched, farted, and exclaimed, "We'll leave the thinking to you Druids! 'Tis what you do the best. But I," he winked at the wench beside him, "I'll tend to making honey in the hive."

Cathbad sighed and shook his head as Fergus rose, tossing the giggling wench over his shoulder, and strode quickly toward the sleeping apartment reserved for him. Then his brow furrowed deeply in thought as he tried to separate the images he had seen in the coals from thought.

X.

IN THE SHADE OF THE oak tree, Deirdre reached out and moved a piece on the *fidchell* board, then smiled with satisfaction and sat back, waiting for Naisi's reaction. The move had left Naisi only two more moves before the game would be hers. She sat back, her hands folded primly in her lap, anticipating his reaction: the slapping of his brow with his hand, his pretended anger, then his lunge over the board to kiss her.

But Naisi sat quietly, frowning at the board. Suddenly she realized that his eyes were not on the board but on something in the past and a shiver raced down her spine like ice water. A wren wrinkled her thoughts with a happy song. She looked up in the branches of the oak tree beneath which they sat and admired it perched against the leaves dappled August colors. Her black mood fled, she gave a small laugh, and his eyes clicked like marbles made of blue agate to stare into hers. Her rich lips curved up in a smile as she nodded toward the board.

"I've got you!" she said triumphantly.

He glanced down at the board, then shrugged and leaned back on his elbows, staring across at her. He glanced up at the oak tree. "It's only a game," he said. "I've lost far more than a silly game."

Her happiness fled. She felt a lump form in her throat as she realized how much Naisi and his brothers had given up for her. "Are you unhappy that you came away with me?" she asked quietly.

He frowned at her. "Unhappy? Yes, I'm unhappy. Sorry? No. It is a choice that was made. But I'm unhappy about having to choose."

"You miss the Red Branch, then?"

"Yes," he sighed. "I miss the Red Branch."

Hot tears fell from her eyes, and he leaned over the board to smudge them away with his broad thumb. "Now, we'll be having none of that. 'Tis a fine fall day made for laughing and not crying. You've won one game; let's see you take another."

She laughed and snuffled back her tears. They sat up the board and had just begun to play when a cry echoed up from the beach. Naisi cocked his head, listening. A strange light came into his eyes. "If I don't miss my guess, that is a familiar cry. 'Tis a man of Ireland."

"No," Deirdre said quickly. She moved a piece. "No, it is only a man from the mainland of Alba." She laughed. "I fear, my husband, that you have been thinking so long about the Red Branch that you hear the hurly-burly of Emain Macha in the wind through the oak leaves."

Naisi pressed his lips together, then laughed. "Yes, you're right."

The shout came again, hard on the heels of his words, and Naisi nearly upset the board, leaping to his feet.

"It *is* an Irish shout!" he exclaimed.

"No," Deirdre said anxiously, for she had heard the shout, too, and recognized the war cry of Fergus Mac Roich. "No, you are mistaken. It is only the wind from the sea."

A third time the shout rose. His brothers rushed up to stand beside him, staring down the slope of the hill to where it curved around to the sandy beach.

"What's that?" Ainlé demanded, clutching his sword in one hand, a javelin in the other. "Sounds like we have work cut out for us, you ask me!"

"I know that cry," Ardan said, his eyes squinting toward the direction of the cry. "And if I don't miss my guess, that's Fergus Mac Roich bellowing like a beer drunk bull!"

"Better go and see if he's alone, or if the rest of the Red Branch has come with him," Naisi said grimly. "It's been a while since Conchobor has sent any to try us. He's long overdue, I'm thinking! Ainlé, you take the path leading down to the sea while Ardan moves ahead. I'll get my sword."

His brothers nodded and hurried off, Ardan loping ahead like a hungry wolf. Naisi turned to leave, but Deirdre's hand fell upon his arm. He looked down at her.

"There's no need for this," she said quietly. "I knew it was Fergus when I first heard his cry."

"You knew? Then why did you say it was the wind?" Naisi asked.

Deirdre sighed and rose, turning to face the sea:

> "Late last night while I lay sleeping
> Into my dreams there came creeping
> A vision of three ravens[46] coming toward us
> From Emain Macha. I think one was Fergus
> And his sons and Conchobor's son as well
> And they flew to the house where we dwell
> And in each of their beaks were three drops
> Of honey. They left those three drops
> Of honey with us and took away three
> Drops of our blood to a dead oak tree."

Naisi frowned and took her hands gently between his. He searched her face, but there was no laughter in the fine laugh lines beside her eyes. "What do you take this to mean?" he asked.

"What else could it be? Conchobor has sent emissaries to us claiming that he no longer hates us for running away from him. The honey is not sweeter than a message from a lying man."

Naisi's brow darkened with fury. "Then I shall kill Fergus and—"

"No," Deirdre interrupted. "He does not know that he is lying. He is only repeating words that Conchobor has told him." She carried his hand to her breast. "I feel death here," she said anxiously. "Send Fergus away and we shall find another island. I will wear kohl in my hair, and we shall be alone."

"These are the words of a melancholy woman," Naisi said, gently pulling his hand free. "Let us hear what Fergus has to say before we decide anything."

"No," Deirdre answered. "Words are twisted too easily. One sees in them only what one wishes to see. You pine for the Red Branch and, I fear, will believe anything that you want to hear that will allow you to return to it. Our curragh lies on the other side of the island. Let us slip away either north or south—it makes no difference to me as long as we are alone—and live in solitude together."

"We have tried that," Naisi said quietly. "Have you forgotten the past months and years?"

"They seem only minutes," Deirdre said mournfully. "And I fear that we shall have no more of them. Our future is numbered in days."

"Enough of this," Naisi said. He gave her a tiny push. "Go and prepare food and drink for our guests if they come in peace and lay out my weapons discreetly in case there is war behind their mission."

She turned quietly and headed up the path to where their small house, rudely built of timbers chinked with mud and kelp hauled from the sea in wicker baskets, stood on a knoll. The front door faced southwest, where, on a clear day, they could see the faint blue outline of Ireland.

Fergus stepped up the path, his pace quickening as he saw Naisi waiting quietly for him, his hands on his hips, spraddle-legged, his thickly muscled legs like oak roots.

"Hail, Naisi!" he called, and raised his right hand in greeting to show that it did not hold a weapon. He kept his sword, the *In Caladbolg*[47] sheathed and well away from his body so that Naisi could see he came in peace.

"Fergus!" Naisi shouted back, and his face wreathed in a welcome smile as the warrior came boldly up the path and clasped his forearm, shaking hands like a dear, long-lost brother. "It's been a long time since I saw you last."

"Too long," Fergus said firmly. "Too long. But that's what you get when you have a king thinking with his *bod* instead of his head."

"You must tell us all of the news. Right, Ardan? Ainlé?" Naisi said, turning toward his brothers, who kept a close eye upon the others trailing behind Fergus.

"It would be good," Ardan said grudgingly.

"But first"—he eyed Fergus closely—"a bite to eat and drink?"

"Would go well," Fergus said. He grinned. "You remember my *geis,* then?"

"I do," Naisi said, a small smile cracking the corners of his mouth. "And I remember the laws of hospitality as well."

"Then let us seal them," Fergus said firmly, starting up the path. He unbuckled his great sword and carried it by the huge belt that anchored it around his body. His heavy shoulders twitched in anticipation of the drink. "No man may eat honestly of another man's board and lie to him without bringing the gods' wrath down upon his head. And I have no intention of letting a god jig upon mine."

Naisi laughed and clapped him on the shoulder, swinging close as an intimate, as they made their way up the path and to the table Deirdre had set outside the house beneath a quaking birch, its leaves *Samonios* gold. Fergus eyed her appreciatively as he approached.

"I can see, Naisi," he said slowly, "why Conchobor's *bod* was doing his thinking for him. She would be one to give Maeve[48] jealous fits at Cruachan Ai."[49]

"Thank you," Deidre said politely. "And welcome to our house."

"So," Naisi said after Fergus had hung his sword in the birch branches and took his place at the table, "tell me the news from home."

Fergus drained a drinking cup of honeyed beer, belched, and nodded appreciatively. He glanced at the others with him. "Put aside your weapons and join us."

Dubthach pressed his lips together, took off his sword grudgingly, and hung it beside Fergus's. The others followed his lead; then all took their places around the table.

"Well," Fergus said, pausing to drain another cup and rip a large chunk of venison from a cold roast. He bit deeply and chewed loudly. "I have eaten, so there may be no false words between us. The news is good, sons of Usnech! Conchobor swears by Lugh's orb and the mighty heavens that he will not rest during the day or sleep at night until all of the sons of Usnech, his foster brothers, return to Emain Macha. As a pledge, he has sent his own son and mine"—Fergus nodded toward the foot of the table, where they sat eating and drinking quietly—"as a guarantee of your safety. And I," he added, pausing for effect, "offer my sword and arm as further guarantee."

Deirdre stood up, holding her hands at her shoulders, palms out. "It is good that Conchobor has forgotten his jealousy," she said. "And for that, I thank you, Fergus Mac Roich. But I say that we remain here, for the sea between us and our own mountains give us far greater protection than we would have in Emain Mach with the Red Branch sworn to allegiance to Conchobor."

"You doubt the king's word?" Fergus said, waggling his brows at her.

"A king is only a man," Deirdre said gently. "A king may be true to his word, but the man may give the lie to it. There's many a slip between the two, and the man often forgets the crown."

Fergus shook his head sadly. "Lass," he said gently, "it's over, I'm telling you. Over. And now's the time for rebuilding those bridges between the king and yourself. It's been a long time coming, and I say that possibility of peace is worth the risk." He gestured at the sons of Usnech. "These are mighty warriors and the equal of all—save Cúchulainn and myself and possibly Conall Cernach—who share the board at the Great Hall of the Red Branch. And myself you have as well. As for Cúhulainn, he's a warrior of great honor. As is Conall. 'Tis enough, I'm thinking."

She shook her head. "A wily man can fool a warrior and give his truthful words to the wind." She looked beseechingly at Naisi. "I say we thank our guests, but stay. What is there in Ulster that we do not have here?"

"One's own country," Fergus said quietly. "For all its fault, a man can have all the riches in the world; but if he does not see his country around him every day, he has nothing."

"True words, those," Naisi said, looking at Deirdre. "We are rich here, but there is a hollowness to everything. A man in exile goes through long days and longer nights. He may wear his honor on his arm, but it means nothing without his countrymen around him."

"You will be safe," Fergus said.

"You see?" Naisi said. He laughed, throwing his head back and exposing the fine column of his throat. "There you have it! A guarantee."

Deirdre felt a darkness move upon her and in that darkness, she saw vague shapes coiling and moving ponderously.

> "I had a dream last night of the three
> Sons of Usnech, bound by cords of treachery
> And cast into a cold grave by Conchobor
> Of the Red Branch. I saw nothing of honor."

Naisi shook his head irritably. "That's enough of your prophesying, Deirdre. We've heard all we want of nay-saying and needle-pricking! Lay down your dreams, Deirdre! For my sake. And my brothers. Leave them on Alba's hills and on the sea with the sailors and the rough gray stones of the Giants' Footsteps."[50] He looked at his brothers, then back to Fergus. "We'll give you the peace, Fergus, with your guarantee. And we'll take it on good faith from Conchobor."

But Deirdre spoke before Fergus could stretch forth his hand, saying:

> "Hear me, husband! I still hear
> The howling of dogs and see tears
> Of the night in crystal drops before
> Me. I see Fergus taken to another's door
> And Conchobor without mercy in his dun.
> I see Naisi strengthless in battle, his life run
> Out before him. I see Ainlé without
> His breastplate. I see my bitter tears
> Falling on a blood-soaked ground. My fears!"

Fergus belched and shook his head disgustedly. "You may do what you wish, Naisi," he said. "But I've learned not to listen to the howling of dogs who fear the thunder and high winds. And as for women and their dreams—" He shook his head disgustedly. "They see woggles and mumbling hags in the night shadows, I'm afraid."

"I think you are right," Naisi said, giving Deirdre a stern look. She lowered her head and moved away, hearing his last words fall like stones on her heart. "We will go with you."

"Done!" Fergus cried, slapping his huge hand on the table. "And my sword and good right arm will stand with you. Not all the men in Ulster can topple that."

She glanced over her shoulder and saw Fergus and Naisi and his brothers, hands together in a solemn pledge. She shuddered. Above them she saw a red cloud forming slowly.

They left the next day, and as their boat pulled away from the shore, Deirdre stood alone in the stern, watching the heather-clad hills slip away behind in a soft mist rising from the sea. A lay leaped to her lips:

"Farewell, dear land that has held my love
Where the sun rises from its home and doves
Fly in soft song. Farewell to your glens and hills
Where wildflowers grow and the air is clean and still.

"Farewell to your winding streams and sylvan bays.
We go now, but I wish we all would stay
Among Dun Fiodhaigh and Dun Fionn
Where among the hazel bushes red roe deer run.

"Farewell, Innis Droignach and Dun Suibhne!
And Caill Cuan, where Naisi's brother Ainlé
Hunted. I've lost it all, everything surely!
All the happiness of Deirdre and Naisi!

"Farewell, Glen Laoi where I slept softly
Under soft fleece with my love Naisi.
There I ate the flesh of fish and wild deer meat
While Alba's sun-warmed rocks were my seat.

"Farewell, Glen Massan, with its white-stalked
Fields of wild garlic that we picked. We talked
Long of our love there and slept many nights

By the mouth of its river until first light.
"Farewell, Glen Eitche where my first house stands.
Among the sun-dappled woods on fertile land.
Farewell, Glen Urchain, where laughing Naisi
Flirted long and merrily with me!

"Farewell, Glen-da-Ruadh where the cuckoo's song
Sings out on the bending branch through the long
Day on the towering hill above the bay
Where the fish leap and seabirds play.

"Farewell, my beloved Draighen whose sandy
Beach and sylvan waters are like a *pandy*[51]
On my heart! I never would have left you
But for my husband and his brothers, too!"

And slowly the land disappeared in the gray mist behind them while tears fell bitterly from Deirdre's eyes onto the blue soft woolen cloak she had wrapped around her.

XI.

CAREFULLY ARDAN HELD THE BOAT steady as it was swept ashore by the crashing surf. Naisi leaped out to draw it up onto the sand. Fergus and Ainlé followed to give him a hand, and together, they drew it up until the bow lodged firmly like old driftwood in the wet sand left by the receding tide.

The gray day was falling, but Naisi paused and took a deep breath, closing his eyes. A tiny tear trickled through his curling black lashes. He sighed, exclaiming: "Ah, but it is good to be home!" He turned to Deirdre, his eyes shining with excitement. "Smell the land! The heather! Is it not grand?"

"We had heather, too, back in Alba, and on our island," Deirdre said sadly.

"But it isn't *our* heather," Naisi said, taking another deep breath. "There is something about knowing one is home."

"Are we?" Deirdre said mournfully. She looked at Fergus as he climbed from the boat. "What do you say, Fergus? This is your doing. Are we home?"

Fergus shook his shaggy head. "Enough of these metaphysics, girl!" he said. "I'm only an old warrior sent to bring you back. Home? Of course it is! And that's all that I have to say upon that!" He spat and cast an anxious eye up at the leaden sky and the black clouds beginning to gather on the horizon. "And now, we'd better be making our way toward Emain Macha. We need to find shelter before this storm hits."

"I fear that the storm is closer at hand than you think," Deirdre said ominously.

Fergus shook his head in exasperation and, placing his huge hands around her tiny waist, lifted her and carried her ashore above the reach of the waves. "Women! Seeing swords in sticks and heather stalks! The day has enough gloom to it without your moaning! Come!" he shouted, turning to the others. "If we're lucky, we can make it to Dun Borach before the storm hits!"

The others glanced over their shoulders at the gathering clouds and hurried to pick up their bags. They scurried along the shore to a path that led away from the sea. It was a well-traveled path that had felt the footfalls of many a trader, and the way was easy despite the reluctant dragging of Deirdre's feet.

Soon they came to the house of Borach, and Fergus pounded hard on the gate door. "Borach!" he roared. "You son of a scabby goat, open and let us in, or I'll hire a poet to put a curse on your house!"

The door swung open. Borach stood inside, thumbs hooked into a wide leather belt that kept his hanging belly girdled tightly. "I've been expecting you, Fergus! And you, sons of Usnech!" He looked at Deirdre, but she had prudently pulled the hood of her cloak over her hair, hiding her beauty deep within its folds. "And this is the legendary beauty, I'm thinking!"

"Aye, think what you want," Fergus said grumpily. He put a hand on Borach's chest and pushed him back from the door, staggering him. "But we're cold and hungry, and Manannán mac Lir[52] is sending his waters after us! Would you have us stay standing here to be drowned?"

"It'd take a flood of water to float you," Borach said. He gestured. "Come in! Come in!"

They stepped through the door and carefully looked around Borach's hill-fort before following him to the feasting hall. Ainlé sniffed the air suspiciously and frowned.

"Naisi, I'm getting a bad feeling about all of this," he said worriedly. "The place smells like mildew. Borach seems too friendly. Why would he be feasting us? You know how he has always fawned over Conchobor, trying to get into the king's good graces. Maybe Deirdre's right. I say let Ardan and the two of you be off to the Isle of Rechrainn. I'll go on to Emain Macha and see how the weather is there. Rechrainn's not far between Ulster and Alba, and close enough that you can slip on over if the sky is clear."

Naisi bit his lip as he studied his brother, then shook his head. "No," he said softly so only Ainlé could hear. "Better if we stay together. That is our strength.[53] Besides," he said, giving his brother a crooked grin, " 'tis only a wash with lime the place is needing, I'm thinking. Borach's just a bit behind his fall cleaning!"

He attempted a laugh, but the sound bounced hollowly off the walls like a lone echo in a Sídhe wind. A sudden shiver slipped down his spine. He felt the small, cold hand of Deirdre slip beneath his arm. Tiny prickles ran along his forearm. He shook his head.

"Whatever you feel, Ainlé, remember that we're home," he said quietly.

"Are we?" Ainlé murmured. "I wonder."

Borach stood in the center of the Great Hall and motioned to places that had been prepared for them before the center fire. "Come!" he said. "There's a fine meal awaiting you!"

They took their places where Borach had indicated. He clapped his hands. Serving wenches moved out of the shadows, bearing platters and pitchers of honeyed beer. Dark circles seemed gathered under their eyes. Their dresses hung like tattered bags from their shoulders. They left the platters in front of the guests, filled the clay-fired goblets silently, and just as silently left like wafting shadows.

Borach lifted his goblet, saying, "And here's to your return, sons of

Usnech! Would it have been such that you were not forced to wander among the heathens!"

The sons of Usnech lifted their goblets and sipped politely. The beer was thin and laced stingily with honey. Ardan made a face and placed his goblet down away from him.

"Like ass piss," he whispered behind his hand to Naisi. "I've poured better on the ground."

"Shh," Naisi said. "You'll offend him. Remember the laws of hospitality."

"Goes both ways, you ask me," Ardan said grumpily. He cut a piece of cheese and started to eat, then noticed the light tinge of green on its underside and placed it back on the platter. "And the cheese's turned. Naisi, I'm thinking this is a bad sign. I say we leave now before the Cromm Cruaich [54] knows we're here. We'll not get away from his bloody hands!"

"Enough," Naisi said. "If we insult Borach in this manner, we'll draw a *geis* upon us."

"At least, then we'd be knowing what to avoid," Ardan said grumpily. "Sometimes it is a good thing to know what's forbidden."

Meanwhile, Fergus had drained his goblet and refilled it from the pitcher at his elbow. He reached for a large chunk of meat and ripped into it with his strong white teeth. He spat out a piece of gristle and said, "I think you slaughtered an old milch-cow here, Borach! 'Tis as stringy as the Hag's haunch!" [55]

Borach stretched his thick lips in a grin, exposing his long yellow teeth. His suety cheeks gleamed oily in the firelight. "And is there one better suited to be a judge of that than Fergus? [56] The finer meats and ale will be brought out in the feast for you tomorrow."

Fergus slowly lowered the goblet he had raised to his lips and stared hard at Borach. "Now, why would you be doing that, Borach, knowing full well that I'm bringing the lads and lass back to Emain Macha? Conchobor has given his charge to bring the boys back by day or night. You know that, too, I'm thinking."

"Tsh-tock," Borach said, clicking his tongue against his teeth. He shook his head sadly. "Why, a person would think you were seeing bats and goblins—the *gruagach* [57]—in the *dubh ba hoíche* [58] the way you whistle and weep in your beer. I'm half-tempted to withdraw my offer, but that would put the *geis* on me. No"—he waved his fist in the air—"I'll not be taking that on for the likes of you, Fergus Mac Roich. If there's a *geis* to be bearing, 'tis yourself that will do it. You have a feast being laid out tomorrow in your honor. And there's an end to it."

Fergus sat back and eyed Borach sternly, his face turning scarlet until it looked black. Borach cringed away from the gimlet eyes boring into his.

" 'Tis no easy matter to be putting the evil upon a person, Borach. I'm thinking that there is something else mawking about here." He glanced over at Naisi. "What do you think, lad? I'm being made a *braighdenach* by this *aitheach*—"

"Here, now, this is my house!" Borach protested hotly.

"—this churl," Fergus continued, fastening a warning look upon his host. "And it is a serious matter."

"No," Deirdre said. "It is a choice." Fergus glanced over at her, a deep frown falling over his face. "You gave your word to the sons of Usnech to see them safely to Emain Macha. And now you are looking to crawl away from that to eat and drink until you puke. Which matters the most to you? Your honor or your belly?"

"Women!" Fergus snorted, casting an angry glance at Naisi. "Always seeing the gnats instead of the sky."

"What matters most?" Deirdre insisted. "You cannot have them both. The feast or the sons of Usnech? Which will you forsake?"

At that moment, the sons of Fergus entered the hall, and his eye fell upon them. He grinned. "Ah, here is the answer to the conundrum! I'll forsake neither. My sons—Iollan and Buinne—will travel on my word to Emain Macha with you. 'Tis as good as if I myself went, for they are as bound to me as I am to my word."

"No," Naisi said. He pushed the platter aside and stood. He looked down at Fergus and Borach, a dark cloud crossing his face. "No, 'tis not the same. But then, the sons of Usnech are used to caring for themselves. Your word gave us great comfort, Fergus, for up to then, no one had cared for us but ourselves."

"But—but—" Fergus sputtered, but Naisi ignored him and turned sharply on his heel and left with Deirdre beside him and Ainlé and Ardan hard upon his heels.

"Go after them!" Fergus bellowed as his sons looked at him for their cues. "And remember that you are my word! You speak for me!" he shouted angrily as they scurried after the sons of Usnech. He looked blackly at Borach. "And nothing had better happen to them because of this feast," he said. "Or there won't be a stick or stone of your fine home left standing."

And Borach felt the cold gathering in his stomach and wondered if he had not made a mistake by agreeing to Conchobor's plan.

"Ah, now," he said hastily. "Sure and nothing will be happening to those fine boys. Why, would not all of Ireland rise up against the Red Branch if Conchobor should break his word? And is not his word as strong as yours? After all, he is your king."

"Aye," Fergus said, "and his mother my wife. But I was king before him, and it isn't his word that was given to the sons of Usnech, but mine. A man may not sit on a throne to be a king. And there is no jewel as rare as a man's word. You'd do well to remember that, Borach, before you find your house pulled down around your ears."

And again, Borach felt the cold rush over him as if a fairy child had lightly touched his brow with the cold hand of the Otherworld.

xii.

KNOWING THAT THEIR LIVES WERE as worthless as a boar's bristle, Naisi grimly pushed his little company along the shortest back roads he could remember toward Emain Macha. Wearily, the tiny band wallowed through the mud in his wake. At last, Deirdre tugged at her husband's arm until he stopped and stared down at her.

"What is it?" he asked impatiently.

She wiped the rain from her fine forehead with the edge of her cloak. "I have a bit of advice for you, my husband, though I doubt if you will follow it."

A grim smile touched Naisi's lips. "At the moment, a bit of advice might be welcome. What is it?"

"Do what your brother suggested," she said bluntly. "Let us go to the Isle of Rechrainn and wait there until Fergus finishes feasting.

Then we would have the strength of his good sword arm to help us if we should need it."

Naisi pursed his lips and shook his head. He smiled sadly. "Ah. So. You do not have faith any more in our ability to protect you?"

"Don't be using that childish argument with me," she said brusquely. She placed her palm flat against his chest. "I have seen your sword arm—and your brothers'—swing often enough in battle to know your strength. But your strength is not the strength of the Red Branch. If Conchobor's words are as good as chaff in the wind, then all of your strength together is not enough to hold off those warriors."

"We also have the strength of Fergus's word," Naisi said, reminding her gently. She snorted and looked away into the slanting rain.

"But not his sword arm to back it up," she said. "Words are like air. Once spoken, they disappear." She shook her head.

> "It was a day of sorrow for us
> When your friend, mighty Fergus
> Gave us his word that we would
> Be safe back in Emain Macha should
> We decide to return to its green
> Hills and lakes with a mirror sheen.
> And it was yet another sorrow
> When he chose the feast. Oh, woe!
> And it was yet a third sorrow
> When we came on the borrowed
> Word of Fergus with his sons
> To return to Emain Macha's dun."

Naisi clasped his strong arms around her, holding her close to his beating heart.

> "Deirdre, more beautiful than the sun,
> Do not worry about what has been done.
> I do not think that our mighty Fergus
> Came all the way eastward to destroy us!"

And Deirdre leaned her head back to look at him with loving eyes. Tears trickled down her ivory cheek to merge with her rain-soaked cloak.

> "Oh, surely this is my grief! I have lost
> What we fought to gain. We are dust!
> And the beautiful Usnech's sons
> Will soon lose sight of the sun!
> This is my everlasting sorrow
> For soon we will be in our barrows
> With cold earth raised above us
> And all because of the word of Fergus!"

Naisi gently pushed her away from him. "Enough of this," he said. "We will soon be in Emain Macha, and not even Conchobor will be so arrogant to think that he is stronger than the gods to ignore the laws of hospitality."

"But—"

He placed his finger on her lips. "Sh. Enough has been said. There will be no more talk on it. We will be in Emain Macha tomorrow."

They plowed grimly through the rain that slanted down hard against them, often blinding them with a lead-gray sheet. At last, they came to the watchtower on Slieve Fuad. Naisi found lodging for them in the valley, and they fell into an exhausted sleep.

Suddenly, though, Deirdre screamed and awoke, her eyes wild and staring into the dark. Naisi rose immediately and held her close, wrapping his cloak around them to cocoon them against the terrors of the night that Deirdre had seen.

"What is it?" he asked gently to soothe her.

> "Fair-Haired Iollan stood without his head
> And Red-Haired Buinne still wearing his head.
> And although you cried for help, Buinne the Red
> Did not help you! Only Iollan, the Fair-Haired.
> But I saw that of all my four companions, none

Still wore his head. The evil work was done.
Only Buinne lived through the blood-drenched
Night. Conchobor's evil destroyed the Red Branch!
I saw this in a great cloud of blood high above
The willow stand. And from this I can only say
That our time in Ulster is now measured by day
And not by months or years. I tell you now that
We must go to Dun Dealgan and Cúchulainn. That
Is where you will be safe until Fergus is done. That
Is the only place where Conchobor will not dare
To harm us. Remember: his words are only air!
And, O Naisi! Look! The blood-cloud still stands
High above green Emain Macha. The fair land
Is covered with your blood. Do not spend the night
In that house or otherwise you will lose your sight!"

Naisi brushed her hair back from her head and said, "No. That
we will not to do. That would bring dishonor upon us and show our
distrust of Conchobor when he has extended the hand of welcome
to us."

Deirdre remained silent for a long while in his arms, and he
thought she had gone back to sleep. But then she spoke, saying, "I will
give you this last warning, a sign by which you will know if there is
treachery afoot in the Red Branch or if Conchobor has indeed for-
given us."

"What is that?" Naisi asked.

"If Conchobor receives you in his own house with the other nobles
present, then there is no evil in his heart and no plan to kill you. *But,*"
she said emphatically, "if he has you led to the House of the Red
Branch, then he still plans treachery."

"All right," Naisi said soothingly. "That I will accept, for it
would only be appropriate for us to be received in his own house. No
man wishes to bring blood down upon his own house. But in the
Great Hall—" He shook his head. "No, I don't think that would be
right, either, now that I think about it, Deirdre. For if he does

treachery there, then that brings dishonor upon all who are in the hall."

Deirdre remained silent and slowly passed her arms around Naisi, clinging tightly to him. But there was no warmth in her arms, and Naisi shivered, feeling as if the cold arms of Death had just caressed him.

xiii.

HEAVY RAIN STILL FELL THE next day when the small, bedraggled company finally reached the hill-fort of Emain Macha. Naisi took the hand-carved knocker in hand and banged hard on the door.

"Who knocks there?" a heavy voice growled.

"Sure, and if you had your eyes open on the walkway instead of shrinking in the doorway like a mongrel, you'd be knowing who it is," Naisi replied. " 'Tis the sons of Usnech and Deirdre who have come by the bidding of your king, Conchobor, with the safeguard of Fergus in his two sons."

The door cracked open and a scowling face exposed itself. Then the door was swung wide, and the watchman bade them enter.

"Conchobor has been waiting for you," he growled. He hawked and spat disgustedly. "Why you chose to come in this foul weather is anyone's guess. Only ducks and pigs should be out in it! No offense," he added hastily.

"None taken," Naisi replied. "Would himself be waiting for us in his house?"

"No, in the Great Hall," the watchman replied.

"Is it still fit for food and drink?" Ardan asked from behind Naisi's shoulder.

" 'Tis enough for seven armies, I'm thinking," the watchman said. "I'm to take you there, if you arrived on my watch."

He turned and started across the compound. Deirdre placed her hand on Naisi's arm, staying him.

" 'Twould be better if you had listened to me and never come to this place. Had you forgotten that I was raised in the woods?"

"Too late now," Iollan said. "If we turn and leave, we'll bear the mark of the coward upon us. And it would be a grave insult to Conchobor to request his hospitality and then refuse it. That would be enough for him to send the Red Branch after us again, I'm thinking."

"There's that," Ainlé said. He shivered. "By Donn's balls! I'm cold and wet and hungry and thirsty! There are four reasons why we should go forward. A warm fire and a tankard of ale is enough to risk for, if you ask me. It's been a long time since we tasted the good mead of the Red Branch!"

"Aye," Ardan said glumly. "Too long. But the lass has a point here. A good meal and a good drink is enough to bring anyone in out of the rain. But is it enough to risk one's head on the rafters of the Red Branch?"

Naisi stared at him sternly. "You must remember the laws of hospitality," he said.

"I remember them," Ardan said. "But I remember Deirdre's words, too. The *Sídhe* don't give dreams to just anyone, and it's wrong to dismiss them so lightly. And I wonder why Conchobor would be receiving us in the Great Hall instead of his own home. 'Twould have been the right thing to do, you know."

"I know," Naisi said quietly. "But we are home now. And there are others here, too, who were our friends. I'm thinking he'd not be asking them to choose sides."

"Aye, there's that," Iollan replied. "And remember: you have Fergus's bond on it and my own sword-arm as well as Buinne's." He sneezed. "Enough of this gobbing about in the rain. We're here. Let's go in and see where the lay lies."

They walked to the Great Hall and were met by the watchman, who had gone on before them. "Conchobor awaits you," he said. He nodded at Deirdre. "But he says that the woman is to be taken to the guest house of the Red Branch, where she may be bathed and dressed in warm clothes."

"I do not like this," Ardan said lowly to Naisi. "Something smells fishy here, and it isn't Ainle's feet!"

"Stow it!" Ainlé growled. He shook his head. "But Ardan's right; there's mischief afoot here, I'm thinking."

"Watch yourselves," Naisi said softly. Then louder: "We accept Conchobor's kind offer. My wife could do with a rest."

"Naisi—" she began, but he interrupted.

"It will be all right," he said softly. "If treachery's planned, it won't take place in the daylight."

"Night is not far off," she said softly, but then allowed herself to be led away to the guest house by the watchman.

The sons of Usnech entered the Great Hall of the Red Branch, pausing to shake the water from their cloaks. Silence greeted them, and they stood for a moment, feeling the hardness of the silence wash over them. Then Conchobor rose and gestured, saying, "It's been a long time, sons of Usnech! The Red Branch has been the poorer for your absence."

"Aye, and whose fault was that?" Ainlé murmured. Naisi shot him a warning look.

"It is good to be home again, Conchobor," Naisi said. He looked around the room. "I see all is well here."

"As well as can be expected," Conchobor answered. "Come! Take seats! We are waiting on Éogan, son of Durthach, the king of Fernmag to come and make peace with us."

"I wasn't aware that Éogan had not been at peace with the Red Branch," Naisi said mildly. "When did all of this happen?"

"Ah, while you were gone, lad! While you were gone!" Conchobor said. "But we have made meat and drink available to you! Come and enjoy yourselves while we tend to this peacemaking!"

Naisi glanced around at the still faces of the other warriors. "We welcome a bite and a bit to drink," he said, "but we are cold and wet and are not fit to stay in this company. Let us go and wash and bathe and rest while you tend to this business with Éogan. Then we will be better company."

"As you wish." Conchobor shrugged. "I shall send serving wenches to you with clean clothes and food and drink. And here," he said, picking up a *fidchell* board and gaming pieces, "is something to while the time until all are ready."

Silently, Naisi took the gleaming gaming board and left with Ardan and Ainlé with him. Iollan went, too, but Buinne remained behind, speaking as he was to Maine, a son of Conchobor, and Fiachna, the son of Fedelm, Conchobor's daughter.

After the sons of Usnech left, Conchobor stared at the door, the blood slowly rising in his face. He took a goblet of wine and drank it down, holding it out to a passing serving wench to refill. He glanced at her, noticing her beauty, and sighed.

"Ah, what does she look like?" he muttered to himself. "Deirdre, Deirdre! Do you remain youthful and beautiful, or has your hard life in Alba turned your beauty to a hag?" He sipped from the goblet, then pressed his lips together as the anger continued to rise within him. "I must know! I must know if she is still as beautiful as she was and if she is, why, then, I shall bring her out on the edge and point of my sword!" He glanced around the room and saw Deirdre's old nurse silently supervising the serving wenches at the far end of the Great Hall. He called her to him.

"Go to the guest house," he said softly, "and see to your Deirdre. Then come and tell me if her beauty has remained unchanged."

Leborcham looked into Conchobor's eyes and read the darkness there. Her heart sank, but she took herself away to the guest house. She entered and saw Naisi and Deirdre sitting on pillows, the gaming board between them. Deirdre looked up at her, and Leborcham broke into tears.

"Deirdre! Deirdre!" she cried, and held out her arms. The young woman stood and rushed into them, embracing the old woman. She glanced over at Naisi, still seated, watching. "You would do better to be looking to your weapons," she said over Deirdre's shoulder. "Conchobor sent me here to see if Deirdre still has her beauty. I think he means to take her." She looked at Deirdre and broke into tears. "I fear the three bright candles of Ulster will be extinguished tonight."

> "Much darkness will come upon the land
> Thanks to Conchobor's plotting against this band.
> Any of these noble three sons of Usnech could
> Wear the golden crown of Ulster and should

Given Conchobor's treachery. I can see
Ulster fall because of Conchobor's jealousy!"

Deirdre pulled away as Naisi stood and rushed to gather his sword
and alert his brothers and Ioillan and Buinne, who had just returned
from the Great Hall.

"I saw this in a vision," she said bitterly to Leborcham. "But the
others would not believe me. Three times I had a vision, and three
times they refused to believe me."

Leborcham put her fingers to Deirdre's lips, hushing her. "I will go
back and tell Conchobor that life has turned you to a crone and that you
are no longer the beauty that he knew. That will buy you some time.
However, I do not know what you will be able to do with it." She
looked at the sons of Fergus. "Do your father's bidding. Bar the windows and door, and do not unlock them until Fergus returns. Then—
and only then—will you be saved."

She left the guest house and returned to the Great Hall. She told
Conchobor that the great beauty of Deirdre had faded, but that the sons
of Usnech were strong. Now that they had returned to Emain Macha,
Conchobor would surely rule all of Ireland.

"The great beauty of Deirdre has gone.
But the sons of Usnech now belong.
Once again to the Red Branch. This will bring
You to the throne of Ireland as High King."

And Conchobor took great heart at this and called loudly for food
and drink to be passed among all in the Great Hall. But while he was
drinking and laughing with the others, the thought nagged at him
again, and he wondered if the old woman had indeed told him the
truth. At last, he looked around for a man to send, and his eye fell upon
Gelban. He called the man to him.

"Go to the guest house and see if Deirdre is the same now as she
once was. If she is still as beautiful, no other woman on the ridge of the
world or the rollers of the sea will be able to stand beside her."

Gelban went to the guest house, but he found it barricaded to him and the windows barred. He circled the house and found that one window had been left open. He pulled himself up and found himself staring at the great beauty of Deirdre, who had stripped naked and was dressing herself in warm clothes. His eye fell upon her alabaster breasts tipped with ripe plums, her narrow waist, the golden-red triangle between her legs, slim columns of Parian marble. He gasped and she whirled, saw him staring at her, and blushed scarlet as she seized a cloak to wrap around her.

"Naisi!" she cried, and her husband rushed in, holding a *fidchell* piece in his hand. He saw Gelban ogling Deirdre from the window and threw the piece at him, striking him in the eye. The jelly burst.

"Ahh!" Gelban screamed, and dropped down from the window, cupping his hand around his eye. Blood trickled down the back of his hand as he staggered back to the Great Hall.

Conchobor saw him enter and said, "What is this, One-Eye? You leave happy and merry and return in great pain!"

"I have lost one eye, but I would give the other as well if the great beauty I saw were mine," Gelban moaned.

A red rage of jealousy filled Conchobor. He leaped to his feet, roaring, "The sons of Usnech have insulted our hospitality! To arms!"

The men paused in their merriment to stare in astonishment at him. He glared back.

"Are you deaf, men? To the guest house! Seize the sons of Usnech and bring them here!"

"I don't like this," Fiachna whispered to Maine. "How could the sons of Usnech dishonor Conchobor's hospitality? They're still in the guest house, where he sent them!"

Maine belched and reached for his sword. "Are you forgetting that he's your grandfather and my father? 'Tis all we need to know. Besides, I never have liked that smirking Ardan. Let's have a bit of fun with them!"

And so the men of Ulster, who had been drinking heavily with their king, drew their weapons and surrounded the guest house, crying to the sons of Usnech to come out.

"What's this?" Buinne shouted when he heard the battle-cries.

"It is Conchobor," Deirdre said. "A great sorrow has fallen upon us. The king has broken his word!"

"By Donn's balls!" Buinne swore, seizing his sword. "I will stand my father's words!"

He threw open the door and rushed out upon the men, slashing and cutting with his sword until a full three-fifths of the fighting men lay dead or bleeding from the hurts he had savaged upon them.

When Conchobor saw his men reeling away, he cried, "Who does this slaughter among the Red Branch?"

"I do—Buinne the Red!" Buinne roared in answer.

Conchobor came forward to meet the bristling youth. "If you will lay down your sword, I will give you a great gift," he said.

"What gift?" Buinne scoffed.

"A full hundred land and my own friendship," answered Conchobor.

Buinne thought a minute, then laid down his arms, deserting the sons of Usnech. The mountain that Conchobor gave him for this treachery had been green and fertile; but from that moment on, it turned barren with shame and refused to bear. To this day, it is called "Buinne's Shame."

When Deirdre heard the exchange between Buinne and Conchobor, she wailed, "Alas! Buinne has become like his father!"

Iollan became angry when he heard her words. "This is one son who won't!" he cried. He turned to Naisi and his brothers. "Come! Let's take the fight to them!"

They rushed out of the house and began the great slaughter upon the Red Branch warriors. By this time, however, Éogan had arrived with his men and was watching the fighting. Conchobor saw him and approached him, saying, "If you truly wish to make peace with the Red Branch, kill the sons of Usnech for me!"

Éogan sent his men into battle and, seizing his spear, watched for an opening and, when it came, rushed in, stabbing Naisi in the back so that great warrior's spine snapped like a frosted oak branch. Naisi gave a great cry and fell to the ground. When Iollan saw this, he threw himself upon Naisi to save him, but Éogan drove his spear through the body of Iollan and Naisi, impaling them both.

Yet Ardan and Ainlé continued fighting. When Conchobor saw this, he called Fiachna to him and gave him his own great shield,

Ochain, that roared whenever its bearer was in danger, two spears, and his great sword, Gormglas the Blue-Green. "Go and finish the fight!" he ordered.

Fiachna went into battle against Ardan, but Ardan was too strong for the youth and soon pinned him beneath the great shield which roared its warning and the three great waves, the Wave of Tuagh, the Wave of Rudraige, and the Wave of Cliodna, roared in answer. Conall Cernach, who had not joined the others in the battle at the guest house, heard Ochain's roar and, thinking his king was in danger, rushed into battle and slew Ardan. Then, understanding what had happened, he swung his mighty sword and cut off Fiachna's head, then left the battle, searching for Fergus Mac Roich to tell him what had happened at Emain Macha.

Ainle continued to fight, and his slashing sword sent three-fifths of the remaining warriors to the blood-drenched ground until at last, Maine seized Naisi's sword that had been given to him by Manannán, the son of Lir, and struck his head from its shoulders from behind.

Deirdre was seized and brought before Conchobor, who stared at the great beauty with lust. But Deirdre gave him only loathing in return, and he turned away from her and ordered that she be taken to his sleeping quarters.

Thus ended the Battle of the Guest House, when Conchobor broke the laws of hospitality and brought great troubles down upon the Red Branch.

xiv.

ONLY CONALL CERNACH AMONG THE seasoned warriors of the Red Branch took part in that battle, the rest having kept away from it because they were sent out to patrol Emain Macha's borders on the day before the sons of Usnech came to the hill-fort. But when they heard the story of the great battle, they rushed back to Emain Macha.

As they neared the fort, they came upon Fergus Mac Roich, coming from his ale-feast.

"What's this?" Dubtach asked, seeing Fergus. "Why are you not with the sons of Usnech?"

"That bastard Borach held a feast for me. You know my *geis,*" Fergus said. He rubbed his pounding temples and bloodshot eyes. "Aye, it was a noble feast even if the beer was a bit sour. After a while, you cannot taste it anyway, so that matters little—. What's wrong?" he asked, noting the grim faces of the Ulster heroes for the first time.

"Conchobor killed the sons of Usnech and took Deirdre for his bride," Cormac said. "And you sacrificed them so you could have a drunk!"

"My *geis*—" Fegus mumbled.

"—should have been accepted before you surrendered your honor," Cormac finished for him. "Now the Red Branch has brought dishonor upon itself by slaying the noble sons of Usnech to satisfy Conchobor's lust. All Ulster will suffer for this." He gave Fergus a disdainful look that straightened the warrior's back. "This isn't the first time you surrendered your honor, though, is it, Fergus? Wasn't it for Nessa's firm thighs and bouncing breasts that you gave up the throne for a year and lost it forever?"[59]

Fergus roared in fury at this, then calmed down and stared at Cormac and Dubthach.

"We will wait until after the sons of Usnech are buried," he said. "Then we shall reward Conchobor for his treachery."

He took the others with him to Dun Dealgan, where he told Cúchulainn what had happened. Then the Hound of Ulster went up into the hills to mourn the sad affair that had fallen upon the Red Branch.

XV.

FERGUS WAITED UNTIL NIGHT HAD fallen the day the Red Branch buried the sons of Usnech. A sad state of affairs it was, too, for by this time, the warriors of the Red Branch had recovered from the drunkenness and saw in the clear light of day the treachery that they had done.

As they dug the graves, Deirdre lay beside the grave of Naisi, and when they forced her to one side, she said:

> "The lions of Ireland are gone
> But my sorrows will not be long.
> Dig the grave deep and wide
> For 'tis two who will soon be inside.

> "The woodland falcons are flown
> And I am left here all alone.
> Dig the grave deep and wide
> For 'tis two who will soon be inside.

> "Three dragons will sleep beneath this rock
> And deep within my heart I have locked
> My tears. Dig deep that grave, then
> Place inside it three grave men.

> "Lay their spears and bright shields
> Beside them. No, I will not yield
> My place here. You see, these three
> Men used their shields to protect me.

> "Ah, 'tis done. Now, upon the floor
> Of the grave, lay their blades. More
> Valiant men cannot be found here
> And their deaths will soon be dear.

"Place them gently in the grave you
Dug. Gently, I say! There is nothing you
Can do to them now. They are dust
Who once honored Conchobor's trust.

"Gone now are the falcons. Never again
Will they fly above the trees and plain
Of Ulster. Sweet friends, I will never
Again hear your voices singing. Never!

"The sons of Usnech have no breath.
Their lives have been claimed by Death.
But the dishonor is not theirs nor mine.
This I know: Our love knows not time.

"This land is cursed and never will peace
Come to its blood-soaked grass. Cease
Your boasts, warriors! You are all wrong
Who took Conchobor's side to make him strong.

"Emain Macha will be forever cursed
And for Red Branch blood men will thirst
Until the stars fall from the night sky
And fall to the earth like ashes to die.

" 'Tis upon the heads of Clan Conchobor
I pronounce ten curses against its honor.
May his name be forever edged in black
And may the Red Branch honor be attacked.

"Dig the grave wide—do not make it narrow
For soon it will become two bodies' barrow.
I choose Naisi's arms in death
To Conchobor's arms in stealth."

All there had shivered at Deirdre's lament, and filled the graves in
hurriedly. Then they returned to the Great Hall of the Red Branch

while Conchobor took the listless Deirdre to his sleeping quarters.

Night fell, and Fergus led his men swiftly across the grassy plain. Silently they made their way inside the hall, slaying the watchmen near the towers. Then Fergus raised his battle-cry, roaring defiance against the warriors of the Red Branch and Conchobor. He seized a brand from a nearby fire and threw it high upon the roof.

"Conchobor! You milksop warrior! Come out!" he roared.

The warriors tumbled out of the burning hall and met with Fergus's whirring sword, the great *In Caladbolg,* the sword of light that became as big as a rainbow in the heavens when it struck. And now its song sang sharp and clear over the heads of the Ulster warriors. Beside him stood Dubthach and Cormac, and when the Red Branch warriors charged them, Dubthach spitted Maine and Fiachna upon his great black spear that he had steeped ten times in a cauldron of blood. Fergus split Traigtren the son of Traigletha and his brother like a butcher a pig. Before they were finished, blood covered Cormac like a winding sheet.

And then, with the bloodlust full upon him, Dubthach slew the maidens of Ulster, a full three hundred, until Fergus and Cormac could pull him away.

And this deed brought the great split in the House of the Red Branch. Three thousand warriors were with Fergus that night, and all escaped with their lives to follow him to Connacht, where Maeve and Ailill made them welcome.

And for sixteen years, the Exiles showed no love to the Ulstermen who remained behind, mounting raid after raid into Ulster lands until men grew to hate the night and women's wails became commonplace.

XVi.

FOR A YEAR AFTER NAISI'S death, Deirdre was forced to share the bed of Conchobor, but there was no love in that bed, for Deirdre never smiled or let a slip of laughter escape her lips. She ate little food and slept little. Whenever the servants tried to force her to eat, she would say:

"Food cannot hold the sweetness that Naisi's lips
Held for me. Nevermore will that sweetness be sipped
By me. He lived with me in Alba and died heroically
In the land that he loved. Yet one betrayed him for me.

"I remember Naisi's strength in the fire beside our bed.
I remember Ardan's battle with an ox that he bled.
I remember Ainlé's strong back chopping wood.
I remember how tall before me all three stood.

"You ask me to eat this food you have prepared
But nothing can be as sweet as Naisi who dared
To bring me honey from the woods and fish
From the streams and sea. That was a tasty dish!

"I have heard the Red Branch pipes play loudly
But never like Naisi's singing voice so sweetly.
And together with Ardan's deep singing voice
And Ainlé's high voice, I had to make no choice.

"Now Naisi lies sleeping in his dark tomb
For he chose to believe in a king. Soon,
I will join my love and once again run
With him through the woods in the morning sun."

Soon, Conchobor's patience wore thin, and one day, he came upon her with her head upon her knee and pulled her to her feet. She stared at him with lifeless eyes. Her flesh seemed as juiceless as last year's apples.

"Tell me!" he said angrily. "Who do you hate the most?"

"You," she said. "And Éogan, the son of Dubthach, who betrayed trust for your good graces."

"I see," Conchobor said slowly. "And you will never be able to love me?"

"Never," she said.

"Then, I will take your hate," he said, and kissed her. But it was like kissing stone, and he pushed her from him saying brutally, "Éogan comes to Emain Macha tomorrow. I will give you to him for a year. Then you will come back to me for a year. And again to him. That way, your hate will grow strong and give you life."

The next day Éogan came to the Red Branch and, when Conchobor told him what he had decided, Éogan clapped his hands in delight.

"Ah, the fabled beauty in my bed!" He leered at her. "I'll show you a tumble or two and train you well for your new master's bed next year!"

Deirdre refused to answer him, and Éogan laughed mockingly. He turned to Conchobor. "I say let's take her to her lover's grave for one last look! And maybe we can play a game there, a ewe between two rams!"

Conchobor laughed darkly and ordered that Deirdre be bound and placed in his chariot. Taking the reins himself, he invited Éogan to join him. They raced off, with Deirdre tied between them.

"We'll soon have you howling for mercy, my pretty!" Éogan boasted.

At that moment, Conchobor drove his chariot along the edge of a cliff. Deirdre cast one look at each of the men, then cast herself out of the chariot, diving headfirst off the cliff, striking her head upon the rocks below.

Conchobor forebade her burial with Naisi; so, in the middle of the night, warriors moved her body secretly to the same burial place as Naisi's. The next year, two graceful yew trees arched up from the graves, stretched across, and entwined their limbs, becoming, with time, as one.

Notes

1. The famous *gae bulga* was a terrible and magical spear that only the truly gifted warrior could throw. It always found its mark despite dodging and turning of its victim. The spear was always fatal and released deadly barbs when it struck its victim. The meaning of the word is unclear, but it appears to be "forked spear" or "twofold spear" and "the spear of the goddess Bolg," which may associate it with the Fir Bolg.

THE FATE OF THE CHILDREN OF TUIRENN

1. *Rachad a haithle searc na laoch don chill*: I shall go after the heroes, ay, into the clay.

2. The Tuatha Dé Danann, "children of Danu," a Greek goddess, were primarily known as people of great learning, magicians, who reportedly came to Ireland after spending some time in Greece where they studied the arts and magic (P. W. Joyce). According to *Lebor Gebála,* they were quite learned in history, magic, Druidism, and cunning. They were peaceful most of the time but could fight whenever logic and reasoning failed—which it did with the Fir Bolg. Historians and scholars differ greatly on where the Fir Bolg came from. Their name suggests "trouser weavers" or "bag weavers," and historians generally take this to mean that they wore the equivalent of today's pants. This would make them members of the lower social strata. Cecil O'Rahilly suggests that the Fir Bolg of ancient Ireland were part of the tribe of the Belgae, one of the many tribes of Continental Celts. Other historians and scholars suggest that they were a member of the lower order in Greece who made bags to spread over the ground to sack grain. It appears that the Fir Bolg worshiped a god named Bulga or Bolga, a goddess of lightning, although some linguistics suggest "bolg" means "of leathern bags." The Fir Bolg brought five chieftains with them to Ireland—Gann, Genann, Rudraige, Sengann, and Slànge—who partitioned Ireland, establishing the provinces Ulster, Leinster, Connacht, and the two Munsters. This was roughly A.M. 3226 [Anno Mundi time is a continuous accounting]. A.D. is equivalent to the year A.M. 5198. (1972 B.C). The Fir Bolg ruled for thirty-seven years before the great battle of Mag Tuired in Conmaicne, Connacht near Lough Arrow in County Mayo Sligo (sometimes given as the Battle of Moytura near Cong in Country Mayo) when the Tuatha defeated the Fir Bolg by killing 1,100 of them. The survivors fled to Rathlin

and the Aran Islands. They eventually come under the rule of Ailill and Maeve, and are eventually crushed in a series of battles between Connacht and Ulster.

The Tuatha allegedly came from four Grecian cities, where they learned their arts: Falias, Gorias, Murias, and Findias, bringing with them an article of greatness from each city. From Falias they brought the stone of Fal (*Lia Fail*) which was set up on Tara and screamed when the rightful king was crowned. From Gorias came the spear of Lugh, from Findias came the sword of Nuada, and from Murias came the cauldron of The Dagda, which allowed no one to leave hungry.

3. Nuada was the king of the Tuatha at this time. He was the son of Echtach, the son of Etarlam, the son of Ordan, the son of Ionnaoi.

4. Conn-sneachta: "Conn's snow," after which the province took its name "Connacht."

5. Sreng: A Fir Bolg warrior who was sent as an ambassador to the Tuatha Dé Danann. He met with Bres, who originally suggested that Ireland be divided between them. Sreng was very impressed with the weapons the Tuatha carried but rejected the offer. Consequently, the great battle of Mag Tuired was fought. One account of this battle has Sreng cutting off Nuanda's hand; another account has Sreng cutting Nuada's arm off at the shoulder. Either way, Nuada was provided with either a hand or arm of silver by the great physician/god Dian Cécht (Diancécht) who weaved an enchantment over it so that it functioned like a normal arm. Nuada was referred to after this as Nuada of the Silver Hand. But the silver arm was not entirely like a normal arm and, consequently, Nuada lost his kingship as only one who was whole could rule the Tuatha. In Connacht, people well into the seventeenth century claimed they could trace their lineage back to Sreng.

6. Oghma: the god of eloquence and literature, he was a son of Dagda. Among the Tuatha, he was the most skilled in dialects and poetry and exceptional as a warrior for he did not depend upon brute strength alone to win a battle. In some myths, he is credited with being the counterpart to Charon or Hermes as a conductor of souls to the Otherworld. He was sometimes called Oghma Grian-aineach (Oghma of the Sunny Face) or Oghma Cermait (Oghma of the Honeyed Words). He is credited with inventing the *Ogham* writing. Among his children were Étain, who married Diancécht. Oghma was the ruler of *Sídhe Airceltrai*.

7. Diancécht: also Dian Cécht. A mythicál physician in early Irish literature. His name apparently means "he who journeys swiftly," which could have been a pseudonym for the "god of healing" similar to Hermes in Greek mythology. He is also "an arbitrator on leeches," which would suggest that he settled arguments between other physicians. This would seem to have some association with "The Judgements of Dian Cécht" in the Brehon Laws (Eriu Vol. XX). He has been described as "the healing sage of Ireland" and as "going great roads of healing" in various Irish texts. He and his three brothers are mentioned significantly in the First Battle of Mag Tuired. In the Second Battle, however, he appears along with two sons (Miach and Omiach) and a daughter (Airmed). Together, they make a well (the Tioipra Sláine) into which they cast all the known herbs of healing. The wounded Tuatha Dé Danann are lowered into the well and healed when Diancécht and his family chant an incantation above them. It is he who makes the silver arm of Nuada when Nuada's arm is severed in the first battle. Since Nuada now has a blemish, he cannot serve as a king and must give up the throne to Bres. Diancécht's son, however, Miach, upstages his father by removing the silver arm and restoring Nuada's original arm. Jealous of Miach's skill, Diancécht kills Miach and buries him. Three hundred sixty-five herbs grow up from his grave, one for each part of the body. Airmed attempts to sort them, but they are mixed up by Diancécht and thus man loses his chance at immorality.

He is also connected with snakes, destroying those that have infested the heart of a son of the Mórrígan and killing a great serpent that threatens to destroy the countryside surrounding the river Barrow in south Leinster. This suggests a relationship to a dragon and may be the source for later stories in the Arthurian Cycle, where the Knights of the Round Table fight dragons. He is also credited with restoring the eye of Midir that is lost in an accident and with curing Tuirenn by making an emetic draught for him.

8. Argatlam: silver-arm.

9. Fomorians: dwellers under the sea or from across the sea. In legends, they are said to come from Lochlainn (Scandinavia) and may be the ancestors of the later Vikings. They were considered rude and crude giants who generally are seen as the evil gods within the Irish myth, perhaps the Giants of later Norse mythology who are seeking a way across the bridge Bifrost to defeat the pantheon of Norse gods in Ragnarok, the Norse Armageddon. The Formorians sometimes appeared with only a single foot, hand, or eye, but their power was great. They are generally associated with Tory Island off the Donegal coast (c. 2300 B.C.) They are traditionally seen as the lords of darkness and death while

the Tuatha Dé Danann are seen as the lords of life and light. It has also been suggested that the Fomorians were once associated with the worship of the moon and darkness in early Ireland, while the Tuatha were associated with the later worship of the earth and sun.

10. Elotha: the king of the Fomorians who had an affair with Ériu, the wife of Cethor (also called Mac Gréine). She gave birth to Bres, who was to become the king of the Tuathas in an attempt by the Tuathas to maintain peace in the land.

Ériu was a queen among the Tuatha Dé Danann and one of the daughters of Fiachna, a grandson of Oghma. Her sisters were Banba and Fódla. In the *Lebor Gabála* we read:

> Cethor, great and pleasant a fellow is he
> and Ériu, his wife, a generous woman is she.
> When the Mílesians attacked Ireland around A.M. 3500 (1698 B.C.)
> Ériu said to Amergin, their leader, that the attack was an unjust one.
> When Amergin said that the Mílesians still intended to rule the land,
> Ériu said, "Grant me one wish, then: let this land be named after me."
> And since Amergin was taken with her beauty, he agreed. The land
> became known as Ireland.

11. Balor's Hill: the hill where the Tuatha Dé Danann had to gather after the First Battle of Mag Tuired to pay taxes to the Fomorians. The hill was named after Balor Béimean (Balor of the Mighty Blows), who had one eye in the middle of his forehead and another at the back of his skull. The eye in the back of his skull was an evil eye that could with its "beams and rays of venom" strike people dead at a single glance. He kept this eye covered with his long hair unless he wished to destroy his enemies. In Irish, this is referred to as Súil Bhalair, Balor's Eye. A Druid told him that he would be killed by a grandson named Ó, so Balor had his daughter imprisoned in a tower on the top of Tor Mór on Tory Island off the coast of Donegal. A chieftain known as Mac Kineely had a cow known as the Glas Gaibleann. Balor stole the cow and Mac Kineely, with the help of a *leanán sídhe* (elf with magic) who dressed him in a woman's clothes, went over to the island from Port na Glaise (the port of the green cow). He found Balor's daughter, left her pregnant, and took his cow back to the mainland. He was captured by Balor and beheaded at Kineely—Cloch Chinn Fhaolaidh (Bloody Ground)—in County Donegal. His son avenged his father by thrusting a glowing rod from the smith's furnace into Balor's evil eye.

12. Hill of Usnech: at Ráthconrath in Company Westmeath. This allegedly was owned by the father of Naoise, Ainlé, and Ardan, who are featured in "The Exile of the Sons of Usnech," the oldest of the "Three Sorrows of Storytelling." Usnech was married to Ebhla, the daughter of the Druid Cathbad and Maga, a daughter of the love god Aengus Óg.

13. The laws of hospitality were very complicated and differed slightly from region to region. But basically, a host was required to give a traveler seeking shelter the best room and bed that he had in the house, the best food that he could afford, gifts, and even a woman for the night to serve him in whatever capacity the traveler wished. Failure to abide by this would be enough to bring a *mallacht* or curse upon his house. Even one's enemy was safe if he had requested shelter.

14. *Darb-dóel*: a black beetle like a cockchafer or cockroach that fastens upon a man or a woman and sucks the goodness and life out of him/her.

15. *A nimdibe colnide* appears to be related to *mo tholcholnide* ref. *carnalis sum* which I have chosen to translate as "sensuous." I wonder, in this instance, if the reference is almost Jungian in which man's vision of the perfect woman is described as she who is not only wife, but mother and whore.

16. This seems to indicate a Continental belief that there is a difference between commoners and royalty and that difference can always be ascertained. This is a familiar episode in several stories where a royal personage exchanges places with his *doppelgänger* for a variety of reasons. But the *doppelgänger* is always uncovered, suggesting that royalty has a special place with the gods. One of the most famous stories regarding the exchanging of places is Anthony Hope's *The Prisoner of Zenda*.

17. Airmed: also Airmid. She was the sister to Miach and Omiach and daughter of Diancécht, the god of medicine. She was equally skilled at healing as her brothers and father. When Miach proved to be a better physician than his father, he was slain and his body buried near Tara. From his grave grew healing herbs, one for each of the body's three hundred sixty-five parts. Airmed gathered the herbs, carefully sorting them upon her cloak. But Diancécht scattered the herbs, costing man his immortality. Airmed is also credited with helping her father establish the Well of Healing (the Tioipra Sláine at Lough Arrow), by which the Tuatha Dé Danann were healed during the Second Battle of Mag Tuired.

18. An *ioldánac* is similar to a jack-of-all-trades.

19. *Fidchell*: a game like chess.

20. Lugh Lamfada: Lugh of the Long Arm, who led his army from the fairy-mounds. He is one of the most important of the Irish pantheon. He was the son of Cian and Ethlinn, the daughter of Balor of the Evil Eye. He is associated with Lugus in Gaul and Lleu in Wales. He is the god of arts and crafts, similar to the Greek Apollo. His story parallels that of Oedipus, in that he was rescued from death when Balor tried to avoid a prophecy that he would be killed by his grandson. His foster-father was Manannán Mac Lir in most tales, although a few list his foster-father as Goibhniu, the god of the smiths. When he reached his maturity, Manannán bestowed upon him his wonderful mail coat whose wearer could not be killed above or below it; his breastplate that could not be pierced by any weapon; his sword, The Answerer, from whose wound no one ever recovered; and his horse, Enbarr of the Flowing Mane, a mare as swift and clear as the cold wind of spring and who could travel equally over land or sea. He fulfills the prophecy by killing Balor and becomes the ruler of the Tuatha Dé Danann when Nuada is killed. He is the father of Cúchulainn by the mortal woman Dechtíre. In *Táin Bó Cuailnge*, he fights beside Cúchulainn when his son needs help. According to legend, he is last seen in Ireland when he emerges from a magical mist to help Conn of the Hundred Battles (High King A.D. 177–212). He foretold Conn's reign and the number of children that he would have. When the old gods are driven underground, he ceased to become important and became a simple craftsman who was called Lugh-chromain ("crooked-back Lugh"). From this, we get our modern term, "leprechaun." The Feast of Lugnasa (Lughnassdh) was introduced by him to commemorate his foster mother, Tailtu. Lugnasa became one of the four major pre-Christian festivals. It was basically a celebration of the harvest. After the advent of Christianity, Lugnasa became Lammas. The Irish name for "August" (*Lúnasa*) comes from this feast.

21. Tír Tairnigiri: the Land of Promise. One of the many "land tales" (*Tír*) that give varying descriptions of heaven or paradise.

22. Manannán Mac Lir: the Irish god of the sea. He is the son of Lir, who ruled from Emain Ablach (Emain of the Apple Trees) in Tír Tairnigiri (Land of Promise). His wife was Fand, the Pearl of Beauty, who fell in love with Cúchulainn and had an affair with him. Manannán broke up the affair and shook his cloak between the two of them so that each would forget the

other. This is found in *Serglige Con Culainn* (*The Wasting Sickness of Cúchulainn*). When Manannán appeared to Fand in a magic mist, she recognized him, saying:

> "When Manannán the Great married me
> From his land beside the sea
> He found me to be a wife worthy
> Of his greatness. He gave me
> A bracelet of well-tested gold he
> Gave me as price for my blushes. . . ."

Manannán is also associated with birds, dogs, and pigs. His pigs are always alive the next day after being eaten in a feast the night before. He had a magical bag made from a crane's skin that contained all the treasures of the Tuatha Dé Danaan. Among these were his shirt and knife (or sword), the king of Lochlainn's helmet, a smith's hook, and the bones of Asal's swine. The bag comes from the story when Dealbaeth's daughter, Aífe, was turned into a crane by Luchra out of jealousy for a lover. Her skin was made into the bag.

At times, Manannán is seen as the overlord of the Tuatha and the one who distributed the *sídhe* to them. In other stories, he brings Cormac Mac Airt into the Otherworld, and establishes the Fled Goibnend, the feast which gives the Tuatha eternal life. He is the father of Mongán in a story that resembles the conception of Arthur by Uther upon Igraine. In this story, Manannán appears to Fachtna, the king of the Dál nAraidi who is getting the worst of it in a battle, and offers to help if Fachtna will allow Manannán to disguise himself in the shape of Fachtna and make love to Fachtna's wife. History tells us that a Mongán ruled Ulster in A.D. 625.

Manannán has a magical horse, Enbarr of the Flowing Mane (Enbarr = "water-foam") and he is referred to as "the rider of the sea." He also had a magic breastplate that could not be pierced by any weapon and a shirt of mail that kept its wearer from being harmed "above or below." He also had a powerful sword called *Fregartach* "The Answerer."

Manannán is associated with the Isle of Man (Emain Ablach=Land of the Apple Trees) which is sometimes associated with the Avalon of the Arthurian Romances and the source of the golden apples of Greek lore.

23. Balor: a champion and general, some say king, of the Fomorians. He is a god of death and the son of Buarainech. His wife was Cethlenn. He had an eye in the back of his head that he kept covered with his long hair. (*Súil Bhalair*) When he parted his hair and glared out with this eye, it would strike men dead (shades of Medusa). This eye had a ring in its lid, which took four men to lift.

Balor gained this eye when he went to watch his father's Druids as they mixed a magic brew. The fumes from this cauldron settled on his eye, giving it its venomous power. There are several other stories told about how this eye gained its power and several snippets in other legends about the damage done by this eye such as why rushes have black tips (scorched by a quick glance from this eye) and why the mountains of Muckish and Errigal are barren. (The vegetation burnt when Balor looked upon them.)

A Druid told him that his only daughter, Ethlinn, would bear a grandson who would be called Ó, who would kill him. Balor had his daughter locked up in a crystal tower on Tor Mór at the far end of Tory Island off the coast of Donegal to keep men away from her. A chieftain, Mac Kineely (or Mac Cinn Fhaolaid), owned a wonderful green cow named Glas Gaibleann that was the pride of his people because it had an inexhaustible supply of milk. Wherever this cow slept, the grass would become rich and nourishing (*LChodail an ghlas ghaibhneach ann*: the glass gaibhleann slept here). One day Mac Kineely brought the cow with him when he went to have some swords made by a smith. Somehow, Balor managed to steal the cow and take it to Tory Island at a place now called Port na Glaise ("green cow port"). A Druid told Mac Kineely that he would not be able to recover the cow until after Balor was killed. Ignoring the warning, Mac Kineely consulted a *leanán Síde* (friendly fairy) and the fairy dressed Mac Kineely as a woman. He then crossed over to Port na Glaise, went to Balor's daughter, and left her pregnant. He returned to the mainland after trying to recapture the cow. Balor captured him and beheaded him at Cloch Chinn Fhaolaidh (Bloody Land), County Donegeal. According to this story, Ó later avenged his father's death by thrusting a glowing rod into Balor's eye in the back of his head (a story familiar to Odysseus and Polyphemus).

A variant on this story is that Balor stole the cow and its calf from Goibhniu, the smith-god, and drove it down into Leinster. But when they reached the coast near Dublin, the cow and her calf balked. When Balor lifted his eye to see what was causing them to hesitate, he accidentally turned them into stone which became the two Rockabill islands off Skerries. In Cong, the rocks there are said to have been men who had been petrified by a glance from Balor.

In *Iuchair and Iucharba,* Lugh is the one who kills Balor, but Lugh also is a grandson of Balor who was responsible for the death of Lugh's father, Cian. According to the story of Lugh's birth, Cian heard about Ethlinn's beauty and, with the help of Birog, a Druidess, managed to reach Ethlinn and slept with her. When Balor discovered that she had given birth to a boy, he cast the boy into the sea to be drowned. Birog saved the boy and he was fostered by Manannán Mac Lir (or, in other versions, Goibhniu). At the Second Battle of Magh Tuireadh, after Balor slew Nuada and Macha, Lugh took a *tathlum* (magic stone) and when

Balor's evil eye looked down, threw it into the eye, knocking it out of its socket. When it rolled onto the ground, it killed twenty-eight Fomorian warriors that its sight fell upon.

Balor is associated with sun-worshiping, as represented by a single eye. As such, he once threatened to burn Ireland unless he was granted special privileges and honors. As a giant, he is associated or compared to the Welsh god Ysbaddaden. T. F. O'Rahilly suggests that Balor the sun god and Goibniu the smith god are the same and in the primitive myth the hero, as represented by Lugh, Cúchulainn, or Finn, kills the evil god represented by Balor, Culann's hound, and Aed with the latter's own weapon which is sometimes represented by a lightning bolt. Both Lugh and Ó are sons of Eithliu, although they have different fathers. I would suggest here that the stories are similar in texture as Lugh is associated with the son as is Ó, whose very name suggests the "circle of the sun" and could be the older version of the story due to the simplicity of his name. We have, therefore, a struggle between three godly figures for control of the "light" or, given the similarity between the stories of Lugh and Ó, the struggle between an old god (Balor), symbolizing the primitive sacrifice needed by mortals to insure the continuance of light in a world where darkness is feared and the new and younger god (Lugh or Ó, who would suggest the "coming to the light" where human sacrifice is no longer needed to ensure the continuance of light in the world. Lugh or Ó would, therefore represent "knowledge." If we carry this a bit further, I would suggest that Ó, whose name represents the twelfth letter in the Irish alphabet (or thirteenth in the Modern Irish alphabet) and the second in the *Ogham* vowel group and known as *omn* or "furze" (ash), represents the acceptance of nature in place of the human sacrifice. "Lugh" could be a natural step further through the celebration of the harvest, but I would suggest that it might be the result of a slippage from the dipthong *ua* (grandson) to *lóg* (value) to *lúg* or Lúgh (most valued?). For further study, I would suggest that the entries for Ó, in *Foclóir Gaedilge Agus Béarla* by Patrick S. Dinneen, M.A. and *Dictionary of the Irish Language, Based Mainly on Old and Middle Irish Materials* by the Royal Irish Academy be consulted.

The story in which Lugh slays Balor with a magical stone seems to parallel the story of David and Goliath and may have been made a part of a recension shortly after Christianity came to Ireland.

24. Il-Dana: the Man of Many Sciences; this was a signalment for Lugh due to his many accomplishments.

25. Nét: associated with fear; I have also found the name written as "Neât"

and believe that this is the god associated with rampant fear as of the unknown. As Balor is sometimes referred to as a grandson of Nét, Eab could be Balor's brother or stepbrother.

26. Donn: the god of death in the Irish pantheon.

27. Lochlann: the Gaelic designation of the country from which the Danes came. Traditionally, this is seen as the country around the Baltic including the southernmost section of Sweden. In Gaelic stories, Berva is always the capital, but its exact location cannot be pinpointed. It might be a real name or an allusion by the ancient storytellers.

28. Frankincense: an aromatic gum used for burning as incense and in the preparation of pharmaceuticals. It is also used for fumigating. When it was beaten into a fine powder and added to white wine, it supposedly helped the memory and settle the stomach. As a paste and applied to wounds, it supposedly would hasten healing.

29. Myrrh: used as incense. As a gum from the myrrh tree, it was used as an antiseptic, astringent, carminative, and stomachic. Myrrh was used as a gargle and mouthwash for sores in the mouth and throat, asthma, and most valuable for cleaning wounds and sores. As a powder, it was sprinkled liberally over open sores and wounds before binding them.

30. Es Dara: literally "second waterfall" which could suggest several places along the west coast of Ireland. I suspect, however, that it is a reference to a place where a fast-flowing river empties into the sea. Although this would seem to suggest Ballysodare in County Sligo, I suspect that it is probably farther south, perhaps in Galway Bay.

31. The Dagda: the father of the Irish pantheon of gods. His name signifies "the good god." He is also called Eochaidh Ollathair (the All-Father), Aedh (Fire), and Ruad Rofessa (Lord of Great Knowledge). Druids regard him as their patron and some sects regard him also as Cernunnos. Usually, he is seen as a man in peasant clothing, carrying a huge club or else dragging it on wheels. One end of the club is deadly while the other end of the club has the gift of life. His cauldron is one of the many treasures of the Tuatha that was brought with them from Murias. No man ever leaves hungry from it. He has a magic harp that was stolen once by the Fomorians, but he recovered it with the help of Ogma Ad Lugh. His black horse is named Acéin (Ocean).

After the Tuatha were defeated, The Dagda allotted spiritual Ireland to his children, the land under the ground, by giving a *sídhe* to each. Only Aengus, the love god, was denied a *sídhe* because The Dagda wanted Brugh Na Boinne for himself, but Aengus tricked The Dagda and got that palace for himself. After the Tuatha departed for their underground world and before they were transformed into fairies, The Dagda retired as their leader and his son, Bodb Dearg, was elected in his place. Manannán Mac Lir refused to accept Bodb Dearg and left, returning to the sea. Midir the Proud also refused to accept Bodb Dearg and began a war against the Tuatha in an attempt to reclaim the throne. The Fianna fought on his side. The Dagda remained separate from all of this, however, and never again took part in any of the affairs of Ireland.

32. Tara: the traditional seat of the *Ard Ri* (High King) in Meath.

33. This is the contradiction that I mentioned in the introduction.

34. Cian: the father of Lugh, who appears to have also been a lesser solar deity. His patronage is uncertain, one tale claiming he was the son of Diancécht, the god of medicine, while another claimed him to be the son of Cainte. His brothers were Cu (The Hound) and Ceithen.

35. Muirthemne: Moy Muirthemne, the great plain in county Louth from which Cúchulainn came and later governed.

36. This would have been a sort of grim humor. The word *"cainte"* means "dog" and suggests the irony of Cian's death: separated from the pigs by hounds.

37. This is a solemn oath, indeed, and one of the most severe. The gods that Brian refers to here are probably Donn, the god of Death; and Scathach, the Underworld goddess; and the Mórrígná, the triple goddess of the battlefield.

38. Éric: a blood fine; the payment that a man would have to make to the victim's family, depending upon the rank of the man who was slain. For example, the old laws said that for a ". . . death main, a great cow shall be paid to the victim's family every night for nine nights." But this was changed in regard to the individual's social standing.

39. Cernunnos: the "horned god" and guardian of animals and the

Wildworld. Otherworld travelers who encounter him are initiated into the secrets of nature. He is the threshold guardian of great cosmic power. He is also the god of the Underworld. The Druids referred to him as Hu Gadarn. He is usually seen sitting in a lotus position with horns or antlers on his head, long curling hair, a beard, naked except for a neck torque. Sometimes he holds a shield and spear, other times a horned serpent. His symbols are the stag, ram, and bull. He is the god of virility, fertility, animals, physical love, nature, woodlands, reincarnation, crossroads, wealth, commerce, and warriors.

40. The ancient laws of hospitality called for Bres to speak first in greeting as he was, at this point, technically the host.

41. There is a bit of curiosity about Lugh's shield here, as the term "chafer-marked" could be taken to mean "marked in many different ways." This would seem to suggest that Lugh's shield might be a parallel to the shield of Achilles that Thetis Silverheels brought back from Olympus where she went at the behest of Achilles to get him new armor from the gods after Hector, the Trojan hero, slew Patroclus, who was wearing Achilles's armor at the time. Hector stripped the body of Patroclus and took it into Troy as an offering to the gods. Achilles's shield has long been the subject of academic debate.

> First, the Fire-God fashioned a mighty and strong shield
> with many wonderful figures upon it. He fixed three rims
> upon its surface that showered glints from the sun into the eyes
> of its beholder and across its width a silver baldric was laid.
> Five plates were welded tightly to the shield and upon them
> the Fire-god carefully carved many mysterious figures around
> the earth and the heavens and the sea. He showed the sun
> and the moon in their glorious splendour and the heavens
> filled with their constellations: the Pleiades and Hyads,
> Orion the Hunter, and the Great Bear that watches over
> Orion and, although her tail occasionally dips into the depths
> of the great ocean, yet her fire is not quenched by the salty waters.
>   Then, the Fire-God fashioned a picture of two cities
> and in one of the cities a great marriage festival was being held.
> A procession of happy revelers carrying torches led the brides
> from their bowers through the streets of the city. Around them rose
> a joyous nuptial song while nimble dancers pranced and paraded
> around the simpering brides in their stately march through the streets.
> There came the sound of the flute and lyre and many maidens

and wives stood in doorways and bowed from windows to watch
the passing pageant. There also stood a minister of justice who gave
stern penalty to one with a blood fine for that which he had spilled.
He appealed to those around him but no one would defend his doing
and all cried for the justices to be served, pressing forward
as the heralds firmly kept them away and gave to the men judging
the staves to speak when they rose in turn to voice their concern
for the judgment ordered. In the middle of the court stood a box
with two talents of gold inside that had been assigned as penalty.

In the other city, however, two armies arrayed in glittering
armor stood impatiently waiting as their leaders met in council
to determine the sack and ruin of the city. Upon the walls stood
the innocent children and the wives with the elders to guard
the city, unfamiliar weapons held in their hands. Others went forth
under Athene and bloody Ares (both cleverly wrought in gold),
godly figures among the small mortals at their feet, to set
an ambush at a river's bed where the armies' herds watered.
Two scouts had been posted to warn those waiting when the herd
approached (all in bronze) and presently they came with two
herdsmen piping them sweetly along, innocent of the death
waiting for them ahead. Suddenly harsh notes rang out and
the slayers waiting in ambush leaped forward and slew
the herdsmen, driving the white-fleeced sheep away. The armies
still sat in council, debating until they heard the din of battle
and the bawling of terrified cattle. Then, they rushed forth
on the backs of high-stepping horses and fought upon the banks
of the stream until the waters ran red with blood, spearing and
stabbing each other with bronze spears. Strife and Tumult rode
with them along with terrible Death who grasped a fresh-wounded
man and another freshly-killed, dragging them by their heels
through the dust while her shoulders ran red with blood.
The armies slew and grabbled with each other, stripping the dead
of the arms dragging them away from their friends.

Next, the Fire-god fashioned a fallow field, rich from
its third plowing while plowers drove their team of oxen
back and forth, throwing up rich black rows of loamy earth
and whenever a plowman came to the end of a row, a servant
stepped forward with a cup of rich red wine to slake his thirst.
Others worked eagerly for this reward and the field showed
a richness more valuable than gold.

And then the Fire-god showed with his cunning work
the land of a king and the reapers who went through his fields
with sickles, felling rich stalks of grain that fell onto the ground
where binders, coming after the reapers, drew the stalks into sheaves.
Three binders worked steadily and behind them came youths
who gathered the stalks for the binders while the king, with staff
in hand, watched silently, rejoicing at the golden harvest. An ox,
freshly-slaughtered, cooked slowly under an oak while women
worked white barley into bread for a feast.

The Fire-God worked a vineyard into the shield with twining
grape vines wrought in gold around silver staffs and the heavy bunches
of grapes in dark metal as where the ditches that circled the staffs
and from them a path in tin led the pickers to their harvest.
Young maids and youths, hearts happy and gay, carried wicker
baskets to gather the sweet fruit of the vines. In their midst came
a handsome youth piping a silvery note while the others danced
lightly to his song and sang happily as they worked.

Then the Fire-God carved a herd of cattle with huge horns
in precious gold, showing them as they plodded from their barn
to their pastures beside the banks of a gurgling river line
with bulrushes. With them came four herdsmen, gently goading
them along. Nine dogs kept the cattle together. But wait! There!
Two lions savagely leap upon a bull and drag him bellowing loudly
away from the herd. The herdsmen and dogs give chase, but the lions
rip the bull apart, glutting themselves with his entrails and greedily
lapping his rich-flowing blood. The herdsmen order the dogs to attack
but the dogs cower away from the growling beasts who crunch
the bull's bones with powerful jaws.

Carefully the Fire-God made a pasture high in the mountains
around the shield with a flock of sheep grazing quietly in the field.
Around the field stood straw-thatched huts and corrals for the sheep.

Next, he worked a square within the small town where
the maidens could dance as Ariadne had danced in the field
at Knossus that clever Daedalus had made for the youths and
maidens of that city. The maidens danced and held the hands
of the youths as they danced with cunning feet, their chitons
swirling to show their fine thighs while the youths followed them,
golden daggers bouncing, feet touching the ground as lightly

as a potter's fingers work upon his wheel. Two tumblers showed
their skill in the midst of the circle of dancers.
> And last, the Fire-God carved Ocean in all its strength
> around the outside rim of the shield.

> *The Iliad*, Book XVIII (478–608)
> trans. Randy Lee Eickhoff

42. This is an emendation that is, I believe, needed to explain the differences that exist in manuscripts as to what happened in regard to the Second Battle of Mag Tuired. In one account of *The Fate of the Children of Tuirenn* no mention is made of Lugh's questioning of the Tuatha who had special skills. Nor is there an account of the death of Balor. Yet, it appears that the battle in *The Fate of the Children of Tuirenn* is none other than the Second Battle of Mag Tuired. Consequently, I have emended the story at this point to clear up the discrepancies that seem to exist.

The only other assumption that could possibly be made is that the account of Balor's death rightfully belongs to another tale that has been partially lost and that between the two battles of Mag Tuired there was another that forced the Fomorians back to the sea, and it was at this battle that Bres was captured. The Fomorians would then have had to return home and Balor again put together a fleet and this time led it himself back to Ireland for the final battle, the Second Battle of Mag Tuired. During the time when Bres lost to the Tuatha and Balor's return, the sons of Tuirenn were sent on their quest to fulfill the *éric* (blood-fine) that was placed upon them for killing Cian. The treasures that they brought back, such as the spear of Asal and the chariot and horses of King Dobhar of Sicily, would have left Lugh better equipped for battle against Balor and the Fomorians.

I believe, however, that over the years *The Fate of the Children of Tuirenn* was altered, and the middle section regarding the Second Battle of Mag Tuired was eliminated from the telling.

43. Again, this calls to mind the funeral games that Achilles held for his friend and lover Patroclus after the latter was killed by Hector at the battle before Troy's walls. Unlike the Greeks, however, the Irish believed that their spirits would join again in the chain of life. Life, to the Celtic soul, is linked to a continuance of life. Yet, we do find some similarity in the fact that games were held to celebrate the death of a hero. These games usually consisted of running, horse or chariot racing, wrestling, and casting (stone, javelin, etc.). Sometimes, in the case of the death of a poet-singer, singing and songwriting were also part of the games.

44. Ard Chein (Cian's Mound) lies in Muirthemne. It is believed to be what is today referred to by some as Dromslian.

45. There is an amazing link with this passage to the charge that Christ gives his disciples when he commands them to go into Galilee and wait for him there. (Matt. 28; Mark 16)

46. Chain of silence: More than likely, this was a chain to which bells had been tied that would be shaken when the lord wished for silence.

47. Micorta: the name of the Great Hall at Tara where banquets were held. The ruins still stand.

48. A similarity is seen in the labors assigned the sons of Tuirenn and the Twelve Labors of Hercules:

1. To kill the lion of Nemea that no weapon could wound
2. To kill the Hydra
3. To bring back alive the stag with golden horns sacred to Artemis that lived in the forest of Cerynitia
4. To capture the great boar upon Mount Erymanthus
5. To clean the Augean stables in a single day
6. To drive away the Stymphalian birds
7. To fetch the Minotian bull from Crete
8. To bring back the man-eating mares of Diomedes of Thrace
9. To bring back the girdle of Hippolyta, the Queen of the Amazons
10. To bring back the cattle of Geryon, a monster with three bodies living on Erythia
11. To bring back the Golden Apples of the Hesperides
12. To bring back Cerberus, the three-headed dog from the land of Hades

49. Aredbair: "the Slaughterer"; a venomous spear owned by Pisear, the king of Persia.

50. Iruad: probably a reference to Norway or Sweden.

51. It would appear that these women are the Amazons.

52. Lochlann: A term used to designate the land from which the Danes come, or the southern shores of the Baltic. This includes, however, also the southern part of Sweden. The chief city is always referred to as Berva, but this could be a fictional city.

53. Scuabtinne: Manannán Mac Lir's curragh, a small boat that would automatically grow larger to accommodate its load. It was a magical boat that could fly across the water faster than a horse could gallop. The name means "Wave-Sweeper."

54. Brugh na Boinne: The palace of Aengus the Magician which lies on the north shore of the Boyne, close by Slane.

55. Fand was Manannán Mac Lir's wife.

56. Tír Na mBeo: literally, The Land of Living. Speculations on the location of this mythical land range from the Isle of Man to the Orkneys. Usually, it is associated with the Otherworld, as are Tír fo Thuinn (Land Under the Wave), Tír Na mBan (Land of Women = perhaps a reference to the Amazons of Greek legend), Tír Na nÒg (Land of Youth), Tír Tairnigiri (Land of Promise).

57. *Seanchaís*: traditional storytellers. They were highly regarded and often accorded a seat beside or near a king. They were the early repositories of history and stories. There were seven grades of poets, schooling took nearly twelve years to accomplish. [Be aware that the Irish *múineact* refers not only to the teaching or instruction, but can also be interpreted as "sing over," which suggests that the ancient teachers knew the value of memorization; a tradition in education that has fallen out of favor today where one would-be school of philosophy of education suggests that memorization has no part in education.] In the first year, the student would study basic grammar and learn 20 stories. The following year, he learned *ogham* and began to study philosophy and poetry. In addition, he would memorize 10 more stories. In the third year, he would learn more about the *ogham*, memorize more stories and the intricacies of assonantal versification. In the fourth year, he learned the *Bretha Nemed* or the Laws of Privileges as well as more stories and poetry. In the fifth year, he would receive a heavy concentration of grammar. In the sixth year, he was taught the Secret Language of Poets and memorized 48 more poems. In the seventh, eighth, and ninth years, the poet was called *anrúth* ("noble stream" = a reference to "a stream of pleasing praise from him and a stream of wealth to

him"). During this time, he learned the *Brosnacha* (a collection of teachings that includes the styles of poetic composition, prosody, glosses, *teinm laeghda, imbas forosna, dichetal do chennaib* (three forms of prophecy or divining the truth), the *Dindsenchas*, several poetic forms, and become the master of 175 tales (that includes the 80 stories already learned). In the tenth, eleventh, and twelfth years, he would be established as an *Ollamh* or Doctor of Philosophy which in itself is subdivided into three grades: *eces* (learned man), *fili* (poet), and *ollamh*. To achieve this, he would perfect poetic forms and composition, learn 100 poems of the *anamuin* genre that are restricted to *ollamhs* (forming a type of rite of passage), and 120 Orations, the four arts of poetry, mastering 350 stories. This was learned, for the most part, "mouth to ear": by rote. Traditionally, the schools were formed around one teacher and his attendants or apprentices. Other poets or teachers would visit for the purpose of examining the students. Although there was a certain herditary process included here, the poets were not limited to a specific class. They could come from any part of society, the chief requirement being intelligence and memory. Poets, however, were not limited to an austere life. They were not celibate or aesthetics for to be so would be to isolate themselves from the normal life in Ancient Ireland. Indeed, to have done so would be to violate the very nature of the poet who must celebrate in song that which he sees and experiences. The would-be poet would dedicate himself to the triad: Three candles that illume every darkness: truth, nature, knowledge—even though most of this learning was in a dark room where the student would not be distracted by daylight.

> The reason of laying the Study aforesaid in the Dark was doubtless to avoid the Distraction which Light and the variety of Objects represented thereby commonly occasioned. This being prevented, the Faculties of the Soul occupied themselves solely upon the Subject in hand, and the Theme given; so that it was soon brought to some Perfection according to the Notions or Capacities of the Students. [Whereby they] . . . shut their Doors and Windows for a Day's time, and lie on their backs with Stone upon their Belly, and Plads [sic] about their Heads, and their eyes being cover'd they pump their Brains for Rhetorical Encomium or Panegyrick [sic]; and indeed they furnish such a Stile [sic] from this Dark Cell as is understood by very few.

> —Daniel Corkery, *The Hidden Ireland*

58. *Striapach*: literally "harlot" or, today more commonly (if erroneously) used to indicate "whore." But, in Ancient Ireland, the term connoted "loose woman" or "woman of loose morals" more than the other more didactic reference. [see Keating's "Three Shafts of Death" (Atkinson, Ir. mss. ser. ii. 1890. Bergin 1931) 2020 . . . *do bhríogh go mbeirann . . . an striapach corp na meirdrighe . . .*] *Nimfeach* or "nymph" referred to a woodland creature, not to be confused with *sióg* or "fairy." A *nimfeachmáineach* (*nymphomaniac*) was a term unknown, as such was not considered to be "unusual behavior" and stigmatized as it is today in a society more rigidly controlled by a code of manners and morals through the aesthetics of a Christian education. Sex to the Ancient Irish (B.C.) was not considered a "forbidden" subject, but rather a natural function of man and woman in a natural world.

59. The Ancient Irish were extremely hospitable, as anyone who was not would be disgraced and dishonored. Strangers were wined and dined before their business was asked. This was the order of things, and asking a guest's business before food and drink had been made available was an insult. A suggestion is made here that this could be a holdover from the rules of hospitality that were laid down in Ancient Greece, in that one never knew if the individual seeking shelter was mortal or an immortal testing the house. We do know that great attention was paid to guests in one house. A marginal note in *Lebor Breac* reads:

Ah, starry king! Let it be known
That whether my house be dark or lighted
No visitor to its doors will be slighted.
And if the seeds of discontent are sown
Let Christ the King cause it to be blighted.

Though the injunction of Christ is made here, the previous four lines appear to be an address to The Dagda or Aengus.

60. Elada: the god of poetic composition, knowledge.

61. An *Imnocta-fessa* is a little reward.

62. Crow men were warriors in the service of Badb Catha (Battle Raven), who was part of the Mórrígna, a triple (triadic) goddess of whom the other two were Macha and Mórrígan.

63. Iurad appears to be identified with either Norway or Iceland.

64. Flidais: Perhaps "Flidias," one of the major characters from *Táin Bó Flidias*.

65. Little is know of the god Tuad (Tuaithe) except that the wave at the mouth of the Bann in county Derry was named after him.

66. Tailltiu: also Tailtu. The daughter of the Fir Bolg king of the Great Plain. She married Eochaidh Mac Erc, another Fir Bolg king, and became foster-mother to Lugh. She cleared the forest of Breg, making it into a plain, but died from her efforts. She was buried at Tailltinn (Teltown, between Navan and Kells). Lugh decreed a feast in her honor which eventually became Lugnasa (Lughnasa, Lughnasadh). The festival became a major event in pre-Christian Ireland with games that corresponded to the Olympic games. According to a poem by Cuan Ó Lathcháin in *Lebar Na Núachongbála (The Book of Leinster)*, the games were held around the graves on the hill. According to *Annálá Ríoghachta éireann (Annals of the Four Masters)* the last official games were held on August 1, 1169 under the Ard Rí Ruairi Ó Conchobor.

67. Usneach Hill: The major assembly point that is said to mark the center of Ireland. Here, where all the provinces meet, is where the great stone Ail Na Mírenn (Stone of Divisions) stands. The five provinces, each with their own king, formed a pentarchy. On this hill, the Fires of Bel were lit on the first day of May (Beltaine). Two fires were lit, and cattle driven between them would be free from disease for the year. Legend has it that the famous Druid Mide lit the first fire and that all the meetings that were held here were held under a sacred ash tree. Although it is not a very tall hill, it has a commanding view of the countryside. The general belief is that fires lit here were seen on other hills where other fires would be lit, forming a loose chain that terminated at the sea. The belief that Tuathal Techtmar lived here is unsupported by archeological excavations. The hill, however, is associated as the place where Lugh was killed by the three gods Mac Cuill, Mac Cécht, and Mac Gréine.

68. This appears to be a reference to Plato's Atlantis, although it is referred to as *Tír-fa-tonn*—the Land Beneath the Waves. It could also be a reference to *O'Brasil* which was a murky island that appeared once every seven years. If we take Thomas Moore's poem, "Lalla Rookh" as a referral, then the island would seem to be the same as the Isles of Perfume that lie

> Many a fathom down in the sea,
> To the south of sun-bright Araby.

THE FATE OF THE CHILDREN OF LIR

1. This is part of a poem by the thirteenth-century poet Gilla Brighde Mac Con Midhe. The translation reads:

> Taillte and Nás Laighean of the slopes,
> Aileach and Eamhain, red with wine
> —no man leaves them sorrowful—
> Uisneach and Cruachain and Caiseal.

The suggestion here is that Tailtiu, a daughter of the Fir Bolg king Mag Mór (Great Plain) was married to another Fir Bolg king, Eochu Mac Eirc, the last of the Fir Bolg kings. She later became the foster-mother to Lugh Lámhfada who, after her death, dedicated a feast to her honor that became Lughnasa on August 1, the day when the Fir Bolg supposedly landed on the shores of Ireland. The festival became a major event in pre-Christian Ireland much on the order of the Olympian festival in Greece, with games similar to the ancient games practiced in Greece. The last games were held on August 1, 1169 under the last Ard Rí, Ruairí Mac Conchobor, which corresponds to the Anglo-Norman invasion of Ireland.

We find reference as well to this in "Temair Breg bale na fían," a poem by Cúán Húa Lothcháin in *Lebar na Núachongbála* also called *Lébhair Laighnech (Book of Leinster)*.

Tailtiu allegedly cleared the forest of Cóill Cúán (the Forest of Breg) and gave her name to the place (Telltown, County Meath) which is consistent with the actions of other earth goddesses who wished to be associated with the land for which they had a love.

2. *Féth fiadha*: the "cloak of concealment" or an obscure magical device by which the Tuatha Dé Danann where able to become invisible to the human world.

3. The Tuatha Dé Danann ("people of the goddess Danu, sometimes 'Anu'") inhabited Ireland before the coming of the Mílesians, who fought a series of battles for control of the land. The Tuatha, however, were more civilized beings than warriors, although they could be fierce fighters when necessary. They preferred, however, to spend their time in more intellectual pursuits and were quite accomplished with the arts and literature. At last, they called for a truce to negotiate with the Mílesians and proposed that the land was big enough for everyone

and why not divide it in half? The Mílesians agreed and said that they would take all the land above the earth while the Tuatha could have all the land below the earth. Although the Mílesians were being ironic, planning on eradicating the race of the Tuatha, the Tuatha took them at their word and melted into the ground to become the spirits and legends of the Otherworld. According to legend, they first came to Ireland from a northern country usually said to be Greece where they had four fabulous cities: Falias, Gorias, Finias, and Murias. They fought the Formorians and the Fir Bolg for control of the land. Because of their gentle ways, however, they are considered as the gods of light and goodness while the Formorians are considered the sinister gods of darkness. Like the Greek gods, they are pictured as humans with the same traits of goodness and vice.

4. The Fomorians were a race of sea-dwelling giants that tried to conquer the Tuatha Dé Danann in several battles. Their name actually means "under the sea." They represent the forces of darkness and death and are associated with water and moon worship. Ultimately, they are defeated at the Battle of Mag Tuired, where Balor of the Evil Eye is killed by Lugh of the Sun. This final battle marks the triumph of the Tuatha Dé Danann over the Fomorians.

5. Battle of Tailltin: the great battle between the Tuatha Dé Danann and the Mílesians, where three kings and three queens of the Tuatha Dé Danann were slain.

6. The *Teach Midchuarta* was the Great Hall or Council Room.

7. The *Fáil (Fál)* is a stone which would roar when the rightful king of Ireland stood upon it. It originally stood near Duma na Ngiall (the Mound of the Hostages) and is now upon the Croppies' Grave. It is roughly six feet long. It is also called *Fearb Cluice, Lia Fáhil, Inir Fáil,* and *Críoca Fáil* It was known as Bod Fhearghais ("the Penis of Fergus") in the nineteenth century. It is granular limestone and stands six feet above and six feet below ground. There are no limestone deposits near it.

8. The identity of this Aengus is vague. Aengus Mac Ind Óg was the son of The Dagda and Boand. He is generally considered to be the harper for the gods and a friend of poets. He is the subject of *Aisling Aengusa,* or *Dream of Aengus.* He could, however, simply be one of Bodb Dearg's sons—Artrach, Aed, and Aengus—who eventually had a falling out with their father and went to LConn ACét Ohathach's grandson, Cormac Mac Airt where they stayed for

thirty years on land he gave them in Donegal. But I believe that the Tuatha Dé Danann were weary of war at this time and were looking for a better life. Consequently, I have chosen to identify this Aengus as the one who was more poet than warrior. This seems to be a fairly logical choice, as Aengus fell in love with a lovely young woman, Caer Ibormeith (yew-berry), who changes into a swam at Loch Bél Dracon during Samhain. When he finds her, he changes into a swan and flies with her to Bruig na Boinne, where they become lovers and the protector of lovers in the Irish pantheon. This is the subject of a poem by William Butler Yeats which is one of the most beautiful and evocative poems ever written:

THE SONG OF WANDERING AENGUS

I went out to the hazel wood,
Because a fire was in my head,
And cut and peeled a hazel wand,
And hooked a berry to a thread;
And when white moths were on the wing,
And moth-like stars were flickering out,
I dropped the berry in a stream
And caught a little silver trout.

When I had laid it on the floor
I went to blow the fire a-flame,
But something rustled on the floor,
And some one called me by my name:
It had become a glimmering girl
With apple blossom in her hair
Who called me by my name and ran
And faded through the brightening air.

Though I am old with wandering
Through hollow lands and hilly lands,
I will find out where she has gone,
And kiss her lips and take her hands;
And walk among long dappled grass,
And pluck till time and time are done,
The silver apples of the moon,
The golden apples of the sun.

9. Mac Cécht was a son of Ogma, god of bards and orators. He was the husband

of Fótla, one of the three goddesses (the other two were Banb and Éire) who asked that the land be named after them. Traditionally, he is seen as one who settles quarrels.

10. The Ancient Irish did not hold the throne as an inherited right, but rather elected their kings through a vote held among the clans. Consequently, the largest clan inevitably elected the king and held that power.

11. *Mucaire*: a swineherd, a boor, or a rustic.

12. *Cáinteac*: a satirist, a fault-finder.

13. The Dagda, is the father of all gods, whose name connotes "the good god." Also known as Eochaidh Ollathair (All-Father), Aedh (Fire), and Ruad Rofessa (Red Lord of Great Wisdom), he is the patron of Druids. He is sometimes equated with Cernunnos (the god of the land). Strangely enough, he is not pictured in the carefully groomed fashion of other gods in other cultures. Rather in the Ancient Irish custom, he is seen as wearing rustic garb, carrying a huge club (sometimes dragging it on wheels). One end of the club kills, the other heals. He also has a black horse named Acéhin (Ocean) and a cauldron from the city of Murias, which is one of the Tuatha treasures. No man can walk away from it hungry. He also has a magic harp.

After the Tuatha were defeated, The Dagda gave a *sídhe* to each of his children in the Otherworld. Only Aengus was not alloted a *sídhe*, as The Dagda wanted that palace for himself. So the love god tricked The Dagda through subtle wording (proving the power of poetry) and gained possession of Bruigh na Boinne in the end. When the Tuatha departed for the Otherworld, The Dagda resigned as their king, prompting a new election. Bodb Dearg was elected instead of Manannán Mac Lir and Midir the Proud. Lir left the proceedings in disgust, but Midir started a war against Bodb Dearg.

14. The use of a wren here to suggest Aobh's voice is very symbolic, as the wren is seen as an omen of misfortune in some areas. It is also, however, called "the Druid bird," because if anyone can understand its song, he or she will know the future. On All-Hallow's Eve, the children dress in various costumes and as "wren-boys" go among the houses, demanding money. If one does not give them this "treat," then bad luck will fall upon the house for the next year.

15. Fionnuala: the name means "the maid of the white shoulder."

16. Donn: the black god of death.

17. "Twelves and sixes": the time between midnight and traditional sunrise when the *bean-sídhes* and goblins most freely roamed the earth.

18. It is not believed that this Cian is the one also known as Scál Balb, the son of Dian Cécht, who gave his son to Tailtiu for fosterage. That son was Lug (Lugh), who became one of the principal gods of the Tuatha, the god of genius and light and the divine father of Cúchulainn.

19. Crom Dubh: this was a golden idol that was on Mag Slecht (The Plain of Prostration) to which the people once offered their firstborn children in sacrifice in return for rich yields of milk and corn and the harvest to be free of blight and disease. The golden idol was reportedly surrounded by eleven lesser idols made of stone. The god Lugh fought against Crom Dubh for the possession of the harvest but, according to tradition, a true victory wasn't had over it until St. Patrick came and overthrew its power by splitting the idol with a sledgehammer and sending the demon-god fleeing to the Otherworld. The idol is also referred to as Crom Cruach in the *Dinnsenchas*.

20. Also called "Darvra" and "Derravargh," this lake lies in West Meath.

21. Another recension says that Aoife was changed into a gray vulture and forced to live in the cold and windy air until the end of time.

22. A pone pin is the pin on an oar that fits into an oarlock.

23. Scale-pans are the pans on a balance scale.

24. According to another legend, Lir was killed by Caoilté, a cousin of Finn Mac Cumail (Finn MacCool) and *Sídhe Fionnechaidh* left to fall into ruins.

25. Here, there is another recension that says the swans made friends with the Lonely Crane of Innishkea, an island off the coast of Mayo. This crane is one of the "Wonders of Ireland" and still figures greatly as an object of folk-belief. According to the legend, the crane has lived upon that island since the beginning of the world and will still be sitting there on Judgment Day. Yet another recension suggests that a man named Ebric owned the land that ran across a shore of the lake on Innis Gluaire. One day, he heard the swans singing and

went down to make friends with them. He is given credit for preserving this story.

26. Here is where there appears to be an intrusion by a Christian scholar upon the story much in the same way that *Beowulf* was altered from its original form. Two endings will subsequently be given for the reader.

27. Sometimes, Kemoc is given as Saint Mac Howg.

28. This suggests a link to *Buile Suibhne*. According to this ninth-century romance, Suibhne (Sweeney) was a seventh-century king who insulted St. Rónán, who was building a church in his territory. Suibhne roared in anger and went to expel the saint. He ran naked into the saint's house, seized his psalter, and threw it into the lake. He was in the process of throwing the saint after his psalter when he was called away to battle. Rónán cursed Suibhne and asked that God punish the king for what he had done. An otter emerged from the lake with the psalter unspotted by water in its mouth. Rónán was called to bless the troops. Suibhne became angered at one of the saint's clerics and stabbed him to death with his spear. He threw the spear at the saint himself, but the spear broke against a bell the saint was wearing. The saint again cursed Suibhne, praying that Suibhne would fly through the air and die of a spear-cast. When the battle of Magh Rátha was joined, Suibhne became horrified at what he saw and raced away. He leaped onto a yew tree and made that his home, living like a bird. For years, he imagined himself a bird and lived in the trees. Eventually, he was slain by a spear thrown by a husband who was jealous of the time his wife, a milkmaid, spent with the madman.

THE EXILE OF THE SONS OF USNECH

1. *Fir ar se ingen fil and agus bid Derdriu a hainm, agus biaid olc impe. cid dia mboi longes mac nusing ni handsa*: Deirdre shall be her name, and evil woe shall be upon her.

2. Fedilimid Chilair Chétach: one of the Red Branch champions.
   Fedilimid mac Dall: also Felim. The son of Dall, he was also the father of Deirdre and the bard of Conchobor Mac Nessa. He was entertaining Conchobor and certain members of the Red Branch society when Cathbad the Druid made the prophecy about Deirdre and how she would bring death and ruin to Ulster.

3. Dall: the father of Fedlimid, who fathered Deirdre. He is a shadowy figure

in Celtic. His name means "blind" or "blind man" and in folk tales he is seen as a seer or the causer of the first darkness. He is seen as a prophet of doom, a prophet of darkness, one who has dark visions that are sometimes brought about by drunkenness.

4. Conchobor became the king of the Red Branch through the wily maneuverings of his mother, Nessa. According to one story, his father was Cathbad the Druid. Conchobor (so named because he was born beside the river Conchobor in Ulster) became king when his mother, who was a beautiful and highly sensual woman, agreed to live with the then king Fergus Mac Roich for one year as his "year-wife" if Fergus would allow her son to be king during that year so that Conchobor would have a royal lineage and be entitled to kingly benefits. Fergus, whose sexual appetite was legendary (he is called Fergus of the Seven Women, as it took seven women a night to satisfy his sexual appetite), agreed to this. Nessa was so great a lover (apparently second only to Maeve of Cruachan, who needed thirty men a night to satisfy her sexual longings) that Fergus was content throughout the year. But while she kept Fergus satisfied in bed, Nessa also made the knights of the Red Branch wealthy through distributions from the Ulster treasury. When the year was up, the Red Branch warriors did not want Fergus to go back on the throne, and they supported Conchobor in that position. Since kings were elected in Ancient Ireland (from the dominant clan), Fergus was relegated to the role of seneschal in the Red Branch court at Emain Macha.

5. This movement or way of serving was a careful ritual that was mentioned in the Brehon Laws, as well as how portions of meat were to be cut and distributed during feasts. To go opposite this method of serving would cast a *geis* upon a house and be a great insult to one's host and/or one's guest.

6. We do not know her name. Normally one would associate such a personage with being a "year-wife": a woman who agreed to be a man's wife for only a year and was paid adequately for her service. There was no shame attached to such a role. But in this instance, since Fedlimid's wife is supervising the serving wenches and appears to be ordering the house, we must assume that she is his "first-wife."

7. Druid: Tacitus tells us that the Druids and Druidesses on Mona dressed in black, but normally they would be dressed in white. The Druid is the historian, the philosopher, and is generally regarded as being the wisest among a particular tribe. In some instances, certain Druids were regarded as being demigods or

semidivine. We really have little information on the Druids, as the secrets of that society were kept carefully. We do know that a Druid usually had at least one student following him around as an apprentice, much in the same way that Greek poets trained young men to be poets or poet-singers. Usually the place of learning or where lessons were conducted was north of a fort or settlement, as north was considered to be the sacred direction. All instruction was "mouth-to-ear" or oral. The initial learning was simple memorization of long lists or chronologies. Although boring, this method of instruction taught the student "memory tricks" or how to remember things. But such teaching was also concerned with practical application of certain things. The basic tenet of the school appears to have been founded on the *viva voce* concept, or the dialogues that were employed in Plato's Academy.

The word "druid" (Irish: *drui*, Welsh: *derwydd*) appears to have been derived form the Sanskrit *veda*: to see and understand. But the word could also have derived from the various words for oak: Gaelic: *dervo*, Irish: *daur*, Welsh *derw*. Oak was considered to be the holiest of trees in the Irish alphabet, which was based upon a certain hierarchy of trees.

The word for wood and knowledge are very close as well. The Irish word for trees is *fid* while *fios* is usually translated as "knowledge."

Consequently, we would suggest that the word "druid" in translation would be a "wood-knower" or one who could understand nature completely.

The reader, however, is cautioned not to think of Druids as magicians in the manner of the legendary Merlin (although Merlin could have been trained in the Druidic arts) but rather as the *aos dana* or "people of the art" or "gifted people." Literally, the term *aos dana* is reflective of the people of the goddess Danu or the Tuatha Dé Danaan who became the mystical forebearers of the *sídhe* or Otherworld beings.

The Druids were well schooled in aesthetics and fully knowledgeable of astrology, cosmology, physiology, theology, and nature.

In essence, the Druid was a shaman who mediated between this world and the next.

8. The raven is a portent of bad happenings. It is a raven that Badb changes into when she flies over the battlefield. In the list of *oghams,* the raven is "H" or *hadraig*, the color *huath* (terrible), and its fortress h-Ocha.

9. Cathbad was the personal Druid or advisor of Conchobor Mac Nessa or the chief Druid of the Red Branch. He appears in many myths and stories of the Red Branch or the Ulster Cycle. One account has him as the father of Conchobor. According to that story, one day Nessa, who was queen of Emain

Macha, was sunning herself when Cathbad passed by. Lazily she called out to the Druid, asking what the day was good for. Cathbad replied, "It is good for begetting a king upon a queen." Nessa took Cathbad into her bedroom and they romped merrily throughout the day and into the night. Nessa gave birth to Conchobor as a result. Because of his importance, Cathbad had eight students with him in his school, not one, which was the usual number. He taught his own son, Geanann.

10. Donn was the black god of death.

11. Sencha Mac Ailella was the chief judge and poet of Ulster during Conchobor's reign. He is a thorn in the side of Bricriu, whose bitter tongue causes a lot of dissent in Ulster (*Fled Bricrend*, translated by Dr. Randy Lee Eickhoff as *The Feast*), and was the one who taught Cúchulainn how to speak.

12. Maeve was the queen of Connacht, the wife of Ailill mac Máta (after being wife to Conchobor Mac Nessa, Tiride Mac Connra Cas, and Eochaidh Dála). She is usually seen as a fertility demigoddess in myth because of her nymphomanic leanings. She is referred to as "Maeve of the White Shoulders" or "Gleaming Thighs" or "White Thighs" or "Thirty-Men-a-Night" as it took thirty men a night to satisfy her sexually. She married Ailill because she did not think he was a jealous man. At the time of her marriage, he was not, but through several of the myths and stories in the Ulster Cycle, we see him become jealous of her many affairs. Maeve also is seen as a standard for woman's equality, as she wanted to be equal to Ailill in all ways. In a wager with him, their fortunes are compared. They emerge equal in all things, except that Ailill posesses a magical white bull, Finnebenach. Maeve wants an equal to the white bull and hears of a black (or brown) bull in Cuailnge in Ulster. She leads an army into Ulster to get the bull. The story of this expedition is the *Táin Bó Cuailgne* (the *Cattle-Raid of Cooley*, Ireland's national epic translated by Dr. Randy Lee Eickhoff as *The Raid*). She is finally killed by Forba, the son of Conchobor Mac Nessa, while she is bathing in a lake with one of her many lovers. (Some stories identify this lover as Fergus.)

13. A note is needed here to explain the strange mixture of poetry and prose in Ancient Irish stories. The bardic singers apparently used a basic narrative style to set the scene or establish the parameters of a story, but reserved poetry for those sections of the story that they considered to be the most important. Usually these had references to those in the pantheon of Gaelic gods who have some affair with the mortals or those times when the *Sídhe*, or members of the

Otherworld are influencing human behavior. The strange mixture of poetry and prose lends a certain mysticism to the story. Although the Ancient Irish poetry in this situation was very aesthetic, I have taken the liberty of translating the intent of the poet and rendering those passages into a poetic form that would be more recognizable and workable for the modern reader.

14. Cathbad is using one of the three methods of Druidic divination here, namely *Dichetal do Chennaib* or "Composing on One's Fingertips," which appears to be a form of psychometry by which the poet/Druid can, by ritual invocation, discover the future.

15. The meaning of "Deirdre" is a source of great argument among scholars. It appears, however, that her name is a compound that derives from *abair*, which means "speak" or, more appropriately "speak the truth" (technically, *abair an fhirnne*), or "sing," as in *abair amhrán* or "sing a song." The last part of the compound could be from *dreach*, or "face," or *dréacht*, or "musical composition," which would suggest that her beauty would be the subject of songs, a great compliment. We would use the term "sweetheart" in the most affectionate syntax as an anglicized equivalent.

16. Lugh is the Celtic sun-god, the Otherworld father of Cúchulainn.

17. Conchobor is planning on becoming a foster-father to Deirdre. Fostering was a popular practice among the Celts. It served a practical purpose in giving the child two sets of parents and helped as well to unite families and clans. A foster-child would be trained in a hereditary career and was returned to his/her birth parents at the age of marriage: fourteen for girls, seventeen for boys. The Brehon Laws were quite explicit on what a foster-parent would teach the child, and even spelled out the fee to be charged for "fostering."

18. Dubthach Doéltenga is the son of Lugaid Mac Casrubae. He is a warrior of the Red Branch and is described in some passages as a man who has never earned the thanks of anyone. He is seen as a loner. His name, Doéltenga, means "backbiter" which indicates the he is also one who stirs up trouble. He was given the magical spear Celtchair Lúin that was found on the battlefield of the second battle of Moytura. He is, however, a supporter of Fergus Mac Roich and is found in *Táin Bó Cuailnge, Fled Bricrend*, and *Togail Bruidne Dá Derga*.

19. Mugain, also Mughain Attenchaithrech, is the daughter of Eochaidh Feidlech and Conchobor Mac Nessa's wife. She is usually pictured as extremely

voluptuous, stripping herself naked on more than one occasion to tease men. In one of her famous scenes, she strips naked and approaches Cúchulainn "full-breasted and bare" when the youth is under the influence of his battle-frenzy. When Cúchulainn hides his face from her nudity, the warriors seize him and plunge him into three barrels of cold water to bring about his sanity again.

20. Emain Macha was the home of the Red Branch. The name means the "twins of Macha." Today, the site is known as Navan Fort, located west of the city of Armagh. During the reign of Conchobor Mac Neasa (Nessa), a celebration was held in which the warriors were obligated to take part. Crunniuc Mac Agnomain's wife had died, and one day while he was sunning himself and bemoaning the tragedy of loneliness a beautiful woman crossed the fields, entered his house, and became his wife. When they left for the celebration, the woman warned Crunniuc not to get drunk and boast, but he did not heed her advice and drank deeply at the celebration. Now, Conchobor's horses were winning all the races and Crunniuc boasted that his wife, now pregnant, could out-run Conchobor's matched blacks. Conchobor demanded that the race be held although Crunniuc's wife pleaded with him to forgive her husband. When he did not listen to her, she appealed to the Red Branch. But they ignored her as well. Conchobor told her that he would have Crunniuc's head if she did not run the race. At last she agreed, saying "A long-lasting evil will come out of this upon the whole of Ulster." At this, the king demanded her name and she replied, "Macha, daughter of Sainraith Mac Imbaith." She ran the race, beating the king's horses easily but as she crossed the finish line, her water broke and she gave birth to twins. As she gave birth, she screamed with her dying breath that all who heard the scream would suffer from the pangs of childbirth for five days and four nights in time of Ulster's greatest difficulty. This curse would last down through ten times ten generations. Only three classes were excused from the curse: women, boys, and Cúchulainn himself, as he was from Muirthemne. She died, and the men were inflicted with that curse from that time to the time of Furc Mac Dallán, son of Mainech Mac Lugdach. Legend has it that an additional curse was placed upon Ulster in which Ulster would never know peace. It never has.

21. A satirist had enormous power among the Ancient Irish, for a poet who had a tongue sharp enough to compose poetry that denigrated another could force that individual to live forever in ignominy. A person's honor and reputation were held sacrosanct among the Ancient Irish and, consequently, anyone who had the gift of poetry was held in high esteem and greatly honored in these days. In a warrior society and aristocracy where one's reputation for the

princely virtues of generosity and courage were considered of the highest social importance, to be denigrated in a satire was greatly feared. Even today, the threat of "giving your name to a poet" is not taken lightly.

22. *La-Bel-Taine*, or May 1, was named after the god Bel, and means literally "the fire of Bel."

23. A rath-fort had ramparts that were basically earth.

24. The Donn Cuailnge or Brown (or Black) Bull of Cooley was the object of the raid by Connacht to satisfy Maeve's desire to be equal to her husband Ailill, the king of Connacht. The Donn Cuailnge was owned by Dáire Mac Fiachna, who had earlier agreed to loan the bull to Maeve, but withdrew his offer after being insulted by one of her messengers. Maeve led her army over Ulster's borders and all of the men of Ulster fell ill with the pangs of birth (see Note 19), leaving Ulster's protection in the hands of the boy-warrior Cúchulainn. The story is known as *Táin Bó Cuailngé* or the "Cattle-Raid of Cooley" and is regarded as Ireland's national epic.

25. The Ancient Irish year was traditionally divided as follows:

>Winter Solstice . . . . .21 December
>Oimelc . . . . .31 January
>Spring Equinox . . . . .21 March
>Beltain . . . . .30 April
>Summer Solstice . . . . .21 June
>Lughnasa . . . . .31 July
>Autumn Equinox . . . . .21 September
>Samhain . . . . .31 October

Of course, there were other celebrations that came during other months, such as the first three days in May and various lunar festivals called "fire-festivals," which were associated with various pastoral and agricultural events. At Samhain, for example, all the beasts were brought into stockades for wintering over, and some slaughtered and the meat dried for use during the winter months. The harvest granaries were filled, and the Irish settled in for the winter. No raiding would be held during these months. At Beltain, herds were driven out for summer pasture, and raiding and warfare would take place between Beltain and Samhain. The major gatherings (we would call them "reunions") and fairs would be held at Beltain, when the doors to the Otherworld would be open, and fairies would dance upon the hills and in the secret glades of the forest. This was a time for marriage (and divorce) and the arrangements of love-matches. Several stories in the Ulster Cycle are attached to the various celebrations as well as stories from the Mythological Cycle and the Fenian Cycle as well. The celebrations were associated with certain sacred sites. Munster was the sacred site of Samhain, Connacht for Beltain, Lughnasa in Ulster, and the Feast of Tara (held every three keeping years) was in Meath. The festivals were also governed by a set of "laws" or "bans" that prohibited violent behavior (given the mercurial temperment of the Ancient Irish, one has to wonder how this one was enforced), abduction, theft, and the collection of debts.

26. Conchobor apparently sent out assassins to the courts of other kings to kill the sons of Usnech. This violates the rigid rules of hospitality that governed the behavior of a host and guest. Undoubtedly, this was also a contributing factor in the actions of some kings to give sanctuary to Deirdre and the brothers for such behavior on the part of Conchobor would be enough for him to be held in contempt throughout the land. Ultimately, this would have a debilitating effect upon the Red Branch warriors as well, for a king must be above reproach, given his elected position. The reader needs to be aware, however, that the strongest clan would elect the king simply through the number of votes that it could muster. Conchobor was from the Ulaid Clan or "wool-gatherers" as it is sometimes translated. This would suggest sheep-herding and weaving centers, although the province itself is associated with witchcraft in the folk imagination.

27. A crannog is an artifical island that was built in the middle of lakes or bogs. The islands were built up layer by layer much in the way landfills are built today. Then logs were driven in to hold the layers together and a stockade placed around the island. Finally, water was trenched around the entire island to provide protection against attack. Over two hundred crannogs have been discovered in Ireland.

28. Ériu was one of the ancient names for Ireland. When the Mílesians sought to invade the island, they came upon three goddess of the land. Banba, Fodla, and Ériu. Amergin the Bard promised each goddess that their name would be given to the land if each goddess would help the Milesians to conquer it. But the Mílesians did not honor the three goddesses and, led by Donn, a war erupted between the gods and the Mílesians in which Donn was killed. Amergin promised Ériu that her name would be used as the country's principal name. Her sisters' names are used only in poetic reference to the land. According to legend, Ériu relented and allowed the Mílesians to live on the

island after they sailed out beyond the ninth wave and came back. They did and Ériu, who was a queen of the Tuatha Dé Danann, was slain in the Battle of Tailtiu (near what is now Telltown, Company Meath) in 1698 B.C. Her name means "regular traveler," which implies that she was a goddess of the sun. In the *Lebor Gabála*, we find the lines,

> Cethor was pleasant and fair and totally free;
> Ériu, his wife, a generous woman of the sun, his god.

After the Battle of Tailtiu, the Tuatha Dé Danann tried to make peace with the Mílesians. The Mílesians said that they would be willing to divide the country with the Tuatha; the Tuatha could have all that lay beneath the land while the Mílesians took all that lay above. According to legend, the Tuatha, having great magic, placed a spell over the island and disappeared into the Otherworld.

29. A curragh is a boat made by stretching hides over a wooden frame and sewing them together, then sealing the seams with pitch. They are still in use in western Ireland today.

30. The Island of Shadows is thought to be Skye.

31. Scáthach's name means "shadowy." Scáthach nUanaind ("Victory") was the daughter of Árd-Greimne of Lethra. Kings from all over the world sent their best warriors to her military academy for training. Cúchulainn was her most famous pupil.

32. The Land of Promise is possibly the Isle of Man.

33. We do not know exactly what constituted the "salmon leap" but apparently it was a maneuver that approximated the leap a salmon makes up rapids while it is migrating back to the place of its birth. Because of the salmon's migratory traits and being able to return to where it was born, the Ancient Irish believed it had great wisdom. Consequently, eating a salmon's flesh would impart that wisdom to them.

34. Alba is the ancient name for Scotland.

35. Here, Conchobor is reminding Fergus that he had once been king of the Red Branch until Conchobor's mother, Nessa, promised to live with

Fergus for a year if he would surrender the crown to her son so that Conchobor would be able to claim royalty in his line. Fergus, who needed seven women a night to satisfy his sexual appetite, knew Nessa's skill in lovemaking and, anxious to sample her skills, readily agreed to surrender the crown. After a year, he tried to reclaim the crown, but by this time, the Red Branch warriors had grown fond of Conchobor and had known greater prosperity under his rule than they had under the rule of Fergus and refused to allow Fergus to reclaim the throne. Nessa had, of course, planned all of this, but to keep Fergus, from leading a coup against Conchobor despite the vote of the Red Branch, she agreed to stay the wife of Fergus if he would leave things as they were. After thinking about the responsibilities he would have as the king of the Red Branch, Fergus decided to let Conchobor remain as the king while he took on the role of Conchobor's *seanascal* or advisor.

36. Cúchulainn had three pupils in each eye, seven fingers on each hand, and seven toes on each foot. These marked him as one of the divine ones, as the numbers had special divine significance.

37. Donn is the Irish god of the dead whose house is at Tech Donn, the assembly place of the dead before they begin their journey to the Otherworld. Donn is usually associated with shipwrecks and sea storms and equated with The Dagda and Bilé Tech Donn was supposedly on an island believed to be southwest of Ireland.

38. Here, Deirdre is referring to the "Pangs of Ulster" or the Ulster Curse. One day, Crunniuc Mac Agnomain, a rich landlord who lived with his sons in the mountains, found his bed suddenly visited by a beautiful woman who called herself Macha and appeared mysteriously out of nowhere. They lived happily together as man and wife for a long spell until one day, they went to a fair in Ulster. After drinking more than he should, he bragged that his wife could run faster than the king's horses. This was considered an insult and so the king, Conchobor, had Macha brought before him and demanded that she prove her husband's boast by running a race against his horses. She protested, as she was nine months pregnant, but Conchobor was firm, declaring that she either run the race or her husband would have his head cut from his shoulders. She appealed to the warriors of the Red Branch, but they refused to intervene. At last, she agreed to the race, but said that no good would come from this. The race was around the hill-fort of the Red Branch. Macha easily defeated Conchobor's blacks, but as she crossed the finish line, her water

broke, and she fell to the ground and delivered twins. In pain and nearing death from the sudden birth, she cried out that all the men who heard her cries would suffer the same pain as she whenever Ulster was threatened down through the tenth of the tenth generation and that the land would never know peace. It never has.

39. This foreshadowing of doom is an international motif that is reflected in many romantic folktales (Type 970) still popular in Irish folklore whereby a young girl and the young boy she loves are forbidden to be together by their parents (echoes of Romeo and Juliet) and, consequently, either die of heartbreak or are killed by either natural forces or arms. The parents, still unrepentant of their hatred for each other, cause the lovers to be buried at the farthest reaches from each other in the cemetery, but a tree grows from the grave of each and stretches out its branches until they entwine like lovers' arms. This story is familiar in the tenth-century Irish tale of Baile Mac Buain and Aillinn.

40. Deirdre's words here are a foreshadowing of the *Táin Bó Cuailngé*, in which Maeve of Connacht and her husband Ailill lead their army across Ulster's borders in the famous raid for the Brown Bull of Cooley.

41. A *geis* is like a taboo. Many warriors had such restraints on them. Cúchulainn could not eat the flesh of a dog because his name meant "Hound of Culann," while Fergus could not refuse a feast or the offer of drink. Breaking the taboo invited disaster.

42. A game like chess.

43. Borach was a minor chieftain who was anxious to improve his state and, consequently, eagerly accepted whatever Conchobor threw his way.

44. Fachtna was one of the Ulster heroes who ran away from the *bachlach*'s challenge in *Fled Bricrend* (*The Feast*, Forge Books, 1999).

45. Loegaire probably refers to Loegaire Buadach (Leery the Triumphant), one of the challengers, along with Conall Cernach, for the "champion's portion" against Cúchulainn in *The Feast*.

46. The raven was usually seen as a omen of war. The Badb Catha (battle-

raven), one of the triad of war goddesses usually appears in the guise of a raven or a *cailleach*, an old crone or hag, sometimes a witch. Sometimes, however, she appears as a beautiful young woman. Together with Macha and the Mórrígan, she makes up the Mórrígan, a triple goddess of the battlefield. Badb is seen not only as a sexual symbol, but as a sinister being as well. She personifies the *femme fatale*, who not only befriends the hero but leads him to his death.

47. The *In Caladbolg* ("hard lightning"), Fergus's sword, is sometimes seen as *Cladcholg*, or "hard striker." It is capable of striking like lightning and is as mighty as the rainbow. This is probably a referral or corruption of *cloidheamh solais,* or sword of light. When striking, it is considered to be as huge as the rainbow in the heavens euhemerized, which would also suggest Fergus Mac Roich as a type of divinity. We see this as well in Fergus's need of seven women a night to satisfy him sexually (or one Maeve who needs thirty men a night to satisfy her sexually) as such a great appetite is usually reserved for those who are demigods. This sword could also, however, be the forerunner of Caliburn, the magical sword of Arthur, from the Welsh *Caladfwlch* that we find in the story of Arthur as related by Geoffrey of Monmouth. Excalibur is really only a Latin corruption of these names.

48. Maeve, the wife of Ailill, the king of Connacht, was famous for her beauty and sensuality, needing thirty men a night to satisfy her lust. She chose Ailill, whom she did not believe was a jealous man and would not mind her affairs with other men as the whim took her. She is seen as a demigoddess of sorts, concerned with fertility. In several of the tales, she appears half-naked, and in the *Táin* spurs her men on to great deeds by riding nearly naked in a chariot around her army. A link with this aspect of her legend and the story of Lady Godiva could be made. However, Maeve's naked or nearly naked appearances appear to be self-motivated, instead of philanthropic, as in the case of Godiva. Although symbolically, the connection between Deirdre and Maeve is made in reference to the beauty of each, Deirdre's beauty is reserved for the sanctity of marriage while Maeve seems to be far more pagan and promiscuous.

49. Cruachan Ai is the ancient kingdom of Connacht. It covered ten square miles near Tulsk, County Roscommon. The pillar stone of Daithi, an ancient pagan king, is there along with Rathcruachan, the largest of the ring- or rath-forts. It is the site of Reilig na Ri, the burial place of kings, and

allegedly contains the entrance to the Otherworld. One cave, the *Sidhe ar Cruachaiy* (Hell's Gate), is the lair of several beasts that come forth to test heroes.

50. The Giants' Footsteps refers to the *Clochán na bhFomharaigh*, which legend says were the stepping-stones of the Fomorians. Located off the west side of Benbane Head in the north of County Autrim, it is one of the world's strangest geologic curiosities. A sudden cooling of lava that burst through the earth's crust in the Cenozoic Period split the basaltic rock into several prismatic columns, hexagonal or pentagonal in shape.

51. *Pandy*: a hard blow

52. Manannán Mac Lir is the Irish sea-god. His name means "son of the sea" and he is often pictured riding landward on horseback through the waves of the sea. This suggests a similarity to the Greeks' Poseidon, who is not only the god of the sea but also gave man the horse.

Manannán is one of the most complicated of the Irish pantheon of gods. In some stories, he is also pictured as a sun god, who is seen in the personification of a horse. A French riddle asks what runs faster than a horse, crosses water, but does not get wet? The answer, of course, is the sun.

An oral tradition on the Isle of Man found also in the eastern counties of Leinster depicts Manannán surrounded by a magical mist inside of which he rolls across the land on three legs. A Manx symbol of the sun with three legs, or a wheel with three legs, is seen as coming from this legend. Surprisingly, we have a similar symbol in Sicily, where it is considered good luck to wear a medallion like this around the neck.

According to legend, Manannán has a great leather bag in which he keeps the most valued treasures of the Tuatha Dé Danann. These include his shirt and knife, Lochlainn's helmet, a smith's hook, and the bones of Asal's swine.

Manannán's swine are magical. Although the flesh is eaten, they never die. These swine are seen in *Fled Goibnend* (Goibneu's Feast) where the Tuatha are fed and given eternal life in the Otherworld.

53. This is a strange comment by Naisi that is reflected in their surname "Usnech," which has a plurisignative meaning. "Usnech" appears to be from "Uisneac" which is the Usnagh Hill in Westmeath. "Uisneac" appears to come from "Uisleann" an early writing of "Usnech." However, this seems to be derived

from *"uṙiabtaċ"* which means "a prisoner." This passage is hermeneutical in its dramatic irony. I refer to situations like this as "homopluristasic" in nature.

54.   Cromm Cruaich: "Bloody Crescent"; Sometimes called Cenn Crûach (Bloody Head) or Cromm Dubh (Black Crom), he is seen as an ancient god of Death. He was represented by a golden idol on Mag Sléchta (the Plain of Adoration) where his worship was traditionally started by Tigernmas (Lord of Death) who was the son of Follach. Tigernmas was slain during one of the more frenzied worships of this god. This story greatly resembles the Greek story of Dionysus, who was torn apart by bacchantes. In *Dinseanchus,* his worship on Mag Sléchta allegedly involved human sacrifice, most notably the firstborn at the feast of Samhain.

55.   Although Fergus may be referring to another old woman (hag), there is a possibility that this poet may be referencing *Caillech Bérri* (The Old Hag of Beare), which is an old Irish epiphany dating somewhere around 800 A.D.

CAILLECH BÉRRI	THE OLD WOMAN OF BEARE

Sentainne Bérri cecinit íarna senad
don chrini:

The Old Woman of Beare said this when senility
had aged her:

Aithbe dam cen bés mora
    sentu fom-dera croan;
toirsi oca cia do-gneo
    sona do-tét a loan.

The tide has ebbed from the sea
and old age has yellowed me.
Although I may grieve its coming,
it approaches its food joyfully.

Is mé Caillech Bérri Buí,
no meilinn léni mbithnuí;
    in-diu táthum dom séimi
    ná melainn cid aithléini.

I am Buí, the Hag of Beare.
A new smock I used to wear
But today my estate is so poor
I don't even have a used smock to wear

It moíni
cartar lib, nídat doíni;
    sinni, ind inbaid marsaimme
    batar doíni carsaimme.

It seems only riches you love.
There are no men that you love.
But when I lived young
It was men that we loved.

Batar inmaini doíni
    ata maige 'ma-ríadam;
ba maith no-mmeilmis leo,
    ba becc no-mmoítis íaram.

We loved the men whose plains
we rode over. Those plains
we loved, too. And the people
boasted little who lived on the plains.

In-diu trá caín-timgairid
  ocus ní mór nond-oídid
cíasu becc don-indnaigid
  is mór a mét no-mmoídid.

Carpait lúaith
  ocus eich no beirtis búaid,
  ro boí, denus, tuile díb—
bennacht for Ríg roda úaid.

Tocair mo chorp co n-aichri
dochum adba dían aithgni (áichne?);
  tan bas mithig la Mac nDé
  do-té do brith a aithne.

Ot é cnámacha cáela
  ó do-éctar mo láma—
ba inmain dán do-gnítis,
  bítis im ríga rána.

Ó do-éctar mo láma
  ot é cnámacha caela,
nídat fíu turcbáil, taccu,
  súas tarsna maccu caema.

It fáilti na ingena
  ó thic dóib co Beltaine;
is deithbiriu damsa brón:
  sec am tróg, am sentainne.

Ní feraim cobra milis,
  ní marbtar muilt dom banais;
is bec is líath mo thrilis,
  ní líach drochcaille tarais.

Ní olc liumm
ce beith caille finn form chinn;
  boí mór meither cech datha
  form chinn oc ól daglatha.

Today you make many claims
from people. But you do not give claims.
Though you do give little
You boast about receiving claims.

Swift chariots and steeds carried
the prizes away. A flood of them buried
hatred then. A great blessing on the King
who allowed them to be carried.

My bitter body seeks a home
where the afterlife is known.
When the Son of God picks the time
let him come and take me home.

Look: my arms! All bony and thin!
Once they practiced pleasant loving.
Many times they were placed
around willing and happy kings.

But now, my bony arms
are not worthy of my charms
and I do not any longer seek
youths to favor with my charms.

Maidens are joyful when Beltaine
comes their way. But grief deigns
to be my lover. I am miserable—
an old woman is not for Beltaine.

No honeyed words are for me.
My wedding will be the sea.
My hair is scant and gray.
I need a full veil to cover me.

I do not grieve if a veil of white
covers me. I once wore white
and many other colors when
we drank ale to our delight.

Ním-gaib format fri nach sen
inge na-mmá fri Feimen;
    meisse, ro miult forbuid sin,
    buide beus barr Feimin.

Lia na Ríg i Femun,
Caithir Rónáin hi mBregun,
    cían ó ros-síachtar sína;
    a lleicne nít senchrína.

Is labar tonn mora máir
ros gab in gaim cumgabáil;
    fer maith, mac moga, in-díu
    ní frescim do chéilidiu.

Is éol dam a ndo-gniat,
    rait ocus do-raat;
curchasa Átha Alma
    is úar in adba i faat.

Is mo láu
nád muir n-oíted imma-ráu!
    Testa már mblíadnae dom chruth
    dég fo-rroimled mo chéthluth.

Is mó dé
Damsa in-diu, ci bé dé,
    gaibthi m'étach, cid fri gréin:
    do-fil áes dam; at-gén féin.

Sam oíted i rrabamar
do-miult, cona fagamur;
    gaim aís báides cech nduine,
    domm-ánaic a fochmuine.

Ro miult m'oítid ar thuus;
    is buide lem ro-ngleus:
cid becc mo léim dar duae,
    ní ba nuae in brat beus.

I envy no old one—except the Plain
of Feimen. I have worn the same
old people's clothes for years.
Yellow crops are on Feimen's Plain.

The Stone of Kings in Feimen,
Rónán's Dwelling in Bregun,
both are long from storms
but they are not old and withering.

The great sea's waves are loud
and raised high by winter's shroud.
Today I do not expect I will see
a nobleman or slave's son around.

I know where they go
off Áth Alam's reeds they row.
The dwelling where they sleep
is cold in winter's blow.

Alas! I will not sail on the sea
of youth. My beauty has deserted me.
My great, wanton ways
have long deserted me.

I rue the day when the sun
demands I cover myself. The sun
is no friend to age.
I recognize the old ways are done.

The youthful summers were lovely.
Even autumns were good to me.
And now the age of winter overwhelms
everyone, including me.

I wasted my youth in the beginning
but I am satisfied with that beginning.
When I finally left my home to roam
a ways, it was not that new a beginning.

Is álainn in brat úaini
    ro scar mo Rí tar Drummain.
Is sáer in Fer nod-llúaidi:
    do-rat loí fair íar lummain.

My King has spread a green cloak
over Drumain. The nubbing on the cloak
is rough, though, and wool covers it.
My King is noble for giving the cloak.

Am minecán! mórúar dam,
    cach derc caín is erchraide,
iar feis fri caindleb sorchuib
    bíth i ndorchuib derthaige.

I am cold indeed, and my day
is spent as the acorns begin to decay.
After feasting with bright candles,
the oratory darkness is like bright day.

Rom boí denus la ríga
oc ól meda ocus fína;
    in-diu ibim meduisce
eter sentainni crína.

I once sat with kings drinking wine
and mead and although well we dined,
I now live on whey and water.
Poor porridge in place of good wine.

Rop ed mo choirm cóidin mide
    ropo toil Dé cehcam-theirb;
oc do guidisiu, a Dé bí,
    do-rata cró clí fri feirg.

Now my ale is a little cup of whey
and I think that is God's way,
His will. I pray, however, that God
does not make anger my way.

Ad-cíu form brot brodrad no-aís;
ro gab mo chíall mo thogaís;
    líath a finn ásas trim thoinn
    is samlaid crotball senchroinn.

My cloak bears the stains of age—
Reason has left me. I am no sage.
My gray hair grows through my skin
like when an ancient tree has aged.

Rucad úaimse mo shúil des
dia reic ar thír mbithdíles;
    ocus rucad int shúil chlé
    do fhormach a foirdílse.

My right eye has been taken from me
to be bartered for a land for me.
My left eye has also been taken
to secure that same land for me.

Tri thuili
do-ascnat dún Aird Ruide:
    tuile n-oac, tuile n-ech,
    tuile mílchon mac Luigdech.

Three floods near the for of Ard Ruide:
a flood of warriors, a flood of steeds,
and a flood of swift grayhounds,
all owned by the sons of Lugaid.

Tonn tuili
    ocus ind í aithbi áin:
a ndo-beir tonn tuili dait
    beirid tonn aithbi as do láim.

What the wave of one flood brings
is taken by its swift ebb that brings
only emptiness to your hand.
I must live with what the flood brings.

Tonn tuili
    ocus ind aile aithbi:
dom-áncatarsa uili
    conda éolach a n-aithgni.
	The flood and the ebb and flow
	have become familiar to me. So
	I now know how to recognize
	the flood and the ebb and flow.

Tonn tuhli, nícos-tair socht mo chuile! Cid mór mo dám fo deimi fo-cress lám forru uili.	May my cellar's silence stay a secret to the flood-wave. In the dark I feel a hand coming upon me like day.

Má ro-feissed Mac Maire
    co mbeth fo chlí mo chuile!
Cení dernus gart cenae
    ní érburt 'nac' fri duine.
	Had the Son of Mary known
	what seeds He has sown
	beneath the house-pole in my cellar.
	I have been liberal; I said "no" to none.

Tróg n-uile
    (doíriu dúilib in duine)
    nád ndéccas a n-aithbese
feib dorr-éccas a tuile.
	Oh, the pity! Man is the most base
	of all of God's creatures. The case
	of the flood is reason enough.
	He has not seen it, not a trace.

Mo thuile,
    is maith con-roíter m'aithne.
Ra-sóer Ísu Mac Maire,
    conám toirsech, co aithbe.
	My flood has guarded well
	that which was given me. I dwell
	with what Jesus, Son of Mary,
	has left me. I am not sad where I dwell.

Céin mair insi mora máir:
dosn-ic tuile farna tráig;
    os mé, ní frescu dom-í
    tuile tar éisi n-aithbi.
	It is well for upon the great sea
	I find an island that has come to me.
	The food comes after the ebbing.
	I expect no food later to come to me.

Is súaill mennatán in-díu
    ara taibrinnse aithgne;
a n-í ro boí for tuile
    atá uile for aithbe.
	Today I cannot find a place
	I can recognize. The space
	of time has takenthat from me.
	What was once flood ebbs from that place.

A similar poem is François Villon's *"La Belle Héaulmière"* ("The Regrets of She Who Used to Be the Beautiful Armorer"). See *Le Grand Testament, "Ballade des dames du temps jadis"* ("But where are the snows of yester-year?")

56. The reader needs to remember that Fergus had a *geis* on him that kept him from refusing a banquet, a feast, or an ale-feast (drunken revel) without bringing disaster down upon himself.

57. *gruagach*: hairy goblins.

58. *dubh ba hoíche*: literally "the black of the night" but connoting the evil part of the night when the bad spirits are up and about.

59. Nessa, the mother of Conchobor, was a great beauty, and Fergus, then king of Ulster, who needed seven women a night to satisfy his lust, yearned greatly for her. But she ignored his overtures until he promised to let Conchobor sit on his throne for a year, during which time she would be the wife of Fergus. Fergus agreed to this arrangement but during that year Nessa made the other nobles rich, so when the year was up, the nobles of the Red Branch refused to let Fergus back on the throne. As the king was elected from the ruling clan, Fergus had to be satisfied with keeping Nessa for his wife and being the *seneschal* to Conchobor. This actually suited Fergus better as he cared little for the duties of the king, being a warrior of the old school.